ETTA

Harry Longbaugh and Etta Place in 1902.

ETTA

A Novel

GERALD KOLPAN

BALLANTINE BOOKS

NEW YORK

Copyright © 2009 by Gerald Kolpan

All rights reserved.

Published in the United States by Ballantine Books, an imprint of The Random House Publishing Group, a division of Random House, Inc., New York.

BALLANTINE and colophon are registered trademarks of Random House, Inc.

ISBN 978-0-345-50368-8
eBook ISBN 978-0-345-51289-5

Printed in the United States of America on acid-free paper

www.ballantinebooks.com

2 4 6 8 9 7 5 3 1

FIRST EDITION

Book design by Dana Leigh Blanchette

For J. S. W.

From the

NEW YORK *HERALD TRIBUNE*

December 9, 1960

LORINDA JAMESON CARR, 80: PHILANTHROPIST, HORSEWOMAN, "SURE SHOT"

MANHATTAN—Mrs. Lorinda Jameson Carr, wife of the late Ralph Worthington Carr, died at her Fifth Avenue apartment late Wednesday morning.

The formidable Mrs. Carr was known as much for her high spirits and her ability to command a horse and fire a rifle as for her numerous charitable works in the cause of the urban poor.

Mrs. Carr was seen often at the country's most prestigious equestrian events. For over 40 years, she was an officer of the famed Devon Horse Show held outside of Philadelphia, the city she always described as her home town.

"There was no one like Mother," said her daughter, the noted poetess Mrs. Etta Chase Harlan of West Hampton. "When she wasn't down on the Lower East Side or in Harlem trying to help someone, she was on some horse farm in Virginia breaking a stallion everyone else was afraid to even look at. That is, until the stallion looked at Mother."

She married Mr. Carr, then one of the city's most eligible

young men, in a civil ceremony in 1912. "It scandalized all the bluebloods, their not having a proper wedding," Mrs. Harlan recalled. "For a time, Father was disowned by my grandparents. Mother didn't care. She said she would have rather spent Father's money on food for a starving child than a Paris gown." From 1928 on, Mr. Carr was chairman of his family's firm, the venerable Carr Burton Brokerage. A pilot, independent socialist, and adventurer, Mr. Carr was also a member of President Franklin D. Roosevelt's "Brain Trust." He died during World War II while serving as the president's liaison to the United States Special Services. He was aboard the plane carrying bandleader Glenn Miller and members of his orchestra when the aircraft disappeared over the English Channel on December 15, 1942. Mrs. Carr never remarried.

In the years prior to World War I, Mrs. Carr was a celebrated beauty much sought after by many beaux in New York society. She was a leading light of the Settlement movement and an early and vocal proponent of female suffrage. An orphan living on inherited wealth, she led an independent life, flouting the conventions of her day and often appearing in public alone and unescorted. The famous salon at her Manhattan apartment, and later her summer home on Lake Waramaug in Connecticut, welcomed influential figures from Albert Einstein to Max Ernst.

Although her politics had moderated considerably by the nineteen fifties, in that decade Mrs. Carr once again rode to the rescue of those accused of un-American activities. She offered financial and moral support to writers, actors, and even some State Department officials affected by the blacklist. Still stylish and beautiful well into her 70s, she was linked to many famous and prominent men, and her rumored affair with blacklisted radio personality John Henry Faulk, many years her junior, kept gossip columnists busy in 1952.

A close friend and advisor to former First Lady Eleanor Roosevelt, Mrs. Carr served as a delegate to the 1932 Democratic National Convention, which nominated Mr. Roosevelt for president.

In a statement, Mrs. Roosevelt said, "Both I and my family are deeply saddened by the loss of this unique and talented woman. By her independence, her indomitable spirit, and her charitable works, she has set an example for all women of goodwill. I will greatly miss my longtime companion and friend."

In addition to her public philanthropies, Mrs. Carr was also noted for her tremendous skill with both rifle and shotgun, abilities she claimed to have acquired from her father. From 1915 through 1935 she participated in the ladies' division of the American Winchester Competition. Winning first place 17 times, she never ranked lower than third. "She would get very upset when we would call her 'Little Sure Shot,'" Mrs. Harlan remembered. "She always said that title belonged only to Annie Oakley."

Little is known of Mrs. Carr's early life. She claimed to have been born in Philadelphia in 1880, the daughter of prominent socialite G. David Jameson. After Mr. Jameson's untimely death in 1898, Mrs. Carr was sent to live with relatives in Colorado.

"Mother never talked about that time," said her son, W. Harold G. Sperling Carr, president and chairman of United States Trust Company. "We always believed it was too painful for her to mention. I think interrogating her about it all would have been, at the least, impolite. And while she was rather secretive about her writings, Mother was quite the autobiographer, and now that she's gone, my sister will be reading some of her diaries while I pore over a pile of scrapbooks. So perhaps a bit of light will be shed on that subject."

At time of publication funeral arrangements for Mrs. Carr are incomplete.

ETTA

Among all the other things her father liked to call her, he could now add "thief."

He had always had pet names for her. He would refer to her as "lamb" and "angel" and "picky," which he explained was short for "pick of the litter." When he was the worse for drink, he had other names for her. If the spirits had made him happy, he called her "pharo," after his favorite game of cards; "lucky" if he was winning. If the whiskey had turned him maudlin, the tears running down his cheeks, he would sometimes confuse the girl with her mother. "Anna," he would cry, "Anna, you've come back," though the fantasized return would bring no comfort to him. When demon alcohol turned him angry he would accuse her of being disloyal or spoiled. He would even say she was never wanted.

And always in the sober light of morning, he would beg her forgiveness; always she would grant it.

Over the years, she had learned to dismiss both the drink and the words. He was her father, and she preferred to think of him only at his best: the father who had taught her what he knew, the father who, she became convinced, had loved her as best he could.

He had bought Bellerophon in Virginia only the year before from a genteel man named Mr. R. C. Campbell. A month prior to the purchase, the breeder had stood helplessly by as the stallion bit and kicked two of his stablemates to death. Campbell had sold the horse to Father at a bargain price, stating that he was "doing the Lord's work by lowering the tariff on a devil." Less than five minutes after the deal was struck, Father was astride the giant animal, digging his spurs into the fat sides and galloping across the green meadow, his crop driving the demon toward ever-higher speeds. Whooping and hollering, he had disappeared from sight for over an hour, and when he finally returned the horse was covered in foam and he himself drenched in sweat. As the big man dismounted, the stallion reared and attempted to trample him. Father reached up and grabbed the bridle of the beast, pulling hard and laughing. With the help of half a dozen grooms, he managed to return the stallion to his paddock, complimenting the astonished Campbell on the quality of his stock. "This devil will do fine for me," he told the breeder. "Either he will kill me or I will kill him. In either situation, the world will be minus one more ne'er-do-well."

Now, as Lorinda rode Bellerophon through the fields she knew so well, the stallion felt ready to rebel beneath her; and so she rode him close, her mouth nearly kissing the black of his mane. It had been the work of months to get this far. She had waited until dusk every day, when she knew her father would be in the library of the main house, seated beneath his hunting trophies and too drunk to hear or interfere. As they raced across the lawns of the estate, she murmured as if to calm the horse, trying to allay both her own fears and his instincts to murder. The wind's tears welling in her eyes, she flew with him, her auburn hair strung behind her in near-perfect imitation of his swirling tail, her stomach vibrating with thrill and fear.

The hours in the saddle that began with her first pony, the equestrian competitions she had begun winning at the age of six, and all Father had taught her had led to this moment. As she plucked the Winchester 94 from her saddle, the long gun buzzed with an electricity that seemed to flow through her arms toward trigger and stock. With the strength born of a life on horseback, she clamped her legs to the leather of the hunting saddle and, using only her thighs to guide him, maneuvered the demon around the circle of four targets.

Crack!

The first shot was wide of the center, landing in the red area of the target a centimeter or two from the dark bull's-eye. She kicked Bellerophon nearly deep enough to draw blood, battling him into posi-

tion, and then fired from fifty feet. The black of the second target exploded, the paper shredding into ribbons.

Crack! Crack!

With the stallion dead between the next two targets, she twisted her
body first to one side of his mane and then the other, destroying the dark
centers of the two final bull's-eyes. With the last report of the rifle, she
sheathed her weapon just as Bellerophon reared in an attempt to shake
her from his back. With no time to spare she leaned into his mane, holding fast to the thick leather reins. Facing the wind, a large dollop of his
foam brushed her breast and neck. Now she could hear his front hooves
regain the ground and fall into a gallop. The calming speeches were gone.
She cursed and commanded the monster, her message clear: It would
take a better man than him to break her heart.

Crack!

A fourth shot rang out, soft and distant. For a moment she looked
down at her side, straining to determine if the Winchester was still
sheathed in her saddle; if somehow in her excitement the weapon had
come undone and fired. But the shot had echoed from a distance. It vibrated inside her with a menacing sustain. It was, she remembered later,
a sound to change a life.

She pulled hard on the reins of the bridle, causing the Spanish bit to
slash hard against the stallion's mouth and tongue. Nearly exhausted, she
managed to turn him to the right and toward one of the hedgerows that
crossed the estate. Her eyes blurred with tears and sweat, she dug her
heels deep into each black haunch. As Bellerophon landed hard on the
far side of the hedge she swore at him again and again, spurring him to
higher speed.

When she reached the house, the chief groom looked up in terror at
the sight of the hell horse in hands not those of his master. Covered with
foam, his tongue bleeding from the bit, Bellerophon slowed down only
long enough for the young woman to jump from his saddle and race toward the door of the great house. Snorting and pawing, the big black
kicked high in the air as the grooms garlanded him in lariats.

At the entrance to her father's study, the housekeeper stood in the girl's way. "No, miss," she implored. "Please! Please don't go in, for the love of the Savior, Miss Lorinda! For our Savior, miss!"

The girl was tall and strong and dwarfed the tiny Scotswoman. She gently but firmly placed a hand on each of the housekeeper's shoulders and in one hard motion moved her from the door.

Her father had been in a sitting position when she heard the shot's echo and so he remained. Graham David Jameson was as always elegantly dressed. His collar was pure white, offsetting the subtle blue stripe of the shirtfront below. For this occasion, he had chosen a dressing gown of mandarin scarlet with oriental symbols embroidered in its silk. The Navy Colt revolver hung still in his left hand beside his sharply pleated charcoal trousers. His face bore no expression, neither of peace nor horror, grace nor curse. The left temple, where the bullet entered, was neatly penetrated. The right, where the slug had made its exit, was a red mass stretching to the shoulder, punctuated here and there by the gray of brain and the cream-white of bone.

Lorinda's pale face became a mask, unreadable and plain. She stood for a long moment before the weeping servants and then, with one swift motion, removed a flowered and fringed cloth from a nearby table and covered her father, head to waist. She was in charge now. There were no older brothers; no married sisters to lean upon. It would not do to fall apart before the retainers who had served her father for so long, tolerating his benders, pretending that the women in his private apartments of a Saturday morning were the sort worthy of a Jameson.

Lorinda glanced sidelong at the housekeeper. "Mrs. Reeves," she said, "I will ask you to kindly clear all the staff from this room, as I would prefer my father neither to cause upset nor to be made a spectacle by his current condition. If you will do this, please, I will telephone the police and in due course engage the services of Kirk and Nice."

At the mention of the venerable undertakers, the Scotswoman crossed herself, then wiped the tears from her eyes and complied. The room was shortly empty of all souls save the daughter of the deceased. Lorinda picked up the newly installed telephone, asked for the operator, and only then turned in hot tears from the gory husk that had been David Jameson.

From the

PHILADELPHIA *PUBLIC LEDGER*

May 6, 1898

JAMESON SCANDAL WORSENS: SUICIDE BY
BANKER LEAVES CREDITORS FUMING,
DAUGHTER PENNILESS

FAMOUS "CEDARS" ESTATE TO BE AUCTIONED,
ENTIRE CONTENTS SOLD TO HIGHEST BIDDERS!

WHEREABOUTS OF MISS JAMESON UNKNOWN.
YOUNG BEAUTY DISAPPEARS FROM PUBLIC VIEW,
SAID TO BE IN SECLUSION

By our correspondents

The strange case of noted local banker G. David Jameson continued today amidst fresh allegations of both financial and personal
wrongdoing, all adding to the sordid revelations of the past two
months.

As is now well known, police have determined that on or about
March the first, Mr. Jameson, 55 years of age, took his own life inside the study of The Cedars, his 100-acre estate at Germantown

Outside the lead casement window, Bellerophon reared one final time before the grooms led him to his stall. As Lorinda fell to her knees, all she could hear was the drumming of his hooves, threatening to shatter the paddock door.

Then, through her tears, she noticed for the first time, nearly hidden in the upper corner of the desk blotter, the small sheet of monogrammed notepaper. It was upon this rich pure-white stock that Father had always sent the most personal of his messages. On it she had read his congratulations for every ribbon won at a horse show, every fine grade earned at school, every expression of gratitude at her forbearance, every apology for this or that weakness.

Lorinda reached for the note. The paper felt more like cloth in her fingers, so fine was its weave. But now, instead of some last comfort, its message led only to a last bewildering rage. *My dearest Lorinda,* it began, the greeting followed only by the single letter: *I.*

Below were two marks. One was red, a spot with a long tail that ran to the paper's edge. The other, a gray streak, ended in a sudden burst, like the period on a sentence her father would never write.

Avenue and Etta Place in the Chestnut Hill section of the city. The weapon of choice was an S. Colt model 1851 Navy percussion revolver, which Mr. Jameson had carried with some distinction throughout his captaincy during the War Between the States.

In recent days, numerous creditors have come forward and are demanding payment of what they claim is over two million dollars in debts incurred by Mr. Jameson, the former assistant chief officer of the Seaman's and Merchant's National Bank and Mercantile Society. Along with police, that institution is now investigating allegations of embezzlement by the deceased man, which, if so proven, could add additional monies to the total upon which various elements now lay claim.

Though able to trace his lineage to the earliest days of the Republic, the doomed financier had no living relatives and no male heir and so was known to Philadelphia society as "the last of the Jamesons." Some who knew him claimed that Mr. Jameson had been permanently altered by the death in 1880 of his wife, the former Anna Pepper Reese, who expired giving birth to their only child, Miss Lorinda Reese Jameson, now 18. During the past decade, they say, a slow deflation had taken place within the unhappy banker, a decline rumored to be fueled by alcohol and the abuse of a doctor's script of laudanum.

Chief among Mr. Jameson's creditors are the Shippen and Vare Real Estate and Trust Company, which holds a mortgage of some consequence against The Cedars. The company has stated in court documents that Mr. Jameson had allowed the property to slide into arrears over the past five years. On February 23, President Judge Mr. Harris W. Wilkeson, Jr., of the orphan's court, ruled that Messrs. Shippen and Vare may proceed toward auction of the entire estate and its various contents. This includes all furniture, books, paintings, and statues and over 20 of the finest horses in the region, including Spanish and Argentinian quarters and a black stallion.

As of publication, the whereabouts of Miss Lorinda Jameson

are unknown. According to the Society editors of the *Public Ledger,* Miss Jameson created a sensation among the young men considered suitable at her coming-out ball earlier this year. Tall and slender, with large green eyes and auburn hair, she is considered by many to be the most comely of all Philadelphia's debutantes. Although she had been present for the majority of the court sessions, Miss Jameson has not appeared in public in the past week and has contacted no friends or classmates of the Agnes Irwin School during the recent unpleasantness. According to neighbors, she was last sighted two days ago walking away from the horse stables on the Etta Place side of the property.

At the hearings, Miss Jameson's lawyer argued that the jurist's decision would leave his client without resources and little method of making her way in the world. No appeal on this account, however, is currently planned, upon the theory that there are now insufficient funds to mount such an endeavor.

Lorinda peered through the small side window of the black landau as the dusty progress of City Hall drew near. The vast building had begun construction twenty-six years ago in 1872 and seemed no closer to completion than the last time she had seen it. Even as a child she could remember the spirited, even heated discussions her father and his cronies had carried on about its size and cost and the dubious taste in which it had been designed. "Calm yourselves," he would assure the nervous men. "This public work will be a fine thing for our fair city and—dare I add?—our friends."

Now, along with everything else, the graft that Father had received over decades was gone. Lorinda smiled slowly and briefly, knowing that even the waxed and shining carriage in which she now rode would shortly make its way to a family of their acquaintance: the same family that had scooped up her driver and two stable hands and purchased Bellerophon for a song. Old Hicks, who now drove the perfectly matched bays toward the business district, was the last of the servants still living at The Cedars. His wife Nancy, the family cook, had already moved on to the Moffitts, as had many of the staff. Clara Moffitt had always envied the Jamesons their retainers, especially the efficient Mrs. Reeves—who, rather than work for the celebrated dowager, had opted to return to Edinburgh. By week's end, the bays themselves would be transported to the Dagits in Bryn Mawr. At least Lorinda had never been introduced to that family, which somehow made it easier for her to bear parting with the horses.

As she stepped from the carriage, her hand fell into the big rough glove of Hicks. Since childhood those hands had supervised her dis-mounts, holding her firmly about the arms and shoulders and swinging her down with a laugh from the cab. His huge mustache, once the color of the carrots he fed the bays, was now white with a hint of rust. And his eyes seemed bluer now for their moisture at the knowledge that they had completed half of their final ride together.

"I'll be waiting, miss," he said, taking a second longer than usual to release the green satin of her glove.

"Of course you will, Hicks." She smiled. "And what else would my dear Hicks do?"

Hicks gave a short stiff bow. The unfinished tower of the City Hall threw its shadow over South Broad Street as she made for the entrance to number 106.

It was not a new or luxurious building and clearly had seen its share of transactions through the years. In the elevator she asked the operator for the offices of Larabee, Hay & Litch, attorneys-at-law. Silently, the op-erator pulled back the brass and mahogany handle long enough to gain the third floor. Off the elevator and to the right stood the Larabee office, and although Lorinda had never been here, she knew instantly that Messrs. Hay and Litch were either long gone or dead. No secretary greeted her, no assistant offered her tea or water. The dust stood thick on the outer desks neatly piled with paper portfolios, some overflowing with testimony, others long unfiled or unread. From the private office of Mr. Rodman D. Larabee III, Esq., the half-built tower of the new City Hall seemed close enough to toss her hat upon. Emerging from a small cham-ber at her right, Larabee himself rose to greet her, bade her sit and re-turned to his chair.

Rodman Larabee was another of the many prominent men Lorinda had known all her life. He had been her father's lawyer and her grandfa-ther's. The old man had been a frequent guest at The Cedars but, unlike her father's other friends, he never came to hunt or drink or share bawdy jokes and low opinions of women about whom low opinions were de-served. His position was clearly that of counselor, a man to be paid mind. To Lorinda, he had seemed changeless, eternally one of those men who were never young. His manner of speaking was formal and stentorian. He always wore the same black frock coat, the same old-fashioned collars, high and stiff. And like many men "born old" he had aged to a certain point and then gone no further, his features frozen. There would be no additional wrinkles or crow's-feet, only a profile as sharp as a falcon's and as serious as a lawsuit. Lorinda thanked God for him. He was now the only remaining soul in the wide sweet world who had not deserted her over her father's profligacy and its resultant scandal.

At the hearings, she had learned that Larabee had spent the better part of the past decade attempting to keep her father out of either the jailhouse or the grave. As she sat in the courtroom day after day, she came to understand why the old lawyer had stormed out in a rage so many times and why she had not seen him visit The Cedars for at least the past two years.

"You are a strong young woman, Lorinda," the old lawyer said, fixing her with his hawklike gaze. "You were a strong infant and a fearless little girl as well. Therefore I shall forgo placing my words in a honeyed envelope. Quite in truth, if your father were not already dead, I should like to make him so. I would like to wring his neck for the great misfortune he has visited upon you, his innocent child.

"And so it is my sad duty to inform you that of your father's estate there is nothing left. In fact, there is less than nothing. As you are doubtless aware, his debts to the bank, his creditors—everyone, in fact, down to the horse farriers and haymakers—amounts to a sum that has cost you your home and lands, everything . . ." His voice trailed off.

"Please, Uncle Rodman," Lorinda said, fixing the old man with a withering gaze, "it is no good now reporting the misdeeds of the dead. The esteemed Federal Court of Philadelphia quite did its job of telling me just how much of a wastrel I had for a father. But if they now seek to have me renounce him, they will be disappointed. This was my father. And I believe there should be at least one soul to hold the memory of who he was before grief brought his downfall."

The old lawyer leaned in closer to his young client and briefly pressed his palms to his eyes. "I understand, dear child. And I wish that the sour-ing of his reputation were the worst of it. But in recent months it has come to light that your poor father had been laid to considerable debt by a cabal of gamblers, unscrupulous and desperate men who preyed upon your father's weakness for horse betting, no doubt with his enthusiastic support. Like the remainder of his creditors, these villains have contacted this office and informed me of their need to be remunerated. They have also advised that if they do not quickly receive what they believe is theirs, they shall be forced into actions that will mean suffering for any whom your father loved in life. I need not tell you who that is."

Lorinda felt a chill at her back but neither moved nor spoke.

"I would not uneccessarily alarm you, Lorinda, but these are men to whom evil is second nature, Sicilians who have come here to mock our way of life. They tell me they have studied your whereabouts, your comings and goings, and if they do not receive recompense they shall punish you in your father's stead. They are aware of your beauty: I daresay they have described it to me in the crudest of terms. They have also described the method by which, should payment not be received within a fortnight, they intend to disfigure your face by means of vitriol."

The cold along Lorinda's spine expanded. She had read of such attacks. It was not an uncommon occurrence among some dark men who ran strings of prostitutes within the city's seamier quarters. By one account she had read only the month before, a poor young woman had had a bottle of the acid slowly dripped upon her by her employer, a man the papers decribed as belonging to something ominously called "The Black Hand." When his evil work was completed, she was described by the newspapers as "half-pretty, half monster" and blind in the left eye. Unable to imagine that there were very many men in Philadelphia vicious enough to perpetrate such an act, Lorinda concluded that they must be the same fiends who now demanded their due from the old man.

"Uncle Rodman," she finally said, "how great is the sum in question? I have a small amount of money of my own put by. Perhaps that will satisfy them."

"I would be greatly surprised, my dear, if you were in possession of such a sum. The amount your poor father owed is in the general neighborhood of twenty thousand dollars."

Lorinda did not reply, but no words were neccesary to explain that she had no such amount and no means of obtaining it.

Larabee rose to his feet and walked toward a painting of a steamship tossed upon the ocean. "Take heart, Lorinda. I did not summon you here today to introduce despair without offering hope. I have cherished your family far too much and for far too long to leave you with no option but misery."

He gripped the painting along its side, and it swung away on a hinge. Behind the boat was an iron safe, which Larabee swiftly unlocked.

"You are to go away from here," he said. "Far away."

From the safe's interior, Larabee took a small alligator box. He lifted the lid and removed several different-colored envelopes waxed with the seal of his firm, a small leather purse, and some papers in various colors. Tears welled in his eyes as he cleared his throat.

"For now, this small packet will be your freedom. It contains some money from my own humble resources, a train ticket, and these letters. The ticket will provide you safe passage out of Broad Street Station and will bring you to Chicago, Illinois. There you will meet my agent. The papers in the purple ribbon are personal identification documents: your certificates of birth and baptism and your references."

"Uncle," she said softly, nearly laughing, "how could I have any references? I have never worked for anyone. And I can't imagine that anybody is looking for a too-tall girl who knows little but how to muck a stable and clean a rifle."

"Where you are headed, such skills may not ultimately prove wasted. As for your references—well, I may be an honest man, but I am still an attorney. Your curriculum vitae, as it were, is, I am afraid, a forgery—and, I may say without undue modesty, an excellent one.

"I also hope that you will quickly adjust to your new name. I understand that it is indeed traumatic to submerge one's identity, even for a short time. Please do not think me supercilious for my choice, but I had to devise something quickly. Believe me when I say there was no attempt on my part to be humorous."

"But what will happen to you? Isn't it conceivable they will soon discover that I am gone? They will know who informed on them. What will stop them from taking revenge on my only friend?"

The old man smiled faintly, the nostrils flaring beneath the hawk's beak. "I have lived a long life and a good one, Lorinda. One need only look to these humble surroundings to know that I took no opportunity to profit overly from my practice. For more than fifty years I have defended poor and rich alike, often discovering that the first couldn't pay, the second couldn't be bothered to. I owe no man money or favors. I have no children, and my wife is long dead. Worry not about me. Anyone who settles accounts with Rodman Larabee will find himself poor indeed. As to my bravery, have no illusions. It is fairly as much for my safety as your own that I urge your escape. I am a lawyer, not a soldier, and certainly no hero. Should they attempt to torture me I know not how long I would last. But, given their skills and experience I would not wager on a long session."

Larabee turned to the window and faced City Hall. A workman was struggling to set a window below a gigantic effigy of Moses.

"I often wonder what might have been had your dear mother survived. You are so very like her. The same beauty . . . the same spirit. Perhaps, had she lived, your poor father would have been blessed with sons, and you would have had a normal girl's upbringing: parasols and lawn parties instead of rifles and shotguns and horses."

"That was all he had to share, Uncle," Lorinda said. "And, bless me, I loved every moment. To be raised without the stupidities of a rich girl was the gift that made me love him. If I could have banished every tutor and silly instructress in etiquette from our home I would have, if it meant I could have spent one more minute in the woods hunting down a deer or one more second on horseback racing him to the barn."

Larabee nodded, replaced everything in the box and handed it to Lorinda. "I would ask that you not linger unduly over these papers. Right now the deadline the gentlemen in question have set for their payment is drawing very near. Every day you stay in Philadelphia, your life is in peril. I beg you to trust me that this journey is the most advantageous solution. I understand it will be difficult for a young lady of your upbringing to make her fortune in the world. But happily it is a world that is fast changing for your sex and, from what I have seen of you in a horse barn, hard work holds no fear for you.

"As for the future, the police are on the case, but I fear that in our fair city justice has not yet replaced bribery as the driving wheel of ambition. There may come a time, and God grant it be soon, when you will return to us. But for now, you must go and go quickly. I will do the very best I can to maintain contact with you by letter and wire. And please know, dear child, that you will remain in both my thoughts and my heart."

The young woman and the old lawyer rose from their chairs, and her hand slipped into his. "Thank you, Uncle. I shall do as you instruct. My father and I attended more than one horse exhibition in Chicago. I . . . always liked it there."

Rodman Larabee's cheek was wet when Lorinda kissed it. Before the lawyer could even bid her a formal goodbye, she squared her shoulders, turned without a word, and walked through the grimy outer office into the dim corridor. Stepping to the window, she breathed deeply. She removed her gloves, opened the box, and untied the purple ribbon. The cream-colored envelope atop the others was addressed with her name. The letter inside began:

My Dear Lorinda,

Enclosed you will find complete documents legal and proper pertaining to all aspects of your personal history. You will also find an itinerary of your journey. I pray you read it carefully. As time is of the essence, it will explain everything I have not been able to, and answer the many questions I am sure you wish to pose.

As your schedule states, you will proceed from Philadelphia to Chicago, where you will be met by Mrs. Loretta Kelley, who has been alerted to your arrival. Upon that meeting, Mrs. Kelley will accompany you and several other young women to your place of employment. Please be assured that your work will be of the most respectable nature.

I pray that you will have a pleasant and not uncomfortable journey. Please also know that I shall work tirelessly to bring you home as soon as possible.

May our Lord hold you ever within the hollow of His hand.

I remain, very truly yours,
Rodman D. Larabee III
Attorney-at-law

Replacing the letter, Lorinda began to examine some of the papers. A ticket here, a document there. And then, as she raised her handkerchief to dry her filling eyes, she caught sight of a yellow label affixed to a very formal letter of introduction: a stiff paper label bearing her new name.

She laughed aloud.

The ink on the label was as green as the spring fields of The Cedars. Above a blank space it read "kindly return to" and below, "The Pennsylvania Railroad: Standard of the World."

In the yellow center, scrawled in black upon the first of two green lines, was her saving alias. Uncle Rodman had made certain that the memory of her home would never allow her to forget it.

It read simply: *Miss Etta Place.*

JOURNAL OF LORINDA REESE JAMESON
10 May 1898
Aboard the Pennsylvania Railroad train Chicago Arrow,
Sleeper Car Ralph Waldo Emerson

Diary,

How beautiful the view is from my little moving window.
I had always thought that little could match our home . . . the
surrounding green, the noisy magnificence of the cities of
Philadelphia and New York. But the farther we go toward the
prairies, the more glorious the country becomes. Past the black
fog of Pittsburgh there is an exquisite nothing for miles and
miles, with only a farm or perhaps a single home standing
bravely alone among chestnut and buckeye. West, it would seem,
is the proper direction of paradise.

It would be well that I remain satisfied with the magnificence
of the scenery, as the food has been entirely another matter.
Of course I am spoiled, but one need not have been raised in
wealthy circumstances to retch at the swill the Pennsylvania Railroad sees fit to serve its second-class passengers! This evening my
meal consisted of ham, half of which was green and shiny, and
potatoes that I suspect had been scraped from a previous diner's
plate, owing to the presence of cigarette ash. The mince pie

smelled for all the world like an old woman's saddle mixed with beeswax. The rest of the meals have been equally nauseating. Having merely looked at yesterday's luncheon (veal loaf, the like of which might be Sunday dinner for the devil), I have managed to survive mostly on bread (which they seem to stock fresh from depots along the way), butter (which apparently is consumed in such large quantities on this train that there is little time for it to go rancid), and tea.

But perhaps even more disgusting than the food itself is the fact that a goodly proportion of the passengers seem to have no problem with it at all. They down it with, if not relish, then at least calm acceptance. Well, most of them anyway. There was, of course, the small boy who vomited on his mother this morning after munching on what was barely recognizable as bacon. I nearly gagged myself to see barely cooked slabs of fat sitting astride a cold and viscous poached egg. But one must maintain some semblance of the lady, Diary, even under such noxious conditions.

All in all, it is a "hell" of a way to spend one's eighteenth birthday. Perhaps when I change to the Union Pacific, the culinary experiences shall change as well.

The victuals aside, my enforced lack of contact with other passengers has made for a lonely ride. But Uncle Rodman has admonished me to keep all contacts with other passengers, even those with seemingly suitable young men or girls my age, to an absolute minimum. I suppose he is right. It is possible that this "Black Hand" ends at a longer arm than we suspect. The sad result has been that I have spent the majority of my journey inside my little cabinet, reading and writing and venturing out only as needed for meals (I shall never eat bread again!) or for those functions required by nature. I long, Diary, for two things: a contemporary to talk to and a hot bath. I vow that once I am settled in Chicago I shall speak to whomever I choose, go wherever I choose, eat whatever I choose. Villains and poor chefs be damned!

On the eleventh of May, the newly christened Etta Place stepped off the Chicago Arrow and on to the platform of Dearborn Station. Near the end of her long ride she had hoped for some time to drink in the magnificence of the city, but no sooner had a cool blast of the town's famous wind blown a railroad cinder in her eye than she and her cohorts were confronted by a jagged line of boys, evenly staggered up and down the platform and stretching the length of the train.

Each one appeared no more than ten or eleven years old. Their faces were as scrubbed as the cement below them was grimy, washed as if their mothers had bathed them only moments before and specifically for the occasion. They wore crisp red tunics with gold buttons and black woolen knickers leading to matching hose. On their red caps were shining brass buckles emblazoned with the name of Etta's new employer. They looked, she thought, like curious little bellhops about to page an important personage in a grand hotel lobby. As they paraded along the platform, each carried above his head a stiff cardboard sign affixed to a slim wooden stake, and every placard bore in dark blue ink a single neatly lettered word: HARVEY.

"All ladies please to come with me!" they cried, in the cracked tones common to boys their age. "All ladies please to come with me! Gather around me, please!"

From all parts of the train, Etta could see young women step quickly toward the boys and their signs. Some were clearly older than she, others younger; some strode confidently across the platform, others walked slowly, heads down and shoulders hunched, their eyes filled with fear.

Two brunettes, possibly cousins, linked arms with each other for support. Others read the cardboard plaques for those girls who could not. All were dressed in their best.

The girls appeared to hail from many walks of life. Etta reckoned some to be shopkeepers' daughters or perhaps former millworkers. Even more appeared fresh from the farm. None, however, seemed as rich as Lorinda had once been. She began to feel conspicuous in her fine traveling clothes, tailored to her measure and purchased by an aunt who had lived in Paris for thirty years. But no matter how rich or poor in dress, Etta knew in an instant that she was one with these women. They were sisters in loneliness and confusion—and all far from home.

"All ladies please to follow me! Please be so kind as to follow me quickly into the station!"

Once all the girls had formed knots around each boy there began a parade of sorts. Etta looked down the long stained slab and saw the lad at the farthest end of the train lead his ladies up the platform to meet the next group. Then the two boys bade the women follow them to the next gathering and so on up the line. By the time they had reached the last boy, they were easily forty strong, coughing in the shadow of the belching locomotive. Etta peered over the head of the lead boy into the large waiting room of the old station. Looking back, she saw only a sea of hats and, below each, a youthful face nakedly betraying its emotions of the moment.

There was a plumpish redhead, her cheeks a sea of freckles, eyes red with crying; a dark girl, tall and slender, her face impassive, her eyes as black as the hide of Bellerophon; two squat strong-boned blondes arm in arm, smiling and laughing and chattering in some Slavic tongue. Amid so much anxiety and so many tears, Etta wondered just what kind of life these two were leaving to be now so suffused with happiness.

On orders from the pages, the women crossed the arched threshold into the waiting room, boots clattering like the hooves of cattle on the hard granite. The old station echoed with the calls of conductors and the laughter of black porters. To the left of the giant archway, hawkers stood at their stalls, selling fresh fruit and sausages cooked in beer and sauerkraut.

At the end of the grand hall, directly beneath a bas-relief depicting one of the major battles in the Civil War, stood a florid and handsome woman perched atop a wooden apple box. Beneath her hat, her hair was a sleek chestnut, pulled tight and only beginning to gray at the temples. She was dressed simply but in perfect taste. Her ochre satin suit was subtly accented by velvet and lace, its short waistcoat piped in white. The high cream collar of her blouse was partially hidden by a large pink ascot tied at the knot with a silver brooch emblazoned with the letter *H.* From her fine brown and white boots to her nearly luminous Directoire hat with its upstanding green leaves, everything about her cried that this was a modern woman, a woman of business, a woman to be respected. Above her left breast she wore a card framed in silver that read simply *Mrs. Loretta Kelley.*

Mrs. Kelley made no move to call the group to attention or remonstrate for silence. She simply stood still and waited for the women to quiet, looking down from her box in silence. Though she could not have explained it, Etta became aware of a feeling of warmth and security as those red cheekbones broke into a dazzling grin. And all around her, as if by instinct, the gathered girls smiled too, even those who only seconds before had seemed nearly overcome with fear of the unknown.

"Welcome, ladies," Mrs. Kelley began. Her voice was like spun sugar flavored with Irish whiskey.

"I am Mrs. Loretta Kelley, the Fred Harvey Company personnel director for this region, and I wish to welcome each and every one of you to the city of Chicago. I know that for many of you the journey has been long and exhausting, so for now I will dispense with unneeded information and pleasantries. All of you know why you are here and, quite frankly, none of you would have been accepted for your positions had you not been of the finest character and reputation.

"You will work and work hard, girls. But you will be treated with the respect due a professional, housed in clean and pleasant surroundings, and fed sanitary and—and as you may know, we pride ourselves upon this—delectable meals. I know that some of you have spent these past many hours in tears because you long for those families you have been brave enough to leave behind. I know this because I once was one of you: a little girl from Lowell, Massachussetts, who had never been even so far as Boston taking what seemed like an endless train ride. For the next few days, I hope you will think of me as a mother. I know I cannot replace the fine women whom you have left behind, but, should it become necessary in this trying time, I pray you will confide in me. For those girls who are orphans and used to relying upon themselves, this confidence is even more important.

"But plenty of time for talk during entrance interviews tomorrow. Please note that it is now ten o'clock. I ask that you all follow me and our little pages to the Hotel Rochambeau across the street. There you will be assigned your rooms and roommates, and a light luncheon will be sent to your quarters. Following the meal, you will meet me and the boys in the Rochambeau lobby promptly at twelve thirty. Please bring with you a separate suit of clothing appropriate for the city, as well as all"—and here she whispered—"unmentionables."

The women tittered at the naughty word.

"At that hour," Mrs. Kelley continued, "you will enjoy what we hope will be a special treat. As we of Harvey like to say, a clean girl is a happy girl. And now, please follow me. An adventure is always better enjoyed among friends. Let us begin this one together and leave all fear and tears behind."

From the
JOURNAL OF LORINDA REESE JAMESON
11 May 1898
Hotel Rochambeau, Chicago

Diary,

I can hardly contain my delight! As I record these words, I luxuriate in a clean bed with real linens. My fondest wish for a sweet warm bath has been met beyond my expectations, and for this I bless the name of Mrs. Loretta Kelley.

To think that up until today I believed that the Turkish bath was something used only by old men: immigrants and those otherwise unfortunate enough to make do without proper plumbing. But this place was magical, all white and pink granite with gleaming porcelain tile. The shy girls among us looked nervously about the great entrance hall with its scalloped Moorish design and giant columns and capitals. As we made our entrance, Mrs. Kelley informed us that there was no cause for undue modesty since the Fred Harvey Company had secured the entire Luxor Baths for our healthful enjoyment, so that for this afternoon it was ours alone. At first, I was afraid that the two Slavic towheads I encountered at the station were about to be overcome with fright or anxiety until I realized they were clutching each other, and jumping up and down, not with fear but with unrestrained joy.

"Bania!" they cried excitedly, waving and attempting to attract the attention of a few other girls within the group, seemingly familiar to them. "Bania!" they cried again and, gesturing to all, bade us follow them through an ornate atrium and into the belly of the giant bathhouse.

Over the next few hours the Russian girls—sisters named Nadia and Katia—were our happy, enthusiastic tour guides. In their New York–accented English, they instructed us in the finer points of the lady's Turkish bath. Without a shred of false modesty they stood naked before us, showing us how to properly tie our long towels. We followed along as they laid the cloth about their big white breasts—over the right shoulder, under the left—and soon the dressing room was filled with female Roman senators, splendid in their blue and white togas.

We were led into a large tiled room filled with hot menthol-scented vapors. As impassive attendants poured cool water over our exhausted heads, we perspired away a thousand miles of railroad ash. Some of the girls could only stand the steam for a few minutes, but I could have sat on that hot slab of marble an hour, the vapors cleansing me of a million worries and the memory of death.

Next came a hot pool so large that, had we so desired, we could have held a swimming race. Here, sweet cake and hair soaps were provided. Some of the women who knew one another or those who were related lazily scrubbed each other's scalps or backs. And it came to me as we stood or sat, shy within our towels or brazen upon the marble, how nakedness creates all women equal. No fine or dowdy clothes separate us, no elaborate foundations hide the flaws or accentuate the assets of our bodies. In nakedness, there is no class, no money, no poverty. We are simple creatures composed of twos: eyes, ears, arms, breasts, legs. By the time I reached the dressing room once again, I was as one reborn, a babe created from sweetness and pleasure.

Now I am returned to the hotel. By some fluke or mistake—

and unlike every other woman among us—I discovered that I had not been assigned a roommate. In my previous life I might have welcomed such privacy. But here, gazing at the narrow empty bed opposite my own, I felt strangely as if I had been deprived, shortchanged of something all the others had been given. Still, my nearly complete state of relaxation did not allow for any truly sad emotions, and soon I slept.

By the time the noise awoke me, the light outside my little window had gone from yellow to orange. The woman bustling through my room was clearly taking no pains to protect my rest. She clomped across the floorboards like a fisherman navigating a dock. Considering her small size and slightness, I was amazed that she could even produce such a clatter. Although I was now awake, I did not rise but secretly observed the bold intruder.

She could not have stood more than five-foot-three inches. She appeared lean and lithe, but her movements were ungraceful, mannish. She wore a two-breasted woolen traveling suit of dark camel with a white blouse and spotted bow tie. It was neither cheap nor expensive and bore all the marks of the hard journey.

Her face was a remarkable combination: Her hair was as black as a Spaniard's, tied back tight and undressed by pins or pomade. She had a sallow complexion, and her eyes, beneath heavy lids, were gray. Full lips and a strong chin bespoke a more Anglo-Saxon heritage, but most striking of all were cheekbones that cut her face in sharp quarters; planes so high and chiseled they suggested a heritage of the red Indian. And although it was true that this woman was not beautiful, it was equally true that this would never matter.

She stripped off the jacket, threw her traveling case upon the bed opposite mine and proceeded to unpack. Out came a skirt, a blouse, a corset, and underclothing. I began to rouse myself from my pillow to greet the stranger when a voice like a darning needle pierced my words dead center.

"Laura Bullion," she said. "Texas by way of Tennessee. Better wake up, pretty. Dinner. Ten minutes."

She turned back to her work, apparently uninterested in any reply. I rose, catching sight in the mirror of the rat's nest my hair had become since I had washed it at the Luxor. Standing, I combed and dressed it, gaining a higher angle of sight over Laura Bullion's suitcase. I hate to admit to such prying but, given the result, I am glad my feminine curiosity caused me to spy. For peeking from the lining of a pair of green and gold slippers was a glint of hard silver.

I have spent my life in the company of too many guns not to know a derringer when I see one.

Dear Miss <u>PLACE</u>,

Enclosed please find your Contract of Employment.

I ask that you please read it carefully. Should some of the terms seem unfamiliar to you, or if the actual reading of the document should prove difficult, myself or a member of our staff will be most pleased to aid you or to read the contract aloud to you.

We welcome you to the Harvey family and look forward to working with you in the coming year.

Very truly yours,
Mrs. Loretta M. Kelley
Directoress of Personnel,
Wabash Region

The Fred Harvey Company
LEAVENWORTH, KANSAS

*Providing only the finest in food and lodging for
elite rail travelers since 1876*

Binding Contract of Employment

Whereas, the **Fred Harvey Company** (which shall be known hereafter in this indenture as the **employer**) has seen fit to secure Miss <u>Etta</u>

S. Place (who shall be known hereafter in this indenture as the **employee**), of St. Monica's Orphan's Convent School, Philadelphia, Pa. in a position of work, this **Contract of Employment** is issued and shall, under its terms and conditions, be legally binding upon both **employer** and **employee** for a period of time no less than and not to exceed ONE YEAR from the date indicated. Such time shall be known in this indenture as the **period of employment** and shall include all days inclusive from the date indicated through 365 days from said date through the date of termination.

Article I During the **period of employment** the **employee** agrees to perform any and all such duties related, but not limited to, the hygienic handling and serving of foodstuffs in the assigned restaurant owned and operated by the **employer,** during such hours as to be decided by the **employer.**

Article II Attendant to this last, the **employee** agrees to maintain at all times a clean and wholesome appearance consistent with the prevailing traditions of taste and refinement that have become associated with all establishments maintained by the **employer.** The employee agrees to wear and maintain the Harvey Girl uniform and to at no time appear anywhere within the assigned establishment without a clean white starched apron, all such clean uniforms and aprons to be provided by the **employer.** The **employee** also agrees that at no time will she apply facial cosmetics of any kind, chew tobocco or chewing gum, smoke cigars or cigarettes, or take snuff. Such limitations shall occur in all situations, public or private, for the indicated **period of employment.**

Article III The **employee** agrees that for the aforementioned **period of employment** she shall not marry or enter into any other such arrangement that may simulate, imitate, or otherwise resemble in any manner, shape, or form, wedlock.

Article IV During the **period of employment** the **employer** shall provide clean and pleasant lodgings and board, including bed linens, pillow, blankets as needed, three wholesome and adequate meals per day, and clean uniforms and aprons. A curfew of ten (10) o'clock P.M. shall be strictly enforced for all employees so housed within company facilities. The **employer** shall also provide full transportation for the **employee** both to the assigned establishment and from it at the conclusion of this indenture. Transport shall be limited to locations within the continental United States. **Employee** salary shall total $17.50 per month in United States currency and shall include **four days off per month,** which shall be determined by the **employer** and only after adequate notification in advance to Harvey management by the **employee.**

   Article V Employee stipulates and/or proves that she is of a legal age of no younger than eighteen (18) years of age and no older than thirty (30) years of age and therefore may lawfully sign and enter into this indenture.

   The Fred Harvey Company welcomes you to the august ranks of The Harvey Girls.

Contract dated 12 May 1898

Frederick H. Harvey
Frederick H. Harvey, Founder and President

Loretta M. Kelley (Mrs.)
Loretta M. Kelley, Company Representative

_____
Employee

ASSIGNED HARVEY HOUSE RESTAURANT/HOTEL
Grand Junction, Colorado

"Mrs. Kelley, I'm not quite sure I understand this part here at the bottom," Etta said.

   " 'Assigned Harvey House or Hotel.' That little slash mark means *or,* my dear. Don't worry. It simply means that you have been assigned to work in one of our nicer and newer establishments in the city of Grand Junction in the state of Colorado."

Etta looked around the small, sparsely furnished private bedroom that now served Mrs. Kelley as an office. All day long girls had been coming through, sitting for their final interviews and signing their contracts. When her turn came, Etta had assumed there would be no surprises; then she took note of the parchment's final line.

"Please, Mrs. Kelley, don't think me ungrateful, but my father's attorney led me to believe that I would be working here in Chicago. Is there no way for this to remain the case? I would be more than happy for you to redraw the contract under terms more favorable to you and your company. Less salary, perhaps . . . or longer hours?"

Mrs. Kelley's high-colored face broadened to a slow and sympathetic smile. The gaelic lilt in her voice was much like that of the poor Mrs. Reeves who had found her father; made by God to soothe.

"Miss Place, we of Harvey do not maintain facilities in such great cities as this. We are, instead, outposts of civilization along the rougher rails of this country. So even if I had a position to give you here or in your beloved Philadelphia or my sorely missed Boston—it wouldn't matter as there would be no restaurant or hostel in which you might work. I beg you not to be afraid of tales of the Wild West, with its heathen Indians and badmen. It is, after all, 1898; and even to the far hills and mountains the modern world has come."

Etta flushed, as if admonished by a teacher. "I meant no offense, ma'am. I am certain that, even in the loneliest parts of the country, your company operates respectable and efficient places. It is only that I am city bred. Used to the uproar of the horse cars and paper hawkers that ran by our dry-goods shop. It is difficult to imagine myself surrounded by the prairie's silence."

Loretta Kelley leaned forward. "You need not pretend with me, child. The attorney for our Wabash region, Mr. Bledsoe, is an old classmate of your good counselor Larabee. He has entrusted me with your full story. Therefore I know your true name and recent history, and I offer my condolences. I can readily imagine that your imminent departure for parts west is something of a shock to you, but your great friend wished it this way. Knowing you to be of a strong and independent nature, he worried that you might refuse to come here had you known your true destination. And so this small deception about Chicago was devised."

Mrs. Kelley rose from her desk and gently entwined Lorinda's hands in hers.

"I said yesterday that I hoped you all would think of me as your mother, but I know that, for you, no such good woman has ever been present. I also know of the degree of danger that looms for you. The men who seek you have ears at every wall, and—believe me—the gangs of Chicago with whom they are surely affiliated are far more cutthroat than any to be found along the Delaware River. Although the kind of work in which you are about to engage is far different from any you have ever known, a young woman of your education and breeding can be a positive asset, not only to your employer but most certainly to the other girls as well. I realize you are frightened, but trust me when I say that just as your background sets you apart from them, your fear also provides you much in common."

Mrs. Kelley released Lorinda's hands from hers and reclaimed her chair. Across the room she could see the girl's beautiful head stiffen in resolve, or perhaps defiance; although she adjudged herself to be an expert reader of young women, there was no hint in those green eyes as to which emotion claimed dominance. Or perhaps, she thought, I have misinterpreted this one altogether.

"Have you a pen, please?" she asked.

Mrs. Kelley dipped the nib of a long glass quill into the purple ink she kept for these signings—and these signings only. A harmless affectation, she had always thought, a unique color to remind the central office that these were "Kelley's girls," unique even among the fine specimens deemed good enough for such an enlightened concern.

Lowering her eyes, the woman who would be known as Etta Place signed the contract, gently gripping the clear cut-crystal pen.

It felt in her hand like an icicle.

In 1898, the town of Grand Junction, Colorado, was officially sixteen years old in a state that wasn't much older. It stood like a small interruption at the foot of the Little Bookcliffs, whose rocky terra-cotta walls reach to the summits of rugged mesas. Only a few years before, the buildings had been plank wood, hastily constructed and makeshift, built in a fever to establish the practical and mercantile. Just a year prior to its birth, Grand Junction, with Washington's aid, had given permanent walking papers to the Utes, banishing them forever to reservations elsewhere in the state and far west into Utah. Thus were the miners and farmers left undisturbed to carve a new life from the virgin land without fear of being carved up themselves by the ax of the Indian.

The railroad that provided service to this growing outpost was far less luxurious than the Pennsylvania. There would be no bed for Etta over the four days that it took for the El Capitan to wend its way from Chicago to the Grand Valley. Like the other women under contract to the company, Etta's ticket reserved only a parlor-car seat. When fatigue seized her aching muscles, she would console herself with the spectacular scenery flashing across the train's windows: the vast long grass of the Missouri prairies and the shorter paler plains of Kansas. Through her sleep-worn eyes she tried to imagine what they might have been like when black with buffalo, beasts now mythical for having been slaughtered.

She took solace, too, in the courage and good humor of the other girls. Some were born performers, singing or telling stories bawdy enough to make most of the car blush. Others were more serene, listening or nodding or obeying the call for a song, happy to be included in

anything that might approximate a family. These last were usually also
the ones who watched over the shy or terrified among them, comforting
the girls who cried whenever another would mention a father or perhaps
a sweetheart. Etta had assigned herself this role although she knew that
her manner of speech might quickly mark her as fancy or high-toned and
thus less of a support to her sisters, so she consoled the sad ones not with
words but with touch, caressing the hands of the grieving, cradling the
heads of the homesick.

Still, this leg of the journey held a pleasant surprise. To Etta's great relief, it came from the kitchen.

The El Capitan was a train of the Atchison, Topeka & Santa Fe railroad and as such had contracted with the Fred Harvey Company to operate its food service. There would be no hog swill aboard a Sante Fe
train! Instead, breakfasters would awaken to fresh eggs fried in butter and
biscuits baked aboard. Luncheon might consist of a fresh tomato, hol-
lowed out to admit a mixture of meats and cheeses. Dinner took advantage of the West's bounty of beefsteaks, with huge tender slabs offered up
beside roasted potatoes and stewed collards. Broiled capons rested gingerly on beds of pure white rice. Apple and peach pies were rich with
fruit and lard and fragrant with allspice. If this was the caliber of fare on
the railroad, with its small kitchen cars and tiny staff, what then must
await her at her final destination? Even in her anxiety, Etta was comforted by the thought that at least if she had to earn her own bread, it
would not be stale. And if she had to serve food to earn her keep, at least
it would be fare she could serve with pride.

By the fourth day of travel, however, no amount of cinammon or sage
could disguise the odor arising from the women, not to speak of the
men. As the train traveled on, it picked up scores of rough fellows seeking fortunes in the new mines and mills and who boarded the cars already reeking. As for the Harvey employees, the sweet scent of the Luxor
had long deserted even the most dainty of them, let alone those who
were used to waiting a week or even a month between baths. Etta and
some of the others devised whatever methods of toilette they could.
Some used daily applications of soap and water. Others relied solely on

perfume, although this was frowned upon by Mrs. Kelley. Cologne, she said, when applied to an already redolent body, was enough to sicken the sensitive.

For diversion, Etta read one of the volumes she had managed to rescue from her father's library. *Thompson's New Compact Encyclopaedia of the Horse* seemed the perfect traveling companion. By day it was thorough enough to provide fresh knowledge of her favorite subject; by night, boring enough to help induce sleep in her uncomfortable chair. But afternoon or evening, try as she might, Etta could not concentrate on fetlocks or hooves or the proper proportions of hay to oats. Ever since spying the ornate double barrel of the derringer, she had spent much of her time in observing Laura Bullion.

During their short cohabitation and on the journey since, Laura had spoken little and then in an odd and choppy manner. Somehow, she had learned to economize on her sentences, as though she were saving words for a day when they would be scarce. For example, the article *the* had disappeared from her speech, as had the personal *I*. One morning when she and Etta sat down to breakfast, Laura Bullion indicated the butter with a slight smile and said, "Looks good. Toast, Pretty? Jam?" It took Lorinda a long moment to make the translation. She had meant, *Doesn't breakfast look good! Would you pass the the toast and marmalade, please?* For one so laconic, it had also struck Etta as odd that, although her erstwhile roommate had never bothered to ask her given name, she had assigned her the sobriquet "Pretty."

At first, Etta had been worried that Laura Bullion might be a female agent sent to punish her for her father's bad dealings. But there had been too many opportunities to kill or maim her in Chicago, the easiest of which would have occurred as she slept in their shared room. And then there was Laura's inexplicable habit of staying close to Etta in all situations. By the time they reached their destination, Etta realized that the dark girl had managed to sit by her side all the way from Chicago, making sure they took all their meals together, even though each one was ultimately consumed in silence.

Once they reached Grand Junction it was much the same. Laura Bullion had been just behind Etta when the girls queued up for their first baths; she had secured a bed next to hers in the dormitory that occupied the entire floor above the restaurant; she had received her uniform just before Etta was issued hers and sat to either her right or left through all their training classes.

Her reticence did not deter Etta from attempts at conversation. "Such a beautiful day today, Miss Bullion," she would suggest. "One would certainly wish to be in that lovely field yonder with a handful of those spring poppies." Her reward might be a half smile or a nod of the head and the reply, "Yeah. Nice, Pretty." Sometimes it would only be the smile. Sometimes only the nod.

Before long, however, Etta and the other young women would have little to concentrate upon but work. The new Harvey House, Grand Junction, Colorado, was gearing up for its maiden meals. Every woman had to learn the company's precise technique, its famous "system." Day after day the core principles of the concern would be drilled into them: posture, cleanliness, friendliness without fraternization, a clean apron, a clean apron, and, again, a clean apron. A Harvey Girl was a handpicked angel, expert in a scientific method that allowed a full-course meal to be served to the traveler in less than thirty minutes while his or her train picked up passengers and mail and took on water. A woman who worked for Harvey was not merely a waitress and was never to be referred to as such. She was a Harvey Girl, a spotless symbol of all that was sanitary and civilized, even here in the wilderness: the American ideal laden down with steak and eggs.

PINKERTON'S NATIONAL DETECTIVE AGENCY
Founded by Allan Pinkerton, 1850
"We Never Sleep"

ROBERT A. PINKERTON, New York
WILLIAM A. PINKERTON, Chicago

REPRESENTATIVES OF THE AMERICAN
BANKERS ASSOCIATION
$4,000 REWARD
INTERNAL MEMORANDUM. CONFIDENTIAL.
DO NOT REMOVE FROM FILES

November 1, 1898, about 2:30 P.M., MONTPELIER CATTLEMEN'S AND MERCHANTS BANK, Montpelier, Montana, was "held up" by highwaymen who took tellers and patrons hostage and opened the main safe by the use of dynamite.

After robbing the establishment, the bandits mounted horses and rode away. No patrons or bank staff were injured.

SUSPECTS IN THIS ROBBERY

Description of GEORGE PARKER

NAME: GEORGE PARKER, alias "BUTCH" CASSIDY, alias GEORGE
CASSIDY, alias INGERFIELD

AGE: 30 years	HEIGHT: 5 ft, 9 inches
WEIGHT: 165 lbs	BUILD: medium
COMPLEXION: light	COLOR OF HAIR: flaxen
EYES: blue	MUSTACHE: sandy, if any
NATIONALITY: American	OCCUPATION: cowboy, rustler

CRIMINAL OCCUPATION: Bank robber and highwayman, train robber,
cattle and horse thief.

MARKS: Two cut scars back of head, small scar under left eye, small
brown mole on calf of leg.

"BUTCH" CASSIDY is known as a criminal principally in Wyoming,
Utah, Idaho, Colorado and Nevada and has served time in Wyoming
State penitentiary at Laramie for grand larceny, but was pardoned
January 19, 1896.

Description of HARRY LONGBAUGH

NAME: HARRY LONGBAUGH, alias LONGABAUGH, alias "KID"
LONGBAUGH, alias "SUNDANCE KID," alias HARRY ALONZO, etc.

AGE: 30 to 35 years	HEIGHT: 5 ft, 11 inches
WEIGHT: 165 to 170 lbs	BUILD: rather slim
COMPLEXION: light	COLOR OF HAIR: black
EYES: black	MUSTACHE: if any, black
NATIONALITY: American	OCCUPATION: cowboy, rustler

CRIMINAL OCCUPATION: Bank robber and highwayman, train robber,
cattle and horse thief.

MARKS: Black birthmark over lip above mustache, right side of face.

HARRY LONGBAUGH served 18 months in jail at Sundance, Cook Co,
Wyoming, for horse stealing. In December 1892, LONGBAUGH, Bill
Madden, and Harry Bass "held up" Great Northern train at Malta,

Montana. Bass and Madden were tried for this crime and sentenced to 10 to 14 years respectively; Longbaugh escaped and has since been a fugitive. June 28, 1897, under the name of Frank Jones, Longbaugh participated with HARVEY LOGAN (alias "KID" LOGAN, alias "KID" CURRY), Tom Day and Walter Putney in a Belle Fourche, S.D. bank robbery.

All were arrested but Longbaugh and Logan escaped from jail at Deadwood, Oct 31, 1897 and have not since been found.

LETTER TO JOSIAH LONGBAUGH
12 State St., Phoenixville, Pa.
10 November 1899

Dear Father,

There is no further need to worry about your captured lamb as I am broke out and have hit the highway. In no time flat I will be safe among my fellows where John Law and his brothers will never find me in a thousand years. Ha-ha! Only trouble I have these nights is to keep warm in this South Dakota territory, but I am used to such hardships and will survive well. There is plenty to hunt, and as I managed to borrow a rifle from my jailer (and six-gun as well), I have had no problem arranging feasts for myself. South Dakota and Wyoming have the biggest hares you have ever seen, and they are fine for eating.

You will also be glad to know that I am not alone in the wilderness. Harvey Logan—we call him Curry here—is with me just as in Belle Fourche. He is not always the best company and I have spoken him down harshly over the bloody beating he gave the turnkey before we left town. He did not really need to do it. But Logan said the man had mistreated him by telling him just before bedtime that he would soon do a rope dance. God help him. Cruel is his way, but maybe it is good for any group of no-goods to have at least one man with no conscience. Butch and me have him.

I hope I am not too much of a disappointment to you after these fourteen years. But when we lost the farm to the bank I just couldn't take watching Mother grow thinner and thinner and her hair fall out in patches. I figured a boy of sixteen ought be able to care for himself, and when the cousins left for Durango I counted it my best chance. I have so far killed no man and robbed only those richer than their fair share. And me and Butch have made a pact that we will give something to the poor people when we can, so that maybe we can help balance the money scales. And though it may be achieved by the goods of a thief, at least now I can afford to help a woman or a child that's been made sad and beaten down.

As soon as I get to where I am going I will send some money to you, if you will accept it. And I promise you that when I do return someday it will be as a man of property. And then no bank nor no one else will never take a farm nor a mother nor nothing else from a Longbaugh again.

Please wait for word of me. Where I am going there are only caves and tents and no mail cars. Give my love to my brothers and read over Mother's grave for me, as I am afraid that the prayers I say come from too far away for her to hear.

My best to you and for your health, Father.
Affectionately, your son,
Harry Longbaugh

In the months she had been in Grand Junction, Etta had learned all the nuances of Harvey service: how to greet the diners as they emerged from the trains hot and dusty in summer, freezing and sooty in winter; how to make them comfortable in their chairs, and how to make sure they didn't take too much time choosing their dinners. After all, the trains stopped for only half an hour, and in that time she was expected to serve a four-course meal, complete with cake or compote.

As it had with every aspect of its business, the Harvey system (or "the Company," as it was called by those in its employ) had reduced every detail of food and service to a nearly exact science. There was, for example, a code for every beverage. If the waitress placed the cup right-side up in its saucer, it meant the patron had ordered coffee; upside down was the signal for hot tea; upside down but tilted by the saucer meant iced tea, and upside down to the side of the saucer meant milk. Once these table-side signals were established, a drink girl would appear as if by magic and fill each astonished diner's cup with the correct requested liquid. It was only one of many tricks the company used to save time and increase efficiency; if a girl had a good memory, her day could be made considerably easier by it. During the past months, Etta had seen all the women with bad recall unceremoniously dispatched back to their homes, farms, orphanages, or pimps.

For those who remained, the Harvey life may have afforded toil with dignity but it was far from ideal. Because the restaurant served all trains, no matter what their schedule, it was usual for a woman to awaken at two in the morning to rendezvous with hungry passengers debarking the

2:27 from Indianapolis. And even at such an hour, the Harvey Girl was required to greet all comers with a smile and the utmost courtesy. Never mind that most of the customers were allowed to be as cranky and sleepy as *they* desired and thus were more prone than usual to bark orders or snap fingers.

But the most difficult part for Etta had been the uniform, a set of garments often described as "a cross between a nurse and a nun." It consisted of a black ankle-length long-sleeved dress with a wraparound skirt and a black ribbon knotted below the white collar in the manner of a man's bow tie. This was combined with black hose, black shoes, and a starched white apron that stretched from collarbone to hem and hung exactly four inches from the floor. No more was allowed and certainly no less. Reflecting Fred Harvey's seeming obsession with the sanitary, the dresses were washed and ironed after every shift and any apron despoiled by so much as a dollop of gravy or a speck of chutney was quickly exchanged for one stiff and spotless. Etta found the outfit rigid, unforgiving, and far more suited to a woman less well endowed than herself.

This preoccupation with dignity and order sometimes seemed laughably out of place in the roughness of Grand Junction. And while travelers from the East might feel somewhat at home within the civilized cocoon of the Harvey House, the local miners and cowboys and rustlers were more than a little amused by such pretensions to decorum. With such a coarse coterie of regulars, there were many days when the women wished, first to themselves and later out loud, that some enterprising go-getter would take some of the heat off them by opening a grand saloon overflowing with prostitutes. In the street, Etta and the other women were whistled at, remarked upon, and otherwise humiliated by the catcalls and unwelcome propositions of sprinkle-toothed louts. Instructed to ignore such ignorant taunts, many soldiered on while others gave as good as they got. Some even eventually succumbed to a particularly handsome blacksmith or traveling dry-goods drummer, against all the rules of their employ.

Such a case was Laura Bullion, although it would be hard to say that she had succumbed.

Late in February, a tall man had appeared in the restaurant between trains and was quickly seated. Except for his enormous height, Etta took no notice of him as Blanche, a sweet and shy girl from a Baltimore blacking house, arrived to take his order. When Etta turned back from the salver she was polishing, she saw that Laura Bullion had dismissed Blanche and was now serving the giant herself. She made no small talk with him, betrayed nothing that was contrary to Harvey regulations, but Etta thought she sensed something passing between them. If she were to have chosen a man for Laura, she thought, he would probably be like this one: dangerous, with matching revolvers strapped to the hips of his gabardines, and handsome, with heavy-lidded blue eyes and a luxurious mustache.

"Miss," the giant said to Laura, "I believe you may be the prettiest girl I have ever seen in this old town."

Laura Bullion stared at him for a moment and then pointed toward Etta. "No," she said. "Her."

"She's all right if you like that type," the man said, grinning, "but contrary to what might be believed, I don't prefer no ginger Amazon but someone more petite and dainty-like, what represents the meekness of the fair sex. Someone small and dark such as yourself, I believe, would suit me to the ground."

Etta thought she saw the beginnings of a smile cross her friend's face.

"Food?" Laura Bullion said.

As the weeks went by and the tall man appeared every day, Laura Bullion could not easily hide the fact that she and Ben Kilpatrick, as the man was called, had been previously acquainted. At each luncheon, Laura remained the girl of few words. The nights, however, soon confirmed Etta's suspicions.

When bed assignments had been given out, Etta and Laura had drawn what was called the Leftover, a tiny cell off the main dormitory directly above the kitchen. It was, like most things here, mixed in its blessings. Unlike the other girls, Etta and Laura Bullion had a certain measure of privacy, but the room's outer wall faced north. When the winter temperatures dropped deeper than anything Philadelphia had ever known, they could see their breath by a bright moon.

Beginning almost as soon as Ben Kilpatrick appeared, Laura Bullion began to disappear from the Leftover in the smallest hours of the morning. Etta suspected how her roommate and the tall man were occupying their time and was soon proven right.

On the first warm spring night, Etta awoke to the soft sound of a female moan and rose from her bed to peer from the window to the alley below. At first she was confused at the sight. Here was Laura Bullion, her hands pressed hard against a hitching post with her black skirt draped around her waist and the tall man moving like a pendulum behind her, his hands gripping her slender hips. Was this base, violent, beautiful? Etta knew only that she was unable to leave the window, her throat constricting slightly as she watched her roommate back into Ben Kilpatrick, caress his face, and twist around to kiss him. As they met and parted, his movements threatened to drive her into the rough wood of the post or even onto the ground. What passion is this? thought Etta. Surely, they had had their time in his hotel. And to still be unsatisfied? To want yet more of him here in the grime and dust of an alley?

As Etta filled the window, Ben Kilpatrick seemed to stiffen and Laura Bullion rose once again to meet him, her back flat with his chest. She looked now to Etta like a goddess, her two hands reaching up behind his neck, stretching her trunk like the Winged Victory, her face a mixture of submission and triumph that only another woman could understand. Not base, not violent, but beautiful.

As spring wore on, Laura Bullion never bothered to swear Etta to secrecy, never asked to be covered for, never searched her roommate's face for an open eye in the middle of the night. Somehow she had known that Etta would never report these flauntings of every rule of both employer and society.

Indeed, Laura Bullion had chosen her companion well. Over the course of three hundred years, the polite classes of Philadelphia had made an art of minding their own business.

From the
JOURNAL OF ETTA PLACE
12 March 1899
Harvey House, Grand Junction, Colorado

Diary,

I might never have thought so, but in many ways I seem suited to this work. With some highly notable exceptions (Mr. Earl Dixon's attentions become more and more alarming by the day), our clientele is mannerly and considerate, and they are appreciative of all we do to meet their needs. Often, though it is not permitted, they will leave a small gratuity behind as a token of that appreciation. Miss Hortense kindly looks the other way at this contraband largesse. She was one of us once and knows well that a little tip can often spell the difference between wearing a coarse hair ribbon or a fine one on one's day off. And how we look walking amid our fellow citizens is as important to the Fred Harvey Company as serving the correct beverage or a meat done precisely as ordered.

If nothing else, having this job has confirmed that I am not quite as coddled as I might have been. I suppose I can thank Father for that. He never allowed the servants to do what I could do for myself. Though I complained, he forced me to muck the stables, feed and water and curry the horses, clean my own rifles, and patch my own wounds. "Being rich can be a curse, Picky," he would say. "It can make you into something softer than horse's shit and twice as stinking. The Jamesons have lasted this long because when the soldiers came or the slaves deserted, we could do for ourselves."

In any case, it is fortunate for me that I have found some solace and distraction in my role here, as the news from home seems all bad. Our friend Rodman Larabee informs me that two weeks ago the very last of our belongings went to an estate auction house. A little man in a grimy coat carted off the kitchen utensils and the last of the hay and oats from the stables, although these were rotted and filled with worms.

But worse, it seems that the Hand has struck once again, and this time at another young woman. Last week, Uncle Rodman writes, the papers were full of another horrific incident involving a young woman in their employ. The girl, a Miss Roseanne Maria Simonetti, age eighteen, was the daughter of a local ice and coal jobber. She was the product of a local convent school and by all accounts respectable. The Public Ledger surmised that she had begun keeping company with a young man named Dante Gabriel Cichetti, a known associate of the Hand. The constables believe that the vehemence with which the crime was committed points to its being somehow romantic in origin. The poor girl was found in the empty back garden of her parents' house. Her throat had been sliced neatly, she was nearly decapitated, the word "puttana" inscribed in her forehead with a knife. Apparently, it is the Italian word for "whore."

This is not the first time Uncle Rodman has mailed me such ghastly news. I surmise that he believes me to be headstrong, capable of throwing all caution to the wind and making my way back to Philadelphia at any moment, the Black Hand be damned. With every warning and dire clipping, he implores me to stay put and assures me that, in time, arrangements will be made for my safe return. It is true that I am bold and always have been. Father would have allowed for no less. But as near as I can tell, my good friend thinks I am ignorant of the difference between bravery and folly.

Rodman Larabee need not worry. As of this moment, I believe I would do well to save my neck for something better than the blade of a mad Sicilian. Of course, I yearn to see my beloved Philadelphia once more, but not badly enough to be killed for it. After all, homesickness is a disease from which one might recover.

Murder is not.

No one who knew Earl Charmichael Dixon was surprised that his behavior would one day lead to a gunfight.

Earl's father had struck a rich vein of silver in 1875 and had sent the boy back east to be refined, rather like a piece of rough ore in search of a good polish. Earl Dixon hadn't done particularly well in any of the eastern schools to which he had been shipped. Some said the damage had been done before he had even left; that the boy had been coddled so much, by the time he reached Boston he was as spoiled as a six-week-old mackerel. But although calculus had flown over his head and he had simply not attended his lectures in business and finance, he had absorbed most of the attitudes of the wealthy young men with whom he associated. And the cardinal tenet of privilege he learned, was that whatever was the finest, the most well made, the most beautiful or expensive, by rights belonged to him.

No one in Grand Junction at that time could doubt that the most well-made young woman in town was one Etta Place, the Harvey Girl. The male diners she served in the restaurant invariably remarked on her beauty.

The compliments varied in their content according to the diner's degree of sophistication. A Christian gentleman from Hartford might remark to his wife, "Mother, it seems we're to be served here by the prettiest girl in the county, present company excepted." A lout might proclaim, "Darlin', there's only one thing I see around here sweeter than this puddin' and I'd like a lick o' that too." Both in and out of the dining room, Etta was the subject of considerable discussion and even more jealousy among the mothers of young women of marriageable age, the kind of parents who considered the Dixon boy Grand Junction's prize bull.

Earl Dixon had begun his campaign by merely annoying her. At first, it had been enough for Etta to simply put him off with a wan smile and the short speech that the company had trained each girl to repeat whenever accosted. "I am sorry, sir. Although your offer is flattering, we Harvey Girls are not allowed to keep company with any gentlemen diners during our employ here. But thank you once again."

With persistence, though, Dixon had risen from the merely irritating to the openly offensive. His position of prominence in the town allowed him to request Etta's table and be assured of receiving it every time. As her robotic refusals continued, Dixon's frustration turned to open attempts at humiliation. It had begun as "Miss Etta, we would make a great match, you and I. For in this town only you are good enough for me. Intelligent enough. Elegant enough. Beautiful enough. I hope you will take all this as a compliment." But over time such politeness had metastasized into "You think you're made of gold? You think you can do better around here? I once thought to keep you in luxury or perhaps even marry you. Now I'll just have you, mark my words. Remember who I am. And who you are."

Etta knew that no one would dare take the beady-eyed swine by his collar and waistband and fling him to the street. As the bile of anger rose in her throat she again repeated the company mantra as she poured his coffee. "I am sorry, sir. Although your offer is flattering, we Harvey Girls are not allowed. . . ."

On the day Earl Dixon threw down his napkin and stormed from the table, Etta hoped he had at last absorbed her message. She discovered otherwise early the next morning, just before serving the 5:53 A.M. from Los Angeles.

The location of the staff quarters above the Harvey House forced the girls to make their way down an open-air iron staircase that ended at the exterior door to the kitchen. This design was intentional. Fred Harvey believed that his waitresses, as domestic staff, should never be seen using the same halls or stairways as paying customers. Besides, it appealed to the romantic in him to have his girls appear seemingly from nowhere as if they were sweet, attentive apparitions, servile ghosts floating over hardwood floors.

Etta rubbed the sleep from her eyes as the late May dawn broke over the last step. Two months before she had been made Leading Girl, a sort of assistant to the manager. As such, she was always the first to brave the morning chill of those metal stairs, the first to prepare the dining area and confer with the chef while the others pinned and brilliantined their hair or tied their aprons. Earl Dixon knew this, as he knew everything concerning her movements; knew that for a few moments she would be alone behind the building. It would be all the time he would need.

Etta heard not so much as a footfall as he took hold of her from behind.

"I told you I would have you," he hissed in her ear. "If you're a virgin, I'll ruin you." His right arm was pressed against her neck, half crushing her windpipe, while his left held her tightly about the waist so that when he pulled her away and under the stairs, her heels nearly left the ground.

His plan was not so much to force himself upon her but to degrade her so that her will would be sapped of any future resistance. He would also make certain that word of the incident was soon spread but in a different form from the truth. Over their washbasins the town matrons' would tell the story of how the whore from the East had rutted with him in the dust of an alley. It was a method Earl Dixon had employed before.

With a single pull, he managed to tear the white apron and black blouse from collar to waist, but he had seriously unestimated the physical strength of a girl who had grown to womanhood battling angry colts and recalcitrant stallions. As his hand rose from her belly to her breasts, she caught it between her teeth and bit down, even as her left hand reached for his face and tore four fine slices from his cheek. With another lunge of her nails, she turned the side of his face into red latticework as he bellowed and was forced to release her. Whirling, she brought the pointed toe of her boot up even with his ribs and kicked. The blow did not so much pain as enrage him.

As Etta tried to run, Dixon pushed hard against her shoulders, pinning her to the horizontal slats of the building. Using his chest to hold her fast, her lifted her skirt to her waist and undid his buttons. Amid the blood rushing in her ears, Etta thought she could faintly hear the voice of her father over the click of poker chips. "Never weaken, girl. If he thinks you're his, you will be."

For an instant, it passed through Etta's mind how sad it was that the first time she would hold a man it would be not to bring pleasure, but pain. Steeling herself against disgust, she channeled a lifetime of controlling horses into her grip. He bellowed in pain and the pupils of his eyes rolled into his head. Seeking escape, he slapped her hard across the face and then fell moaning to the earth of the alley.

Attracted by the ruckus, a small group had gathered: a few girls and a Chinese cook from the kitchen; the owner of the dry goods whose back door abutted the alley; some early rising layabouts whose names and faces she did not know.

Etta did her best to replace her dress and apron in a position sufficient to cover her underclothing. "You saw him!" she cried to the throng. "You saw what he tried to do to me! Call the constable! I want this man arrested for trying to violate me!" No one moved or spoke. Through tears of rage, Etta allowed them all a decent interval of shock, but when still not one soul attempted to aid her or call the law, she recalled where he and his family stood in this town and his arrogant words came back to her.

Remember who I am. And who you are.

Now what Earl Charmichael Dixon wanted for the insult was her life. She saw him reach to his side for one of two ivory-handled revolvers and point it at her head. As much as the long black skirt would allow, Etta ran, hoping to create a moving target until she could reach a bay horse tied and saddled hard by the livery just across the dusty yard. The first shot whistled close by her ear, the second was wide of the mark, and by the third she was in the saddle, tugging at the reins.

But Earl Dixon was not to be denied. At the fourth shot he ran toward her, trying to bring his fire as close as possible. She cursed him through tears and gritted teeth, rearing the animal in his face. The next two loud reports turned her clean white apron crimson, dyed edge to edge by a cascade of blood.

She felt no pain, saw no wound to herself, but looking down saw the horse's chest and throat laid bare and red to the bone. As her mount began to fall, Dixon aimed one more time. Etta ducked behind the bay's neck and the animal's skull exploded twice just above her head. As the horse fell, her leg only narrowly missed being pinned beneath the big body.

Etta lay atop the dead bay, her mind seething with hatred. Almost by itself her hand found the stock of the Winchester 73 rifle cradled in the saddle holster. As Dixon pulled the second revolver from beneath his frock coat she shouldered the weapon. And before his finger could bring pressure to the trigger, Etta Place cocked the handle and fired.

From the
GRAND JUNCTION, COLORADO, *CITIZEN'S NEWS*
May 30, 1899

"HARVEY GIRL" GUNS DOWN PROMINENT CITIZEN!

EARL C. DIXON SHOT IN COLD BLOOD!
LEFT TO DIE IN THE STREET!

LOCAL AUTHORITIES CALL FOR INVESTIGATION!
MISS PLACE JAILED!

By Francis Xavier Dixon III

Early yesterday morning a so called Harvey Girl took the life of one of Grand Junction's most prominent and important sons, the noted mining heir, Mr. Earl Charmichael Dixon.

The dastardly and cowardly act was carried out by Etta S. Place, originally of Philadelphia, Pa., who has worked for the past year as a waitress for the Harvey House restaurant at Gold and Main streets, an establishment that up until now has enjoyed no such blemish upon its reputation.

By all accounts, Miss Place is a young woman of the lowest character and breeding, and it was well known that she had come to Grand Junction as a Harvey Girl (as such waitresses are called) to gain the trust of local real estate interests so as to initiate the building of a brothel. Prostitution, it is rumored, had been her profession in the East.

According to his father, Mr. Francis Xavier "Fitz" Dixon, Jr., proprietor of the Clean Strike silver mine and publisher of this newspaper, his son had been the object of months of unwanted advances on the part of Place.

"She thought because of her good looks she could snare my son into an arrangement or even marriage," said the elder Dixon. "Many women have tried to do this because of our good fortune and social standing in this community. He resisted them all. Apparently, this waitress would not take no for an answer. And now my boy is dead."

Eyewitnesses say that about dawn of the morning in question, Miss Place stole a horse belonging to Mr. Roderick L. Kurwood from the Poe and Peters Livery, which stands directly across the back alley from the Harvey restaurant. She rode up to Mr. Dixon and, as in the past, made such advances as were alleged by the father of the dead man, even going so far as to partially undress herself to gain the young man's attention. Receiving yet again an unsatisfactory reply, Miss Place produced a powerful Winchester rifle from the horse's saddle and, in a rage, proceeded to shoot at young Dixon. Although practically dead on his feet, Mr. Dixon managed to get off six shots from his revolver, but in his distress succeeded only in killing the stolen beast, which Place had cruelly used for cover.

The woman is now being held in the new James C. Denforth City Jail, charged with murder in the first degree, possession of an instrument of crime, horse theft, animal cruelty, and creating a public disturbance. She is due to be arraigned today and will remain in custody without bail until the circuit judge arrives in two weeks' time.

Etta Place is believed to be the first woman ever to be charged with murder in the history of our city.

Chester Braithwaite, Jr., was never happy about having a woman prisoner. Not for this long, especially.

There had been others in the past, of course: prostitutes, drunks, hellraisers of various kinds. He could even remember one evening when Calamity Jane herself had been his guest

She had spent the night drunken and howling and awakened the next afternoon in a pool of her own spew. A well-dressed dude with a glass eye had paid her fine and bundled her into the caravan of a medicine show, but not before she had twice fallen in the dusty street. As the wagon pulled away, Braithwaite could see a large painting on its side depicting a vigorous Jane astride a proud palomino, training a rifle on a terrified buffalo. DR. OMAR PIERCE'S NUMBER 17 SOLUTION, it read, THE PANACEA THAT CURED CALAMITY JANE.

Like Jane, most of his ladies stayed only a night or two, just long enough to make their bail or dry out sufficiently. And then they returned to their boyfriends or outraged fathers or procurers. Etta Place, however, had been the county's guest nearly a month, occupying cell number three from the time of her arrest throughout the whole of her trial and the construction of the gallows. These formalities dispensed with, she had only two days left until her execution, and as far as Braithwaite was concerned it couldn't come soon enough.

Not that Braithwaite was eager to see such a beautiful young woman wasted by a rope. Throughout her ordeal, Miss Etta had remained calm and composed. She was unfailingly polite to him and never seemed to take his role of jailer as any personal affront. She was respectful, too, always referring to him as Deputy Braithwaite, a term no one else in town ever used, even on the most formal occasions. Accordingly, she received his respect in return. They played eights and checkers, talked of his family (though never hers), and established the kind of rapport he rarely enjoyed with anyone similarly condemned.

Still, having a female inmate in his charge for thirty days had made him excessively nervous; and he was often embarrassed by the tasks required to accommodate the needs of her sex. Twice a day, it was necessary to erect a makeshift screen before her cell so that she might change her clothing in privacy. An additional organdy shade also had to be placed over her rear cell window to discourage the gaggle of Peeping Toms who appeared day and night, standing on produce boxes or hay bales to get a glimpse of the infamous beauty, hopefully in some stage of undress.

But far worse than this were the mobs.

On every night save Sunday, hordes of townspeople would gather before the tiny prison demanding that justice be served upon the trollop within. They chanted in unison and sang hymns of the old-time religion. The slogans on their placards were clearly visible in the light of their torches. HANG HER stated one sign. JUSTICE FOR DIXON another proclaimed. Every day there was another editorial in the *Citizen's News* demanding swift justice for the innocent scion of the paper's founder, its relentless drumbeat whipping the populace into a self-righteous lather. It had taken all of Braithwaite's courage plus that of Sheriff Becker and ten federal marshals to keep the crowd from storming the little building and dragging the prisoner away.

Happily for Chester, what nightly resolved this situation was the fact that Grand Junction was a rural community. Everyone rose early to their business, and the ranchers and miners and cowboys often beat first light to breakfast. The hardworking's need for slumber being what it was, most nights Braithwaite could expect the crowd to disperse at a reasonable hour. In fact, the only thing that would have kept the majority awake past 9 P.M. was actually seeing the figure of Etta Place decorating the nearest oak. Barring that, even the most vociferous rabble-rousers could be counted upon to leave the jail's courtyard no later than ten and be in their beds by eleven.

Ben Kilpatrick, Laura Bullion's tall lover, had taken note of this too, as he had all the comings and goings in Grand Junction. It was fine for a dime-novel outlaw to shoot his way out of a bank or defy the red faces of a lynch mob, but this was God's own life Ben was living, and to put himself at any more risk than necessary would be, at the least, ungrateful. His months of careful surveillance in the little town had produced a body of intelligence perfect for the jobs at hand. Walking the streets in the evening, he noted when the locks were locked and the relative strength of each one; he knew the hour the sheriff went home to his wife and the seven children who ran him ragged; and he knew just when the federal detail would change guards, leaving only Chester Braithwaite Junior between Laura Bullion and Etta Place—and his father, Chester Braithwaite Senior, between Ben himself and the contents of the First Grand Junction Bank and Trust Company.

Ben knew the time for action would be short, less than one hour between four and five in the morning. But he deemed it sufficient to carry out both the robbery and the rescue without waking decent people still abed and dreaming.

In the event, the first of the tasks proved as simple as expected. At such an early time of the morning, the only guard on duty at the bank was, in fact, Chester Braithwaite Senior, father of the man who had so long stood guard over Etta. Braithwaite Senior had made a career of keeping his eye on things: night watchman, security guard, and, like his son after him, deputy sheriff. He had passed on his skills (such as they were) to his boy, who had also spent his working life standing between what someone had and what someone else wanted. This night, however, such long experience would do neither of them any good.

As she made for the rear jailhouse door, Laura Bullion could see the face of her friend shadowed in moonlight by the bars of her window. It was the work of seconds to disable Chester Junior; she merely approached him in the partial darkness, placed a gun barrel to his temple, and spoke with her usual economy.

"Cell. Keys. Dead. Alive. Choose."

Braithwaite obeyed. He handed the keys to Laura Bullion, who threw them to Etta.

As Etta put those keys to the lock and her erstwhile roommate bound and gagged the astonished deputy, the Tall Texan arrived at his destination less than three hundred feet away. Using the jagged tip of a pocketknife, he opened the lock to the home of First Grand Junction president Bainbridge Kenilworth and silently climbed the back stairs. He entered the master bedroom and whispered its occupant awake.

"Mr. Kenilworth," he intoned in his slow drawl, "I would first like you to know that I have never in my life killed a man."

Kenilworth was unable to reply, as the tip of an Army Colt was pressing on his tonsils.

"Please know, sir, that this is an unpleasant task for me, and were you a married man I probably would not carry it out for fear of alarming your wife. But as you are a bachelor, and the only keeper of your bank's keys and combinations, I must ask you to please turn them over to me pronto, or I may have to spoil my spotless record and spend your money with a guilty conscience."

Kilpatrick removed the gun from the banker's mouth long enough for Kenilworth to recite the combinations. Ben calmly wrote each one down, several times politely asking his captive to repeat a number or the direction of a twist. The banker then unlocked the top drawer of his desk and produced his set of master keys, each one neatly labeled with the location of its corresponding lock. With a thank-you, the Tall Texan quickly hog-tied the president and then gagged him with a convenient doily. This is the way things should be done, Ben thought. No dynamite, no fisticuffs—just a few simple threats, a big gun down the gullet, and several feet of rope. It's regrettable that people must be frightened, but it's worth it if no one is harmed. The bank may not like it, but in the end the First Grand will still be rich, and now, Lord be praised, so will I.

Kilpatrick looked at Kenilworth one more time. "On the bright side, sir, an incident like this may get you to thinking about marriage. Forgive me for saying it, but a man of your age and position in this community without a bride? It's, well . . . unseemly."

Ben gave a small salute of parting to Mr. Kenilworth and then made his way back down the stairs and around to the rear door of the bank. He glanced at his gold watch: quarter past four.

Kilpatrick knocked on the back door as if it were his own home. When Chester Braithwaite Senior opened it, his eyes peered out into a night full of stars provided first by nature and then by the butt of the Colt. Ben filled Senior's mouth with his bandanna and secured his wrists with the old man's handcuffs.

Using the president's keys, the Texan unlocked the bank's inner door and then did the same for all of the cash drawers and the smaller of the two safes. No sense being greedy. Too much money meant too much weight. Too much weight meant a slow getaway.

He filled a large duck bag with all it would hold, fastened it shut, and then walked out of the bank, into the alley, and four buildings down, entering through the front door of the jail just in time to see a freed Etta Place sighting down the barrel of a taxpayer-funded Winchester. Laura Bullion stood motionless in the center of the room, her gun still affixed to the deputy's temple.

Ben frowned when he saw the state of Chester Braithwaite Junior. The poor man was sweating and trembling. He gently pushed Laura's iron away from the deputy's head. Hadn't he told her time and again that instilling such terror in a subject was unnecessary?

"Woman," he said, "don't tell me you haven't informed this gentleman about the terms of his confinement."

Laura Bullion looked at him. "Did."

"No, I don't mean saying 'Unlock it. The cell. Or I shoot.' I know that's a dictionary for you, but you needed to tell Mr. Braithwaite here that if he cooperates he will not be harmed. Did you tell him that?"

"Didn't."

"Did you inform him that all we desire is freedom for our friend and not his blood. Did you tell him that?"

Laura Bullion simply glared at her lover, apparently having used up that evening's quota of words.

"Do you understand our intentions, Mr. Braithwaite?"

Chester Junior nodded eagerly through his gag, visibly calmed by the Texan's reassurance.

"All right, then," he said. "Thank you for your cooperation." Turning to Etta, he tipped his hat. "Can you ride?" he asked.

At first she gave no answer, and then a grin of the most complete happiness spread across her face. Ben nodded back, picked up the canvas bag, and made for the street, the two women close behind.

As they gained the horses, Etta put a gentle hand on her friend's sleeve. "You and Mr. Kilpatrick could have so easily been captured. Why did you risk so much to rescue me?"

Laura Bullion swung into the saddle and smiled. " 'Cause you shut up, Pretty. Let me love all I wanted. Could've rat me out. Better for you. Worse for me."

She paused as Etta sat her mount. Before their gallop began, Laura grabbed Etta's bridle in one gloved hand and fixed her partner in crime with those black eyes.

"Did . . . what friends do."

Later, when questioned by his superiors, Chester Braithwaite Junior would state that through the cell's front window, he could see but a single horse. He recounted that Etta Place flew into its saddle, for an instant seeming to hang suspended in midair, silver in the moonlight, like a beautiful earring on a fine woman. Then, as the mount reared up, she leaned in tight, pressed her face to its mane, and was gone.

Diary,

It has been many hard days I have spent on the hidden trails of two states, and I have finally reached my destination (such as it is).

Hole-in-the-Wall, Wyoming territory. Somewhere between the beginning of nowhere and the end of nothing.

Even in such a place as this, freedom is sweet. I sleep at night in a canvas tent. My toilette in the morning is performed by a frigid stream. Dust is my face powder and rouge. At night the coyotes sing to chill the heart, and the stillness through which their voices cut is quiet as a crypt. But preferable to jail? Most assuredly.

I suppose I should be afraid of these rough characters, but not a soul among these godforsaken canyons has yet crossed the line to lewdness or filth as was so common in the train stations of Chicago and the streets of Grand Junction, to say nothing of the half-elegant confines of Mr. Harvey's dining room.

And regardless of my short time here, I have never been treated as anything but a respected member of "society." Perhaps this stemmed from being recommended by longtime inductees of the group. At first, this struck me as funny: something akin to being recommended to the Union League by a high churchman or a pompous banker.

I can imagine the official certificate:

Know All Ye by These Proceedings that
~~LORINDA JAMESON~~
ETTA PLACE
having met the requirements of leadership and
community standards . . . and also being wanted for
FUGITIVE MURDER
is hereby accepted as a member in good standing of
THE HOLE-IN-THE-WALL GANG
and as such is entitled to all rights and privileges
pertaining thereto.

Signed,

Benjamin Kilpatrick
President and General Manager

Laura C. Bullion
General Secretary

It is also strange that here it feels somehow natural to be referred to by my new name. Back in the world, I seemed never totally able to accept Uncle Rodman's humorous rechristening. Whenever a fellow Harvey Girl or chef called "Etta," my first impulse was always to turn round to see if she was standing behind me. Perhaps being cut off from all comforts and rules encourages one to new birth. Or maybe it is just something that accompanies administering a bullet to another's brain.

Of course, I am not alone here in having an alias. Only a few of the members seem to go by their Christian names: Ben Kilpatrick is one, Will Carver another. But Laura Bullion is known to friends and the hated Pinkertons as Della Rose. It sounds like something out of a dime novel, but so far I haven't been able to determine which is the <u>real</u> name and which the fake. And with Laura's (or Della's) sparing method of communication as much in practice here as it was in Grand Junction, I'm unlikely ever to find out.

Of course, in such a place as this, one expects to find more than the usual number of characters; and one is not disappointed. For example, today beside the cook tent I observed Frank Elliott, known as Peg Leg, the show-off of the group, as he performed amazing rope tricks before his hooting fellows. With a laugh and a whoop he would spin the lariat about his person and jump through it at every angle, dirty-blond cowlicks flying, punctuating each feat with a cornpone witticism or an old joke. Then he would heel-and-toe and make on like a lady fan-dancer, his feminine movements eliciting piercing shouts and bellows of approval. Perhaps because they were somewhat the worse for drink, Dave Lant and Elzy Lay both got up and joined Peg, and I laughed in spite of myself at this kick line of thieves and cutthroats.

Still, not all the men here are high in spirits and sweet in nature. Some are simply dangerous misfits, the flotsam and jetsam of the western criminal element. Many are drunken and silent, sprawled for days in stupor or engaged in fistfighting or gunplay over the smallest of slights.

And, hidden among the drunks and degenerates are a few men who possess the kind of nobility that would shame our blue-blooded Easterners. The living example of this is the acknowledged leader of the group, a jocular and charming Irish towhead who upon our first meeting grandly introduced himself (with courtly bow) as Robert Leroy Parker. But I had seen enough Wanted posters since coming west to know I was being addressed by the notorious Butch Cassidy.

He stands three or four inches shorter than I, with a wide and florid face and a grin that proudly proclaims a complete set of teeth, a rarity hereabouts. He is, like all of them, rough and ready, but his sweetness of manner and innate respect for womanhood have made me think of him as a sort of brother-in-arms.

Since my arrival in this rugged land there has never been a moment when Mr. Cassidy, bless him, has not done all he could to make me feel a confident and comfortable member of the band.

In camp, he strolls the landscape like a local politician seeking votes. He slaps backs, inquires after children, and nods with sympathy at tales of illness and injury. But even such grace cannot mask the resolve required to rein in this unruly horde. Cassidy's strength may be quiet, but it is strength indeed; there can be no doubt that it is Butch who sets policy for this gang and Butch who enforces it.

Only yesterday, the stinking, drunken reprobate known as Tom O'Day dared to challenge Cassidy, probably over the plans for some new crime. For what seemed like an hour, O'Day raged at him, spitting invective and insults before the assembled band. Still, throughout the abuse, the leader remained magnanimous; the more O'Day drooled and seethed, the more Butch portrayed the soul of reason, the patient voice of diplomacy, urging rapprochement.

"Now, now, Tommy," Butch said, "you're deep in your cups. You don't want to take punishment for something you won't remember tomorrow." Yet despite this fair warning, O'Day persisted. Worse, his curses had begun to stir some of the men nearby to nodding heads and their own whispered oaths.

And then it was as if a switch had been thrown inside Butch Cassidy. Seizing a handful of dust from the dry ground, he flung it into the red eyes of the drunkard. O'Day opened his mouth to bellow and Cassidy kicked high. His boot caught the villain hard in the stomach, drawing all air from his lungs. As he began to fall, Cassidy caught him with a right hand beneath the chin. O'Day rose for a moment and then crumpled in the dirt.

The encounter lasted not a second more than needed to acomplish its purpose. There was no note of revenge or cruelty, no show of pride in victory. Throughout the beating, Cassidy's wide serene face never changed. It was the same face I observed

on the day I met him and every day since, the face he presented
to all in camp any hour, day or night, the face that slapped backs
and asked after babies. Watching him, I felt both a thrill and a
shudder: frightened by the violence of which this man is capable
but joyous in his victory over the kind of mindless brutality that,
left unchecked, could only bring chaos to our domain.

The thumping complete, Butch walked to his fallen hat and
returned it to his head. Turning to the assembled outlaws he
began matter-of-factly to issue instructions, his manner never ad-
mitting the slightest possibility that they would not be obeyed.
Tom was to be carried to his bed and cold compresses applied to
his chin. His ration of whiskey was to be increased for as long as
the pain persisted, and no man was to mention the fight to him
or remark upon his defeat, even in jest.

Butch then brushed some dust from his chaps and walked toward me, still smiling but with eyes full of contrition. "Forgive
me, Miss Etta," he said. "I'm very sorry you had to see that." He
touched the brim of his hat, squared his shoulders, and walked
off toward his tent.

Chilling as it all was, perhaps it is also a lesson: that power
may stem not only from the lead of bullets or the skinned flesh
of the fist but also from the simple authority of one who domi-
nates without the burden of malice and rules in the absence of
anger. In these times, perhaps it is the only way to govern. Cassidy knows the modern world is coming, even to the bandit
country. He sees the new ways of catching a man and the new
breed of man so skilled in those ways. He knows of men snared
by the telegraph, the horseless carriage, the new female agents
and methods of disguise. And he sees perhaps more clearly than
anyone else that the society of the desperado is ending, and any
money still to be made had better be taken with the smallest
amount of fuss and the minimum number of corpses. If, in the
end, all this modernity is to get us caught, better to be seen by
the jury as a thief than a murderer.

Cassidy's second in command is a young man named Harry Longbaugh, who is referred to by all hereabouts either as "Kid" or (to distinguish him from numerous other "kids" around here) "Sundance," this last being the name of a jail where he apparently spent some time. In any event, he is a fine-looking lad: tall and broad-shouldered with eyes like the hide of my dear Bellerophon, hair and mustache matching. And although the sun has given us all the skin of day laborers, it has only turned Mr. Longbaugh a luminous gold. His posture is far less that of the cowboy, who seems to sit tall only in the saddle, than of the soldier, upright at all times, as strong and unbending as the flowering desert paintbrush.

Such beauty considered, when he strides across the grounds of camp he is invariably accosted by our ladies. Some are bolder in their propositions than a sailor fresh from a Schuylkill wharf, others catcall and even whistle as if he were the prettiest girl on a Tombstone corner. I suppose none of this is helped by his long eyelashes or the small black birthmark just above his mustache, the kind that fashionable ladies in the court of Louis XIV spent hours to create.

Even in this happy hell of bandits he remains clean-shaven and fastidious. It is well known that he steals away four or five times a week to bathe in the small stream that provides us with our single sustaining trickle of water. And although they are never said to his face, his constant ablutions are the subject of much joking here, as naturally they would be in a place where the calendar can turn twelve pages before a man comes in contact with any liquid other than whiskey.

If it is day, Harry Longbaugh is usually found sitting alone, apart from the card games and roistering. If it is evening, he can be found immersed in his summer-warmed water, attempting to remove the dust of hideout and trail and, I suspect, something else.

A hurt, a lover, a memory?

Something, in any case, deeper than skin.

The encampment to which Laura Bullion and Ben Kilpatrick had taken Etta Place was as well hidden as a Harvey Girl's crinolines.

The spot they called Hole-in-the-Wall was surrounded by sheer rock faces hundreds of feet high. The only entrance or egress was through a single narrow pass that was hidden from the main trail and passable only by horse or on foot and then only in single file. The surrounding canyons formed a sort of natural fortress. Its battlements were high stone cliffs, and its ramparts were rocky escarpments providing lookout points covering all directions. Butch Cassidy had told Etta Place that over the years a few of Mr. Pinkerton's detectives had succeeded in locating the redoubt, and all had received proper rites of Christian burial on the property.

Perhaps Etta would not have loved the rocky hiding place so much had it not come with the freedom to gallop it horseback. From the day of her father's death until her rescue at the Grand Junction jail she had lived the life either of a pedestrian or a passenger. She had walked, been hauled by hansom, shared a wagon, or stared from the windows of trains. But here, as an outlaw, she had ridden and ridden hard. Ridden fast, ridden every day.

Some of the animals had been quicker than others; some were skittish, some courageous. But she had extracted all there was from each, forcing the lazy to bolt like steeplechasers, the frightened to leap from ridge to ledge, the stubborn to obey like champions in a show ring.

Now, most of a year had passed, and whatever horse was beneath her, Etta was able to traverse the calloused landscape like a seasoned bandit.

Familiar with every stone and cactus, she committed the ways of every species of bird and beast to memory, absorbing from each their ways of speed or stealth. Likewise she had learned the ways of each man in camp: the drunks and the players, the horsemen and the pederasts, the card cheats and the rustlers, the professional gunfighters and the nearly professional gunfighters, and the farmhands and cowboys who yearned to become gunfighters of any kind.

And then there were the women and girls who, by their continual fornication with multiple members of the Bunch, brought a kind of comfort and peace to this odd society of troubled men. Etta had dubbed them the Prairie Saints.

In many ways they reminded her of the girls with whom she had served in Grand Junction. Some hailed from the ranches of the West, others from the less reputable precincts of its cities. But they had been far less fortunate in life than her Harvey sisters. Most had been prostitutes, and those who had escaped that profession were the few deemed too unlovely or malformed for its purposes: Clara with her withered arm; Maria, the harelip; the slow-witted Belle; the balding Jeanine. It had been heartbreaking for Etta to hear their tales of hungry nights alone in the snow or rain, outcasts abandoned by all—parent, church, and law. After such an existence, Hole-in-the-Wall proved a kind of paradise. A place where the male population was less choosy where they took their pleasure; where a homely orphan was welcome, even if only as a warm body. In return for their skills and affection, the Saints asked only for a canvas roof under which they could perform their duties and whatever victuals could be eaten in gratitude.

Indeed, if anyone had asked, Etta would have freely admitted that, yes, these men and women were the scum of the earth and, yes, for better and for worse they were now her family. All the family she had in this world. And bless them, one and all.

All save one.

Harvey Logan was known as Kid Curry to the bandit world and whatever unlucky law enforcement encountered him. He stood no taller than most of the women and the smaller women at that. Everyone in camp knew he did all he could to increase his stature by a combination of high heels and carved deer-horn lifts secreted inside his boots. On the few occasions that Etta had met him, he had done little but stare and nod.

Sometimes Curry would not be seen in camp for weeks, and even when he did appear the little man could keep silent for days at a time, ignoring all greetings or invitations to gamble, eat, or drink. Compared with him, Etta thought, Laura Bullion was a gossipmonger. But unlike her taciturn girlfriend, Etta had also seen Kid Curry launch into rambling and violent rants: obscenity-laced speeches filled with conspiracies and fueled by loathing. She could recall how, about a month into her stay, she overheard a casual discussion between Dave Lant and Bob Lee about the recent rise in ticket prices on the Union Pacific. Curry, silent for days, had suddenly turned on his heel and aimed a spitting tirade at the pair.

"It's an invention of the Freemasons!" he shouted at the two cowboys. "It's them what causes these fares to rise for American folk. The Masons in New York City set them prices according to what jewels and furs their wives still need. How I would love to get ahold of some of their fat women! The lessons I would teach them they would remember longer than any commandments from their prophet."

Now, as she knelt to gather water for the midday meal, she heard a muffled scream. One of those lessons had begun. And all in camp knew who the "pupil" would be.

Over the months she had been at Hole-in-the-Wall, Etta had caught brief glimpses of a tiny Indian woman peering from the rocky cave where Curry made his home. Sometimes she would emerge from its opening to discard refuse or tend the fire and then quickly scurry back inside. Everyone in camp referred to her as Little Snake.

Etta knelt to fill her water bag and again heard the woman's howl. This was not like the moans she had heard from the tents of the Prairie Saints. This sound was joy's reverse. The Indian language notwithstanding, Etta understood her words, each one begging Harvey Logan to cease whatever acts could cause such suffering. In the space between her cries she thought she could hear Curry laugh, or make whatever sound such a monster made in place of laughter.

Curry's "lesson" over, Little Snake would not be seen for days at a time. Others in camp had told Etta that the man's squaws usually lasted him about a year before they vanished. "Run off," Curry would say, before beginning his hunt for a fresh one.

"Your pardon, Miss Place, but you're getting that water all down your dress."

The man's voice seemed to snap like a dry branch. Etta looked down to see the leather sack overflowing. Placing it on the ground before her, she straightened her skirt and shook the water from her hands. As she stood, her knees trembled slightly. She turned toward Harry Longbaugh and murmured a too-quiet thank-you.

"Not at all," he said. "Can I get something to dry you down, maybe?"

"No. No, thank you, Mr. Longbaugh. You're most kind."

Harry looked at her long enough for his eyes to soften and then put his forefinger to his hat. He bowed slightly and began to walk off across the compound.

"Mr. Longbaugh, wait."

Harry stopped and turned to face her.

"Mr. Longbaugh, this is a delicate subject, but I am sure you could not fail to notice the sounds being made by the Indian woman who shares that cave with Mr. Curry."

"Yes, ma'am. Hard not to."

"Well, as a Christian, how can you stand by? Those horrid cries. My God! I've been told of the fate worse than death. If it has a sound, I imagine we have just heard it."

Harry Longbaugh took two steps closer to Etta. The toe of his boot drew a circle in the dust. "Miss Etta, here in camp a man's business is his own. This is where the laws of the world are evaded, not just the money laws or the property laws but the laws between man and woman. Now, if she was a white woman, Butch might see fit to interfere. But the Indian is made different from the human. Organs in different places, brain smaller. And though them sounds might be to white ears terrible, it could just be the savage way of female satisfaction. Until Butch says different, it ain't our'n to come between man and wife or whatever they call themselves in a place like this. Now, I could rustle a few huskies to move your tent as far away from Curry's hole as this acreage will allow. It won't stop the noise from bouncing off the rocks, but farther away is farther away."

Etta drew herself up to her full height. A vein in her left temple colored and began to pound. "No, Mr. Longbaugh, I am afraid that would not be satisfactory. You see, it is not the hearing of the act to which I object but the doing of it. I am used to hearing such nonsense about location of organs and displacement of the brain. In Philadelphia we often are subjected to similar stupidities about our blacks. But no matter where her heart might lie, in your own you must know that this is a human, your stupid code be damned. Can it be that the great Sundance is either so ignorant of pain or so afraid of Kid Curry that he cannot put a stop to such perversion in his ranks?"

Harry Longbaugh's eyes flashed for a moment and then turned sad. "No, Miss Etta. I am certainly not ignorant of pain."

Etta approached him. She placed one hand on his forearm and looked up into his dark eyes. "And this woman, Mr. Longbaugh. If she were I?"

Harry Longbaugh paused for a moment and then turned toward the screaming. Etta picked up her skirts and followed him. She could hear the jangle of his spurs as his heels crushed the alkali. At the entrance to Curry's cave, Harry stopped and cupped his hands around his mouth.

"Logan! Harvey Logan!"

Perhaps twenty seconds passed before Curry emerged. The little man was in shirtsleeves and blinked at the light of day.

Behind him stood the even smaller figure of Little Snake, her dark eyes darting left and right. Her face was filthy with grime and smudged with tears. Her buckskins were torn into rags and stained here and there with blood. The beautiful beadwork that had once adorned her breast and collar had been wrenched away, leaving only the odd lonely bangle amid a line of broken threads. And perched upon her head, bent at its center, its plumage stripped to ribbons, was a single eagle feather, placed there as a cruel parody of what once had been an ornament of pride. As Etta got her first close look at the tiny Indian she realized that the girl was little more than a child, sixteen years old at most, and she began to tremble in horror and fury.

"We'll get right to it," Harry said. "Them screams from your squaw are upsetting Miss Place."

Curry spat in the dust. "And why should I give a mule's damn about what upsets Miss Place?"

Longbaugh hooked his finger in his belt. "They upset me too."

Curry inhaled the contents of his nose, swallowed, and smiled. The sight chilled Etta like a first frost. "I see," Curry said. "What upsets Miss Place upsets you. And what upsets you upsets Miss Place. Ducky. Well, last I looked this was Hole-in-the-Wall, not San Francisco or—where is it you hail from?—Phoenixville-goddamn-Pennsylvania. I can't help what an Indian sounds like when she's taken. What would you do, Longbaugh, stifle all the whores here from hollering their pleasure?"

"No matter, Curry. It's pain. And we'll have no more."

"And what about *Miss Place* here, Mr. Sundance? What kind of noise does she make?"

Harry Longbaugh reddened from cap to collar. He strode toward Curry and, with one jerk of the little man's linen, lifted him until their eyes were even.

"This is the only way we're the same size, Curry. And just as I'd not beat a child, I'll not fight a dwarf. If you'd prefer we get equal by iron, then we'll settle it that way. Otherwise give me the woman."

Curry glared hatred but gave no answer. Harry dropped him to the ground.

As the dust rose around Curry, Little Snake bolted from the mouth of the cave and through the center of the camp. Etta gave chase, following her to the edge of the tents and through a maze of rock and brush. When she emerged into a stony clearing, Etta shaded her eyes against the setting sun. The girl had disappeared.

She could hear the clatter of her boots upon the flat stones. How could she track the woman here? This land was the birthright of the Indians, and not even a hundred years of white theft had been enough to negate their magical ability to dematerialize into it. Then, between two jagged crags, she saw the twisted dirty-white eagle feather standing only an inch or two above the rock. Etta clambered over a long flat stone and into the crevasse.

The girl was curled into a ball, her face tight up against a rock wall, arms encircling her legs. Her eyes were wild with fright, her teeth bared in defiance. Etta approached her slowly, speaking soothing words she knew Little Snake could not comprehend but hoping that their tone would convey her good intentions.

And then, as if called by memories of comfort, Etta began to hum a soft melody. It was a lullaby her nanny would sing to her whenever she was afraid.

> Hush-you-bye, don't you cry.
> Go to sleep, you little baby. . . .

She murmured the lyrics carefully, individually, long breaths between each. And as she sang she recalled the cradle of those soft black arms and how every note had felt like the balm of Eden.

> When you wake, you shall have
> All the pretty little horses. . . .

By inches and over hours, nearly still but for her lips, Etta approached Little Snake. And when she was within a hand's distance, she felt the trembling girl's head upon her breast. She was dirty as a miner and smelled as if she slept amid horses. Her breath came in short desperate gasps, like a victim of consumption. But Etta Place held tight to her in that crack of jagged stone. And for the first time since she had discovered her poor father dead in his mansion, she wept.

Detective Charles A. Siringo was never comfortable in this much store-bought wool.

He was a cotton man, a leather man. That was the uniform one wore astride a horse, hunting takers of property and enders of lives. Suits and ties tended to hang on him like a scalp from a Sioux wickiup. No tailor ever seemed able to drape his whippet's frame with the exact amount of cloth to make him appear a proper gentleman. They either used too much, the fabric making banners of his arms and legs, or too little, so that he looked like a scarecrow escaped from the field. He remembered well what one poor seamstress from St. Louis had said: that dressing him was like trying to cover the Eads Bridge; his bones the iron girders, his muscles the steel cables.

Of course, when meeting the swells, his blue serge was the uniform of the day and little could be done about it. And once Siringo laid eyes on the sartorial spendor that was Mr. Fred H. Harvey, he was thankful he had not arrived at their meeting underdressed.

One could have cut a fresh-baked loaf on Fred Harvey's lapels. His suit was of the richest gabardine, at first appearing black but then turning an almost iridescent gray-blue at the smallest refraction of light. The ensemble, like all of Harvey's clothing, was tailored on Savile Row in his native London. He made two trips there each year for this express purpose. His vest was a lemon brocade, set off by a black silk cravat and a gold and diamond stickpin large enough to proclaim his wealth but small enough to establish his taste. Harvey's plus fours were a perfect match for the waistcoat. They wrapped themselves around boots that gleamed like a millionaire's landau. Taken as a whole, there was no outfit to match it in in all of Leavenworth, Kansas, other than its brethren within Harvey's own cupboards.

Like the man, Harvey's office was clean and sharp. The desk shined like a new saddle, attesting to the application of twice the layers of stain and shellac a master craftsman would have called for. The bookshelves behind him were laden with the finest volumes stamped in gold and morocco: all of Mr. Dickens, the complete Shakespeare, and Harvey Company records so elegantly bound as to seem sacred texts. No speck of lint marred the rich oriental carpets, no thumbprint marred the fine woodwork outlining the huge room. The red damask adorning the walls must have amounted to ten years' salary for one of his girls. The windows were so clear as to appear glassless.

The world Harvey moved in was one of order hard won. Order carved out of wide spaces in roads masquerading as towns, their ramshakle kitchens striving to replace hog swill with cuisine. The disturbance that Etta Place had caused within his universe had now rankled for many months. The incident had created a flood of disastrous publicity for the company, something hitherto unknown.

And then came the train robberies and killings. Near Medicine Bow, Colorado: Cassidy and his so-called Hole-in-the-Wall brigade utterly destroyed the mail car of the Union Pacific Overland Flyer, blowing it to bits with dynamite and making off with over thirty thousand dollars. Apparently not satisfied, the gang exploded a baggage car at Table Rock in Wyoming, making off with nearly sixty thousand dollars. And at every scene, bystanders were astounded to see a stunning woman, dressed in the finest riding clothes and astride a luminous English saddle. It was she who was assigned to make her way through the first-class cars and rob the ladies of their jewels.

A manila folder on Harvey's desk was open to one newspaper account:

Mrs. Delbert W. Hatcher of Minneapolis, aboard the train to join her husband at a California mining venture, described the young female thief thusly: "I don't think she was more than twenty or twenty-one, and she was most beautifully attired and groomed. I would swear that her hat and veil were from Paris or at least New York. Her clothing reminded me of the style used by fox hunters in England when they ride to hounds. She herself was most lovely, with deep green eyes and lustrous auburn hair. Her diction was perfect and she held no weapon on us but smiled sweetly, politely asking each lady for her jewelry. Whenever she sensed anything had some sentimental value, such as a locket or a wedding ring, she very politely refused to take it, explaining that she was only here to relieve of us of our gold and silver, not our memories. To tell you the truth, she very much reminded me of Jane, my sister's girl."

"Jane!" Fred Harvey bellowed to Siringo. "My sister's girl!"

He slammed the cutting down on the desk's gleaming top. "Mr. Siringo," he said, in his clipped accent, "I pay the Pinkerton Detective Agency a considerable sum to keep the peace in such places as I have establishments. I pride myself, sir, that I have brought some small measure of civilization and refinement to every hamlet and dustbin of this land. And now two of my own, this Della Rose whom my people knew as Bullion and this Place girl, have brought untold disgrace upon my enterprise. Moreover, sir, my solicitors inform me that I am now being brought suit upon by the very rich family of the late Mr. Earl Charmichael Dixon."

Fred Harvey sat down slowly in his chair and placed a pale hand to his brow.

"I can fight the Dixons in the courts, Mr. Siringo, but not in print. Every little two-bit newspaper throughout the West is repeating their line: that a *Harvey prostitute* in a fit of jealousy killed their virtuous scion, so full of promise. They print it, Siringo, and the larger scandal sheets in Los Angeles and Denver and San Francisco rip it from the telegraph wires and reprint it in their rags. It matters little that your people have exposed him to me as a degenerate who ruined the lives and reputations of at least a dozen young women—three of them, I have come to find out, girls in my employ. I may know those facts. You may know them as well. But although I am considerably better off than this family of jackals, I have not the means of fighting their news machine and I can no longer abide the bad press."

Charlie Siringo said nothing, made no move to remonstate or defend himself. It was not the first torrent of abuse he had taken in the service of the Pinkertons and would not, he knew, be the last. And so he stood motionless, not even his eyes moving, and remembered Bartlett Janeway, a colonel in the Grand Army of the Republic, who would regularly excoriate his staff officers, Siringo among them; and if such a good man as Bartlett couldn't force an apology or excuse from him, he'd be damned if he'd let this Limey popinjay force his mouth open.

"So here is what you and your men will do, Siringo," Harvey continued. "The Dixon lawyer, damn his eyes and tongue, has informed me that I might avoid wrongful death damages and a long legal battle if I can deliver this Etta Place to his clients for a proper hanging. Believe me when I tell you, sir, that I have little stomach for such an assignment. I have spent my years in this blessed country making the barren beautiful and the rancid and tasteless delectable. Look around you. I am a man who worships taste and order. This so called request is untidy, and if there is anything I cannot abide it is a mess. But I am also in no position to pay out over one million dollars in settlements and legal fees for the sake of some too-spirited tart from Philadelphia, of all damned places."

Charlie Siringo shifted in his chair and ran his fingers across his drooping mustache. He knew no information of any use would be forthcoming from his livid client, and so he allowed his mind to think back over his previous encounters with Hole-in-the-Wall. There had been successes. As recently as July of the previous year his agents had run down two of Cassisdy's minor lieutenants, Elzy Lay and Sam Ketchum. They had been able to bring cases that landed Lay in jail and had set Ketchum at the end of a rope. But the primary figures, the brains and brawn of the outfit, remained elusive. Butch, the Kid, Kilpatrick, Curry, and his brother Lonny Logan all seemed able to melt into the night even at midday. When he had first heard they were traveling with two women in

tow, Siringo had hoped the gang would be slowed down for such purposes as the fairer sex required: shopping for parasols or corsets, perhaps,
or the ladies' daily toilette.

Hc had since learned better.

When four men and a woman who called herself Della Rose had
ended up in a Wyoming jail over Curry's shooting of William Hagen, the
sheriff of Elko, Nevada, the primary witness had been a mousy, half-
witted, near-hunchbacked fourteen-year-old named Sissy Chandler, who
claimed to be the sheriff's niece. Through crooked and blackened teeth
she had supplied the testimony that had driven the final nail into the
Bunch's casket. In a halting voice only slightly above a whisper, she positively identified Kid Curry as the one who had not only gunned down
her beloved uncle but had paused at her hovel in the neighboring county
and raped her senseless. The week before they were all to meet the hang-
man, a stagecoach had arrived from Cheyenne with the reward for the
gang's capture: eighteen thousand dollars, mostly in Union Pacific
money.

That afternoon Sissy Chandler arrived in tears to collect two thousand of it, the portion that the railroad and Pinkerton had deemed reasonable for her participation in the gang's conviction. As deputy Ronald
C. Bradley opened the safe to retrieve her prize, she produced a blue
metal Colt .45 revolver from beneath her ragged petticoats and clapped
it to his head. With the utmost politeness and a diction that was preci-
sion itself, she requested that Bradley please turn over all eighteen thousand of the reward money to her and to kindly provide all cell keys
appropriate to the release of Messrs. Longbaugh, Cassidy, Kilpatrick,
Curry, Logan, and Miss Rose. Thus had Etta Place not only freed her
compatriots but collected the reward for their capture.

Fred Harvey thought he detected a slight smile on the detective's face.

"Quite frankly, Mr. Siringo, I don't care what Pinkerton does with
Laura Bullion or Ball of Roses or whatever she might be calling herself
today. She is merely for me a matter of embarrassment, not of finance.
But I need this Etta Place girl, preferably alive but at the least identifi-
able. Obviously, the farther away she is found from Grand Junction,

Colorado, the less desirable, as her remains will not last over a long distance of ground. Should it be necessary to kill her, it is essential that your men engage the services of a photographer. The Dixons are demanding proof of identity in order to restrain themselves from the aforementioned legal actions. It will come as no surprise to you, sir, that a family that could raise such an accursed bastard as young Earl is indeed a pack of bastards themselves.

"I also hope it is plain to you that discretion is of the utmost importance. That means no bulletins to local idiot sheriffs. No reporting of movements or tips to helpful U.S. marshals. Not even any general knowledge of this girl's whereabouts to any but your closest operatives. The last thing I need is glory-seeking or credit-taking on the part of Pinkerton. *You* are to find her, Siringo, not some headline-happy lawman or mick cop who wants his mother to see his name in the papers."

Charlie Siringo rose with his host. He pulled down hard on his coat and vest, the white collar digging into his neck. "Seems a pity, Mr. Harvey," he said, looking at the crude drawing of Etta that accompanied the article. "Such a pretty young woman."

Harvey colored, from his well-starched collar to his perfectly delineated hairline. "The pity, Siringo, is that the newspapermen are now asking if *I* knew the woman. They're asking me just what *my* relationship with her was. I know what they're after. I know the story they so long to write. You've got to find her! It's costing me thousands in free luncheons, dinners, and liquor to hold them off. In Cleveland and Phoenix I had to hold *press appreciation days* with oysters and beefsteak and God knows what all. Two more such feasts are planned for Rapid City and Los Angeles."

Fred Harvey's hand shook slightly as he handed Charlie Siringo his tan Stetson.

"They say that in this country you can have any newspaperman for the price of a drink; that buying the press is a bargain. That may be true, Siringo. But not when you are faced with the purchase of every reporter in America."

Dear Diary,

It has been entirely too long since I have written you, and much of consequence has occurred. More than anything, I am amazed that in this hard place filled with hard people, something as fragile as love can bloom and that I should be among those to pluck its flower. Even more astounding is that the former misery of the Indian girl called Little Snake should yield my current joy.

Would that I had been so happy with her heretofore! It has been the labor of weeks simply to get the girl to uncurl from her tiny ball, and I sang every one of my old nanny's lullabies simply to get her bathed. During this difficult time she refused to see anyone but your correspondent, and even her trust in me was not complete. The girl would not take food or even water in my presence and refused to meet my gaze, as if the green eyes of a white woman could bewitch her back into slavery.

Yet at night, when she was most afraid, she would demand that I stay by her side, hiding beneath our rough blankets so that not even her black hair might be seen. And in time, once she was certain no monster, real or imagined, would come to wound her, she would slip wordlessly into my arms and lie still within them until daybreak.

And a lovely child she is, blessed with the fine high cheekbones and crow-dark hair of her race. Her figure is lithe and slender, and when, in these past few weeks, she began to stand and walk bedside me, her graceful posture recalled the ballerinas of my beloved Chestnut Street Opera House.

Still, July had long turned to August before she would allow even such a disreputable society as ours to witness this beauty, so great was her shame over Curry's savagery. She need not have worried.

On the day she finally emerged from my tent and walked among us, the Prairie Saints wept for joy. Over those difficult weeks a goodly number of our women had supported me in my effort, offering the poor girl food and clothing and, most vital, the sympathy of their experience. Conversing with them, I would learn to my horror that many had been similarly maltreated: by their procurers, their clients, their husbands, and even their fathers. I can only surmise that to them, the redemption of a child who had endured tortures equal to a dozen of their number must be somehow a victory shared.

Now I know why the Indian enjoys his reputation for fighting spirit, for I believe that the girl's return from Curry's world of brutality is due not to my ministrations but to the grit and courage of her ancestors. I cannot imagine a single white girl, your correspondent included, who would have escaped with her sanity from such afflictions.

But as remarkable as all this is, there was to be one more miracle, and it arrived two days ago in the person of a peddler.

From about our third week together my little friend had begun to shake her head and hiss in a most agitated manner every time I would address her as Little Snake. After several such instances, I at last guessed that this was not her given name but one more humiliation bestowed by Curry. Hence, I had dispensed with any name for her, making do with the soft cooing sounds to which she had so far responded.

Then, Mr. Eli Gershonson appeared. As he is everywhere in this territory, Mr. Gershonson is trusted here at Hole-in-the-Wall. For thirty years he has been known far and wide as a cheerful man who does his business and keeps his mouth shut. The worst of bandits are his friends, the most savage of Indians his valued clientele. On his ragged Conestoga wagon, Mr. Gershonson carries all manner of factory goods, rare finds in these territories where catalogs don't reach: pots, pans, knives, and scissors, silver and china, and (Lord be praised!) bolts of good cloth. I am told he is usually led into our redoubt once or twice a year to do his trading and that he is not only honest but religious, conducting no business on Saturdays, even in a place where most people couldn't tell you which day it was in the week.

As Mr. Gershonson and I were haggling amiably over a particularly fine piece of green velvet, my young charge shyly took up a bolt of Irish lace and, running her hands over it, spoke a few words in her native tongue. To my astonishment, Eli Gershonson replied to her with a torrent of words and intricate gestures of his hands. At first I could not imagine that an Indian would be conversant with the language of the Hebrews, but she replied to him and, for the first time since she became my charge, evinced a slight smile. Over the next few minutes they both spoke animatedly, their hands fluttering in the air like pairs of crazed sparrows.

When their conversation was concluded, the old peddler nodded gravely and then turned to me. "Your poor little friend here is a Sioux," he said. "She wants you to know that when, as she puts it, the snow last fell, she was captured by another tribe and kept as a slave. One of your men here apparently traded two rifles for her, and from what she tells me he wasn't very nice. She says she owes her life to you and that she will always be your koda—your friend. Oh, and one thing more, darling. She wants you to know that her name is a fine one and has nothing to do with snakes."

I was amazed, but not so much that I couldn't ask what her name actually was. Mr. Gershonson turned to her and said three or four more words. She said only one.

"Hantaywee."

"Hantaywee." The peddler smiled. "It means *faithful.*"

Faithful. I could not imagine a more worthy name for the child I had come to so love. But this is not the only love I have found here. I am only amazed that my emotion is requited, and in a place where its object is desired by so many. But then, mere lust for Harry Longbaugh would be easy for any woman. I have more than once recounted here his abundant charms.

But it was his rescue and subsequent protection of my little Indian, my Hantaywee, that changed for me his stature as a human being and brought forth an affection far beyond the base or carnal. A passion of the body, yes, but also of the soul. Since the very first moment she emerged into our little world at Hole-in-the-Wall, Harry Longbaugh has made it his mission to ensure the girl's protection. Harry Longbaugh, who told me an Indian's heart is where his kidneys should be! Even weeks before she finally emerged into camp, he made it clear to our assembled reprobates that any man who attempted so much as a whistle in her direction would deal with him directly. And since that courageous debut, he has approached her as he might the most refined of white women, speaking gently, touching his brim at her approach, bowing slightly before taking his leave.

Last evening, I encountered him standing by the river. In one of his pensive states, he acknowledged me but said nothing. As we stood alone I could hear the ripple of the water. Feeling the approach of winter in the newly cold wind, I brought my great buffalo robe close about my shoulders.

"Mr. Longbaugh," I said, "I must thank you for all your kindness toward the Indian girl. But I also must ask: What could have precipitated such a change of heart that you now treat her as you would me?"

Harry put his head down for a moment and then, gently taking my robe in his hands, pulled it more tightly around me, warming me against the cold. "I did only what was right," he said, "and I knew it was right because it was what you wanted." His dark eyes reflected the orange of the dusk.

I put my hand on his cheek and brought his splendid head down toward mine. I kissed him deeply and for a long time. Perhaps it was the wind, perhaps it was the same instinct that had caused me to tremble, but as he brought his lips to my neck, I felt him shiver. It was then I remembered the story of how an Indian maid proves she has accepted the love of her brave. I stretched out my arm and, opening the robe, gathered him inside.

I had never so realized my own softness until I embraced his sinew; never so delighted in the smoothness of my skin as when contrasted with the rough texture of his face and hands. It took all the will within me to part from him, though why I should have bothered I now cannot guess. Perhaps the last traces of the girl I once was still imagined a fine and upright husband gently taking me in a big clean bed of marriage, the two of us freshly consecrated by the laws of heaven and earth.

But this is Hole-in-the-Wall. There are no laws here, save only those one carves for oneself. And by these I am certain that I shall soon be known among our band as the lover of a chief, a bride sealed in a union made holy only by the spirit of these canyons, the woman of the Sundance Kid.

Suspect in This Robbery

Description of HARVEY LOGAN

NAME: HARVEY LOGAN, alias "KID" LOGAN, alias "KID CURRY"

AGE: 30 years   HEIGHT: 5 ft, 2 inches

WEIGHT: 135 lbs   BUILD: slight

COMPLEXION: light   COLOR OF HAIR: black

EYES: black   MUSTACHE: black, handlebar

NATIONALITY: American   OCCUPATION: cowboy, rustler

CRIMINAL OCCUPATION: Murderer and highwayman, train robber, cattle and horse thief, rapist, and sodomite.

HARVEY LOGAN is known as a criminal principally in Wyoming, Utah, Idaho, Colorado, and Nevada. Unlike CASSIDY and LONGBAUGH, who eschew gunplay when possible, LOGAN seems to have a penchant for killing. He is currently wanted in Johnson County, Wyoming, for the murder of miner PIKE LANDUSKY. Additionally, he is the prime suspect in a revenge killing against Montana rancher JAMES WINTERS, who is suspected of killing Harvey's brother LONNY LOGAN in self-defense. Of all of the so-called "Wild Bunch," LOGAN must be considered the most dangerous. He has stated publicly that he hates all lawmen and will not miss the opportunity to kill one. He is also suspected in several brutal rapes in Colorado and New Mexico.

PINKERTON'S NATIONAL DETECTIVE AGENCY
Founded by Allan Pinkerton, 1850
"We Never Sleep"

REPRESENTATIVES OF THE
UNION PACIFIC RAILROAD CO., INC.
$8,000 REWARD
INTERNAL MEMORANDUM. CONFIDENTIAL.
DO NOT REMOVE FROM FILES.

June 2, 1899, about 5:30 P.M., Medicine Bow–Wilcox, Wyoming, the express car of the Union Pacific Overland Flyer was "held up" by highwaymen, who ordered the engineer and conductor to slow the train so they might gain access to the car. They then proceeded to open the main safe by use of dynamite. The safe was blown open and the car totally destroyed. Such a method would indicate the involvement of GEORGE PARKER (alias "BUTCH" CASSIDY), HARRY LONGBAUGH (alias "KID" LONGBAUGH, alias THE SUNDANCE KID), and HARVEY LOGAN (alias "KID" CURRY).

From their first meeting, Kid Curry had hated Etta Place.

He hated that, unlike most women of his aquaintance, she was neither a prostitute nor a full or half-breed Indian. He hated the way she insinuated herself into the world of men and was rewarded with near-instant acceptance by the members of the Bunch. He hated her perfect English and the way she poured coffee by a campfire as though it were tea at the Palmer House. He hated her abilities with horse and gun. They aroused his envy and irritated rather than impressed him.

He hated that the meddling of Etta Place had cost him the use of Little Snake. An Indian, yes, but still flesh for his needs. He hated that now this Little Snake could laugh with the others, who would take grand pleasure in his humiliation; laugh with the likes of Dave Atkins, who now courted her as if she were a white Christian rather than a red, ruined pile of his own leftovers, too ignorant to even speak the American tongue.

Even more than this, he hated the insult of Etta Place's height. A squaw is only a squaw, but Etta, like every man here, towered above him, the heels of her fashionable boots and haughty posture serving to aggravate the situation.

But perhaps most of all, Kid Curry hated the fact that he owed Etta Place money.

Curry was not alone in that situation. Little more than a year after her arrival, Etta had become the Hole-in-the-Wall's banker, mostly by virtue of the fact that she was the single member of the gang who could keep company with a dollar.

After a robbery, all involved would be given equal shares, Butch and Harry being democratic leaders and not inclined to take larger portions for themselves. Plunder in hand, the men would descend upon the nearest town and get about the serious and expensive business of drinking and whoring, followed by a search for the West's most unkind pack of cards. By the time a week was gone, even the bandits themselves would be shamed by the sheer amount of money they had lost to those whose profession is the skillful trimming of suckers.

But Etta refused to squander her treasure as the men would. Her money might buy a few yards of fine woolen fabric, later to see new life as a tailored suit or riding skirt. More might be allotted for a long-wished-for bath and the clean sheets of a hotel bed. And a few coins might go to share a good dinner with Laura Bullion, the meal often served at the closest Harvey House (on such occasions Etta would find the meal doubly delicious, served as it was with a side dish of irony). Rarely would the total of these luxuries exceed ten or perhaps twelve dollars, hardly a king's ransom even in these scattered towns. The rest she consigned to a purse, then a Gladstone bag, and finally to a large duffel of canvas duck.

Thus did Etta Place eventually become the primary financial institution of the Hole-in-the-Wall Gang and their assorted outlaw brethren.

Initially, her loans were small: ten or twenty dollars until the next robbery. But the meaner the cards and the dice became, the larger grew the loans: three hundred dollars, five hundred dollars, a thousand dollars. As a proper broker's daughter, Etta charged only the current rate of interest, carefully researched by telegraph whenever the Bunch happened near civilization.

The largest loans were invariably made to Kid Curry himself. His luck at cards was second only to his subtlety with the opposite sex. Butch often said that the gang would only have committed half its number of offenses against decent society if Curry could keep his cards off the table and his cock in his pants. As it was, his losses were staggering, and even one as feared as he could ill afford the reputation of welsher. There were only so many games in any given state or territory; once a man was marked as a reneger on his debts, no decent group of cardsharps would welcome him, even if his skills were as rudimentary as Curry's.

By October of 1900, with interest accrued, Etta was by far the richest of the Bunch, having received over ten thousand dollars in payments and interest from Curry alone. On the first of every month, the men, sometimes as many as twenty-five, would form a line outside her tent or hotel room and settle their obligations. The young ones were silent, ashamed to be in debt to a mere girl (or perhaps they were simply intimidated by her beauty). The older and more confident exchanged pleasantries and passed the day along with their currency.

Not so Kid Curry. "Here is your money," the little man would say, "and may you choke on it. You and your fellow Freemason bankers."

Having heard this recitation before, Etta would calmly glance through her green ledger and, in her neat hand, make the proper additions to the lengthening column of figures. "I am afraid you are mistaken when you honor me as one of that fine society," she would say. "However, I accept your compliment and I thank you for your continued patronage. Here is your receipt. Please come again."

Kid Curry would spit into the dust and stomp away. The only thing he found more mortifying than borrowing money from Etta Place was paying it back, and the only thing more humiliating than this was his failure to discover where she hid her funds.

It was difficult to follow her. Harry Longbaugh kept a wolf's vigil on the girl, and when they traveled from hideout to hideout, robbery to robbery, her strongboxes were well concealed and protected by young outlaws whom she could well afford to pay for their service. Curry believed that if he could only find the hole or mine or dead tree that served as her vault, he would become a man of independent means, able to buy off the Pinkertons and sleep among the most costly of whores.

This would be no theft, he thought, no dishonor among thieves. It was, after all, his own money he was seeking.

Of course, honor would also demand punitive action for such usury. The disgrace to which he had been subjected was unendurable; and more than justification for his fantasies of vengeance.

As far as Butch Cassidy knew, the horse beneath Etta Place had no name.

It was one of his few incontrovertable edicts. No one among his band was to name any mount for any reason. Not even numbers were allowed. If a horse was to be referred to at all, it was as "the bay," or "the roan with the star," or "the paint," or "the little paint." At any time, Butch reasoned, he needed to be able to assign the horse best suited to the task of the rider. On one day, Harry Longbaugh might need speed but not courage; another day, Dave Atkins might require courage but not jumps. It was Cassidy and only Cassidy who reserved the right to create these strategies. It kept his band from getting personal instead of practical with their mounts.

Etta's horse today was the one they called "the big dapple." He was a twelve-hand gelding, nearly solid black at his hindquarters. From the hooves up he was stippled with spots of black on a gray that grew lighter toward the head. Based upon his most valuable quality, Etta had broken Butch's rule and secretly given him a nickname: Won't Spook.

On that morning Etta rode him into the town of Powder River dressed in new riding togs. The costume had arrived only the week before and she was excited to show it off, especially considering the trouble and expense to which it had put her. It had taken over three hours for Laura Bullion to outline her figure upon an enormous sheet of paper (itself the product of a two-week wait as it traveled from Meininger's artist suppliers in Denver to the post office in Buffalo, Wyoming). Laura had carefully measured every length and contour of her friend from leg to hip to head. What with letters and instructions and measurements changing hands between Buffalo and Henry Poole & Company, London, the whole had taken three months, but Etta reckoned the result worth the wait.

The jacket was a smooth Italian black velvet, longer in the back than the front and with only the faintest hint of a lapel. Beneath it, she wore a white chemisette with tight bodice and wing collar, topped by a green silk tie. Its color matched perfectly the delicate organdy band that ran the circumference of her stunted black silk topper. The skirt of the habit was generous; had one not been paying full attention one could imagine that its rider preferred sidesaddle. But to suit Etta Place, the skirt had been designed to act like a pair of giant pantalones so that, in the event of a chase, its wearer might grip the sides of her mount, lay to with her spurs, and travel. Its sheer size might also prove handy when it came time to hide whatever might need concealing: a rifle, a bullwhip, a shotgun, or a bank bag.

On this morning the task had called for the skirt to conceal a large canvas sack containing a six-foot diamondback rattlesnake.

This early, Main Street in front of the Powder River Farmers Bank and Trust Company was deserted, but for a few drowsy horses tied to a hitching post. After a sharp look left and right, Etta slid the bag from beneath her blowsy folds and with a single clean motion dropped the snake to the rough boardwalk. Almost before the rattler hit the wood, the nearby horses began to whinny and rear, stomping and whistling in panic all but Won't Spook, who remained stock-still amid the chaos

Normally, the bank guard would have been alerted by the confusion, but this morning William "Big Bill" Williams was absent from his post. The night before, Williams had been drinking in the Queen of Swords and encountered a young man who called himself Peg Leg. The cowboy said he had just come off a long cattle drive, and so, flush with cash, was buying. Never one to insult his host, Williams took full advantage of the new friendship and imbibed both beer and whiskey in quantity. (The day after the robbery, Big Bill attempted to explain to Mr. Helm, the bank's president, that he had been "slipped a mickey" by the girl Peg had purchased for him, and so his absence was justified or at least understandable. Helm called him a numskull and banished him from the bank, even as a depositor.)

As the morning sun began to cast its light past the bars of the teller cages, Helm and teller J. R. Finlayson jumped at a woman's shrieks from the street. They rushed through the big double doors and were dismayed to find a girl in a riding habit, near hysterical, shaking and pointing to the ground. They looked down to see the gigantic snake, in full rattle, coiling about the wooden leg of the hitching post. With the arrival of the bankers, the young woman's screams grew more dramatic, bringing other citizens running and causing the postmaster to faint.

At the moment that Helm and Finlayson ran through the front door, Butch Cassidy and Harry Longbaugh were walking through the back. Between Etta's fourth and sixth screams they had picked the lock; as the electric alarm rarely saw use this far west, the intrusion had raised no warning. Butch had estimated that Etta's diversion would keep the locals busy for approximately three minutes, long enough to gather a reasonable amount of cash and achieve their getaway. If it did not, he had strategically placed several of his lieutenants throughout the town, their numerical strength hopefully sufficient to minimize any unwanted gunplay.

Outside, a young man in farmer's clothes had attempted to take the situation in hand. As the snake clattered and hissed, the farmer poked at it with a rake while imploring the distressed young woman to mount her horse and ride away. Etta only screamed louder in answer and swooned into the arms of Mr. Helm, who, being not much bigger than Kid Curry, had considerable trouble not dropping her in the dust. Women shouted for water, men for whiskey.

Twenty yards up Main Street, Curry stood before the main corral of Bradley's Livery and consulted his pocket watch. At exactly three minutes after nine, he began firing his two Navy Colts into the air, the shots bursting loud and in quick succession. At the sound of the pistols, the crowd in front of the bank all looked north, the two thieves exited the rear door, and Sheriff Fisher Holley, who had been walking toward the Queen of Swords in search of coffee, dove headfirst into the alley between the dry goods and the barber.

As soon as his irons were empty, Curry jumped on his horse and rode for the town limit. In three more minutes he was met by Butch, Harry, and twenty-five thousand dollars. By this time, the farmer and two mail clerks were attempting to brain the rattler with ax handles retrieved from Gordon's General Store. So brave was this display that no one noticed that Etta had gathered her petticoats and quickly mounted the dapple. As she wheeled hard and began to gallop in the direction of her comrades, she could hear the confused Mr. Helm calling after her, inquiring as to her well-being. She was almost out of earshot when his words of concern dissolved into a fading string of curses.

Well out of town, Harry turned his horse around to wait for Etta. He worried little about delay or capture. Butch had chosen the town because it had only two lawmen, and Holley, a well-known coward, counted as less than one. When she at last galloped into his sight he was, as always, amazed at her presence, even at a distance of two hundred yards. Her riding habit billowed behind her like the wings of a raven, and its fluid blackness brought high contrast to the white of her face and her cheeks, now flushed crimson. Harry was proud that she rode with the practiced style of a champion, back straight, head high; but what thrilled him was the undisciplined abandon of the girl: the bank thief, the snake dropper.

She was laughing.

As she pulled within a horse's length of him, she reared the dapple up and suspended him there like a trick rider in a circus. Whooping like an Indian, she crashed Won't Spook to the ground, spun him around three times, and then shouted at Harry in happy, breathless defiance.

"We are rich once again, Harry Longbaugh! I wonder if even now they know what hit them! But I refuse to give up such elation so quickly! Race me to the river, Harry Longbaugh! Or does the Sundance Kid decline?"

For a moment Harry was dumbstruck. The rider's wind had defeated her hat pins, and she now taunted him bareheaded. As it always did in sunlight, her hair had turned to flame, and the scarlet strands that had escaped her careful fastening seemed to him like wildfire around her head. Then a smile slowly spread across his face and the race was on.

Over the next few miles Etta would cut in front of him, whip him with her crop, and goad him when he fell behind. She reached the river first and jumped down from her saddle, releasing to her waist the auburn hair he had never seen undressed. A second later he dismounted and she ran to him.

Never forgetting who she was, Harry tried to be a gentleman. He caressed and fumbled, not quite sure if one handled this kind of woman the way one did the usual kind. There were, after all, so many hooks and eyes, so many fine pearl studs, and, underneath, so much lace. His hands moved across her as if she would break, faint caresses slowly giving way to the unjoining of this and the untying of that.

Etta would have none of it. The woman whom all of Powder River was likely cursing as a she devil wasn't about to stop being one now. She kissed him and tore at him, ripping buttons and pulling leather. What he couldn't remove quickly enough, she did, until they stood by the river in a pile of cotton and leather.

They paused as if in midair and then blended together in a sea of warmth and chills. At last they kissed and he took her hand, guiding her into the river, and there they bathed in the water and the light. She hooked a long leg about his waist as he stood tall and still, bracing her gently against the currents. She cried and bit the hump of his shoulder as she took him, then lifted her head, holding his firmly between her hands and peering into his dark eyes.

"Look at me," she said.

She broke their embrace and leaned back from him, locking both legs around him and holding his forearms tightly. She did this so that he might see her, all of her.

Up until this moment, being beautiful had never been anything Etta treasured. It was merely an inheritance, something easy and unearned. But now it was no longer hers. The eyes, the lips, the neck, belly, and breasts, all of the parts the world had always seen as perfect now belonged to him. And so she filled his eyes with her beauty, bestowing it upon him as a balm and a gift.

Then she enfolded him again and they slipped into the river, still joined. The water rushed around them, cold from the mountain snows, and when they rose again, it was as something new. Something finer than a rich girl and a sad young man. Something purer than two thieves.

LETTER TO JOSIAH LONGBAUGH
12 State St., Phoenixville, Pa.
14 September 1900

Dear Father,

I hope this finds you well and in no ways put out by news appearing in the presses that makes me out a murderer. And I am very sorry that policemen and agents of the Pinkerton have come to our home and questioned you and my brothers.

I cannot tell you that I have not shot at men in the heat of battle or at those who shot at me first. I may be a gunman but I am no liar. Yet so far no one lies dead of my weapons. And if I may have the luck that seems to elude the Longbaughs then this way it will remain.

Just as it is a lie that I am a killer, it is the truth that I am a thief. I am good at this and have amassed a small fortune through my efforts. But please know that those who gets taken off by me and my band are only those that steals the greater from people like us, folk with naught to spare.

For more than any other reason I write you to say that in the midst of the world's misery I have at last found love. She is most beautiful and dear and some ten years my junior. She is also near a hometown girl, hailing from Chestnut Hill in Philadelphia, and is as refined as that place produces. She talks right and proper and can eat with three forks when she has them and alas, like all of the quality, cannot cook so much as a bowl of beans.

But for all that she holds no airs and takes the good with the bad like Mother would have. She sleeps on the ground when we do. Even when we are cold or hungry, she does not complain. She can ride and shoot so clever, she is now considered within our bunch a full partner. We have not as yet had benefit of clergy but live as man and wife, happy.

And Father, she is kind like few are. There was a little Indian girl here who was being hurt by one of our men. I didn't do nothing. But my Etta, she rescued her and nursed her to health. Just this morning that little girl left our camp with one of our young bucks called Dave Atkins, who has courted her all this year. They hope to go back to Texas, where he has people, and maybe ranch or rustle.

Like us all, my Etta is wanted. For the men of my band this is fair enough, as we are guilty of our charges and more besides. But my girl is innocent of what they say she done, and I tell you now that I will kill if it comes to that to save my love from regulator or lawman.

I don't ask your blessing nor pity for the life I chose. What I ask now is that you pray for me and her. Pray that God in heaven not now consign me to fire over all I have done, just at the moment He has allowed me to find this love.

And if it is true that love may bring grace, then a bad man like myself and a good man like yourself may yet meet one day in paradise.

My best to you and for your health, Father.
Affectionately, your son,
Harry Longbaugh

Diary,

We slept last night in this good hotel, and today Harry says he will take me shopping for jewelry. It is typical of him to be so thoughtful, jewels being the kind of gifts a poor boy imagines a rich girl likes. Actually, I would be just as happy to remain here in these sheets, warm against him, and continue our intimacies of the previous evening.

But one must meet the world, <u>non</u>? I only worry that every woman in the street who sees my smile and looks at my man will know the source of my joy.

Bedroom, sidewalk, or dime museum, I am more than ready for a respite from our adventures, especially as our deeds seem increasingly hazardous, the danger coming not only from the law and the Pinks but from the little serpent in our bandit Eden.

Every time we emerge from hiding to do our work, I thank the Lord for Curry's craven fear of Butch and Harry. I have seen with my own eyes his open and excited willingness to take the life of a bank teller or conductor without even token hesitation.

But Butch says it is better to have his fearless skill with us today than against us tomorrow. If only I could believe that the stories Butch tells are not just an Irishman's blarney: how Curry saved his life, dispatching the leader of a hijack crew even though his throat had been cut; how, unarmed, he fought off a wolf intent on devouring the infant of one of the Prairie Saints; how with only two pistols, he broke Elzy Lay from the Moab jail—leaving three deputies wounded, their shotguns unfired—and then took their dinner for the ride back to camp.

Still, I wonder if such courage is worth its madness. I feel I am not being immodest when I say I can outride and outshoot Curry (something I would not say about Ben Kilpatrick or even Peg Leg) and get my work done without leaving a mess. Were I the leader of this gang, I would dig a hole in the sand, deposit the evil dwarf inside, and be gone by the time he managed to climb out.

Curry's bloodlust notwithstanding, no lives have yet been lost in our escapades, although we did come perilously close on the two occasions in which we encountered a young fool named Woodcock, who seemed to believe that the contents of the Union Pacific's treasure car belonged personally to him. During the Wilcox job last year, I hear they practically had to shoehorn him from the car so that the dynamite could do its work. Thank goodness he realized resistance was useless by the time we robbed his second train at Tipton. On that occasion Butch greeted him in his usual avuncular manner, almost as a long-lost friend, and congratulated him on his bravery in the first incident. Just the same, they once again blew his car to kingdom-come-alleluia.

Do I seem a much-changed girl from the one who used to write of cotillions danced and ribbons won? Oh, yes, my friend, I am. Of course, I was raised with the teaching that stealing is immoral, that "he who takes what isn't his'n/must pay up or go to prison." But out here, the moralities are not at all the same as in the polite society from which I came.

Here, the railroads control everything and everyone. Their greed is relentless. I have seen whole towns—man, woman, and child—evicted from farms and homes for the need of a railroad right-of-way. I have cried more than once over their treatment of the cruelly exploited Chinese—an ancient and noble race, judging by those I have met—who have been worked to death driving stakes and laying track. And then there are the hapless Indians. For the railroads' profit, they have forfeited entire villages and been death-marched to remote areas. Here they starve for want of the now-slaughtered bison that once served their every need. This, while "dudes" from the East shoot the few remaining specimens from the windows of private railcars.

I contrast all this, Diary, with Harry and Butch, who have often come to the aid of such unfortunates. The woman with the pox for whom Butch rode over three states to retrieve medicine. The young Indian boy whose pony was shot from under him by Pinkerton goons and who would surely have died in this rough country without a mount. Harry gave him our finest: a fleet bay mare Thoroughbred quarter, stolen from a shipment of polo ponies bound for a Connecticut millionaire. There was even U.S. Marshal Eben Walsh of Rio Blanco County, Colorado, who was suffering the takeover of his domain by renegade soldiers armed to the teeth. Harry and Butch, along with Ben, Della, O. C. Hanks, Dave Atkins, and a few others, managed to drive them off without firing a shot. Butch's considerable charm figured prominently here, but the soldiers, being cowards, had no stomach for taking on seasoned gunfighters. Their usual competition, after all, was likely to be but a single lawman and a few frightened homesteaders.

Even in my capacity as "highwaylady to the ladies" I have learned by their example. Before I relieve any woman of so much as an earring, I ask myself the following questions: What is the quality of her shoes, how expensive is her dress, is her hat bespoke, and is she traveling with a personal maid? If by these inquiries I determine she can weather the loss, I gladly take her baubles, as they will be easily replaced—and in any case, she (like the railroad) is likely to be insured. At all times I do my best to set these women at ease and convey to them the idea that I am of a similar social class as they and that being robbed by me is far preferable than by someone rougher.

In my work, I try always to smile . . . and I have become adept indeed at spotting those trinkets that mean the most to the lady: a particular brooch, a ring given in celebration of a child's birth, a wedding band. These I never take, just as I never take even so much as a stickpin from a maid, farm wife or daughter, Chinawoman or prostitute, unless the lady has achieved the status of house madam. (During the Tipton job, I was approached by one such woman who offered me employment on the spot, allowing as how we would both make as much in a month as I was making in a year and that it would be from pleasure and joy instead of terror. I smiled and politely declined. She gave me her card "just in case.")

Tomorrow we leave for Fort Worth, Texas, and the wedding of our erstwhile colleague, Mr. Will Carver, to Miss Lillie Davis, an employee of Madam Fanny Porter. I have been informed that not only does Miss Davis possess a beautiful singing voice but that she has never in her career been subject to any of the various and sundry diseases associated with her calling. This is due in part, I am told, to the carriage trade that is Mrs. Porter's clientele and the excellent medical attention provided to all ladies in her employ. It will be a drive of something like a week, but Messrs. Longbaugh and Cassidy have engaged a private stagecoach for the occasion. The traveling party will include only the finest of outlaw society: the aforementioned gentlemen, Miss Place, Miss Bullion, Mr. Kilpatrick, and, for spice (Lord help us), Mr. Curry.

PINKERTON'S NATIONAL DETECTIVE AGENCY

Founded by Allan Pinkerton, 1850

"We Never Sleep"

REPRESENTATIVES OF THE

UNION PACIFIC RAILROAD CO., INC.

$10,000 REWARD

INTERNAL MEMORANDUM. CONFIDENTIAL.

DO NOT REMOVE FROM FILES.

On August 29, 1900, about 2 P.M., Tipton, Wyoming, the express car
of the No. 3 Union Pacific was "held up" by mounted highwaymen
armed with rifles and sidearms. Safe was blown open and the car totally
destroyed. The similarity of this incident and the events of June 2,
1899 at Wilcox, in which another Union Pacific train was exploded,
indicate the involvement of the so-called HOLE-IN-THE-WALL GANG,
lately also known in the press as THE WILD BUNCH. Express Clerk
WOODCOCK, once again the poor victim of such a robbery, positively
identified gang members ROBERT (formerly GEORGE) PARKER, alias
"BUTCH CASSIDY," HARRY LONGBAUGH, alias THE "SUNDANCE
KID," FRANK ELLIOTT, alias "PEG LEG," BEN KILPATRICK, and the
murderous HARVEY LOGAN, alias "KID CURRY." Courtesy agent C.

Siringo, the young woman riding with the group has been positively identified and is described below.

PLEASE NOTE: ALL STATISTICS BELOW ARE ESTIMATES, AS THE YOUNG WOMAN IN QUESTION HAS SO FAR NOT HAD CONTACT WITH EITHER PUBLIC OR PRIVATE LAW ENFORCEMENT AND NO PHOTOGRAPHS OR DRAWINGS OF HER ARE CURRENTLY AVAILBALE.

SUSPECT IN THIS ROBBERY

Description of ETTA PLACE

AGE: 19–22 years	HEIGHT: 5 ft, 9–5 ft, 11 inches
WEIGHT: 125–130 lbs	BUILD: slender
COMPLEXION: light	COLOR OF HAIR: red-brown
EYES: green	MUSTACHE: none
NATIONALITY: American	OCCUPATION: prostitute

CRIMINAL OCCUPATION: Associate of outlaws, thief, murderess.

ETTA PLACE is known as a criminal principally in Wyoming, Utah, Idaho, Colorado, and Nevada and is known to travel in the company of her paramour or husband HARRY LONGBAUGH, alias "KID" LONGBAUGH, alias THE "SUNDANCE" KID. Over the past year or so, PLACE has been known to acompany LONGBAUGH and his comrades in the outlaw brigade variously referred to as THE HOLE-IN-THE-WALL GANG and THE WILD BUNCH. According to the Grand Junction (Colo.) *Citizen's News,* she emigrated west from her native Pennsylvania to establish a house or houses of prostitution. She is currently wanted in Colorado for the May 29, 1899, slaying of EARL CHARMICHAEL DIXON, a prominent citizen of the city of Grand Junction, an offense for which she was tried and convicted. With the aid of unknown confederates, PLACE escaped from the Grand Junction jail, 30 June 1899. Despite her polite demeanor, considerable beauty, and fashionable clothing, PLACE is an active participant in the group's nefarious doings and is both an expert rider and a crack shot, especially with a rifle. She is believed to have recently helped her fellow road agents in the robbing of the Powder River Farmers Bank and Trust Company in Powder River, Wyoming, using a rattlesnake as a diversion. Agents should be advised that, if captured, all courtesies due a female should be followed as dictated by procedure, but be warned: underestimating this young woman could be a fatal mistake. In the event of gunplay, no special consideration is to be afforded ETTA PLACE.

3

John Swartz had made many fine images in his ten years in business, but he truly believed that this time he had triumphed. Artistically speaking, it was the best group photograph he had yet produced: five men, all attired in their finest, their ties perfectly knotted, each with a shining new bowler atop his head. If they hadn't been somewhat rough in manner and smelling strongly of whiskey, Swartz might have taken them for the core sales force of a local concern or even a group of North Texas oilmen come to document their big time in the city of Fort Worth.

Within the frame, two of them stand at the rear, right hands upon the shoulders of their seated brothers. These were the shortest of the men and thus were assigned the upright positions, lest they be dwarfed by the taller three. Even seated, the man at the center, the one they called Ben, is nearly half a head taller than those on either side. Gazing at his work, Swartz remembered that the gentleman who had initiated the transaction, one Robert Parker (seated, far right), was particularly jovial and friendly, so much so that by the end of the session Swartz was referring to him by the same nickname used by his fellows.

"All right, Butch," Swartz had said, "a little taller in your chair, please. Relaxed, right hand on chair arm, and . . . hold it."

Nothing could have surprised John Swartz more than the reaction of the shortest man, the one with the huge handlebar, upon the explosion of the flash powder. As it popped off in black smoke and lighted the room, the little fellow let fly with an oath and then tucked and rolled toward a corner of the studio, coming up with a silver .38-caliber pistol. Swartz hit the floor just as the first shot shattered the lens of his great nine-by-twelve-inch Dierdorff. The second shot landed harmlessly in the ceiling as, by now, Mr. Harry Place, the second tallest and by far the handsomest of the five, had tackled the small man. He was followed by Mr. Parker, Mr. Kilpatrick (the giant seated center), and a thin fellow whose name Swartz never did get. The small man railed as he struggled with each of them, screaming curses against their parentage and loudly proclaiming that Swartz was, in his words, "a Jew name." In their turn, each of his cohorts had exhorted him to calm. "Curry," they shouted, "it's a camera, not a goddamn gun!"

It took all three men to remove Mr. "Curry" from the studio, leaving behind only the shaken photographer and a sanguine Mr. Parker.

"Hell of a thing," Parker allowed, panting from his exertions.

"Yes, Mr. Parker," Swartz replied, wiping new perspiration from his forehead. "Hell of a thing."

"Now, now, John! It's been *Butch* all day and I hope this regrettable incident will not change the friendship we've developed, just as I hope you'll forgive us this trespass. We are rough fellows newly in from the nether regions farther west, where we were doing our best to convert the heathen redmen to the ways of the Savior. Our friend Mr. Curry has endured many horrors and privations during our service, and ever since he was staked out on an anthill by the Oglala, he has been a different man. At the slightest provocation, he tends to go into a defensive posture, as you, I'm sorry to say, have witnessed. Please believe me when I tell you that we had no idea that he had even purchased, let alone was carrying, a firearm. Had we been aware of such a thing, suffice it to say we would have done all in our power to separate him from it and prayed long and hard that his formerly calm and holy disposition would return to him."

Parker quickly surveyed the studio and the damage to both camera and ceiling. He reached calmly into his pocket and produced the largest roll of cash the photographer had ever seen. "It seems it will be necessary to replace your device and its lens," he said. "It also seems that the tin of your ceiling will want repair. Tell me, John, how long will it take before a new camera—even a better one—can be sent here from wherever such exotic instruments come?"

"Well, Butch," Swartz said, his eyes widening, "the camera must be sent from Germany to the distributor in New York. From there, it must be shipped overland freight to my studio here."

"And how long will this take?"

"I expect that the studio will do no business for the next five weeks or so."

Parker nodded. "If you will then do me the great honor of computing a sum that will include the price of your new camera, five weeks of business, repair of the ceiling, and, of course, the cost of today's session, then I and my fellows will do what good Christians must surely do: offer you complete restitution."

"But Mr. Parker—"

"Butch."

"But . . . Butch . . . this is a great sum. We are a highly successful studio. I daresay, one of the most successful this far north. These cameras are quite dear. I'm not sure that even the amount you hold in your hand could cover so much damage and lost revenue."

"An estimate is all I require, brother. God will provide."

"Well . . . Butch . . . such a camera runs about twelve hundred dollars with its lens. Our average weekly take here is between one and two hundred dollars. Averaging that to say, one hundred fifty, at five weeks that's another seven hundred and fifty. All told, that seems to come to nineteen hundred and fifty dollars."

Butch nodded, reached into his vest pocket, and pulled out another roll, larger than the first. "Let's make it an even two thousand, John . . . for all your trouble and allowing for any delays that may occur in shipping and so on. I ask only that you not mention this incident and transaction to anyone, as I would wish to spare Mr. Curry's wife and seven children any potential embarrassment. Lord knows, we need not add to the burden they will surely carry as we pray for him to recover from the illness brought on by his ordeal with the savages. OK, brother?"

Butch peeled off twenty one-hundred-dollar bills from the two rolls and placed them in the photographer's hand. With a smile and a tip of his bowler, he turned on his heel and left the shop. Swartz stood at the door and watched as he strode easily down Main Street. At the second corner he could see Mr. Parker rejoin his fellows and engage in what appeared to be some relaxed conversation. Swartz was amazed to see such good fellowship punctuated by Parker's boot engaging Mr. Curry's groin. The little fellow doubled over and Mr. Parker smashed his left hand across his chin. Mr. Curry fell to the ground and rolled into a pile of fresh horse manure. As he lay insensible in the dung, Parker leaned over his body, reached into Curry's vest pocket, and pulled out what appeared to be another roll of bills. Led by Mr. Harry Place, the four men then picked up their moaning companion and dragged him down the street and out of sight.

Swartz would have spent a few moments pondering just what kind of Christian sect engaged in such violence, but he had his camera to see to. It was true that the bullet had shattered the lens and lens board but, as luck would have it, the slug had curved up and lodged in the box behind it. The cherrywood cabinet and bellows were untouched, as was the negative holder at its rear. Upon further inspection, the photographer discovered that the glass plate containing the image of the five most notorious members of the Wild Bunch was completely intact.

Two days after the session, Swartz sent word to Field's Hotel. His note read:

Dear Mr. Parker,

I hope this message finds you well. You will doubtless be glad to learn that, in the incident of Saturday, the damage done to my camera was far less than estimated. Therefore, you are due a great refund, as it will be necessary for me only to order some replacement parts for the camera instead of an entirely new device itself.

I also have the happy news that the photograph of you and your companions was in no way damaged by the event and that a suitable proof print is now available for your inspection.

I also hope that your friend Mr. Curry is fully recovered from his illness of the other day. He will remain in mine and Mrs. Swartz's prayers.

> Very truly yours,
> John Swartz
> Swartz Photographic Studio
> 705 Main Street, Fort Worth, Texas

Swartz gave the letter to his page and then placed a large framed print of the picture in the studio's front window. He did this partly as a pleasant surprise for Mr. Robert Parker but even more as an advertisement for the type of first-class portraiture available within.

To his great disappointment, Swartz's messenger returned within half an hour and told the photographer that Mr. Parker and his fellows, in an apparent hurry, had checked themselves out of Field's Hotel early the preceding morning.

As events ultimately unfolded, Robert Parker and the other Christian gentlemen would have no use for the picture.

Charlie Siringo would.

They were the only two souls on the platform that morning, but that was two more than the locals were used to in Yellow Jacket, Colorado. Most days, the stop was good only for taking on water or mail or the occasional group of workers arriving from or returning to Mexico.

The man was dressed for this rugged land. His outfit was that of a cowhand: worn Stetson, vest and chaps of leather, and trousers of heavy denim. The woman, however, was enough out of place to appear an apparition, a page from *The Delineator* or *Godey's* magazine. The high velvet collar of her three-quarter-length traveling coat framed a face designed by God for angels: the sort of face that women in these parts lost early to wind and sun and care. Her long skirt was of the same fabric: alternating horizontal stripes in light and deep green velvet, the whole trimmed in black and set off by mint silk lapels sweeping nearly to the shoulder. Her blouse was fastened by ivory studs in a barrel shape, kept in place by four chevrons of a rich rust brocade. She was crowned by a broad black hat; its brim rising high, the right side a mass of green moire ribbon and a matching ostrich plume.

Beside her on the platform lay four large trunks with shining bronze locks, exactly the gear one would expect to accompany someone who would bother to wear such a costume where the only audience was buzzards and prairie dogs. In the dry chill of early fall, she fell against her cowboy, seeking shelter from the uncertainties before them.

By now, John Swartz's group portrait had been distributed to Pinkerton agents from Texas to Montana and from Idaho to Missouri. Although the Bunch had never seen it, the photograph hadn't escaped the notice of Fairhill P. Dolan, a middle-level detective in Pinkerton's Fort Worth office. He had run into both Butch and Harry on more than one occasion, and Logan had once smashed a beer mug against his head in a little town near Odessa.

Charlie Siringo had personally negotiated the contract with Swartz that allowed the company to buy the rights to the heads of the outlaws. A photographic bust of each man was isolated from the group and enlarged, providing as much detail as a sheriff or bounty hunter could ask. The photographs were then printed on cards and Wanted posters and mailed to law enforcement across the West. By the time Etta and her friends had crossed the border into Oklahoma, a small army had joined in their pursuit. There were U.S. marshals from as far away as San Antonio, farm boys with rusted shotguns seeking reward and reputation, regulators, eastern reporters, and the scum of the Texas earth. It was only Butch's knowledge of horseflesh that saved them. He always knew where a fresh mount could be bought or stolen, and he never failed to choose the animal that could run a fraction faster than those giving chase.

Butch knew no one could find them once they disappeared into Hole-in-the-Wall. And even if someone did, the place was so isolated by rock and cliff it could be defended against the Grand Army of the Republic by two men with rifles and someone to cook. But what good would it do them to hide, sitting on the fortune they had accumulated? There could be no significant gambling on the floor of a cavern, no drinking and carousing inside a tent. No, if ever they were to enjoy their profits, the money had to be moved to a place where it was spendable. And considering the degree of heat that had been generated by the Swartz session, that task could only be accomplished by someone with a face not in wide circulation.

Once the decision was made, Butch's first order of business was to sucker-punch Kid Curry into unconsciousness and then bind him hand and foot inside one of the caves. He allowed later that he could have gotten the little man drunk and unconscious, but given Curry's hollow leg, it would have taken too much time. The faster Etta was sent to New York with the money, the faster they could follow it east and indulge in what it bought.

That money now lay within the largest of the fashionable trunks piled beside the man and woman standing on the platform in Yellow Jacket: eighty thousand dollars, some in banknotes, some in gold. Even as she wept against Harry's collar, Etta remembered how amazed she was that money enough to keep a family in home and food for a lifetime could fit into a space small enough to water a foal.

Harry didn't know whether to hold her tight or lightly. The night before in their small hotel he had been as desperate for her as she for him. To lie naked beside such a woman as this, even once in a man's life, was an honor; to be loved by her, a miracle. And now, in tribute to all that had been given him, he chose to hold her sweet rather than strong. His time had come to be remembered, and he wished to be remembered as gentle.

Across the north wind they could hear a long whistle. She nearly laughed aloud as she recognized it as the sound of the Prarie Zephyr, a train they had robbed twice.

"Have you got everything?" he asked her. "Is there anything you have forgotten?"

Etta laughed. "Well there is the little matter of about sixty thousand dollars buried near Estes Park."

Harry was unamused. "That's your money. You earned it banking for those wastrels."

"Anything I have is yours. And if it was up to me, it too would be headed for your little bank in Brooklyn right now."

"I've told you before. Outlaw's insurance. Now, please. I ask you again. Is there anything you've not remembered?"

The lace along the edge of her handkerchief scratched at her nose. "No, Harry," she said. "And before you ask, I am suitably armed for the journey. Derringer in sleeve, revolver in handbag, stiletto inside jacket pocket. You packed the money, so you know it is here. I am heading toward safety. But even more than the Pinkertons, my worry is Curry. He fairly foams at the mouth with insanity. And I fear every day that he will seek vengeance upon you and our dear Butch."

"It's no never mind," Harry said, taking her face in his hands. "We have been handling Logan for years and we'll handle him still. There's no reason for you to worry. We are full-grown outlaws and used to caring for ourselves. My only trouble now is that a cruel and careless woman has worn me out with love and ruined me for the services of skilled professionals. Until this awful woman returns to me, I'm doomed to solitude and the company of dog-ugly men."

He kissed Etta full on the mouth and could taste her tears at its corners.

"I'll be in New York before you can whistle," Harry said. "All the arrangements have been made with your landlady by telegram. But please be careful. I hear that Chinamen capture girls to be white slave whores. A woman like you could make someone's fortune."

Etta laughed. "You are dear and ridiculous, my love. Have you forgotten that I too am a dangerous outlaw and used to caring for myself? No, I am far more concerned about how you will cotton to a city so big and bright. You who once lived a short ride from Philadelphia and never visited."

As the locomotive gained the water tower, they embraced once more. Harry could not hide the tears of parting and so made no effort. He turned to tip the black porter as he hefted the four trunks. When he turned back, Etta was gone.

The sun was now high behind the third car, and for a moment he was blinded. Then, as if from a sunburst within his eyes, he saw her through the window. He made to raise his hand in a grand salute of farewell but thought better of it. This was not a gesture one made toward Miss Lorinda Reese Jameson of Philadelphia. And so his hand rose only to the level of his shoulder and he contented himself with a single wave.

Diary,

New York is very much as I remember. Everything is <u>too</u>: The buildings are too high, the clothing too fashionable, the women too beautiful, the rich too rich, and the poor <u>far</u> too poor. Is it any wonder that, living as I do a life of extremes, I should so love a city that often seems all one way or all another?

The trip here was also <u>too</u> something: it was too damn <u>long</u>!

Luckily, as I am now a lady of some means, I traveled in the most comfortable of circumstances. I took a private compartment and had my meals served therein. I suppose I should have enjoyed my journey, as it will be the last chance I have for any degree of luxury for some time. Here in New York, I must live modestly and quietly, so as not to call attention to myself from any inhospitable sources, most notably the Pinkertons.

Of course, it is natural that I was chosen for the honor of accompanying our treasure far from the deserts of the West. Although I am now myself a wanted person, no one doubts that the so-called law will be concentrating its efforts on the menfolk of our group. Perhaps most significant to my mission, there are no Pinks who have seen me at close range. And thanks to the artistry of Mr. Swartz, I am now the only one of whom the police have no picture.

As to our money, it currently resides in a safety deposit box in a bank deep in the city of Brooklyn. We have placed it there rather than in Manhattan to minimize the chance of encounters with any old employees or friends of Father. Too, there is also always the question of the Philadelphia villains. As Uncle Rodman once observed, their reach is long, and my dear hometown is a mere ninety miles away.

As I am alone, my landlady, Mrs. Taylor, has become my greatest friend. She is, like so many who keep boarders, a widow, her husband having died in the same influenza epidemic that took their seventeen-year-old son. She has allowed me to stay in her establishment, rather than have me seek shelter at a ladies' hotel, because of what she believes is the imminent arrival of my husband, the respectable Mr. Harry Place.

I wish I was as sure of that arrival as she seems to be. Harry and Butch are now over a week past our date of rendezvous, and as I have had no word of either of them I am more than a little concerned. I do not expect a letter, as it is probable that any area in which they may currently be found is without convenient post. A telegram is even less likely, as in the country where they are riding the only wire is likely to be barbed.

But more than loneliness, it seems my chief tormentor these days is tedium. Now that I have been here over a week, filling my time has become a major preoccupation. At first, it was enough just to watch from my window the ever-changing parade of types: the tradesmen and the shopgirls; the Negroes carrying out their thankless tasks; the Jews with their tall hats and beards and long locks of hair; the handsome and mysterious Italian boys. Everyone is selling something to everyone else in a different language, and yet business is transacted. For one who has only recently shaken the dust of the plains, it is quite a human exhibit.

But these entertainments last only so long. I can safely say, Diary, that I have never been bored in my life, but staying in my little room amid chintz and linen is beginning to drive me to distraction. And as I am supposed to be the wife of a prosperous western businessman (I had the bad taste to tell Mrs. Taylor that my husband was involved "in the railroad business"), finding paying work is out of the question. Even here, among the bohemians of Greenwich Village, there is a limit to the number of times a woman can be seen wandering about unescorted without some specific destination in her eyes. As Della would say in her inimitable way, "I'd give my left tit" to be useful again. Whenever I see a streetcar go by, it has been only with the greatest difficulty that I have avoided the temptation to board it in one leap, take the conductor prisoner, and collect every purse.

In her career as an outlaw, Etta Place had learned to abide many privations without complaint. During those times when Hole-in-the-Wall was on the run, she did without the most basic of women's needs: a clean blouse, a horsehair brush, even the proper mainstays needed during those days when her body insisted on asserting its feminity. But whenever the gang got close to civilization, Etta would take any opportunity, even risk capture, for the chance to be clean: to immerse herself in anything that could wash away the filth of the trail and the weight on the heart. Even in the backroom of a barbershop, with the boiling kettle fired for a twenty-five-cent bath, she would instantaneously become the most spoiled of rich girls, laying claim to hot water and soap as if they were a God-given right.

Never had she forgotten those life-restoring few hours in Chicago when she and her new Harvey colleagues had discovered what the Russian girls called their "bania." If Chicago had such a magnificent palace of cleanliness and health, didn't it stand to reason that New York must surpass it? As soon as she arrived in Manhattan, Etta had sought out the finest bathhouse in the district. The Alhambra exceeded all her hopes and expectations.

As she walked up to its double iron door, Etta expected little, given the squalor of the exterior. All around the columned entrance were the signs of hard work for little pay or work for no pay at all. The emaciated children of the Lower East Side roamed the nearby streets in rags, some barefoot in the September wind, dodging the fetid leavings of the horses that stood in great mounds in the gutter. To and fro, peddlers far more ragged than those in Greenwich Village screamed beside their pushcarts, hawking their wares in half a dozen tongues as well as in an English not so much broken as smashed to bits.

But stepping inside the Alhambra, all her fears were allayed. Yes, like the city itself, the Alhambra was *too*. By comparison, the Luxor was a mere introductory course in the Turkish bath. Where the Luxor had one hot pool, the Alhambra had three. Where the Luxor had two steam baths, the Alhambra had five. Here, Italian marble replaced granite, ceilings soared thirty feet to the sky, and the attendant who brought you your towel was uniformed in a white brocade coat and a silver turban set fast with a pure gold clasp.

Once Etta had discovered the place, she visited twice a week to be bathed and massaged by the mighty and wordless Slavic women who asked not to be appreciated, only obeyed. On this October Sunday she had spent from ten o'clock in the morning until two o'clock in the afternoon within the sweet confines of the palace. And as she would sit in the ladies' steam bath or shiver in the cold fountain, she could feel her cares—Earl Dixon, the Pinkertons, Curry, her loneliness—all being washed away.

As she reluctantly left the Alhambra and turned dreamily down Orchard Street, Etta felt that all was truly right with the world. By now she knew to treasure the bliss, knowing it would last only until the front door of Mrs. Taylor's. Once inside the boardinghouse, there would be only the hours divided between boredom and despair as she waited for word of Harry and their friends, now delayed nearly a month. She closed her eyes and savored the tingle at her scalp and the deep rest in her shoulders that she knew would soon desert her.

At the corner of Rivington Street, Etta had turned to make her way toward the more civilized quarters of Greenwich Village when she heard, among the joylessness and squalor of poverty, perhaps the most cheerful sound of her life. It was an odd combination: a solo piano, slightly out of tune, bouncing out the happiest of polkas, laid over every five or ten seconds by a sweet and dignified voice offering words of encouragement, and punctuated here and there by crystalline laughter.

"Yes, yes, that's right . . . jolly good! . . . Capital, Malka! . . . Oh, you're doing very well!"

The voice had come from a large but modest tenement, its front door open in the October afternoon. A gilded sign over the building read RIVINGTON STREET SETTLEMENT HOUSE. Etta walked up to the large window of the brownstone and peered inside.

The joyful sight that met her eyes was a perfect match for its sound. She saw a large room, obviously designed for grand functions but bare of furniture or carpets. Against the far wall stood a line of perhaps a dozen girls, the eldest not more than sixteen, all dressed in simple white uniforms of a sailor design: full blouse, wide skirt, black hose, and shoes. Their eager faces indicated their ancestry as probably Italian or Jewish, as befit the population of the neighborhood. Since her arrival in New York, Etta had seen these faces hundreds of times every day: young faces made old by unending work in the sweatshops, darkened by the frustration of early marriages or betrothals to men they had never seen.

But today every face was bright with fine humor, every pair of hands clapping along to each beat of the piano and the warmth of that fine and cultured voice.

Perhaps it was still the intoxication of the Alhambra, but to Etta the couple in the center of that big room seemed almost a mirage, like one of the new motion picture strips come to life: two women engaged in a blissful moment of what was clearly a dance class. A plump red-haired young girl, dressed in the uniform of the settlement house, was being whirled and twirled about the floor by another girl a world different from herself, a most astounding creature, by turns as beautiful and as ugly as any woman Etta had ever seen.

She was dressed in a white silk blouse with a tall collar, a gather of lace at her throat. Her skirt was silk taffeta, long and black, cinched at her narrow waist by a circular buckle of pure silver. She was as tall as an Amazon, close to six feet in her fine bespoke boots. Taller even than Etta herself.

As her splendid head whirled by the window, Etta admired her lustrous golden hair, piled high and tied with a white damask ribbon. Her eyes, holding a laughter all their own, were each as large as a hen's egg and blue as a robin's. Her nose was slightly turned up in the aristocratic manner, but the face seemed to go bad below it. Her enormous thick-lipped smile revealed teeth nearly as large as those of a horse and set in a pronounced overbite. Even this might have been a charming feature, but the face ended in a weak and receding chin that robbed her of any claim to beauty by the shallow standards of the world.

Yet in motion she was like a goddess come to earth, towering over her little partner, kicking up legs that seemed to have no end, holding the girl in long and graceful arms. When that ruined mouth smiled, the world seemed to light. And as that gorgeous voice cried instruction, Etta could well imagine a poor girl might believe that all things were possible in this new world if a woman like this could teach her to dance.

As the tall young woman reached over to pull a thin dark-haired girl from the line, Etta found herself drawn irrevocably inside: first to the foyer, then the hallway, and finally the archway just outside the large room. The blond woman now counted as they whirled. "One and *two* and three and *four*! Capital, Donatella! That's right!"

And then the piano gave a final low bump and the music was over. The instructor bent in a low and courtly bow. The Italian girl seemed lost at first and then brightened and curved herself into a curtsy as perfect as any Etta had seen at a Philadelphia cotillion. As she returned to the line she was grinning, her hand to her heart in breathless and joyous fatigue. The rest of the girls greeted her as a hero, chattering away in native tongues and fractured English until their mistress quieted them.

"Very very good, girls!" she told them. "*Bellissima! Mazel tov!* As usual, you all have learnt your lessons most admirably!"

The silver laugh chimed again, joined by the half of the class that understood English well enough to receive the compliment.

"Being able to dance properly is an important part of life in America. After all, what fine young man will be at all interested in a dull girl unable to kick up her heels? Dancing is as important to becoming a true American as applying for citizenship or the woman's right to vote—

which, God willing, we shall win this very year. As important as your own name. Malka?"

The stout red-haired woman took a step forward.

"Yes, Miss Eleanor?" she said, in an accent as thick as a Ukraine noodle.

Miss Eleanor slowed her speech. "Please introduce yourself to the class like a good American girl."

The young woman smiled. "Hello. My . . . name . . . is . . . Malk— *Molly* . . . Berger . . . and . . . I . . . am . . . very pleased . . . to make your . . ." —She paused for a moment and then smiled broadly— *"acqvaintance!"*

The class burst forth in applause and Molly Berger colored from collar to hairline in pride.

"Excellent! Excellent, Molly! You are obviously working very hard in your English classes and soon you shall speak like a native born! Remember that here you are *Molly* Berger, an American girl. But remember, too, that I have had the pleasure of meeting the handsome Mr. Radomiselski, your intended. And you will have to work even harder to match the excellence of *his* speaking!"

Half the girls erupted in laughter and then translated for the others, who laughed as well. Molly Berger blushed again.

"Thank you, thank you all, ladies!" the tall woman said, and then uttered a few awkward phrases in Italian and Yiddish. "I will see all of you back here next Sunday."

As they melted away into their harsh world, Miss Eleanor took notice of the stranger peering through the ballroom archway and approached her with a purposeful stride. Close now, Etta could see that that she was probably younger than many of her European charges. Her skin was flushed and flawless, a light gold that seemed nearly to blend with her hair. Her clothing was of the finest quality, almost certainly designed and hand sewn abroad.

She flashed the brilliant equine smile. "Yes, madam. May I be of some service?"

Etta hardly knew what to say. Her three years' experience as an outlaw had trained her to lie almost as a reflex.

"Please excuse me, Miss . . . Eleanor," she said, "but I was walking down the street, returning to my hotel, when I was . . . captivated by the beauty of the music emanating from your hall."

"Oh, yes," she replied. "Madame Kisleikoskaya does play most wonderfully. In her native Moscow she was a renowned concert artist, and we at Rivington consider ourselves fortunate indeed to have the benefit of her talents."

Madame Kisleikoskaya gave no sign of understanding this praise. She picked up her sheet music promptly and efficiently and left the room with only a nod to her young mistress.

"But you seem to have the advantage of me," Miss Eleanor said.

"Oh, I beg your pardon. My name is Mrs. Harry Place and I am from Colorado. I am currently staying at Mrs. Taylor's house in Greenwich Village while I await the arrival of my husband, who is still in the West on business."

"Well, Mrs. Place, thank you so much for stopping. I hope you enjoyed watching our young women dance. There is so very little to brighten their lives. I believe it is incumbent upon women like you and me to provide some short respite from the grueling work that is, sadly, their entire lives. Wouldn't you agree?"

"Oh, yes!"

"It is veritable food and drink for me to come here, Mrs. Place. I am lucky enough not to be spending my time at piecework or living in two rooms with a dozen people. There but for the grace of God, as they say. . . ."

"But to see the way you speak to them, Miss Eleanor. Even though they can hardly understand a word. And yet they smile and laugh at your every thought and gesture. It seems, if I may say, miraculous." Etta paused and looked about the empty room, still feeling the hope of the now-vanished dancers. "How I envy you your work!"

Eleanor nodded and smiled. But as she did she shrewdly appraised the status of the beautiful woman standing before her. Clean as a whistle and scented with a French cologne. Hat straight from the pages of *La Nouvelle Mode.* Coat of the finest black camel hair, its collar trimmed in fox.

Boots of two-tone kid, more than likely molded to her foot at great expense. All of this and new to town with little to do but wait for a wealthy husband to make his way back to her.

"My work can be the work of any person of goodwill. If I may ask, Mrs. Place, how are you passing your days while you await your husband's return?"

"I am afraid that I have very little to occupy my time these long afternoons. And I have received as yet no firm commitment from Mr. Place as to the date of his arrival."

The blue eyes seemed to brim with a sympathy Etta hadn't felt from anyone since Mrs. Kelley in Chicago. It seemed a lifetime gone. "How very lonely you must be, Mrs. Place! I hope you will not think me familiar, but I well understand loneliness. Might I make a suggestion?"

"By all means."

"By your clothing and demeanor, you are clearly a gentlewoman. And your speech . . . Philadelphia, is it not? Well, then, if you will not think me outrageously forward, I shall get right to it. Do you think you might help us here a few hours a week? The need is so great. If I could only tell you of the killing work, the early marriages and constant pregnancies, the cruelty and drunkenness of both fathers and husbands. A woman such as yourself could set the kind of American example that we are trying so hard to foster. We teach many things here: citizenship, music, mathematics, and, of course, proper English. You, of course, would not be required to continue past the time of your husband's arrival. But the intervening days would pass more quickly for you. I know this to be true because that is precisely what this wonderful place has done for me."

Through the window Etta could see a shiny black coach pull up to the house. Miss Eleanor reached for a shawl of coarse silk and with a smooth motion wrapped it about her shoulders.

"I will most certainly consider it," Etta said. "I have little enough to fill my time. But do you believe there might be something I could really teach?"

"Everyone has something to contribute," Eleanor said, pushing a golden pin through her Berlin hat. "Perhaps you will join me for luncheon this week and we can discuss it further? We have had the telephone laid on at home and the number is within the city directory. I really must fly now. My coachman is an old grump and hates to be kept waiting. And my aunt, with whom I stay these days, is far worse. May I drop you somewhere? I fear it has become quite cold outside."

"Oh, no. My rooms are only steps from here."

"Then I shall look forward to seeing you very soon. This has been a pleasure. Please don't forget to call. Goodbye." She pressed a cream-colored calling card into Etta's hand and, with a wave, flew down the steps.

As she watched the black carriage move down the crowded narrow street, Etta stood nearly breathless in the wake of the young woman's sheer life force and something inside her heart leaped up at the thought of once again seeing its owner. The brougham finally pulled out of sight, and Etta looked down at the card in her now-open hand. It read:

Miss Eleanor Roosevelt

Etta quickly put the card in the deepest pocket of her black coat—the place where she put everything she could not bear to lose.

As she stood in the freezing foyer of the townhouse at 11 West 37th Street, Etta was not sure she had arrived at the correct address. Could this gloomy cave really be home to the niece of the president of the United States?

Looking into the library, she could see that the furnishings were dark and worn, their cheap lace doilies soiled, the room's carpets stained and threadbare. The deep green velvet draperies covered far more of the windows than they should have on such a bright winter's day, and the marble of the foyer floor, which would have been the pride of any such house, was softly cracked at its corners. Etta had difficulty imagining that such a dreary place could actually contain the living ray of light she had encountered in the settlement house or, indeed, shelter *any* member of one of the country's oldest and most respected families.

Eleanor Roosevelt emerged from a side door into the foyer and held out both her hands.

"Oh, Mrs. Place!" she said, beaming that crooked grin. "I'm so glad you've accepted my invitation to luncheon. I hope it wasn't too sudden."

"The pleasure is mine, Miss Roosevelt," Etta replied. "I have so looked forward to this, it would have suited me to the ground had it been sooner still."

"I suppose neither of us is all that keen at the thought of eating yet another meal alone. Please, come this way."

Eleanor draped her arm through Etta's and led her through a small warren of narrow rooms into the kitchen. There, in the far corner, close to a cheerful, blazing hearth, was the servants' table, elegantly set for two, with a nearby sideboard neatly prepared for tea. A young maid stood next to the huge old cookstove.

"As you come from the West, Mrs. Place, I took the liberty of supposing that a certain lack of formality would not altogether offend you. And, quite truthfully, I had to make a choice between whatever elegance the dining room might provide and your personal comfort. As you have no doubt already realized, this old barn is as cold as an Alaskan Christmas, as my father used to say—and I thought that you might enjoy our meal more if you did not have to shiver through it."

Etta's grin ignited Eleanor's own. "Who doesn't love the kitchen?" she said. "When I was a little girl, there was no place I would rather take my meals, and that continues to this very day. My father, God rest him, often joined me there, and we ate and talked before a warm fireplace very like this one. Oh, no, Miss Roosevelt. Your charming kitchen has put me right back in Chestnut Hill and, I daresay, given me a wonderful appetite."

Eleanor politely dismissed the maid and served the lunch herself, sweeping through the kitchen with the grace and aplomb of the finest French waiter. Etta couldn't help but think of the plentiful tips such skills would earn her in a Harvey House.

"Will your aunt be joining us?" Etta asked.

Eleanor sighed. "I am afraid my aunt has decamped for the country with my grandmother. She has had a frightful time of it of late, as one of her beaux has . . . once again . . . flitted off for parts unknown."

"You are alone here then?"

"Quite alone." Eleanor deposited half a steaming squab and a helping of rice onto Etta's plate and, sitting down, turned to her guest. "I hope you will not think I am prying, Mrs. Place, but from what you have told me I believe that my situation is similar to yours, in that I suspect we are both orphans."

"Yes," Etta said. "My mother died giving me life, and my father . . . well, let us just say that he died far too young."

"I can see we already have much in common. My mother is gone these ten years and my father . . . well, let us also say that he was young as well."

"But who chaperones you?" asked Etta. "Are you really here by yourself in New York at such a young age? I have done a little detective work . . . and surely a prominent clan like the Roosevelts must be concerned about the possibility of one of their lambs going astray."

Eleanor's laughter was like the jangle of a silver chain. "Well, truth be told, Mrs. Place, the Roosevelt clan doesn't bother too much about me. My uncle Theodore's wife doesn't invite me, as she is afraid that our portion of the family is eugenically predisposed to all manner of unpleasantness. Drunkenness, mostly. She would rather that my presence not infect my cousin Alice, who is my peer in age and, if I may say so, very little else, being both vivacious and beautiful. The rest of the family seems to have had quite enough of me, as I have been a serial guest in most of their homes since the age of fourteen. Oh, no, Mrs. Place. Believe me when I say it is far preferable for me to have the freedom of the orphan than the pity of the poor relation."

Etta placed her hand over Eleanor's. She thought then of all the undeserved benefits she had received merely because of the way she looked. How teachers had endowed her with wisdom and morality she did not possess; how men would court and compliment, all the while ignorant and uncaring as to whether she had either heart or brain.

And then she imagined what the world was like for this extraordinary creature. Even her own family had failed to discover her courage and generosity of spirit. She could only wonder at the cruel indifference of the men whom her circle would consider *suitable*. Worst of all, she seemed to have taken these messages deeply to heart, where daily they became a hundred small arrows, each taking its turn at wounding her.

"Well, then," Etta said, "I am a respectable married woman. If you will allow it, I shall be your chaperone and accompany you on your many interesting journeys. And before you know it, your settlement girls will enjoy a supporting wage and you and I will sign the ballots together to elect a woman president!"

The two laughed heartily. As Eleanor poured tea, Etta lied cheerfully about her life, about her Harry's cattle interests, and about the ranch they were building in Wyoming. But even in the interest of self-protection she could not manage to disguise her beginnings in Philadelphia or anything relating to her father save his name, which she now conjured as Mr.

G. W. Cassidy. Somehow, Etta sensed that if this friendship were to grow there must be at least some common ground untainted by her shield of untruths. So she would cling to the one truth that was unassailable. The tale of two orphans, young and virtually alone, their mothers dead, their fathers destroyed by the same demon.

By the time four o'clock came, Etta and Eleanor had both laughed and cried. They lingered into four-thirty and then five o'clock before Etta insisted that she must go or she might not leave at all. Eleanor reluctantly led Etta to the big hall cupboard, helped her into her coat, and then spun her gently around and took Etta's hands in hers.

"Mrs. Place, I cannot tell you how enjoyable this afternoon has been for me. I hope you will come and see me again. That is, if you can stand the abject worship of a little sister."

"But would my little sister refer to me by my married name? From now on I must be Etta for you, and only Etta."

"And I, Eleanor to you—or even. . . ." Eleanor's face darkened and then the huge smile spread shyly across it.

"Yes?" said Etta. "Come now. No secrets between sisters."

Eleanor paused and cast down her eyes in embarrassment. "In his letters, Father used to address me as his Little Nell. He was the only one who ever called me that. No one else has even known it was his name for me. I loved him more than anyone else in my life. If someone would call me that again, it would be a great comfort."

Etta enfolded her companion in her arms and held her, brief and tight. "I shall be honored," Etta whispered. "I shall be your sister and your friend. And you shall always be Little Nell to me."

Eleanor called for her aunt's carriage. As it rolled up to the curb, its canvas top battened down against the wind, Eleanor again took Etta's hand. "George will take you back to your hotel. And any time you wish to see me, you need only send word and he shall be there quick as Mercury."

With that, Etta was down the front steps and into the carriage. As she waved from the window and looked back down 37th Street, she could see her new friend raise her arm only once and then, with a gesture graceful as a swan, bring her hand lightly to her throat.

From the

NEW YORK WORLD

October 25, 1901

"WILD WEST" PROVIDES MUCH DIVERSION FOR NEW YORKERS

Colonel Cody's Show Features Thrills and Spills Aplenty

Cowboys, Indians, Arabs, Cossacks, and Gauchos in Celebrated "Congress of Rough Riders"

Miss Annie Oakley Amazes with Trick Riflery but Leaves Stage Early

Madison Square Garden manifested a veritable living "dime novel" this Wednesday past as Colonel William F. Cody—better known to the public as Buffalo Bill—brought his Wild West extravaganza to New York.

There was no shortage of thrilling exploits for the youngsters gathered therein as the famed former Indian fighter and showman brought a plethora of exciting actors to the great dirt floor of the edifice, performing feats the likes of which have never before been seen hereabouts.

Featured in the evening were the numerous members of the Wordwide Congress of Rough Riders. These include cowboys of the Western plains attired in buckskin and leather and their South American cousins known as gauchos; red savages in their curious feathered headdresses and war paint; Arab horsemen in flowing white robes, and the fur-bearing Cossacks, those fierce knights of the Russian steppes. Each man was astride a magnificent animal that was likewise attired in the decorated saddle and bridle of its native land. During their portion, the Rough Riders performed trick equestrian feats and staged mock battles for those assembled who, it can well and truly be said, were demonstrative in their hearty approval.

Colonel Cody's troupe also treated the audience to a historically accurate re-creation of the death of Custer at the Battle of the Little Big Horn. The horseman portraying General George Armstrong Custer fair succeeded at becoming his double, and the native who dispatched him is authentically acted by a full-blooded Indian humorously named Kicking Bird. Indeed, this red man is reputed to be an actual descendant of Crazy Horse, the bloodthirsty Sioux chieftain who carried out Custer's brutal murder during the legendary massacre.

The night's only disappointment was the curiously truncated performance of a longtime favorite, Miss Annie Oakley, of sharpshooting fame. The diminutive Miss Oakley assayed some of her trademark manoeuveres: she shot a cigarette from a man's mouth and hit a target reflected in a mirror while aiming her rifle backward. But after only five minutes' time, she abruptly left the arena, followed closely by her husband and assistant, Mr. Frank Butler, all to the great displeasure of the throng. No explanation was evinced as to the cause of Miss Oakley's early departure.

"Buffalo Bill's Wild West" will reside here for a fortnight and will include special children's matinees.

LETTER TO ETTA PLACE
234 West 12th Street, New York, N.Y.
25 November, 1901

Pretty,

Know not best to write where you are. Sorry to put you in danger but pray luck holds.

Unhappy news. We are captured, 8 November. Butch and Harry and most others by greenhorn marshal, Abilene, Kansas, Ben and me taken by Mr. Charles Siringo of Pinks, St. Louis. Fair man. Showed Ben respect. Funny. After all we did and escaped, finally done in by a bank teller name of Jaquemin. Made Ben from poster in Abilene Trust. Kind of place we used to knock over easy as knitting.

Us inside but Curry on the run. Wouldn't know to ask God where. Whole time you gone he swearing blue to find you. Git his money.

Have a care. Curry clever as foxes.

My Ben got fifteen years in calaboose, me five. So you must keep his goods and mine. World being as is, probably never see you no more.

Siringo ask me about you. Five hours over two days. Tell him shit. He brung in a artist to try and draw you from my words. Habit of quiet a fine thing.

Only got this to you by bribing the turnkey with only thing I still got. And it still works. Ha-ha.

Know this: Won't never forget how you kept my secrets and was my friend. Know you honest. Won't spend a penny of mine or Ben's. Don't care if you do. For all this thieving, one of us should get a good life. If it's you, good.

As to Sundance Kid, heart shouldn't break over outlaw. Forget. Live.

Hope they do not take you. Rope would look silly with your pretty lace. Ha-ha.

Your friend,
Laura Bullion

As Christmas approached, Etta's desolation was near total. She was able to draw some comfort from the softness of the falling snow outside her window or a cup of sweet tea shared with Mrs. Taylor, but even the smallest portion of happiness requires hope, and Etta was as short of that essential as she had ever been.

The sheer number of charges against Harry Longbaugh virtually guaranteed a lengthy sentence, perhaps totaling the remaining years of his life: train and bank robbery, horse theft, fraud, property destruction. The accumulation of his calumny probably continued for pages. If his trial had not been completed by now, it soon would be, and barring a miracle or a jury addled by drink, he would surely grow old in prison.

Worse, Etta had no direct contact with Harry. In order to assure that she remain undetected by the law or jailhouse censors, all their correspondence was conducted through Laura Bullion, and the strange code they established in her letters only added to Etta's frustration and helplessness. For a young woman in love, *I hope this letter finds you well was a* poor substitute for *this letter arrives with all my love.*

Eleanor was her only solace. She could, of course, never reveal the true source of her sadness, confiding in her friend that it was merely the absence of her "Mr. Place" that prompted the frequent onrush of tears.

The two women saw each other first once a week, then twice, and finally nearly every day. They took long walks through Central Park and skated on its frozen pond. They ate sweet rolls and drank Turkish coffee in tiny Village restaurants. They were content to be silent as they brushed each other's hair to glistening, one hundred strokes and more. And they talked: first about things small or jolly—music, art, horses—and then about their fathers, who, each in his way, willingly took leave of this world; David Jameson by a pistol to the temple, Elliott Roosevelt by demons in a bottle.

Only later came the far more painful subject of their mothers. Etta had only known hers from a few photographs but had inherited her magnificence and then some. Eleanor had known her mother well enough to realize that she would be found forever wanting for not matching her in beauty. They laughed at their mutual finishing of sentences and cried through smiles and intertwined fingers.

But as elated as she was by her new friendship, as the weeks went by Etta found herself increasingly concerned with the practical. How ironic it seemed that she, the holder of a fortune buried in Colorado, was growing increasingly short of funds. The classes she taught in English Pronouncement at Rivington Street were some of the finest hours she had spent in her young life, but they offered no compensation. And, with the law and Pinkertons everywhere, it would have been worse than foolhardy to dip into the Brooklyn goods. Soon, she knew, it would be necessary to find employment of some kind. But who would have work for a girl fit only to break horses and rob trains?

In the event, that employment came to her in a ball of flesh and leather hurtling through the door of a saloon.

She had only just kissed Eleanor goodbye on the steps of the settlement house, turned right up Orchard and left on Houston when a man flew through the swinging doors of the bar. As he sailed through the air, his fist caught the large bow that decorated the hip of her greatcoat. The two fell hard into the dirty snow; she fuming in rage at the indignity, he clearly in no mood to apologize.

As they rose from the slush she recognized him at once. He was a lot less sunburned than she remembered and his usual alcohol flush was gone. But it was him, all right. There was no mistaking the squinty eyes and the lick of dirty-blond hair that fell across his forehead. His clothes were cleaner than she had ever seen them and his hat shinier, but this was

Frank Elliott, sure as sunrise, Peg Leg himself. When he was riding with the Bunch, no one ever commented upon the nickname or why it had been given to a man with two good legs. It was one of many things never explained. Laura Bullion had one theory. In her laconic way, she had intimated that a whore from Albuquerque had told her that it had to do with his "stature" as a man or, more accurately, his stature somewhere between man and mule.

As surprised as he was to see her, Peg Leg was even more astonished when she clapped her hand firmly over his mouth. "Greet me, Peg," she said, "but speak neither too loudly nor too clearly."

"Whatever you say, Miss Etta," he mumbled through her fingers.

She lowered her hand to her side and suggested that they repair to a local tearoom. Peg Leg seemed little the worse for the bum's rush, but then he had always been the sort who could fall from a horse, a coal car, or a two-story building and walk away whole. Butch liked to say it was because his brain didn't function well enough to tell his body it should be hurt.

Back at Hole-in-the-Wall, Peg had never shown any interest in male fashion. But as Etta accompanied him down the street she marveled at his gear. He wore a Stetson beaver sombrero with a black and gold band. His coat was of natural buckskin festooned with fringe about the breast and down each arm. The leather of the chaps concealed dungarees of corduroy striped with silk brocade, and the ensemble was completed by timber-rattler boots, each sporting a silver spur at the heel and matching tip at the toe.

A few blocks up Houston, they came to a small dingy café. The waiter led them to a table and Etta ordered tea and cream cakes. Peg allowed as he had never had tea, as he heard it was a drink only for ladies. Etta assured him that, here in New York, men drank tea as well as women. Reluctantly, Peg agreed to try a sip, but not too much. Overindulgence, someone had told him, could cause a man to shrivel some.

"Well, Peg," Etta said, placing a napkin in his lap, "either you've taken someone off big or you and the boys have found my goods and made the split. Never have I seen so fancy a cowboy."

Peg Leg looked wounded. "No, none of that, Miss Etta. I been work-ing legit, and that's a fact. I bought these duds with wages such as a hon-est man can earn."

"Where in the world could you possibly have made enough money to buy such an outfit? Those boots alone are two months' salary for a gen-tleman of your skills and education."

"But I don't need no skills of education, Miss Etta. I'm in the show business."

It was Etta's turn to be astonished. "The show business? I knew you could do rope tricks and tell funny stories, but I never quite pictured you performing the works of Shakespeare."

Peg Leg blushed. He was amazed to find Etta Place in New York City and more than a little flattered that a woman of her beauty and grace (and Sundance's woman in the bargain) would invite him to a table of any kind.

"I'm no actor, nor singer neither. I'm currently in the legal employ of Colonel William F. Cody and the famous *Buffalo Bill's Wild West.* We're touring the country and selling out the house at the Square Garden. De-pending on the time of day or the degree of another man's drunkenness or illness, I can be any one of the Congress of Rough Riders."

Etta laughed for what felt like the first time in a year.

"No, Miss Etta, it's true. I been a Ay-rab tribesman, a Confederate *and* a Union soldier, a Tartar, and a Cossack, as well as a cowboy like my-self, roping and riding. I get treated awful good, Miss Etta, and the colonel pays me as befitting my expertness. Outside of Harry and Butch, he is the best man I ever knew. And the show we put on! Why, only last night me and my fellows enacted the whole Battle of the Little Big Horn with twenty redskins and Kicking Bird hisself making pretend to be Crazy Horse."

"It must be thrilling to ride every day and every night!" Etta said, her eyes shining. "Lord, it sounds wonderful."

"I been to France and England and Russia, too. Them people was nice, and apart from the food I had myself a time." Peg Leg reached for a cream cake. "But Miss Etta, what are you doing here? Is the Kid with you?"

Etta cast her eyes down. She would have liked to unburden herself to this simple boy but could not bear to explain her love's imprisonment. Besides, the Philadelphian in her had decided it was none of his business.

"No, Peg, I'm afraid Harry is still in Colorado. He'll join me here in a few months' time. Meanwhile, I could very much use a job. Could I dare hope that you might speak to your Colonel Cody on my behalf? You know I have some degree of riding and shooting skill. But I would muck the stables just to earn my own supper and inhale the scent of live horse-flesh once more."

Peg Leg swallowed a second cake nearly whole. The tea sat before him, steaming and untouched, as an eager grin spread across his face. Etta was comforted by that smile. It was the same one she had seen on Peg every time he leaped from his horse into an engineer's compartment or asked a bank teller politely if he had said his prayers that morning.

"Miss Etta, your timing could not be better. We are going to have some trouble replacing a lady performer what has walked out this very day. The colonel is pulling out that long hair of his, trying to find a lady who can handle iron even half as good. You knocking me down in New York? I swear, it's a miracle.

"But if I was to secure you employment, you would have to be ready to leave here right quick, as we are headed south in about two days. I do believe the colonel would like to make your acquaintance, and I would not be surprised if he did take you on. We would have to make an appointment with his people on the double."

"Then see him I shall."

As they rose, Peg Leg took the last two remaining cream cakes and a white napkin from the table. Wiping the last few flakes of sugar from his face, he pocketed the linen in his vest. Then, with Miss Etta Place on his arm, he exited the café, looking left and right, hoping to see the eyes of envy upon him.

Outside, on Houston Street, he helped Etta aboard a horse trolley. As the driver rang the bell and the car began its journey uptown, Peg Leg Elliott sighed. Already he could picture her, calm and polite, pistol in hand, robbing all the passengers.

From the
PHILADELPHIA *PUBLIC LEDGER*
December 6, 1901

TERRIBLE MURDER OF PROMINENT ATTORNEY!

MR. RODMAN D. LARABEE FOUND
STABBED TO DEATH IN OFFICE

POLICE BAFFLED, CAN FIND NO CLUES

By our correspondents

Last night, somewhere between the hours of seven and eleven o'clock, a person or persons entered the Center City offices of Mr. Rodman D. Larabee III, Esq., and fatally stabbed him in the chest.

The unfortunate man was found lying near his desk inside the offices of his firm, Larabee, Hay & Litch. Police said Mr. Larabee had been stabbed several times with a slender knife. The weapon was not found at the scene of the crime and, as yet, the police have no clues as to a possible motive for the crime or the identity of the wrongdoer.

Mr. Larabee, 73, was considered one of Philadelphia's outstanding members of the bar. He was general counsel to both the

Lehigh Stone and Quarrying Company and the Speakman Manu-
facturing & Shirtwaist Corporation. He was also instrumental in
the recent purchase of new acreage for the proposed expansion of
the John B. Stetson Hat Company.

Mr. Larabee was a member of many of the city's most prestigious clubs, including the Union League and Pickstocking. Long
admired as a champion of the destitute, he defended the poor in
criminal and civil cases, work for which he sought no monetary return.

Mr. Larabee was also the attorney in the sensational Jameson
matter of 1898. In said case, he served as counsel to Miss Lorinda
Reese Jameson, daughter of the bankrupt suicide Mr. G. David
Jameson, who died owing hundreds of thousands to creditors.
Miss Jameson disappeared toward the end of the case and has not
been heard of since. Mr. Larabee's gruesome death has raised fresh
fears that she too may have met with foul play.

Mr. Larabee was the son of Rodman D. Larabee, Jr., and the
former Fannie Phelps Dagit of this city. The attorney was a widower and leaves no family.

Over the years, Detective Charles A. Siringo had devised quite specific rules concerning interrogation.

If he presumed the person being interrogated was innocent, he would do his best to gain any necessary particulars by gentility and persuasion. If the subject was a lady, even one of dubious reputation, he would become the soul of discretion and calm. In either case, the use of violence of any kind was ruled out, owing to company policy and Siringo's own Catholic upbringing and respectable background.

In situations involving known miscreants, however, Siringo's long experience had persuaded him that such lofty considerations invariably proved unproductive. His research into psychology and the inherited traits of specific ethnic groups had convinced him that a certain class of criminal was, by nature, predisposed to lie. His studies had also shown him that this propensity was in direct proportion to the number of years spent in nefarious enterprises and, of course, time spent in jail.

This December evening, Siringo was applying these theories to the eyes, nose, mouth, and abdomen of a Mr. Dante Gabriel Cichetti of Philadelphia. As Cichetti bounced off the wall in the cellar of Pinkerton's Denver, Colorado, office, Siringo's left fist came up just under his chin, its force lifting his feet from the ground.

Cichetti had been found in Grand Junction; he had not been hard to spot. He was swarthy, yes, but his complexion was not the giveaway; it was more his clothing and manner. He was too flamboyantly dressed to be an Indian and not polite enough to be a Mexican. This, and his accent, had led Pinkerton's well-trained operatives to identify him as Italian, and his pinkie rings and stickpins and the bulge in his coat were all they needed to deduce his affiliation: *Black Hand.* It was standard operating procedure for the company to detain any such vermin, and when the detectives had found a wrinkled note in the pocket of his silk vest, they knew to wire Charlie Siringo immediately.

The sound of Cichetti's lower teeth breaking against his uppers was sickening. He spit purple blood from his lips and nostrils as he collapsed to the floor. Before the dark young man could catch his breath, Siringo pulled him to his feet by the material of his vest and slapped him twice across the face.

"Where is she, *paisan*?" Siringo demanded. "You went all around Grand Junction looking for her. Described her to everyone you met. How tall. How pretty. How dressed. I didn't have my men spend two days hauling you here to Denver to hear silence. What is it you want, eh? The money she and that Hole-in-the-Wall trash stole? Where is she?"

Even if Dante had wanted to speak, it would have been difficult. His broken nose had swollen his eyes shut, and his bottom lip had ballooned double. Of course he still had reasons other than pain to remain silent. The cardinal rule of the Hand required him to keep his mouth shut. The consequences of breaking that code would make the current beating seem like his birthday.

But his resolve began to weaken when Charlie Siringo's knee met his groin. After the stars in his head returned to space and he could once again breathe, Dante unburdened himself as if Siringo were his priest and he a contrite confessioner.

"She ain't here, mister. You gotta believe me. She ain't here. Please don't hit me again."

Siringo was relieved at the hood's words. Now he knew this unpleasantness was nearly at an end. Once he heard the first cry for mercy it would take only one, or at the most two more blows to prove his own ruthlessness definitively and end the bloody dance. The Pinkerton took Dante's olive-skinned wrist in his and bent it back in one motion, forcing the young hood to his knees.

As the boy burst into tears below him, he reverted to his most understanding tone, the one that seemed to say, *I am your father and all will be forgiven.*

"All right, Dante. . . . I'm listening."

Siringo released Cichetti's hand and allowed him to crumple to the floor. He walked to a corner of the room and, dipping some water into a tin cup, handed it to the boy. Cichetti thankfully drank it down, ignoring the searing pain coursing through his lips. Siringo brought up a hard wooden chair and bade Dante sit in it. Then he drew up another and sat facing him.

"I was sent by my boss to take care of her. Owes us money and won't pay it back. Comin' to Colorado don't mean nothin'. Goin' to the moon don't mean nothin'. We don't care how far you go or how long it takes. You're birthin' a baby? We find you; you pay us. You're on your deathbed? We find you; you pay us. You pay us or you're dead and your family pay us."

Siringo narrowed his eyes. "How'd you find out she was out here?"

"My boss sent me to get it out of that old fuck lawyer of hers. A couple of twists to the balls and he gave it up right away. But by the time I got to that Grand Junction town she was long gone. Whore killed some rich guy, and the cops and you Pinks was after her, they said. Come to find out she's been gone more than two years. But this was the only lead we had, so I followed it. I swear, mister, it's true. On my mother, it's true."

"I don't take the word of dago trash," said Siringo in a measured tone. "You all love to leave important things out. Like for instance, you didn't tell us anything about the little note we found in the front pocket of your vest. Now, why would you do that?"

Dante stared for a moment at Siringo. It was long enough for the Pinkerton to determine that the hood was either not going to answer or was going to lie, so he backhanded him once more, this time opening up a purple bruise just below the Roman nose.

As Cichetti rose from the floor, Siringo handed him a handkerchief. The kid wiped the blood from his nostrils and the tears from his eyes as Siringo read the letter out loud:

Stranger,

I hear you been inquiring around town about a girl name of Lorinda Jameson.

According to your description, anyone you meet in these parts will tell you that the woman you seek here once went by Etta Place.

I know who her friends are and where they may be found. This woman is a associate of dangerous outlaws. She owes me very much money. Meet me tonight at 8 at the Four Star, room 5, top of the stairs. You and me both might could benefit.

H. Logan

Siringo chuckled. *Might could.* Kid Curry was no English professor.

"Please, mister. This note, I got no idea on earth who sent it. It was just under my door in the hotel two days ago. Your men grabbed me up before I could meet the guy."

Siringo folded the note and placed it neatly in the pocket of his waistcoat. He opened a door and called to an assistant.

"You'll take Mr. Cichetti here back upstairs to the lockup and see to it that he gets medical attention. After that, I want him on the first train to Philadelphia. His boss will know what to do with him."

As the detective turned to escort Cichetti from the room, Siringo put his hand on the young man's shoulder and looked deep into his black eyes.

"This little conversation never took place, Dante. You'll tell no one—cops, feds, your boss, your mother, no one. What is it you greaseball punks say? Oh, yes." Siringo put one finger up to his pursed lips and whispered, *"Omerta."*

The assistant hustled Cichetti through a side door. Siringo walked slowly up a back staircase and into a small room. He washed his hands and dried them on a pure-white towel. Then he changed his clothes; everything from his linen and collar to his boots. Finally, he replaced his weapons: gunbelt at the hip, knife in breast pocket, derringer tucked neatly into left cuff.

When he felt clean again, he took a paper dossier from the nightstand and studied it. LOGAN, it read, HARVEY R, Alias KID CURRY. He combed through the list of aliases, the age, the weight, color of hair, the various and sundry crimes from horse theft to murder. Not included in the dossier were those facts deemed too noxious for a proper agency: the animal cruelty, the beatings and sexual brutalization of women both high and low born, the twitching eagerness to turn a routine robbery into an occasion to kill. Charles A. Siringo cursed at the thought that a scrawled note could have led his men to this Lorinda Jameson and now that opportunity had vanished.

Now, he knew, Kid Curry had ridden safely out of Grand Junction taking with him the true identity of Etta Place.

Diary,

I am at at a loss. The event of yesterday turns over and over in my mind and fills me with confusion.

Even so, I must be strong; a great friendship is at stake.

The incident itself was small, lasting only a moment. But I now fear that this tiny fragment of time threatens all that Nell and I have built these past months. Since its occurrence it has been all I can to to comfort my companion and ease her mind, assuring her that no single indiscretion could ever be enough to alter our mutual affection. Would that I were so sure; for it is the nature of that affection which now seems in question, and I wonder if I possess the fortitude to see both myself and my fragile friend through this trial.

Over these last precious weeks I have learned much about my wonderful new companion. We have walked, ridden, taken in museums and theaters, and charted the blessed waters of the Alhambra. From the very first we have been not the least bit shy with one another, discussing all things pertinent to both spirit and body.

These conversations have been . . . to put it politely . . . most frank. As befits a girl of her age and background, Nell is yet a virgin, and we have spent many hours side by side in the sitting room of Mrs. Taylor's while I have patiently and honestly answered her endless questions about men and what joy and sorrow they may bring. When they love you do they hurt you? Unclothed are they beautiful or ugly? Is their scent agreeable or not? Is it true that a woman can reach a kind of rushing ecstasy, like a man?

Such sweet ignorance is more than understandable. As she has grown to womanhood without a mother or father (and as a living ghost to the remainder of her family), most of Nell's knowledge of love has come from the schools she has attended, where she consorted only with women or other young girls. In England, at the academy of her beloved Mademoiselle Souvestre, she had transformed into a popular pupil and the subject of many a schoolgirl "crush," as she charmingly puts it. During that time, it was not unusual for her to return from a weekend away and find her room bedecked with flowers and admiring billets-doux from some smitten fellow student. Such innocuous writings are not unusual among upper-class girls at school. I myself often received—and sent—such breathless notes.

Upon the morning of the odd occurence, Diary, I awoke early, dressed, and hurried to post a note confirming my appointment with the famous Buffalo Bill. I had been surprised at how quickly Peg Leg Elliott had been able to secure the meeting, and I could only guess that the great man himself was either desperate for performers or reacting to the great pile of lies Peg had surely deposited upon his assistants.

When I arrived back at Mrs. Taylor's, there was a letter upon the sideboard, which I now paste here as I do all things lovely or precious.

Etta Dearest—

You have, as only you could, turned my loneliness to most ecstatic happiness!

Thank you, my dear one, for sharing your secrets with me.

I will meet you at the appointed hour, and together we shall explore the magical pictures of your scandalous Miss Cassatt.

All my love, your
"Little Nell"

I saw nothing untoward in this. Our letters back and forth had always been effusive in their affections. But in rereading this one now, perhaps I should have noted a transformation: the word "ecstatic"; the pledge of her love in total.

Just before ten this morning, Nell and her George came by and we made our way toward the gallery downtown. She was in high spirits and spoke animatedly of the audacious paintress who had abandoned her country and the role of heiress to the Pennsylvania Railroad for the sake of her work. Mary Cassatt: a woman who, like us, came from a class that frowned on impropriety.

"Oh, to be like her, Etta!" Nell exclaimed. "To someday live one's own life without the hand of society or the eye of dead ancestors upon one!"

Of course, observing the art, it would be hard to imagine anything untoward about its maker, except perhaps that she was a woman daring to create. The paintings themselves were largely of mothers and their children posed in pleasant surroundings: parlors and salons and gardens. The gowns of the women were of the sweetest whites and pinks and pale blues; their sons' short-pantsed suits like black holes in the canvas, their daughters' taffeta dresses tiny mirrors of the mother's couture. At first, Nell thought the work odd. "All these little pieces of paint," she remarked to me. But as the hour extended I could see her blue eyes bore into each subject. When she had seen all the works, she returned to one particular canvas. Its title, translated to English, read, Reine Lefebvre Holding a Nude Baby.

The painting was of a lovely young woman, dark in eye and face, silhouetted against an ochre ground. In her two strong arms she held a naked child about two years old, its sex indeterminate (as its back is to the viewer) but so soft and beautiful that I could not imagine it being anything but a girl. I took Nell's arm as she observed the happy pair, smiling slightly but saying nothing. I needed no words for her to tell me that this picture was a window into a world in which she longed to dwell but from which she had been cruelly excluded, a wonderland where all children are loved and cared for: never lonely, never ugly.

Afterward, we retired to a nearby restaurant for luncheon and, as the afternoon grew chill, returned to the brougham and settled in, the warm carriage blanket enveloping us, Nell's gloved hand firmly in my own. Through the window we could see a light snow begin to fall and, through it, the refracted lights of the shops, newly dressed for Christmas. We were, in that moment, women full: full of the fine food of that restaurant; full of Cassatt's lovely vision; full of the warmth of our shared friendship. When Nell's coach came to a stop before Mrs. Taylor's, I expected the usual lingering goodbye that had become so essential a part of our excursions.

As Nell's face drew near mine I happily anticipated our traditional farewell: an embrace in the French manner with one kiss upon each cheek. What I received instead far more befit a lover than a friend.

Nell's kiss was different from that of a man. Being female, she was of course more gentle, her lips more soft, and she did not press my mouth to hers as an excited male might do. She dared not linger very long, being unable to predict my reaction, but still the kiss seemed to suspend me in a place between satisfaction and shock: satisfaction that such a fine creature should think so much of me that I might take the place of a man in her life, but shock that she could believe I would respond in kind, woman being made for man, no matter what pleasure such feminine sweetness might provide.

God forgive me, I did not mean to be cruel, but when at last our faces separated, I fear my eyes were harder than they should have been, colder than I meant. One look into them caused my friend to commence to weep and lay her face hard against my hand like a supplicant begging alms.

"Oh, my dearest," she said, raising her head from my gloved fingers, "please forgive me. Please! I am so very sorry!"

I looked at Nell for a long moment and knew I must choose the better between indignation and compassion. I embraced her and stroked her trembling back as I had once caressed the frightened Hantaywee. I said nothing but held her tight to me as she vibrated with sobs.

"You are," I finally told her, "my Little Nell. And my Little Nell you shall remain. Nothing, especially nothing so small as this, can change that."

Needing courage, I fought back my own tears and, at length, broke our embrace. At first she refused to look at me, trembling and averting her eyes in shame, but I took her face in my hands and coaxed those huge blue eyes into meeting mine.

"Still, my dearest, I am not a man and cannot be treated as one. I am also a married woman. And would you not think less of me if I proved a deceiver, no matter who that deception was with?"

I embraced my Nell once more as she again dissolved in tears.

"But oh, my darling, kiss or no, do you honestly believe I could ever give up what we are to each other over this one thing? Never, dear Nell, and again, never! One does not cast one's sister into the cold world because of a single moment. No. We shall speak of it no more and all shall be as it has been."

And so, Diary, my predicament. I cannot imagine a life that does not now include Miss Eleanor Roosevelt. And though I lament the possibility of encouraging her affections beyond what my heart can offer, I cannot desert her. Her heart is now one with mine: as much a part of me as my visions of Harry Longbaugh, or my memories of Utah, or the derringer in my left sleeve.

"I know *who* she is," the little man insisted. "You know *where* she is."

Laura Bullion would have laughed if she hadn't known all he was capable of. The priest's collar and robes were so incongruous as to make him seem something from a comic opera, a vision from the four-a-day vaudeville. But the blazing eyes, now as always dark pools of madness, removed from her heart all thoughts of merriment.

"Today I am your father confessor, bitch. No screws, no wardens listening. I've come to take your confession."

Laura looked at the false priest through the bars of her cell. She had always been afraid of Kid Curry. Everyone was, save Ben and Butch and Harry.

"There are two things you can give out, and as far as I am concerned one is as good as the other. You can tell me where she hid our goods, but I figure for that you got no answer. So you can tell me where she is, and I'll dig it up. You and Kilpatrick will get your cut; I'll enjoy her a little before she dies—or maybe even after."

"Fuck you, Curry," she said.

"I know you're a brave girl, Laura," Curry said, "and I admire you for that. But Etta Place is a dead girl. And the dead ain't worth your life."

Laura lowered her head as she spoke, avoiding the two freezing coals fixed upon her.

"Never give her up," Laura said, spitting the words at Curry. "Kill me? Do it and hell welcome you. Maybe I'll beat you to it, shit heel. I'm here for five years. Kilpatrick's got ten more. This skirt'll hang me good. This belt too. That gun a yourn'll do just as fine."

Curry began to feel the temperature of her fear begin to rise. A slight smile came to his lips. "Your living or dying means precious little to me, girl. And you're right that my killing you buys silence, not talk. But my intention is to kill your Tall Texan."

Laura raised her eyes toward him. "Bullshit," she spat. "He's in here."

"No, you're in here, in a nice inside ladies' tier high up over the plain. Kilpatrick—well, he's right off the street with a window for ventilation. I could shoot him dead from my horse or standing on a box or with my eyes shut. It wouldn't even be good target practice.

"But your Ben, now that's different. With Cassidy and Sundance he's conspired to humiliate me ever since we began to ride. They've told me what to do and where to shit and now separated me from my goods and took the food from my mouth."

"You lying shit."

"That's no way to talk to clergy. No, Della, I speak the gospel, and the truth is, if I don't get the whereabouts of your *Pretty* right quick, I am honor-bound to keep my promise in the name of Our Lady and aim my iron through those bars at your man's slicked-down hair and make it explode, brains on stone."

Logan could sense her weakening. For him this was nearly as good as the kill itself. To bend the helpless to his will had been a source of the purest joy since childhood, when dogs and, later, horses were conquered by it. Her despair warmed him up like good wine.

"Brains on stone," he murmured. "Brains on stone."

She trembled more deeply, the first tear mapping her cheek.

"Brains," he said, and paused. "On—"

"New York City," she whispered.

"What?"

"New York City, cursed bastard," she hissed through hot tears. "New York City! No address! All I know!"

She seemed to deflate in grief and her hands covered her eyes.

"You know more," he demanded.

"Devil eat you alive, bastard! All I know and all you will know. All you will ever know. Kill him! Kill her! Kill us all and be damned!"

Kid Curry studied the sobbing Laura Bullion. Had she truly revealed all? It was hard to know without employing the methods he had used all his life. The back of a hand, the quick twist of an arm, or a pistol to the head of a mother's child had always been sufficient to bring him everything he wanted. But here, in an open jail cell and dressed in the raiment of clergy, these options were closed to him. This time, instinct would have to suffice.

Kid Curry rose in his black robe and pushed his wooden chair back into its corner.

"Bless you, my child," he whispered, and, turning on his heel, he sauntered through the cell door.

When she was sure he was gone Laura Bullion collapsed on the small scarred table. She knew Curry would not rest until he had found Etta, and now he knew where to look. It was no comfort that she had provided him with only half the truth: the city but not the street and number. In the days to come, she would gaze blankly into her hand mirror, one of the few possessions allowed her in this place, and ponder her choice. Her man or her friend? To live or to die?

And if she chose not to leave this world of sorrow by her skirt or her belt, would half the truth prove good enough to live on?

The long years in the saddle had ruined the nether regions of Colonel William F. Cody. As a rough youngster, both pony express rider and Indian scout, he had lived atop a horse hour after hour, day after day. Later in life he became a soldier in the Grand Army of the Republic and a famed Indian fighter, both occupations requiring a life lived largely mounted. And so, as the years went by, his equestrian existence exacted a painful toll.

These days, as his show's host and a ruling sultan of the show business, he was only required to appear on horseback ten or twelve minutes of every performance. But all too often even that short time had proven more than ample for the hemorrhoids inside him to assert themselves. Like individual campfires built one upon the other, each seemed hell-bent on consuming some searing fuel upon which he was now cruelly and unavoidably required to sit.

As Buffalo Bill had only just completed the second show of the day this winter afternoon, it was probably not the optimal time to audition before him. When Peg Leg Elliott introduced his beautiful companion to the great man, Etta was surprised to receive not the usual up-and-down appraisal of her charms, but an agonized wince with slammed-shut eyes and a grimace of yellowed teeth. Only after Buffalo Bill had released a long hiss like a rattlesnake in high season did he extend his hand to her. She was disappointed to find his handshake weak and distracted and him short of breath.

"Boy here . . . tells me . . . you are familiar with the . . . workings of the . . . Winchester rifle," Buffalo Bill said, his eyes watering.

"Yes, Colonel Cody," Etta said. "My father raised me to be familiar with both firearms and horses and taught me some proficiency with each."

Buffalo Bill nodded his head before turning to bellow at a young man passing by who was dressed as a tartar horseman. "Riley, goddammit! Where the blazes is my chair. Bring me my chair!"

The young tartar answered in a voice rich with West Virginia coal. "Right away, Colonel—"

"My chair! Get me my fucking chair now!"

"Yessir—"

"GET ME MY GODDAMN FUCKING CHAIR!"

These were not words with which Etta was unfamiliar. Although it had been many months since she had heard such oaths fly freely through the air, she found herself reacting to them as she might have in more genteel days. Cody caught the look of disapproval in her eyes.

"You'll forgive me, Miss . . . Miss?"

"Place," Etta said.

"Miss Place, you'll forgive me my language. But this is a circus, not a Sunday social, and if you're going to live among circus folk, the language is likely to be served with a side order of salt. I myself am especially prone to misspeak when the miseries of the piles are upon me, as they are at this moment."

The tartar returned, carrying the chair Buffalo Bill had sought with such urgency. Etta had never seen its like but soon divined its purpose.

It was an ornate thronelike affair in the finest black walnut, hand carved with scenes from *Wild West* performances: here, the Battle of the Little Big Horn; there, the surrender of the Oglala Sioux. And at the apex, where the sitter's head would rest, the sharp relief of Buffalo Bill himself in profile. Beneath it the legend read, COL. W. F. CODY, PROP.

As Etta and Peg gazed upon the amazing creation, they marveled that it had no actual seat. Instead, there was only a hole surrounded by what appeared to be an overstuffed ring of cotton or horsehair covered in a soft natural cowhide. The material was for all the world like the suede of the jacket the great man wore, minus the long fringes and the silver and turquoise buttons of the Plains redskin.

Buffalo Bill lowered himself gingerly into the great chair and once again expelled a long and tortured hiss. When at last he was seated he looked up at Etta, his eyes brimming with tears.

"Well, Miss Place, let's see . . . what you can do."

Over the next half hour the showman was treated to a spectacle of shooting and riding he would have heretofore expected only from a man, and a dangerous one at that. In that time, Etta's rifle shot six straight bull's-eyes at thirty paces, clipped a cigarette from the mouth of a terri-fied Peg Leg (a trick she had read of in the newspapers and had perfected during the cripplingly dull winter months at Hole-in-the-Wall), shot a playing card through the ace, and, armed with two six-guns, destroyed eight clay effigies of Crazy Horse as she galloped in a circle, alternating sidesaddle from left to right. When she had finished, Etta rode toward Cody slowly and deliberately, somehow managing to turn an ordinary saddle gelding into a dressage medalist. When she finally gained the ground before Buffalo Bill, she dismounted in a single graceful arc, standing before him with a face that betrayed no hint of pride or satis-faction, only the calm, impassive expression that he knew from experi-ence marked a champion born.

Buffalo Bill looked up from his chair, all evidence of pain drained from his face. "And what, Miss Place," he asked, "are your terms?"

"Colonel Cody, I am told by my friend Peg Leg that you are a man of character, and so it thus follows that you are also a man of generosity. Therefore, I would expect that the sums to be discussed would be in line with the other riders and performers in your exhibition."

Etta brushed some sawdust from her skirt and, adjusting her hat, re-placed the Winchester in its saddle holster.

"As I have achieved no fame in this area, I would certainly not expect to be compensated in the manner of a star the caliber of Annie Oakley herself. But I hope my abilities will be useful enough to you and thrilling enough to your patrons that I may receive a fair salary. The only demand I must make is that you allow me to appear under a name other than my own, as my family would disapprove of my involvement in anything that smacked of the show business."

Buffalo Bill leaned back in his special chair, a mistake that produced a full-blooded howl that shook the stadium's rafters. When he finally recovered, he once more appraised Etta Place. "I believe," he said, "that proper monetary terms can be worked out. As to your name, I would estimate that something over half of the artists in my employ are known to the audience under names not Christian to them. This is only natural as they are, in the main, scoundrels and wastrels known in their true identities to both the police and the Pinkertons, not to mention abandoned spouses and fatherless children. In your case, however, I ask only that you allow me to choose the nom de guerre by which the public will know you."

"That seems quite fair, Colonel," Etta said with a grin, "as long as you don't burden me with something like Agnes Criblecobbliss."

"No worry of that, girl," Cody said, a tear leaking through his mustache and into the corner of his mouth. "In fact, of late one of my performers, under the influence of her no-account, no-talent husband, has taken it into her head to abandon me. As many of her talents match yours, and someone of your ability can easily achieve the rest by practice, I propose that you take her place on our upcoming tour of the tank towns down south. It is unlikely that anyone there will notice any difference, although you are probably a head taller than she and, unlike you, this girl has a face like a birthing sow. Against my advice she has sought to begin a rival show in competition with this one, which has been her family these many years. That is, after the long European jaunt that she and the idiot she married embarked on this very morning. I believe that you will be a more than adequate replacement and better, as this woman could shoot all right but couldn't ride for shit or diamonds."

Etta felt excitement building inside her. It would be wonderful to do the trick shooting on occasion, but, oh, the chance to spend every day horseback! To smell the sweet hides, to curry the warm backs. All this and a salary that would allow her to live modestly and avoid the temptation of a dip into the treasure buried in that Brooklyn bank.

"Thank you, thank you, Colonel Cody," Etta said. "I promise you that at every performance I will attempt to satisfy the expectations of your audience and make you proud that you engaged me. I can only hope that this decision is a tenth as wise as the one you made so long ago when you discovered Annie Oakley."

Buffalo Bill leaned forward in his special chair. His mouth contorted again and the tears returned to his eyes. "That's fine, miss," he said. "And I really do reckon you'll like that new name."

Lars Hokanson had eaten Indian fry bread all his life, but never had it tasted this good. The Indian woman who prepared it every day seemed to know just what the white men liked. The bread itself was standard fare but fine: crisp and brown at the edges, pillowish in the middle, and made in a skillet that saw frequent changes of oil. But to this she added ingredients he had never known an Indian to use: sweet pork, chicken with the tang of pepper, beef with salt and onions.

When she had first appeared outside the Dickinson County jail, she seemed no different from other local hawkers, just another shy, tattered soul selling her wares from a small metal box. Attracted by their rich aroma, Hokanson had purchased a pork-and-peppers for fifteen cents, was transported by its flavors, and bought another. At the end of a week, the squaw had needed a second, larger box to satisfy the demand of the turnkeys—as well as any prisoners who had the price of such a delicacy. At the end of two weeks, she was invited inside and instructed to deliver the bread directly to the men, all of whom, free or not, reckoned they had better things to do than line up in the street for a sandwich.

The woman usually arrived at noon to begin her rounds. As she neither spoke nor understood English, she finished quickly, there being no opportunity for small talk. On her third Thursday in business, she once again padded through the door of the ramshackle one-story structure and dispensed her creations to each customer. The flavor of the day was ham with roast potatoes.

Having delivered all she had prepared, the woman smiled and gave a small wave to Murrow Graham, the guard whose post was at the end of the final block. When she returned to his desk near the front door, Lars Hokanson grunted at her through a piece of potato and smiled, expecting the woman to simply grin, nod, and scurry through the door.

This day she did not.

It was hard for Hokanson to imagine that a woman so small could handle a shotgun so big. But the twelve-gauge held no apparent awkwardness for her. Before Lars could make a move for his rifle, the woman leaped onto a chair and placed the performing end of the gun squarely in line with his eyes. Turning toward the outside door, she shouted in her native tongue. The cry was answered by a reedy young white man, who strode quietly through the door and into the antechamber. He looked at Hokanson, touched the brim of his hat, and cocked the handle of his Winchester.

"Mr. Lars," he said, "I believe you are holding Butch Cassidy here. And Harry Longbaugh and Ben Kilpatrick. This will go much easier on you and us if you would release them into my custody. And I suggest you allow your three other guards to finish their lunch in peace. Raise an alarm and I will send you to the next world."

Hokanson thought of his twenty-dollar-a-month salary and looked into the holes of the shotgun. He rose slowly from his chair and unlocked the iron door that separated the antechamber from Cell Block Number One. With the young man walking behind him and the Indian woman creeping backward before his eyes, Lars made his way down the block's long corridor.

"Any of you yardbirds makes a hoot, I'll kill him right here," the young man stage-whispered to the astonished prisoners, "so eat that flatbread and shut up, or by God it's your last meal."

Convicts quieted, the young man gestured for Lars to open cell thirteen. Butch smiled as the door swung open, and he accepted a Colt .45 from the squaw.

"Much obliged, Little Snake," Butch said, tucking the pistol in his waistband.

"You know that ain't her name," the lanky man whispered down the row of bars.

"Sorry, Dave," said Butch. "Force of habit."

By the time he had apologized, they had moved on to cell twenty. Dave Atkins kept his rifle trained on Lars Hokanson as he opened the door. Harry Longbaugh did not smile or speak. No use exchanging pleasantries with a woman who wouldn't understand. He gave a quick nod of gratitude to Hantaywee as she reached beneath her serape and dispensed a second Colt. Hokanson and the young man proceeded toward cell twenty-three to release the Tall Texan.

"Mr. Hokanson," whispered Atkins, "I'm sorry we have to bind and gag you, but I guess you knew the rules when you signed up for the game."

"I guess I did," Lars said. "Shame of it is, all I can think of is how much I'm gonna miss that bread."

Within minutes, the three outlaws and their liberators were clear of the town. As usual, their mounts easily outpaced the nags of the deputies. They were also aided by the fact that, while Hantaywee was delivering the bread, Dave Atkins had flung the lawmen's saddles into the manure pile at Compton's Livery.

In the wooded area around the Lyon Creek, they stopped to regroup.

"That was brave, what you done," Butch told Dave Atkins. "Figure to come with us back to the Hole?"

"No," Dave Atkins said. "The missus and me are fed up with the life. She only agreed to help because it was Harry, and then only because, to her, Harry means Etta. No offense, but you and Ben are just a bonus. Anyways we figure, with the way the bread went over with them jailhouse screws, we might as well try selling it someplace else legit."

Butch laughed. "No doubt it was the best thing about this particular pokey. Think you'll make a go of it?"

"Hell, yes," Dave said, with a grin. "Last time I had this much money, we turned a mail car to kindling. What about you, Harry?"

Harry Longbaugh shook his head. "Business. Back east."

Ben picked the rifle from his saddle sleeve and began to load it. "I'll meet you in Philadelphia soon as you need me," he said, "but I better stick here a little longer. Maybe figure some way to spring Laura. Who knows? I might even get two words in gratitude."

The bandits shook hands all around. Hantaywee formed a sign in the air that the white men figured meant goodbye. With a whoop of triumph, Dave Atkins and his bride headed south for the long panhandle of Oklahoma. Ben Kilpatrick searched the flat horizon for a place to hide, then spurred his horse through a thicket and was gone.

With a silent salute, Butch Cassidy and the Sundance Kid spun their mounts in a circle, making for the East and Etta Place.

LOCAL VILLAIN MURDERED IN
HORRIBLE CHRISTMAS MASSACRE!

MAN IS SUSPECTED MEMBER OF
LOCAL "BLACK HAND"!

FOUND BOUND AND CRUELLY STABBED!

POLICE HAVE NO CLUES!
MAN SEEN RUNNING AWAY!

In the predawn hours of one of our holiest days, a man suspected of membership in the City's Sicilian "Black Hand" organization was found bound with wire and stabbed once directly through the heart. The victim, an immigrant believed to be involved in crimes ranging from kidnapping to murder, was discovered in a meat locker at 1061 South Ninth Street in the heart of Italian Town.

The grisly scene was reported by Vincenzo A. Ianucci, the proprietor of Sorrentino Home Meat and Grocery of the above address. The Sicilian said he did not know the dead man and had no idea who would have committed such a sickening act of murder, but that he did see a dark man running from the ghastly scene.

The victim was identified as Dante G. Cichetti of 830 Snyder Avenue. Police told the *Mirror* that Ianucci, far from being unfamiliar with the deceased, was Cichetti's employer and often engaged him to carry out various nefarious deeds. Cichetti was well known to South Philadelphia policemen as a member of the infamous Hand, an organized group of no-goods and street arabs who are involved here in crimes of all descriptions, most of them victimizing their own countrymen.

Reached at his home by telephone, third district police captain Roland V. Dunkenfield told the *Mirror* that he was unsurprised by such heinous goings-on and that, as long as our nation continued to make the mistake of allowing the most lowborn of immigrants onto our shores, such horrors would continue unabated.

"These people not only perpetrate these gruesome horrors," he said, "but they are also known for their treasonous participation in socialism and anarchism. The Italian race is particularly prone to such violence."

From the description of the suspect, it is likely that he too is of Italianate stock. Police are searching for a tall man with dark hair, eyes, and mustache and with a pronounced brown birthmark above his lip. He was described as being "elegantly dressed in the manner of a gentleman" and, incongruously, wearing the kind of high-heeled, pointed boots usually associated only with those in the western cattle trade.

For Etta, the most difficult of the trick shots had been the one called About Face, which obliged one to grip a rifle backward on one shoulder and obliterate a target reflected in a mirror. But with a few days' practice and some advice from Colonel Cody himself, she was able to carry it out, along with the rest of Annie Oakley's repertoire.

Still, she couldn't imagine that anybody would be fooled by the deception. After all, "Little Sure Shot" was world famous and had performed, as the posters proclaimed, "before the crowned heads of Europe."

"Sure, kings and queens have gotten a good look at her," Buffalo Bill said, "but the rubes in Fayetteville, North Carolina, will believe their own eyes and what we tell 'em. Just like when we tell 'em that a bunch of plowboys from Arkansas are Russian-goddamn-Cossacks. They'll believe us because it's in their interest to believe us. They paid their hard-earned money for you to be Annie Oakley, and by God, as long as you don't screw up, you'd be Annie Oakley to them even if you was two heads taller than her, 'stead of just one, and them two heads was side by side. Besides, a tall and pretty Annie Oakley adds value to the price of the ducat."

Etta had laughed at the image of a two-headed girl shooting at both heads on a Jack of diamonds as the crowd applauded, but Cody seemed to know what he was doing, and so far no member of the cast had expressed doubt of any kind that she could pull off the charade.

"But just to be on the safe side," Cody had said, "we'll get you an extra-big horse—make you look smaller. I guarantee they'll love you more than they ever did the original."

Cody was as good as his word, and wherever they traveled, Etta's act was greeted with delight, no questions asked. Now, as she waited behind a purple curtain for her opening music, Etta no longer feared discovery. All would be well, Cody had said, as long as they kept "Miss Oakley" away from reporters and dumb-shit local politicians who might have met her before or wanted their picture taken with the phenom.

Far more difficult than learning the trick shot over the shoulder, Etta mused, had been leaving her "Little Nell." She had made certain that, despite the incident of the kiss, her relationship with Eleanor remained unchanged. She knew, if she did not maintain their usual schedule of work, luncheons, and walks, that her sensitive friend would read such a change as displeasure, even disgust. And so they saw each other as often as always, and Etta never hesitated to tell Nell how much she reveled in the pleasure of her company.

Together they dedicated themselves to the Rivington Street Settlement, dealing every day with the beaten and scorned women of the slums and sweatshops. Eleanor continued to teach dancing and champion Rivington to her wealthy friends. Etta taught the intricacies of English and, when necessary, handled a broom or mop with the aplomb she had once applied to a Winchester rifle or Army Colt. And several times a week the two repaired to the Alhambra, where, amid steam and privacy, they sought to dissolve the cares of loneliness. With the passage of time, Etta had even resumed speaking to Nell of her "husband" and how their long separation tore at her heart.

But even the sweet repair of such a valuable association could not forever stave off the evil of the outside world.

When word of Rodman Larabee's murder finally reached her, Etta had been filled with remorse. Were it not for her and her troubles, the kind old lawyer would still be alive. Along with her guilt came fear. Such a gentle old soul could not have been expected to keep silent under torture, so she assumed her secrets were now exposed to the Sicilians: Her false name, her job, her last-known whereabouts—all were now theirs to exploit. Joining Cody's *Wild West* had begun as a way to earn a living without raiding the Brooklyn treasure. Now it became Etta's refuge, providing both an escape from the Black Hand's long reach and an identity so big it allowed her to hide in plain sight.

But staying in New York was out of the question, even as Annie Oakley. If the Hand should somehow discover her charade they would surely have no compunction about torturing the truth from those whom Etta held closest. They had already done so with Rodman Larabee. It required no genius to deduce that the next poor target could be Eleanor herself.

Nor was confessing the truth an option. If the mob could find her, so could the Pinkertons, who in their own way were just as ruthless. Would Nell's status as the president's niece stop them from exposing Etta and destroying her friend's reputation? Would the Pinks travel to the prison where Harry and her friends lay captive and use the methods of interrogation of which every good outlaw had heard and to which so many had been bloodily subjected?

No. She had known she must lie once again. And the lie she would create for Eleanor must be a fine one, simple and easy to believe. A falsehood equal to an outlaw of her stature.

The deception had begun with a short note, the kind the two women exchanged almost daily:

My Dearest Nell,

Good morning!

Dearest, it is urgent that I see you. There has been a very important development in my life . . . and I fear it must now affect yours as well.

I beg that you reply posthaste, as the events surrounding me are by no means patient. Will you come and see me at Mrs. Taylor's, two o'clock tomorrow?

Through all, my Little Nell, I remain your faithful

Etta

The next day, Eleanor had arrived at the appointed hour. Etta had reserved the small sitting room for the hour and ordered tea and cakes.

They greeted as always, kissing each cheek in the European manner. They sat side by side, their hands entwined, and traded the sort of pleasantries that the highborn have always been instructed to exchange, even in the most dire of situations. The river of civilization, they had been warned, did not cease just because one's emotions were in danger of flood.

Etta had looked into those huge hooded blue eyes. She noted the twist of the mouth that had trained itself to remain closed lest its teeth become evident and reveal their owner as imperfect. But all of Nell was beautiful to her now: the golden hair, the prominent nose, even the chin that often seemed as if it wished to hide from the remainder of the face.

"Dearest," she began, "I would not for all the earth injure you or disappoint you in any way. You have been my salvation in this cruel city. You have brought me work and laughter and friendship and love. I tell you right out that I have not asked you here to renounce that love, as I could not, even if I tried.

"But I now do tell you that I must go away for a time, away from my precious Nell. As we always knew would happen, Mr. Place has at last sent for me. His business in the West is now completed but his plans have changed. Instead of coming here to New York, he has wired me to join him in Virginia, where he will be making a series of calls in the near future. Therefore, I must leave for Washington this Tuesday and, I am afraid, be gone many months.

"But oh, my dear, please believe that my excitement at seeing my husband again is matched by the sorrow of leaving you, my only Nell. You who have been left to loneliness so many times."

For a moment Eleanor had sat still, as if failing to comprehend her friend's words. Then she bowed her head like a mourner and wept noiselessly. Etta, too, began to grieve in a manner she could only liken to the tears of parting that fell on that train platform in Yellow Jacket, what now seemed a lifetime ago.

"I implore you, Nell, to have courage . . . because if you do not then surely I too must fall to fragments. And I promise you that wherever I am, small town or big city, I shall write every day, even if is only to remind you that your friend has not forgotten you, that you are ever in my thoughts. Even if it is only to remind you never to forget me."

Eleanor's head snapped up. A tendril of blond hair had fallen from her perfect coiffure and onto her forehead. The immense eyes seemed stricken with a kind of panic but then dissolved into a misery total and immeasurable.

"Oh, no. No, dearest," Eleanor said, "that can never happen! As if I could ever forget one moment of our time. As if I could ever forget the kindness you have shown to an ugly girl by bestowing some of your beauty on me."

Etta had grabbed Eleanor in her long arms and held her tightly. The girl had struggled for a moment and then collapsed in a flood of hot tears against the shoulder of her friend.

"Too ugly," she had murmured. "Always . . . too ugly. . . ."

And then, with a blast of trumpets, Etta's reverie was shattered.

The orchestra began playing her into the arena as the roar of the citizens of Paducah, Kentucky, welcomed Annie Oakley to the center of the great tent. The crowd, swollen by Christmas celebration, was larger even than the one in Charleston.

As Etta steadied her giant horse, she bowed to the throng, a buffalo gun held high above her head. Then she began to shoot: the cigarette from Peg Leg's mouth, the clay Indians from thin air, the five bull's-eyes reflected in the mirror. And at this performance, at least, every blast seemed to strike a target deep inside her own heart.

LETTER TO JOSIAH LONGBAUGH
12 State St., Phoenixville, Pa.
26 December 1901

Dear Father,

On the day of His birth, I have committed a grievous crime against Him that died for us. And yet I know that had the life I ended lasted longer it could have destroyed her whom I prize so much that I would risk my soul's eternity.

Yes, I killed a man. I do not know if his widow or children cry that his life was cut short. But, Father, this was a ruthless man. A Italian of no conscience that kills cold and greedy. And he would have got my girl on but one show of her face.

Once I got to Philadelphia it did not take long to find out where the Black Hand made camp or who their soldiers were. For two dollars, a pair of street arabs told me all about the kid who was going around local taverns, telling tales of the Wild West and the beautiful woman he would kill sure as daybreak. After that, it was all tracking and patience.

I am writing this letter to you from a Papist church in that City of Brotherly Love, inside which I have sat this long hour, looking into the face of His mother, Mary, her that the Catholics worship just as much as Jesus Himself. I have waited here this

long time for the remorse to overwhelm me or to take their confession or to tell my crime to one of their black sisters, but all I
can feel is the chill of the icebox in which the deed was done.
The coldness around my shoulders makes me shiver.

No matter. In cold blood or hot, he is kilt and my love is safe.
And if they do not take my warning, then woe to them they send
to finish his work.

By the time you read this I will have gone where my love is.
The Pinks have done all they can to keep our escape quiet, and I
fear she does not know I am now back in the world. I must find
her quickly, as every hour she believes me in a cage must be, for
her, the devil's own worry.

I think it is only through the warmth of my Etta that I will
ever shake this chill. If I should never find her, then when other
sinners ask me if there is a Hell for what I have done, I will tell
them yes. It is here on Earth. And cold.

My best to you and for your health, Father.
Affectionately, your son,
Harry Longbaugh

4

The young woman pouring his coffee was as plain as the surface of a milk pail, one of those people who, all of their lives, seem doomed to be a single color, all contrast eliminated from crown to collar: pale hair and pale eyes matched with pale skin and lips. Looking at such a washed-out wretch, Detective Charles A. Siringo tried to imagine what it must have been like for a traveling drummer to sit at this very table after an endless train ride and be served by the vision that was Etta Place.

The white-on-white girl took his order and placed a copy of the Grand Junction *Citizen's News* beside his steaming cup. He had read these same stories in every little town on the frontier. Read them more than once.

There was the attempt to form this committee or that (today it was a committee to provide a library). There was also the requisite small-town theft (today's story recounted the theft of a butter churn from the porch of a Mr. C. E. Buckley and family). He wasn't expecting to read about anything as sensational as a murder, let alone the murder of one of his own thugs.

It had been two days since he had received a wire from Weston Sims, Pinkerton's man in Philadelphia. Siringo had assumed that the Hand would eventually deal with Dante Cichetti. After all, no criminal organization could abide providing the Pinks with information. He had expected to hear in time that Dante was found hanging from a meat hook or discovered washed up alongside the Delaware, dollar bill in mouth, but his end had been far less dramatic. Cichetti had been simply and unceremoniously shot in the head. The telegram had included no evidence as to the identity of the culprit.

As morbidly interesting as all this was, Siringo had little time to muse over the demise of another guttersnipe. Kid Curry was now his competitor in locating Etta Place, and the little man's trail was getting cold. He knew Curry hated the girl, and what Curry hated he killed.

Siringo also knew that if Curry caught up to their quarry first, he would certainly bury her where she would never be found; even if he did not, Curry was unlikely to leave enough of her pretty face behind to identify. This would never do. As much as her capture, Siringo's mission was Etta's positive identification. It was all that stood between Fred Harvey and the lawsuit of a lifetime.

"I want her alive," Harvey had said. "More important, *they* want her alive. Those Dixon bastards and their lawyers have made it clear that only a rope will make it nice and legal."

The newspaper was four pages as they always were: one large sheet folded carefully in half. Siringo knew that if he turned past the third page there was apt to be some news from a place other than Grand Junction, and he was right. At the top of page four, in a larger font than usual, he read the words:

PHILA. VILLAIN MURDERED IN HORRIBLE
CHRISTMAS MASSACRE!

At first he was amazed that, in this isolated place, he should read a piece of wire-service copy from a big eastern city about the very man he had recently interrogated. Exactly as Sims had stated, the gunsel's death had come swiftly. Perhaps a rival faction of Philadelphia's criminals had begun cleaning house in a bid to consolidate power or territory or, as was often the case, to take revenge. But the Pinkerton man's theory of the crime was instantly altered as he read the description of the suspect: *of Italianate stock . . . a tall man with dark hair, eyes, and mustache . . . brown birthmark above his lip.*

Charlie Siringo read the item twice and then threw down the newspaper and snapped the linen from his lap. Tossing a dollar on the table, he rushed from the dining room and hurried across the street to his hotel. Gaining his room, he gathered his belongings, quickly retraced his steps, and made for the ticket office of the Santa Fe. Once his fare was paid, Siringo ran across the platform and filed a quick message with a startled telegraph clerk he had awakened from an afternoon doze.

WESTERN UNION
TELEGRAM

TO: MR. WESTON SIMS   JAN 8, 1902

PINKERTON DETECTIVE AGENCY

330 MARKET ST.

PHILADELPHIA, PA

REASON TO BELIEVE H. LONGBAUGH IN YOUR CITY. MAY HAVE DEALT WITH MEMBER OF BLK HAND IN MATTER OF CHRISTMAS DAY. TAKE NO ACTION BESIDES SURVEILLANCE UNTIL I ARRIVE FOUR DAYS STRATFORD HOTEL. POSSIBLE LONGBAUGH MAY SEEK MEETING WITH EP AS YOURS HER HOMETOWN. LONGBAUGH ARMED AND DANGEROUS AS ANY. EP TOO. CAUTION.

SIRINGO

Brown birthmark above his lip. Charlie Siringo could not have been more certain if someone had asked him his own name. He needed to see no Wanted bills, needed to hear no jail-break news. The Sundance Kid had escaped from prison and paid a visit to Philadelphia. He had murdered Dante Cichetti as a warning to the Black Hand. And if Harry Longbaugh was in the East, he was there to rendezvous with Etta Place.

Diary,

It has been some days, my old friend, since I have written. What with the constant practice (at today's matinee I shot out half a dozen candles rotating upon an electric wheel!) and the care and training of Buster (the biggest horse you have ever seen not pulling a beer wagon), it has been difficult to find time for you.

Too, almost all the moments I have reserved to put pen to paper have been carefully reserved for ER. And that paper is truly a tissue of lies. It is especially painful to carry on the deception that I am traveling with my husband and am the happy recipient of all the tender affections that accompany marriage, when in fact I am as lonely and empty as Little Nell herself. But how could I ever tell her that I am pursued on all sides—the Black Hand, the lawmen, the Pinkertons—and that the "husband" to whom I have never been wed is rotting away these precious years in a western prison?

In these days, it seems, my only solace comes at showtime,

when I may truly escape inside the buckskin fringes of Annie Oakley and feel my first sense of accomplishment since I aided the poor girls of Rivington Street. There is something to be said for relieving the daily care of an exhausted farmer and his wife with a few retorts from a buffalo gun, and I now understand why there are those who spend their lives in pursuit of applause. Our own Mr. Elliott is a clear example. To Peg Leg's delight, the colonel has begun to feature him under his own name. The posters now display this addition:

SEE "PEG LEG" ELLIOTT! MASTER OF THE
LARIAT AND SNAPPY REPARTEE!
TRICKS TO AMAZE YOU, JOKES TO AMUSE YOU!

Still, Diary, if anyone had ever told me that living a lie so big would be this easy I would have thought them fit for committing. Under orders from the colonel, no one with the show has revealed my identity to either reporter or copper, and I suspect that the code of the carnival has something to do with that. Nor would I find it surprising if Cody had locked away somewhere a secret about every single "artist" in his parade, full as it is with convicted felons, phony Indians, beautiful girls of dubious reputation, and sundry mountebanks.

In any event, the colonel has so far proved correct in his assertion that the audience in these small southern hamlets is deeply invested in my being who they want me to be. If I am bigger, more "attractive", a better rider and a worse shot than my erstwhile namesake, it seems to matter little as long as people receive their money's worth . . . and I have determined to give them that.

If the truth be known (and at this point some truth should), the most critical problem we have yet faced was getting a much larger suit of buckskins tailored for me in the week we had between New York and the South. A Blackfoot woman who is traveling with us managed to get such a proper outfit done in time for my first appearance, but Lord, it was close! Indeed, she was sewing me into her work of art even as the music introducing me began to play.

Thus does my life become a world of aliases: Lorinda Reese Jameson, debutante; alias Etta Place, outlaw; alias Mrs. Harry Place, newlywed; alias Annie Oakley, trick shot. There are, Diary, hours when I fear I will lose my true self in this morass and others in which I hope that I will. In these last, I think, How grand to be someone else . . . someone at whose heels no dogs are nipping. No Pinks. No law. No bandit lost to me.

And no seventeen-year-old girl alone inside a frozen house in Manhattan, the only victim caught in these lies too good, too sweet, too fine to deserve them.

From the
ATLANTA CONSTITUTION
January 25, 1902

**ATTEMPT ON LIFE OF ROOSEVELT HERE!
PRESIDENT SAVED FROM ANARCHIST
BY FAMOUS TRICK SHOT ANNIE OAKLEY.**

"Little Sure Shot" Foils Encrazed Foreigner!

**Oakley Has Disappeared!
Colonel Cody Says She Seeks No Publicity!**

By our correspondents

As he enjoyed a performance of *Buffalo Bill's Wild West* last evening, an attempt was made upon the life of the president of the United States. The cowardly attack was carried out during a matinee at the fairgrounds in Ormewood, some ten miles from our city.

The would-be assassin, who appeared disguised as a rodeo clown, was described as an anarchist. He tried to shoot President Theodore Roosevelt by use of a small-caliber revolver concealed within his vest. Eyewitnesses said the man approached the president's box via the performing ring and came within only a few feet of the chief executive.

Mr. Roosevelt would almost certainly have been injured or killed, had it not been for quick action on the part of Mrs. Phoebe Anne Butler, known to the world as the famous sharpshooter, Annie Oakley. According to police and audience accounts, Mrs. Butler was performing on horseback when the villain approached the president and she noticed the gun in his hand.

Just as the degenerate shouted forth some oath in an unknown language, Mrs. Butler, who has performed her amazing feats around the globe, exclaimed to the crowd, "Pray get down, everyone!" Then did the heroine of the day gallantly charge her enormous stallion directly at the criminal, knocking him off his feet and causing his pistol to discharge harmlessly into the air, its projectile tearing a hole in the ceiling of the show's great tent. Secret Service agents, who are charged with the protection of the president, then made for the assassin and threw him to the ground.

At first, many in the throng believed Mrs. Butler's selfless act to be merely part of the program with the president playing along. But it soon became apparent that the assassination attempt was genuine and the danger all too real.

After he was released from the grip of the agents protecting him and the tense moment had passed, the president was heard to remark, "Splendid! A bully adventure! I am quite unhurt." Mr. Roosevelt then asked to see the famed "Little Sure Shot" in order to thank her for saving his life. However, after she had dispatched the madman, Mrs. Butler lingered only long enough to ascertain the state of Mr. Roosevelt's welfare and then inexplicably rode her horse through the spangled performer's curtain and did not reemerge. In due course, the president and his party vacated the premises without meeting her.

Later in the day, Colonel William F. Cody, U.S. Cavalry (retired), proprietor and namesake of *Buffalo Bill's Wild West*, held a conference for the press in which he stated that Mrs. Butler was "as any woman would be," in a near-fainting state from the heroics of the day and sought no accolades for foiling the plot of the evildoer. "She believes," said Buffalo Bill, "that any reward or undue publicity resulting from her actions of today would be unseemly. Our Annie thanks the president for his gratitude but says she only did what any patriotic citizen would have done in her place." Col. Cody also stated that Mrs. Butler would not be made available to the government, the police, or reporters until her own health and well-being had been firmly established.

As we go to press, the identity of the blackguard has not been released. He is said to be of middle-European extraction and is more than likely a member of one of the many dangerous anarchist sects that infect that region of the world. No member of the president's party would comment to the *Constitution* about where the insane plotter was being held. At 5:30 P.M. the president and his party returned to Washington aboard a special train. Given his famous indomitable will and iron constitution, Mr. Roosevelt will no doubt be his chipper self by morning, if not sooner.

Considering what she was used to, the trip back to New York was unglamorous and Etta was glad of it. She had had it to the neck with fancy dress and the center of the spotlight. Now her concentration was on simple pleasures. The food on the Great Montrealer was nearly as well prepared as that served on a Harvey train, and the money Colonel Cody had provided allowed her to remain in a private drawing room where those meals could be served to her in peace.

Given a choice, Etta most certainly would have opted for more social surroundings, but she was still a wanted woman. As the idea of remaining in disguise for the better part of two days seemed tiresome at best, she holed up in her compartment like a rich girl, seeing only the faces of black porters and managing always to avert her own in their presence.

For her current luxury, she had William F. Cody to thank. During their final negotiation, the colonel had driven an unexpectedly soft bargain, offering to remit additional monies for her silence. After all, it would not have done for the great showman to be exposed as a fraud, a man whose "Annie Oakley" was not only an imposter but an imposter wanted for murder. But Etta had refused his offer, noting his many kindnesses to her and his generous keeping of her own secrets. The private compartment and a small stipend would be sufficient for her needs.

"I get it," the old man had said, through a thousandth hemorrhoidal grimace. "Trade secrets. You trade me your secret and I'll trade you mine."

Etta's life now seemed all future and no past: a place without home or parent or friend to distract her from her losses. During the month she had toured with the show, there had been at least some diversion from emptiness. In Cody's railroad cars and wagons at night, Etta had sat quietly among her fellow outcasts, raised a glass in their drunken toasts, and turned over cards that won or lost their penny-ante pots. But now even this humble warmth was gone.

All that remained was the smallest and most precious of her lies. Had she been true to her conscience, she would have laid this aside as well. But met with so much emptiness, Etta sought the only thing solid to which she could now cling: the rock called Eleanor Roosevelt, the last person Etta loved not yet imprisoned or killed.

As the train rocked its way through South Carolina, Etta began to write:

10 February 1902

My Dearest Nell,

I can only hope that this letter finds you well and happy.
I must confess that my own life is far poorer for not seeing you every day. And that is why, my most precious darling, with a full heart and your kind permission, I am coming to visit you.

Harry has concluded much of his business here in the South. Truth be told, I believe he needed me mostly as a companion and hostess during the endless balls and parties these rebels like to prepare for themselves. Now, all that is left are the sordid details of money and delivery and suchlike. I think at this juncture he can complete the dullest parts of his ventures without his little wife to distract him.

And so, dearest, I would like to return to you for a little while. As of tomorrow afternoon, I will once again be stopping at Mrs. Taylor's. The telephone is now laid on there and I may be reached in this way, although I know you find such electric conversations public and undignified.

I will contact you when I arrive. To roam New York without my great friend would be like visiting heaven without its greatest angel.

Yours always,
EP

As she penned her last initial, Etta found that she was smiling. She slipped the small cream-colored note into its envelope and heated a stick of purple wax with a wooden match. She sealed the letter, addressed it, and slid it beneath her pillow. All that night, her sleep played hide-and-seek with her hopes, and she was wide awake at dawn when the porters came to collect the mail for posting at Norfolk.

Wherever she walked, Etta Place caused people to stop. The reaction may have amounted only to a slight hesitation of step or a short sharp intake of the breath, but, looking at her, people would begin to wonder things: *How does Nature produce such a girl?* or *Why am I not that tall?* or *Can her hair really be that color?* or *How was I so cheated in love?* These and a thousand other foolish or jealous or obscene thoughts would swirl about her at all hours and in all places. Everyone was subject, no one immune: men, women, even little girls.

In contrast, Phoebe Anne Butler was as unnoticeable as the plaster composing a wall. Less than five feet tall and with few distinguishing features, pointing her out would be like remarking upon the shape of the curb where it meets the street or the cement binding two particular bricks.

Not that she minded. She reckoned blasting a sheroot from the mouth of the Kaiser was attention enough for any girl; she relished the idea that, when not in her buckskin and boots, she was a nobody and looked the part. How tiresome it would have been to be shopping for the most confidential of a lady's needs and have the shopgirl gush and call for her colleagues. No, she preferred to live in disguise right down to her name.

To Phoebe, *Annie Oakley* was like a hat or a pair of boots: something to be put on before a show and removed after. During those short hours that she lived, Annie worked hard. She shot the flames from candles revolving on a pinwheel or exploded a dollar through the eagle's wing.

When she was finished, she was rewarded with wild applause and big bags of gold.

Now, on this cold evening, Phoebe Anne sat across a gilt-topped table from Buffalo Bill Cody. They had taken a private booth at Luchow's and sent the waiter away. Secluded enough, thought Cody, to avoid fools and the gossiping press. Public enough, thought Phoebe, to embarrass her former boss with press-attracting pronouncements if the negotiation failed to go her way. Between the two legends sat Phoebe's husband, Frank Butler, a second-rate trick shot and third-rate husband, known to the world at large as Mr. Oakley.

"Really, Bill," Phoebe began, her tone calm and measured, "this should be a matter for the lawyers. I'm not gone from your sideshow one day but that you find some stretched-out tart to take not only my place but my name."

"Phoebe, Phoebe, Phoebe," Cody replied. "It was really only a borrow. I thought you and Frank here was off on the grand tour, seeing the great capitals of Europe and Asia. How'd I know you was still in America? You wasn't working, and as you wasn't working you really wasn't using the name. You know I never like anything to go to waste."

Frank Butler's narrow cheeks flushed with rage. "Cody, it's an outrage, what you done to my Phoebe! Why, the only reason I ain't as yet throttled you bug-eyed is that my wife won't allow violence on account of her Christian lean-tos! Up to me, I'd settle this like men and no guesses to it."

Phoebe sighed. "Shut up, Frank."

Buffalo Bill shifted uncomfortably in his chair. Aggravation always caused flareups in his hindquarters, and the pillow the maître d' had brought to him seemed to bring more pain than relief.

"If I've offended you, my dear, I sincerely apologize," the colonel said. "But try to see it from my side. My star, my beautiful shining star, leaves the arena practically in the middle of her performance. And in New York City, no less, the town that loves Annie Oakley most! My star *deserts* me over a mere pittance of money to go off around the world. It's not like you was going to perform anywheres of consequence. The tour was just the tank towns down south: tobacco spitters, married brothers and sisters, kids with two heads. I figured it couldn't hurt your reputation for me to—well, *re-create* you for a month or so as long as the girl could do the tricks aright. And meanwhile I had time to figure a way to lure you back to our family—our *Wild West* family."

Frank Butler moved to speak again, but quick as birdshot his wife clapped her right hand over his mouth. "You didn't think it was such a pittance when I asked for it, but you'll give it to me now, and much more."

"And what would cause me to do that?"

"Because now, bastard, I am a hero."

Buffalo Bill stared into those mercilessly accurate eyes and began to feel sympathy for all those targets and candles, those cigarettes cut off in the flame of youth, those funny little cutouts of Crazy Horse.

"Yes, Bill, a goddamned hero. A *national* hero. A hero who saved the life of the President of the United States."

"But Phoebe, now, you know that wasn't really you. I don't think you're being fair, trying to take credit for it."

"But I *am* going to take credit for it, old man. I'll take credit for it right here in front of you, just like you took my name when I wasn't looking. And you'll sit still for it even if it makes them piles of yours burst into the devil's own flame. Because there's money to be made.

"I'm not stupid, Bill. I know you already can't handle all the demands for interviews. A cigar maker wants to put me on a box of Coronas. Some breakfast-cereal magnate is crazy enough that he thinks my picture on the box might sell his mush. And you know something? You're going to be just as crazy as he is. You're going to put my picture on every poster, every lobby card, every advertisement. You're going to fill the lobbies with copies of the autobiography Mr. Buntline is at this moment writing for me, you're going to sell every one, and—"

"My darling girl," interrupted Cody, "be reasonable."

"—and in addition to my salary, you're going to pay me five percent of the gross receipts because I don't trust you to tell me the net. And you're going to do it all with a smile because even when my cut is subtracted you're going to make more money than there was gold teeth in Sitting Bull's yap."

"God rest him," Cody said.

"Yes," said Phoebe. "God rest him." She dropped her hand from her husband's mouth.

Cody stared at her, calculating sums in his head.

"Three percent," he murmured.

"Four."

"Done."

Cody pulled back the purple velvet curtain surrounding the private booth and raised a buckskinned arm to signal the waiter.

"Veuve Clicquot," he whispered to the young man.

In the time it took to finish the first three glasses, Phoebe and Cody had created the rough draft of a statement that would, within a day, be wired to the *Sun,* the *World,* the *Post,* the *Times,* the *Herald,* the *Journal,* the *American,* and all the wire services.

To wit:

Mrs. Frank Butler, known throughout the world as the famous markswoman Annie Oakley, has decided to break her self-imposed silence and speak to the gentlemen of the press about the recent heroics that saved the life of Mr. Theodore Roosevelt, President of the United States. Interviews to be held tomorrow.

Up until now, Mrs. Butler had been reluctant to discuss her fearless achievement, as her natural modesty and deep religious beliefs precluded her from seeking "cheap" publicity. But at the urging of her employer and bosom friend, Col. William F. Cody, famous throughout civilization as the scout, soldier and Indian fighter "Buffalo Bill," she has decided to detail the astounding feat of horsewomanship that saved our beloved president. Mrs. Butler will be available this Tuesday from nine o'clock A.M. until five o'clock P.M., Delmonico Hotel.

Interviews will be scheduled on a first-come first-served basis.

All requests should be wired to Miss Gladys Cooper, Buffalo Bill's Wild West, Plaza Hotel, New York City.

Refreshments will be served. Mrs. Butler requests that all gentlemen reporters maintain forbearance and restraint during these interviews, as the memory of this historic event is likely to cause the international star and legendary sharpshooter to weep openly.

As the weather turned cold in Philadelphia, Detective Charles A. Siringo caught the scent of Harry Longbaugh.

At least the Sundance Kid had good taste. He had chosen to hole up in the Stratford Hotel, easily the Quaker City's finest. If long experience was any kind of teacher, Siringo could soon expect an efficient capture, free of violence.

The procedure was one in which Siringo and his men were well versed: Once the operatives had made certain that the rogue in question was in his hotel room, the final springing of the trap was composed of a carefully coordinated group of tasks, so far foolproof for its creator. One man would be posted in the hotel stairwell, another at the end of the hallway, with Siringo himself, revolver at the ready, directly before the room's door.

When the knock came, it was usually only a matter of answering the subject's inquiry with something designed to appeal to the natural greed of the criminal within. "Who is it?" the scoundrel would ask, and the answer would come back, "Your bank draft has arrived, Mr. So-and so," or "We believe, sir, that we have found your money clip." Once the door was opened, it was a simple matter to take the hunted into custody with little or no resistance. There was no reason to believe the result would be different for Room 6-B of the Stratford.

Siringo had been somewhat surprised that the shadowing of Longbaugh had been so easy. In fact, Sims, the head of the Philadelphia office, had spied him fewer than twenty-four hours after receiving Siringo's wire from Colorado. With the telegram's description in hand, there could be no mistaking the tall elegant figure, birthmark above lip, hair and mustaches so dark their color seemed applied by a City Hall bootblack. Sims had followed every move of those ebony cowboy boots as they strode into Ware's for a quick beer or scuffed themselves against the stalls at O'Leary's bookshop. For a murderer, it seemed to Sims, Longbaugh was making little attempt to hide himself. He had registered at the Stratford under the name of George Ingerfield. When Siringo first heard this, he had laughed out loud at the notion that Harry Longbaugh had decided to sign with an alias normally used by Butch Cassidy. If this was Longbaugh's idea of how to hide in plain sight, he clearly had figured it only halfway.

Etta Place, however, had proved more elusive. If indeed she was anywhere within the borders of the City of Brotherly Love, Longbaugh clearly had her stashed. The Kid had made no attempt to squire her to any of his nightside haunts, nor was she seen in his company by day. But, as Sims had wired Siringo, there was good reason to believe that the girl was somewhere near, as every day the Kid stopped into Bailey Banks & Biddle and purchased some expensive trinket or other. On Tuesday, it was a white-gold chain with a single arrow charm; on Wednesday, a pair of earrings cast in platinum with sapphire insets; on Thursday, a pearl and gilt choker that, upon being subsequently researched, proved to sell for more than two thousand dollars.

But this was no time to muse over money. Now in front of Room 6-B, Siringo unholstered his revolver. He knocked on the door twice before he heard a footfall inside the room.

"Yes?" came a deep and friendly voice from inside.

"This is hotel service, Mr. Ingerfield," Siringo answered, trying his best to sound younger and more callow than his true self. "We have a bank draft here for you."

The room door opened and a tall figure filled the darkened space. Siringo swiftly intruded into the foyer, his Colt .45 already cocked.

The expression on the Pinkerton's face would be something his quarry would remember until the end of his life. First came the look of surprise as one of the now-famous black cowboy boots laid its pure-silver point squarely into Siringo's groin. The detective's face twisted in pain, derived not just from the savage kick but also from the strong right arm, which came down as quickly as the leg had risen and relieved Siringo's hand of its weapon.

From here on it was a matter of taking advantage of what came naturally to the body and the laws of physics. When the testicles are stove in, the chin comes down. When the chin comes down, the fist rises to meet it, using not only its own upward motion but the irresistible force of the victim's entire body quickly bending double at the waist.

The tall man with the black mustache noted that, even crumpled to the carpets and writhing in two kinds of agony, Charlie Siringo, the Pink's Pink, managed to maintain dignity of a sort. Even in defeat, he would give an adversary only so much satisfaction and no more.

"Your men are detained," the tall man said. "They have been waylaid by my own agents. If they were smart, they've sustained not much more injury than yourself. If they were not . . . well, it's likely they are dead. I sincerely hope, Mr. Siringo, that there weren't no reason for them to die for their paychecks. I've not made my reputation by death but thievery, and at this point in life I would hope to be writ in the book of life as a highwayman, not a murderer."

"You've killed before, Longbaugh," Siringo said, through clenched teeth, "and it's no good now trying to say you've got no blood on your conscience."

The dark man reached for a lariat that lay prepared upon the bed. He made no effort to remonstrate with the detective over guilt, innocence, or any other subject. He tied the rope securely about Siringo and, before the effect of the kick to the testoo wore off and allowed him to muster sufficient volume to raise an alarm, filled his mouth with a bandanna. As he completed his task, a confederate appeared at the door, rolling one of the large wheeled canvas baskets the hotel normally used to transport laundry. As he was lifted and deposited into the conveyance, Siringo was astonished to see that this second man was dressed identically to the first: same elegant long coat, same red cravat, and wearing a perfect copy of the black cattleman's boots. His hair and mustache were of the same jet color as the man who had attacked and trussed him. As the third of the confederates arrived, identical to the first two and wheeling a similar basket, it began to dawn upon the detective that his best man in Philadelphia had been duped by a trio of imposters, any one of whom, or none, could have been the true Sundance Kid.

In his undoing, the only consolation the Pinkerton could take was that neither he nor his two operatives had been killed. As each man watched helplessly from his own laundry bin, they could see the fancy clothes fly from the three "Longbaughs." Mustaches were shaved, black hair dye removed with lye soap and hot water. Before Siringo or either of his lieutenants could divine the identities of the triad, the hotel's fine sheets were thrown over their baskets and they were carried down a freight elevator to the street.

Some four hours later in Hartford, Connecticut, a Mr. Peter F. Friel, mail attendant for the Pennsylvania Railroad, stepped aboard the 3:11 from Philadelphia to begin his shift. Making his way toward the baggage car, he heard muffled cries emerging from behind its oak door. Investigating, he found three large wheeled laundry hampers marked STRATFORD HOTEL PHILADELPHIA rocking back and forth in a manner that could never have been created by dirty linen.

A father of five and therefore not prone to engage in heroics, Mr. Friel promptly called for the conductor and asked that he delay departure and send for the railroad detectives. When the three men were freed and Friel was formally introduced to Charles Siringo, the mailman immediately looked into the leather bag he carried for all wire correspondence.

"If you're Siringo," he said, "I reckon I have a telegram for you. Under the circumstances, mister, I just hope it's good news."

It wasn't.

WESTERN UNION
TELEGRAM

TO: MR. CHARLES SIRINGO   FEB 15, 1902
ABOARD THE BOSTON PATRIOT
3:11 FROM PHILADELPHIA
RECEIVED: HARTFORD STATION

SORRY FOR DECEPTION BUT THIS IS OUTLAW BUSINESS. TAKE HEART. IT WAS NOT EASY FOR ME NOR MY MEN. CLOTHES HAD TO BE BESPOKE MADE. HAIR DYE ITCHED AND COVERED MY PRETTY BLOND LOCKS. I LOOK BAD IN MUSTACHE ESPECIALLY BLACK. BIRTHMARKS MADE US LOOK LIKE SODOMITES. WHICH ONE OF US YOU THINK MOST PRETTY SUNDANCE? SHOULD HAVE KNOWN SOMETHING WAS UP WHEN YOUR BOYS SPOTTED HIM SO EASY. DON'T WANT NO ONE HURT AS I PROVED BY YOUR JOURNEY. DON'T LOOK FOR US AS YOU WILL WASTE YOUR TIME. ADVISE NOT LOOK FOR HARRY IN PHILA. NONE OF US WAS HIM. YOU NEVER COULD GET MY NAME RIGHT. WAS NEVER GEORGE. SO I WILL SIGN IT CORRECTLY FOR YOU. AND A HAPPY NEW YEAR.

ROBERT LEROY PARKER

At almost the exact moment Butch Cassidy had finished dictating that message in Philadelphia, Eleanor Roosevelt waited for Etta Place in a tearoom in New York. It was long past the appointed hour of four, but Eleanor dared not leave. Etta had, after all, declined her offer of a coach and driver. Perhaps her dear friend had been delayed by a faulty trolley or been blocked by a dead horse in the street. After all, such things happened every day.

The boy who approached her was the same child who had brought Etta's message of the night before. He was in many ways the typical page of his day: dirty under his uniform, seeking any work that would provide an alternative to the mill's monotony or the pickpocket's art. He asked for Miss *Roos*-velt, pronouncing the surname as it was spelled, and waited as his customer read in silence:

Dearest Nell,

I do so regret that I will be unable to join you today. I cannot explain my actions to you at this moment, but please believe me that they cannot be avoided.

In all the world there is no one I would less seek to disappoint. When we are at last together I will explain all and beg most abjectly for your kind forgiveness.

With much love,
your EP

For a long moment Eleanor stared at the cream-colored stationery and then turned to the boy.

"Any reply, ma'am?"

Eleanor smiled sadly at the messenger. She recognized in his eyes the suffering that had become her old friend at Rivington Street. She noted his red-gold hair and milky coloring. Irish, she thought.

She reached into her purse and produced a silver dollar. "No, young man. No reply. Thank you very much."

The boy stared into his palm and then looked up at Eleanor. Her eyes had now begun to brim. She nodded to him. Without a word he turned and ran down the street, looking once over his shoulder before disappearing around the first corner.

Eleanor brought her white linen napkin first to her eyes and then to her mouth as she took a final sip of sweet tea. She placed two coins on the table, squared her shoulders, and emerged into the fading light and gathering cold of winter.

At almost that same instant, inside a suite at the Waldorf, Harry Longbaugh embraced Etta Place. As she smiled up at him, she could taste her own tears in the corners of her mouth, overjoyed to see his eyes so close to hers. Though they had loved for hours, Etta was still unconvinced that his body was not a dream, that he was not a ghost sent to haunt her with pleasure. All she knew for certain was that he was more beautiful than she remembered him. As he kissed her in the hollow of her shoulder, she twisted herself around him, arm and leg, reluctant to allow so much as a shaft of light to come between them.

The small priest with the black eyes politely thanked his landlady for the two towels arrayed across the narrow bed.

"I'm sorry that yer room has no winda, Father," she said, in a pronounced Scots burr, "but them's all been let. If ye'll just open yer door a crack, there should be ventilation aplenty for ye this time of year."

The priest gave the old woman a short smile, more like a spasm of indigestion than a signal of gladness. "This room will suit me perfectly, Mrs. Davenport. I don't imagine that there is a finer room in all of New York City."

"Then I'll be leavin' ye, Father. I hope that yer stay with us will be pleasant."

"Go with God, madam."

As things stood, the priest was more than happy there was no way to view this city from his cramped and dirty room. Ever since he stepped from the train last night, all he had seen in these man-made canyons filled him with righteous disgust. Hundreds of niggers strode the streets like the equals of white men. Cops stood on every corner, their florid faces as Irish as Paddy's pig, red with drink and graft.

Worse than this, had there been a window in his room he would have seen the pushcarts and makeshift stands of those who had killed Christ for their greed. As he had walked among them on the way to this shithouse, there was a moment when he believed he could no longer endure it. That he would have to reach for the twin pistols beneath his robe. If there were this many Jews in New York, he thought, it truly must be the vile place of which he had heard all his life.

But Etta Place was here. Laura Bullion had told him so. And if she was in Manhattan, so was his money. And if his money was here it stood to reason that the escaped Sundance was here as well, spending what was rightfully his. Still, he told himself, it was only a matter of time before all three of them, the money, Harry Longbaugh, and the woman, would be his to do with as he pleased.

Still, as perverted as New York City was, it had not prevented luck from smiling upon him. Earlier that evening, even before he had secured his room, he had run into a young man on the Bowery dressed in the leather and denim of a cowboy. The friendly drunk allowed as how he was appearing in a great entertainment and that he and a young man who called himself Peg had made great names for themselves among the rough riders and savages of *Buffalo Bill's Wild West* show. "I know the colonel," the drunk had boasted. "Know Annie Oakley too. If they ride, rope, or shoot, they are all my brothers and sisters."

Curry blessed the young man, implored him to avoid strong drink in the future, and asked him if this Peg was likely to be back to the Bowery any time soon.

The cowboy laughed. "I reckon yes, Father," he said. "This is where the girls are."

Now, in the darkness of his tiny room, Kid Curry straightened the white collar eating into his neck and turned to don his long frock coat. Then he strode down the back stairs and into the night.

This world had never seen a day when he couldn't scare Frank Elliott green with a glance. He would return to the Bowery's gutters every night until he found Peg Leg, and Peg Leg would lead him to Etta Place.

Diary,

Tonight I thank God for what He has given an undeserving girl. As I write this, Harry Longbaugh—Harry Longbaugh!—lies sleeping within sight of my eyes.

He is not captured; he is not wounded; he is not dead. He is here! Here with me! With me! With me! With me! As I listen to the sounds made by the soft rise and fall of his breast, my eyes are rimmed by tears.

The tale of his escape is not complex. A warden stupid enough to put Harry, Ben, and Butch in the same cell block. Something about Dave Atkins, fry bread, and a hungry guard. Frankly, Diary, we have been far too busy in this lovely bed for me to glean many of the details.

But his arrival has made me realize what my life has become. It is as if I had been trapped underground all these months, like a miner who carries out all his complicated work by the smallest pinpoints of light. Who crawls through dirt and dust in blackness until he comes upon a single lantern. He moves on, praying to see another lamp ahead, always hoping there will be lights enough to bring him home.

There are moments, usually occurring early in the afternoon, when my boy and I are somehow able to tear ourselves from each other and go walking in the world. Yesterday, we took a cab from Mrs. Taylor's and went far uptown on Fifth Avenue. Oh, it was grand to see the lovely ladies and handsome gentlemen in their fine clothing striding the broad street in the winter's sun! The light seemed to shimmer off the hides of the silver-white horses and the mirror-polished surfaces of the new motorcars. We stepped off at the Plaza Hotel but Harry immediately took my arm into his and began to walk me back southward on the avenue. At 57th Street he fair pulled me into the great Tiffany & Co. store, a place I had heard of all my life and several of whose pieces (until the creditors took them) were to be part of my legacy from Mother.

Once inside, Harry walked up to a man finely dressed in swallowtail and stripes. "Good morning sir," Harry said.

"And you, sir," said the man. "How may I be of assistance? Something for madam, perhaps?"

"The item we discussed," Harry said. "I trust that it is still here?"

"Most assuredly, sir," said the clerk. His inspection of me caused me to color openly.

I must confess, Diary, that this polite conversation made it difficult for me not to titter and soon I began to giggle. The very idea of the Sundance Kid himself cordially exchanging formal pleasantries with a man in Manhattan whom he would not have hesitated to rob in Laramie simply struck me as hilarious. And, Lord help me, the more cross Harry became over my surely inappropriate laughter, the more uncontainable was my mirth. But make no mistake, I calmed down as soon as I saw the magnificent present he had chosen for me.

The watch was in the finest of taste. It was of white gold and silver, the whole covered with a sort of angel's-wing filigree. The face was white pearl shell with Roman numerals in yellow gold and the most delicate slivers of hands.

I attached its chain to the third button of my blouse and Harry pinned it to me, just between collarbone and breast. I had never been so thrilled with a gift. I kissed him full right there in front of the salesman, who did not appear to be shocked in the slightest. He was likely used to the sight of newly wedded women, drunk on endless intercourse, further rewarding their champions for one shiny love offering or another.

And today, Diary, what do you think? We threw caution to the wind and had our "wedding portrait" made at a Mr. De-Young's studio at 826 Broadway. DeYoung's is to the Swartz studio in Texas as the Luxor baths in Chicago are to the Alhambra. Here in New York City, everything must be bigger, grander, MORE. The furnishings were of red velvet, the curtains a heavy blue brocade.

We were greeted by one of Mr. DeYoung's many assistants, an intense young man with a foreign air by the name of Mr. Alfred Stieglitz. He assured us that we would receive the whole of his attention but seemed distracted throughout the process. Our pose was a simple one. We stood side by side, against a backdrop of tall trees and a brook with a bridge that I supposed was meant to represent the Central Park. Harry's one hand was at my waist; the other held his high silk hat. Per Mr. Stieglitz's instructions, we held our poses, addressing our gazes to the camera until the flash powder ignited. When I could see again I told Mr. Stieglitz that I hoped his picture would be satisfactory.

His dark eyes turned warm. "I am sure it will, madam," he said. "Seldom has DeYoung's enjoyed the honor of photographing such a handsome couple. If you will be so kind as to return on Wednesday, we shall most happily prove this to you."

And then, Diary, an event occurred that caused me to cherish my outlaw all the more. As we stepped into the cold air, a newsboy approached us. He was as filthy as a coal stove: ragged, starved, and tiny. Although he could not have been more than eight or nine years old, his eyes and skin had the exhausted look of an old laborer, someone who has seen his life become a part of too many ingots of steel or too many stones in a quarry. As he walked up to us, he paused and, without a word, held up a single copy of the New York World. For a long moment, Harry looked down at him, and then in a voice so gentle I had only heard its like in our bed, he asked, "How many have you got there, boy?"

The lad looked confused, but his hand dove into a canvas bag that was nearly black with soot and dirt. He took a minute to carefully count his papers and then, in a voice that sounded even younger than the age I had ascribed to him, he replied, "Twenty."

Harry looked into the boy's green eyes and reached into his coat pocket, pulling out a silver dollar. "I'll take them all."

The boy seemed incredulous at first, but the twenty pennies he was about to earn meant food for a day and perhaps lodging somewhere other than a doorway. He handed Harry all the papers and my love handed him the dollar. The newsboy's eyes became wide.

"No trouble for the change, boy," Harry said. "I got this money from a very rich gentleman on a train, a long time ago and a very long way from here. There are a lot of gentlemen like him in the world, and any time I want I can go back and get more, savvy?"

The boy nodded, perhaps expecting to be tricked or arrested. At length, he pocketed the coin.

Harry smiled. "Now git."

As the boy fled, Harry gazed after him; then, tucking the papers under his arm, he suggested we go. We hailed a hansom at the top of the block. I rested my head upon his shoulder and we rode back to Mrs. Taylor's in silence.

That night as he lay beside me, Diary, I kissed him deeply,

told him over and over again how dearly I loved him, and tried in happy vain to show him how deep that love went.

And then an odd thing happened. My Harry, usually so reserved, so stoic and even sad, began to laugh. He took me in his arms and rolled me about the bed and tickled me and covered me in kisses. Then, reaching into the pile of papers he had purchased from that poor boy, he began to fling them one at a time into the air until the room was a riot of black and white. As I stared up from beneath him, I too began to scream in joy, watching the day's headlines swirl and fly until they at last fluttered down like great gray birds, blanketing the floor, the bed, and the two of us.

THE UNION BANK OF KINGS COUNTY
6050 Flatbush Avenue, Brooklyn, New York

Telephone: BR 6423   Wire: Union Bank Kings New York

Mr. Harry L. Place
234 West 12th Street
New York, New York

February 3, 1902

Dear Mr. Place,

Please consider this a response to your letter of the 25th.

You may rest assured that the arrangements you requested have been made and your business with our bank on the tenth of this month at 10 A.M. will be both pleasant and efficient in its execution.

We have made note that Mrs. Place will be the agent of retrieval. Upon your instruction we have also made a record of her dress for this occasion. She will present herself as a widow in mourning; a black lace veil over her face will serve to conceal her identity from onlookers.

As you have seen fit to send a lady as your emissary, a fully

armed guard in our employ will accompany your wife into our
special vault room to retrieve the three large bags you have entrusted to our care. At that time, Mrs. Place will sign for the bags
and receive a written receipt for same.

Then, as instructed by you, our guard will deposit the said
large bags into the boot of a black and green brougham that Mrs.
Place shall also use as her mode of transportation back to Manhattan.

Please be advised that all of your instructions will be carried
out to the smallest detail. We have much experience in these
matters and have justly gained a reputation for security and dis-
crection that we believe is unrivaled in all of New York City.
I can also guarantee that I shall handle this transaction
personally.

Should you have any further questions or instructions, please
feel free to contact me by post, wire, or telephone at your earliest
convenience.

We of the Union Bank of Kings County send you our best be-
lated wishes for the New Year.

Your obedient servant,
J. Henry Cavanaugh III
J. Henry Cavanaugh III
Vice President and General Manager

The "carpet" was not a place Charles A. Siringo was used to being.

In the course of his career he had summoned many a junior detective upon it, upbraiding, scolding, on occasion, firing. But it had been many years since he himself had stood before a supervisor and a client and been criticized about his methods.

Robert Pinkerton stroked his long beard and fingered the gold watch that decorated his considerable paunch. Even in the presence of such an irate client, he was careful not to raise his voice. His father had not built a single office into a law enforcement power by upbraiding his best operatives. Any competing agency would be proud to acquire Charlie Siringo and at a higher salary. It simply would not do to have his best detective puff in pride and turn on his heel.

Fred H. Harvey held no such compunction. He was demanding action. It had been the better part of three years since he retained the agency, and Charlie Siringo seemed no closer to finding the girl who had turned the restaurateur's life upside down. Only a combination of company-wide silence and good luck had kept the Stratford Hotel incident from Harvey. Now he lit into Siringo as if he had read of it in banner headlines: A LAUNDRY TRICK FOR PINKERTON DICK!

"You know, Charlie," Harvey began, his voice steadily rising, "it hasn't been easy for me to find fault with you. Up until recent days I truly believed you had done all you could to catch this Place woman. But now my patience has worn to gossamer. Can it be that the great Siringo—and here I quote from your company biography—'star detective and capturer of Black Jack Ketchum,' is unable to find a slip of a girl of twenty-one? Can it be that 'Charlie the Chaser, pursuer of over fifty bandit chiefs and their various minions,' cannot locate a woman so conspicuous by her beauty that she is said to stop horse carts mid-street? Really, Mr. Pinkerton. I tell you I am not satisfied!"

Siringo stood stock-still throughout the berating. It was only his military training and the thorough knowledge that he had so far done his best that kept him from throttling Fred Harvey. That, and his deep respect for his superior.

Pointedly ignoring Harvey, Siringo turned to Pinkerton with the slightest of bows. "Of course, Mr. Pinkerton," he said, "if you order it, I will be happy to resign from this case or even this company. Correct me if I am wrong, but these days it seems that our primary business is breaking the sinister strikes that threaten to cripple our way of life. Perhaps this has become a business that requires new tricks, and I am, admittedly, an old dog.

"I offer no excuses or explanations for my failure to capture Etta Place or her confederates. I leave my fate in your hands and trust that you will quickly find a superior agent who will net Mr. Harvey a happier result."

In the silence that followed, Siringo kept his back to the client, his eyes fixed upon his employer.

"I most certainly do not believe that any such action is warranted, Charlie," Pinkerton said. "On the contrary, I ask you to remain firmly connected to this job. It is understandable that Mr. Harvey is frustrated by the results of this case so far. He informs me that he is daily receiving threats from the lawyers representing the family of that scum from Grand Junction, who claim this girl is a murderer. From what I've learned of the little bastard, it seems she did the town a public service. But it is easy to see how their impatience might spur his."

Pinkerton turned to his client. "But as your advisor, Mr. Harvey, I implore you to follow the course so far charted. This is an especially elusive and clever gang with which we are dealing, not just one *slip of a girl,* as you call her. And I must tell you that to remove the agent who has the greatest knowledge of this case after all this time would mean starting from the beginning. It would be a fool's errand. And Pinkerton's, sir, does not engage in fool's errands."

Harvey had dealt with his share of disgruntled diners. He did not need to hear a raised voice or detect a sneer to know when he'd been told off. The Englishman's face went red with a mixture of embarrassment and rage. But he held his tongue as he had on those occasions when he'd given in to a cheap salesman over an "overdone" steak. As much as he despised the fact, he knew that Pinkerton was right. A new beginning with neither trails nor clues would at this point be like cutting off his own nose and throwing his mustache in as a bonus.

Harvey gestured to the office page, making a mute gesture for his hat and coat. "I am nearly at the end of my patience, Mr. Pinkerton, but my trade is feeding travelers; yours is tracking down perpetrators. I trust that Detective Siringo will carry out his duties with more success in the future. And as I am being sued to death and drowned in bad publicity, I would ask him please to make a quick job of it. Not only am I getting my throat cut, but these bastards are using a dull knife indeed."

Pinkerton and Siringo watched as Fred Harvey turned on his heel and stormed from the office. "My offer stands, sir," Siringo said. "I would be happy to be reassigned or to resign, as your pleasure indicates."

Pinkerton turned to the window and studied the cold scene below. "I prefer that you remain, Charlie, and complete the work to which you've been assigned. A man is not only as good as today but yesterday and the days before that. You have piled up many successful yesterdays for me and should I forget that—well, as the book says, Let my right hand lose its cleverness."

He turned back from the window and engaged Siringo directly. "But, you had better find this girl soon, Charlie, or they'll be carrying both of us out with the dirty laundry."

LETTER TO JOSIAH LONGBAUGH

12 State Street, Phoenixville, Pa.

8 February 1902

New York City

Dear Father,

The events of the past year have taught me much. Mostly, that as a thief I am an amateur. The more I see and read and hear, the more I learn that the true robbers of this land don't hold up banks, they own them. But now I have reason to hope that soon the people of this country will rise up and all within this country will change.

Father, I spent today in a big public square with thousands of others. They wore badges on their clothing and carried signs with names like Socialist Workers, I.W.W., Knights of Labor, Workman's Circle, and a dozen more. As we huddled up against the cold, we listened to people who knew more about this world and how it works than any others I have heard. As they gave their talks, I thought of all the people I have met these years past who no longer had no say over what became of them. Farmers driven off the land by railroads. Miners forced to work underground like the slaves of the Bible. Women who could work all day and night but not vote for so much as alderman.

And then there are the children, like a newsboy I knew. I read about him just two days ago. He had no mother or home. He had fallen asleep near a slaughterhouse and been killed and eaten—first by wild dogs and then picked clean by rats.

These people who spoke to us today said that as long as a few rich hold sway over all the rest, nothing will change and the teachings of the Savior (that you put in me young) will never come about on this earth.

I remember especial the words of a young Jew woman with glasses on her nose and a foreign voice. She spoke for a long time, but I did not tire of her words. She talked about how the sound of the mill had replaced the singing of birds. About how for years poor boys like me have been sent to kill other poor boys so the mill man or the oilman or the railroad man could get richer yet.

Then young girls—some spoke American and others foreign—walked through the crowd giving out pieces of paper with what looked like a poem on it. "Song. Song. We sing," one of them said, in a accent I took to be Italian. Then the people raised up the paper and a man with a concertina took the stage. He did a little introduction and the lady with the glasses counted off for the crowd. Many seemed to know the tune already and we sung it through a few times until some was crying. I kept that paper. The words is like this:

> Let us pause in life's pleasures and count the many tears,
> While we all sup sorrow with the poor.
> There's a song that will linger forever in our ears,
> Oh, hard times, come again no more.

> It's a song, a sigh of the weary,
> Hard times, hard times, come again no more.
> Many days you have lingered around my cabin door,
> Oh, hard times, come again no more.

I thought hard over them words, Father. With all I have robbed I am now rich myself. But never in that time did I harm a poor man or woman. Never did I take the pocket watch of a cowboy or drover. Never did I kill a soul that didn't first threaten the taking of my own life. My targets was banks and railroads, and with what I heard here today I feel proud to have robbed them.

Soon I will be far away, with the woman I love and a fortune besides. I tell you now, Father, that I intend to put this fortune to work for the poor so it may do God's will. What money can do bad it can also make good.

People in the crowd today gave me things to read, things that made sense to me, although I do not understand everything. But I do believe that with a good dictionary (which I can well afford now!) and the fine education of my dear one I can overcome my ignorance and make ready to take my place in the new world that I heard of today.

My next letter to you will come from outside this country so I ask that you be patient and not worry if you hear nothing for a while. You are always in my thoughts, as are the young ones and the memory of Mother.

Please see after your health and remember me in your prayers as I remember you in mine.

Yours for a better world to come and a glorious revolution!

Affectionately, your son
Harry Longbaugh

On a slow night, say a Monday or a Tuesday, the floor of McCreedy's Ale House on the Bowery was a carpet of filth. Its sawdust, changed only when it turned brown, was liberally spiced with the sweet-sour essence of stale beer and garnished with the occasional carcass of a rodent.

But on a Saturday in winter, after pay packets had been issued and alcohol beckoned the workingman, there would be numerous additions of blood. On such nights, fistfights and brawls were as common as lager and pigs' feet. This being the norm, an altercation would have to be violent indeed before the management ejected the miscreants involved. And so it was not surprising that on this Saturday the bartender and bouncers took little notice of the beating being administered to Peg Leg Elliott.

The blows were as savage as they were unneccessary. The mere presence of Kid Curry would have been enough for Peg to tell all he knew. But Curry had not asked Elliott any questions. He had simply tapped him on the shoulder, given him a cheery hello, and then smashed Peg in the skull with his own whiskey bottle. Curry was silent as he brought the point of his boot to Peg Leg's ribs just as the blood from his scalp filled the cowboy's eyes. Cursing at the drunken spectators, he dragged Elliott across the bar's floor and pulled him outside and into McCreedy's fetid outhouse.

"Etta Place," he hissed, "or I start feeding you the shit from these stalls."

Without waiting for Peg to speak, Curry forced the boy's head into the reeking pit, nearly drowning him in an admixture of things rank and human.

"Boy, you ought to get a less public job," Curry said, thumping Peg's head on the rough oaken seat. " '*Buffalo Bill's Wild West*! Back in New York for the grand return of Annie Oakley, triumphant savior of our president! See Peg Leg Elliott! Master of the lariat and snappy repartee!' You always was a hog for attention."

Curry dunked Peg's head again. He would not allow the boy to betray his friend right away. Each time Peg attempted to confess, he found his mouth filled with offal while his brain went red behind his eyes. The false priest was in no rush. Plenty of time to hear confession.

Little by little, Curry got what he came for: Etta's approximate whereabouts, her state of mind, the weapons on her person, her life as Annie Oakley. From here it would be easy, like tracking deer up a mountain or a rabbit through the woods. He'd find Etta Place and follow her until the trail led to the treasure that was his by right.

Curry laid Peg Leg down on the floor of the outhouse and spat in disgust. "I suggest you get cleaned up," he told the cowboy. "Even a hellhole like this won't let you drink on its premises, bloody and stinking like a dog."

Peg Leg tried to rise, but all life had drained from his limbs. And as the shame of the informer swept over him, he began to weep.

"Sad drunk," Curry mumbled. "Nothing worse."

He stepped over the body and picked up the boy's fancy hat. Its brim was crushed, and the mirrors on its band were smeared with the remains of a hundred drunken nights. He dropped it over Peg's face and strode toward the alley door.

"For God's sake, boy," the little man said, "have some pride."

From the

NEW YORK *HERALD*

February 10, 1902

IN SOCIETY

A Jolly Party at Mrs. Roosevelt's . . . Especially for Cousins

Chasing away the winter doldrums was the purpose of a fine party at the home of Mrs. Sara Delano Roosevelt this Saturday past. With the holidays long over and the cold winter set in, the sensible Mrs. Roosevelt deemed it fitting that those of her circle meet in festive merriment while raising considerable sums for the Milk Fund.

Mrs. Roosevelt, well known for the beauty and exclusivity of her events, was surrounded by family and friends at her home, 47 East 65th Street.

Society tongues are still wagging over the attention paid by Mr. Franklin Delano Roosevelt, Mrs. Roosevelt's only son, to his fifth cousin, Miss Anna Eleanor Roosevelt, daughter of Mr. Elliott Roosevelt and Mrs. Anna Hall Roosevelt (both deceased). During the party, the two were described as "wholly inseparable" by one attendee.

A law student at Harvard, Mr. Roosevelt is considered one of our city's most eligible bachelors, with a lineage that can be traced directly to William the Conqueror. Miss Roosevelt, niece of the president of the United States, is known as a scholarly young woman noted for her good works among the lower classes. She is also rumored to be a suffragist.

"I should not be surprised if this meeting results in a marriage," one partygoer informed us. "The Roosevelts have always been known for keeping their bloodline pure: They only marry each other."

Miss Morrow's Death Causes Great Sorrow on the Main Line

There is still much consternation among the best families of Philadelphia over the sudden gruesome death of Miss Emily Katharine Morrow, only daughter of Mr. and Mrs. Hobart R. Morrow II of Bryn Mawr, Pennsylvania, and Newport, Rhode Island.

As has been widely reported in the week since the event, Miss Morrow, seventeen years of age, was trampled to death by her mount during a dressage competition at the Radnor Hunt Club, only a few miles from her family's estate.

The horse, an eight-year-old black stallion named Bellerophon, reportedly bucked Miss Morrow from his back during her last event. Before the eyes of a horrified throng, the huge animal then trampled the unfortunate girl beneath his hooves, causing injuries from which Miss Morrow did not recover.

Her father, the senior investment supervisor of the firm of Banks and Gaily, is said to be in seclusion. Family friends tell us he blames himself for his daughter's demise, as others in the riding community had warned him of the stallion's intemperate nature. The *Herald* has since discovered that, while in the possession of a

previous owner, the animal had kicked two stable mates to death. Mr. Morrow was apparently aware of the incident, but, as it occurred some four years ago, he believed that the horse had calmed with the passage of time.

Funeral services for Miss Morrow are called for Thursday. The stallion is in a police paddock. At the conclusion of the inquest, he presumably will be destroyed.

The Union Bank of Kings County had been built to inspire fiduciary confidence. Its founder, J. Henry Cavanaugh, Jr., had always said he saw no reason why a Brooklyn bank shouldn't have all the accoutrements of one based in Manhattan.

To this end, Cavanaugh had spared no expense on the bank's materials. Its façade was of the finest Pennsylvania limestone, punctuated by bronze framed windows. As an inspiration to the borough, the building's great cornice was decorated with terra-cotta carvings that recalled great eras of history, from the Italian Renaissance to the taming of the West.

Inside, the grand transaction floor was built almost entirely of Venetian marble, polished to a mirror sheen and offset with Brazilian hardwoods. Even the ink pens the customers used to inscribe their deposits and withdrawals were of ebony, tipped with nibs of gold. The Union's vault was among the most modern of its day, a thickness of steel and chrome that most Fifth Avenue banks would envy. Indeed, the *Brooklyn Daily Eagle* noted that when John D. Rockefeller visited on opening day in 1893, he toured the great safe room and immediately instructed a lieutenant to order exactly the same vault for every branch of Chase Manhattan.

It was little wonder, then, that on the morning of Monday, February 10, Henry Cavanaugh III had seen fit to take his charming depositor on a small tour of his father's vision. Later, of course, he was sorry he had done it. That evening, after he awakened in the hospital, he told reporters, "I should have just kept to the business at hand and gotten the lady in and out of the bank. I probably gave that ruffian all the time he needed to rob and kidnap Mrs. Place. Oh, Father will have my head!"

Had he known the whole truth, Cavanaugh might not have felt such remorse. Kid Curry had planned his action down to the last moment, and no heroics by a bank official could have stopped what ultimately transpired. The only thing Curry hadn't figured on was the absence of Harry Longbaugh, as his intelligence had informed him that Sundance himself would be present.

The news produced mixed emotions in Curry. Surely the Kid's absence made his work easier, as only the bitch herself and an old bank guard now stood in the way of success. But Curry had hoped to take Longbaugh hostage as well, the better to enjoy his agony as he took his pleasure with Etta Place.

Besides, had things not gone quite according to plan, he could have at the least killed him on the spot. Her too, if it came to that.

As it turned out, there was more than enough carnage for one morning.

By the time Logan had secured Etta with lariats and loaded her and the big satchels into a waiting buckboard, the old guard and a customer were dead and Cavanaugh the Third, chivalrous fool, had been grazed on the scalp.

Changing wagons in an alley some blocks away, Logan comforted himself with what his mother used to tell him. "Son," she would say, "you can't have everything." And as he drove toward the Brooklyn Bridge with the woman he hated and desired most and the money that was rightfully his, he couldn't help but reflect on what a wise woman Mother had been.

From the
BROOKLYN DAILY EAGLE
February 11, 1902

DEADLY ROBBERY AND KIDNAPPING IN FLATBUSH!

CONTENTS OF DEPOSIT BOX STOLEN!
YOUNG WOMAN ABDUCTED!

BANK GUARD KILLED!
CUSTOMER BRUTALLY ASSAULTED!

VILLAIN DISGUISES HIMSELF AS PRIEST
IN ORDER TO CARRY OUT EVIL DESIGN!

POLICE HAVE NO CLUES!
WOMAN SAID TO BE WIFE OF CATTLEMAN!

EAGLE EXCLUSIVE! EAGLE EXCLUSIVE!

A man disguised as a Catholic priest kidnapped a young woman in mourning at gunpoint and made off with three large bags believed to contain $80,000 in cash during a daring daylight bank robbery in Flatbush yesterday.

Before the robber's horrid work was done, a bank guard lay dead upon the marble floor and a customer had been seriously injured.

Taken in the incident was Mrs. Harry Place, whom the bank's vice president said was the wife of a western cattleman. Mrs. Place was stopping temporarily in Manhattan.

The terrible events occurred at the Union Bank of Kings County, 6050 Flatbush Avenue. According to innocents witnessing the carnage, the scoundrel entered the bank about ten o'clock in the morning, approximately the same time that Mrs. Place, dressed in black with a matching lace veil, arrived to carry out her business. As the man was garbed as a priest, little notice was taken of him at first and there was no suspicion of anything sinister.

Mr. Henry J. Cavanaugh III, vice president and general manager of the bank, was also slightly wounded by the suspect. At the hospital, he told the police and the *Eagle* that Mrs. Place had been sent by her husband to collect three large duck bags from the special safe-deposit rooms inside the bank's vault. She was emerging onto the bank's floor when the "priest" drew two large pistols from beneath his black frock coat and held one to her head. He announced to one and all that this was indeed a robbery, that he had confederates outside the building, and that anyone who interfered with his plans would be dealt with "most harshly." With this, he forced a young bystander to grab the heavy bags as he continued to train his gun on Mrs. Place.

As the thief and his pretty victim gained the door, he seized the three large bags from the accosted man and hit him alongside the skull with a pistol.

What happened next is so far a matter of some dispute. In the confusion there came a loud retort from the thief's gun, and the guard, Mr. Seamus D. McRae of 138 Harrison Street, fell to the cold floor, mortally wounded. With the bank's lady patrons screaming and the men crying for help, the rogue managed to make good his escape. Some of the witnesses noted that Mr.

McRae had made no threatened move toward the killer and had stayed steadfast by Mrs. Place's side throughout the melee.

Flatbush police have at this time no leads as to the whereabouts of the villain and his captive. They are asking the reading public for any information as to their location. The man has been described as between thirty and forty years old, quite small of stature and slight of build with a large dark mustache, eyes, and hair. Mrs. Place is described as in her early twenties, with a pale complexion and green eyes. She was also described as very tall for a woman, towering over her captor.

Mrs. D. E. Gerstenfeld, who was unfortunate enough to be conducting some business in the bank at the time, said Mrs. Place would be a difficult woman for a citizen or policeman to miss, quite apart from her height. "It would be a terrible sin if that horrid little man hurt her," she told us. "When he grabbed her, her hat and veil flew off and I saw her face real plain. I think she was the most beautiful girl I ever saw."

Until he had gone to New York City and reunited with Etta Place, Peg Leg Elliott had lived a life of good luck and high adventure.

His mother had loved him and his father had beat him only when he deserved it. His outlawry had generally been profitable and had never resulted in any dead bodies or the business end of a rope.

His tenure with *Buffalo Bill's Wild West* had taken him around the world, paid him thrice the wages of a ranch hand, and allowed him to eat catered victuals on show days. Everywhere he went there had been money and cards and folks seeking a fine time. The experience had left him far more liberal in his attitudes than he had been hitherto, so that he saw himself as sufficiently educated to converse with those born to higher degrees of sophistication. Yes, he would say to himself, people are people everywhere. Once you've drunk their liquor and had their women, it was hard to hate any fellow human on earth.

But now, because of Etta, it seemed he was forever someone's victim.

First, it had been Kid Curry. With his threats and artillery, he had made Peg Leg ashamed in a way he had never been before. Curry had turned him into what no outlaw wanted to be—an informer—and he had done so in a way that made Peg feel helpless as a jailhouse strumpet.

Now it was the Pinkertons. Once the papers had printed the story about the Union Bank of Kings County and the kidnapping of "Mrs. Harry Place," it hadn't taken the Pinks long to deduce that Etta was in town. Henry Cavanaugh III gave them the address she listed on the safe-deposit paperwork, and when they arrived at Mrs. Taylor's and inspected Etta's room they found a theatrical photo of Peg, grin on face, lasso in hand. He had inscribed it, *To Miss Etta, my partner in crime. Best wishes, Frank "Peg Leg" Elliott.* An operative by the name of Sanderson had attended *Wild West* with his children the previous Saturday and immediately recognized Peg from the performance. All that remained was for the Pinks to abduct him from the Madison Square Garden stage door.

At first, he had thought to charm them. Tell them the kind of casual lies that usually sufficed for law enforcement. But when the wiry detective with the drooping auburn mustache ordered his left arm twisted behind him, it occurred to Peg Leg that he was now faced with a choice: Whom did he fear more, Kid Curry, who had promised to one day cut his throat, or the grim-faced op whose lieutenants were now bringing his bones to their breaking point? As he called out to the Deity, Peg soon realized that the decision had been made for him. The pain of now had trumped the fear of later. All that remained was for the detective to call in a stenographer with his pad and pencil.

At the end of half an hour's time, four pages of that tablet were full and Charles A. Siringo had all the information required to locate his client's quarry. As a bonus, he had also ascertained the approximate whereabouts of the little bastard who had caused so much grief to so many.

It had not been difficult to deduce the identity of the Brooklyn thief. The description of the dark-eyed runt, coupled with the disguise of a priest, was all the information Siringo needed to know that Curry was the man Kings County police were seeking. Still, time was short and the quarry in flight. If this circus clown's information was correct—and heaven help him if it was not—he now had a good idea where Curry might be holding Etta Place.

"Sorry about the rough-up, young man," Siringo said, "but I'm glad you folded as quick as you did. In this business, brave men can be the cause of an awful lot of exertion. We pay for information. Leave me your address, and we'll send you a bank draft with the thanks of the company. I've taken the liberty of bringing some of your clothing and personal items here for you. If you'll pack them into that valise in the corner, we'll put you on the next train to anywhere but here."

"Train?"

"Sure, Mr. Elliott. We don't like to admit of the possibility, but if Curry—or, for that matter, Miss Place—proves to be cleverer than us—well, we're likely dead. And you most assuredly are."

As Siringo and his two assistants watched, the shaken Peg Leg packed his few belongings into the bag. A short agent with a blond mustache handed him his now-empty .44 Remington. Fingers quivering, Peg shoved it into his waistband and turned to gather his clothes.

Siringo placed his own gun in his shoulder holster and turned to the boy. "Mr. Elliott, you know Curry. If he's gone to ground, about how long would you say she's got?"

Peg Leg gave the detective a worried look as he opened the leather grip the Pinks had supplied.

"Well, mister," he said, "he hates Miss Etta and you wouldn't want to see what he does to women he likes. Even if like you say, she's only been gone since this morning, I'd hurry, I was you. If I know the little man he'll take his time with her, but I wouldn't want to find her much past the third day. By then, I reckon if she ain't dead she'll wish to the Lord she was."

Keep him talking, Etta told herself. Talking, he cannot bully you. He cannot strike you or belittle you or violate you. Make him defend himself. Keep him off balance.

And when he is not talking, make him listen. Keep his ears full of your words or his own. Degrade him. Revile him. Say anything to prevent him from sensing the rush of blood to your ears and the quickening of your pulse. Make the little man feel small.

"You can scream if you like," Kid Curry said. "No one will hear you."

Etta looked across the cramped room at him and tested the rope at her wrists. She was seated on an apple box in what appeared to be an attic. Below her, the floorboards groaned at the slightest movement. Above, a skylight loomed. It was nearly black with dust and grime, making it difficult to tell if it was day or night.

"*Scream if you like?*" she said. She began to laugh. "*Scream if you like? No one will hear you?* Oh, Mr. Logan, *très cliché*! Dime-novel threats from a penny-dreadful villain! So the great Kid Curry reveals himself for what he is: a mouse who needs a loaded revolver for protection from a woman with her hands bound behind her."

Curry circled the fetid attic uneasily. Etta Place had been his unwilling guest for more than three hours and had yet to show signs of anything save defiance.

"Your bravado is admirable, bitch. But now I have you at my disposal and at least some of the goods you stole from me. At any moment it pleases me I can separate you from this world or cut patterns in your pretty face and leave you alive, a living horror for children to run from. Do you believe Harry Longbaugh will want you then?"

Etta swallowed. The terror she felt was as deep as the canyons of Hole-in-the-Wall. But she knew that to betray even a trace of fear would be like feeding Kid Curry his favorite dish. He would smell fear as surely as the scent of food. And then he would dine on her.

"You don't scare me, but you do disgust me. As always, Mr. Curry, you are short in stature but long on words."

Curry smiled, pretending that her scorn held no meaning for him. "Perhaps, Etta, I am making this too complicated. Perhaps we will simply become lovers at long last and then I'll kill you. Neat, quick, everybody happy."

Etta sighed as if he bored her. *Talk and keep him talking.* "You *are* a miserable coward, Curry." She laughed. "Untie me, and we shall see who is the better man. Win, and I am yours to ravish, murder if you please. Lose, and I shall spit on you before binding you like a suckling pig and leaving you for the Pinks to find."

Curry made no answer. The darkness in his eyes had become impenetrable, as if they were twin planets of a matter so dense as to swallow all light in their universe. Had she gone too far? Was this, as she had feared, the sign of a madness so complete that he would abandon the pleasures he had sought, leaving only her slaughter to be accomplished?

A pearl of spittle formed in the corner of his mouth. He raised the Colt even with her head.

Etta did not give Curry even a second to cock the iron. Before he could squeeze off a shot, she flew from the box. Her long leg kicked high, aiming for his manhood but catching him just under the chin and sending the .45 flying.

He fell but was up quickly. With a roar one would expect from someone twice his size, he leaped upon her, crashing her back into the wall, hoping to witness through her tears the naked fear for which he had been waiting.

"Ah, hellcat, I can smell you," he murmured, as his lips moved closer to hers.

With all her strength, she pushed against him, her height providing the leverage needed to separate their bodies. Again she kicked at him, missing at first but then connecting with his ribs. She felt a rush of sour air leave his lungs as she kicked the pistol under a rotting chest.

"Come, little man!" She panted. "I am only a woman, and perfect for you. My hands are tied at my back." She skittered sideways across the room, taunting him, urging him forward and away from the gun.

With the speed that the small have always needed, Logan was suddenly behind her. He jumped up on the box and began to strangle her, his short but strong arms forming a vise beneath her throat. Etta fought the panic inside her as she dragged him from the box, but his weight dangling from her neck only added to the pressure on her windpipe. In desperation, she opened the hands tied behind her and, fighting nausea, clutched at his groin, squeezing until, in his agony, he released his hold.

Howling, he fell hard to the floor while Etta struggled to regain her breath.

At that second he read her eyes. In them he could see the beginnings of the horror he so craved, but it was crowded out by loathing and a flicker of pity that he could not abide. Would further battle now lessen his humiliation at her hands? No. All that was left was to retrieve what remained of his honor, and only the death of Etta Place could achieve that end.

Kid Curry dived for the Colt, coming up with it handle-forward. As he cocked the pistol and aimed at her head, a rusted lock, its knob and plate still attached, flew past his head, and Charles A. Siringo burst through the door.

5

The Pinkerton cell had been made sufficient to the needs of Etta Place. The jailers had been instructed to make certain accommodations reflecting the unique needs and privacy concerns of a female prisoner. They had carried in a small table to serve as both vanity and writing desk. The inmate had been provided with a dressing screen and even a mirror, an amenity male prisoners never enjoyed. Charles A. Siringo himself had ordered that cheerful prints of trees and flowers be hung upon the dingy green walls so that a pleasant atmosphere might be provided for his celebrated guest. Etta had no idea if she had been extended these courtesies out of respect for a gallant adversary or because Siringo believed that her tongue could be loosened by luxury.

For Etta, none of it made a difference. If Siringo had expected gratitude for her rescue, she quickly disabused him of the notion. This was a copper, and as with any representative of the police, Etta Place would always be Wild Bunch to the bone. As they met for her first interview, she addressed him with the calm disdain Hole-in-the-Wall reserved for the law.

"If you believe that you have rescued a damsel in distress," she told Siringo, "you are very much mistaken, for I am perfectly capable of taking excellent care of myself. You say I am a criminal, a woman who shoots guns and rides black horses, yet if your files contain arrest records you haven't produced them. You don't have so much as a drawing or photograph of this woman you claim has caused so much trouble. Clearly, you have confused me with some other statuesque person. The motto of your company is We Never Sleep, *n'est-ce pas*? Well, perhaps you should allow your operatives a little shut-eye every month or two. Then they might actually be able to find a woman nearly a head taller than most of them."

Siringo nodded and shifted in his chair. "I don't need a photograph of you, Etta," he said. "There are plenty of reports. And may I say that they do not exaggerate either your looks or your keen sense of fashion."

Etta's eyes narrowed. "Your familiarity, Detective Siringo, only betrays your bad breeding. I would prefer that you please refrain from personal comments and address me as Mrs. Place, as is proper between relative strangers."

"I apologize," Siringo said. "I am afraid that in this line of work one gets used to the dregs of society, and they care little about the niceties of social convention. Still, Mrs. Place, polite or no, manners won't deter me from eventually getting what I want. I've spent too many years tracking you down. I'm not about to lose patience now."

Etta sighed. "For the sake of argument," she said, "let us assume for the moment that I am, as you say, this bold associate of outlaws. If I wouldn't talk to a madman intent on rape, do you honestly believe I would tell any secrets to you? And *if* I were an outlaw, would it not naturally follow that I would hold to what I believe is referred to as the outlaw creed? And *if* I held to this creed I would have only three choices: prison as provided by you, silence, or death by my former compatriots if I break that silence. No, Mr. Siringo, under such circumstances, I would be obliged—no, obligated—to tell you, quite simply and in a far less friendly tone than I use now, to go to hell."

She smiled sweetly at Siringo and then turned to grin to his two lieutenants, one of whom was now stifling a laugh behind his hand.

"That's *if* I were an outlaw."

Siringo was silent for a long moment. He had to admit, she lied with style. "We'll go with *Miss Place,* for now," he said. "I can't apply *Mrs.,* as you've never been married to Longbaugh or anyone else. Still, I must say that it is truly a privilege finally to meet you. Anyone who could have stood up to Kid Curry like you did deserves admiration. It's no wonder you've done so well at your chosen profession."

"Thank you, Mr. Siringo. But one needn't be a bandit to show a little grit. I am only sorry that your Mr. Cathcart took the bullet seemingly reserved for me."

"Those are the risks we take," Siringo said. "What makes Cathcart's injury more difficult for me is that, in my seeing to his wound, Curry made his escape. It only took that second's distraction for him to make his way through the window and over the rooftops."

"I trust Mr. Cathcart will recover?"

"He'll live. And Curry won't get far. Now, if you will please accompany me and our Mr. Armbrister to our processing station, we will take your photograph and fingerprints. At that time, I'm afraid, the laying on of hands will become an unfortunate necessity, but we have obtained a matron for you and we shall keep all contact within the bounds of propriety."

The procedures were carried out with utmost efficiency. After years of anonymity, Etta Place would now be added to the gigantic pile of data the agency kept on the country's lawbreakers. Had the Pinkertons been ordinary police, it would have been Etta's constitutional right to have official charges brought against her. She would have been allowed visitation and legal counsel. But as day became night and then day again, no such charges had been laid and no official record of her capture had yet been prepared. Records could later become defense exhibits; that wasn't the Pinkerton way.

Like any good bandit, Etta knew the agency was a law unto itself, answerable to no one. It employed more operatives than there were members of the United States Army. The state legislature of Ohio had voted to outlaw it, for fear that the company would be hired as a private militia by wealthy clients; Pinkerton money and political connections allowed the firm to operate as a virtual secret police force for those rich enough to afford its services.

Government and local law enforcement had seen no reason to interfere with its activities, as it was often easier to have the agency do the hard work of extracting the confessions that duly appointed authorities later used in court. And if some wrongdoer lost a tooth or bore the mark of a truncheon, the cops needed only state that they were elsewhere at the time of the alleged beating to appear pure before a judge. Besides, Pinkerton needed to show their clients that it was their own efforts, not those of some local constable, that had brought to justice the offenders it had been paid to find. It would be embarrassing indeed if the vaunted Charles A. Siringo had been forced to admit that some beat walker named Clancy or O'Brien had captured Etta Place.

When the photographing and fingerprinting were completed, Etta was escorted to her cell. *May they roast in hell,* she thought. She would go there herself before she would allow any Pink the satisfaction of witnessing her worries or her tears. She reserved displays of emotion for the latest hours, when her captors would be asleep or prowling abroad for other fugitives. In those moments, Etta cried, not for herself but for Harry and what now seemed the incontrovertible fact that, after at last finding him, she would likely never see him again.

On her second morning in captivity, when Etta was served breakfast in her cell, she contemplated refusing the food but realized that she would need all her strength if she had to stand for a grilling or endure a beating. She had no illusions that, once the Pinks reached the point of desperation, they would not resort to the methods that had been so successful in the past. As Butch had often said, it is hard to argue with success.

When she had finished her meal, Siringo appeared. Etta put aside her tray and stood, the better to meet his eyes. Since last night he had bathed and put on clean linen. Etta envied him.

"Good morning, Miss Place," he said. "Or should I say Miss Jameson? Please sit down."

"Really, Mr. Siringo," Etta said. "One would think such a famous man of action would be able to make up his mind. And no, thank you, I prefer to stand."

Siringo chuckled and crossed to the small writing desk. He surveyed its surface for notes or letters. There were none. "At any rate, Miss Place, I would hope that a person as intelligent as yourself would begin to think more rationally of her future, especially as at this point your cooperation is no longer required."

"Then I would assume this case of mistaken identity has been re-solved and I am free to go. Perhaps I shall engage your company to locate the money this Curry person stole from me."

"Not quite," he said. "Since in time the Pinkerton Agency must de-liver you to the authorities, any help you could provide us toward the capture of Longbaugh and Cassidy and others of your associates could shorten your sentence markedly."

Etta stared at the detective, seemingly bewildered. "I know no ladies by those names," she said. "Perhaps they are the wives of some poor min-ers or millworkers whose husbands have had their heads broken by your agents. In any case, I thank you for your offer, but as I am guilty of noth-ing and know no such people, I must refuse it."

"That is a shame. Because four days from now, my operatives and I will be waiting at Union Station in Trenton, New Jersey, to take Kid Curry into custody. Our railroad contacts have told us that on Sunday morning a certain Father Seamus Halligan will be boarding the eleven forty-five Union Pacific at Pennsylvania Station, New York. During that train ride, our agents will be free to locate Curry's ill-gotten gains. We will then arrest him at Trenton, the first stop. Our intelligence further in-forms us that Longbaugh and Cassidy will try to accost him at some time during this journey. Apparently, the Sundance Kid is intent on avenging his former comrade's affront to your honor. So again, Miss Place, any aid you can give us between now and then will count heavily in your favor."

The temperature of Siringo's voice suddenly dropped.

"Of course, once the capture is made, there will be little we can do for you. Then again, there is still much we can do to you."

Etta felt a hollowness in her stomach. The detective's threats meant little, real or idle. But could Butch and Harry actually have been stupid enough to remain in New York, where by now every cop and Pink had their freshly printed photograph? Could those two fools be risking their necks for three bags of money or, even more ludicrous, revenge?

She squared her shoulders. As troubling as these thoughts were, Etta knew she must betray no trace of concern to Siringo. He would receive only what any Pink deserved: scorn and defiance.

"Ill-gotten gains?" She laughed. "It seems that every lout who captures me enjoys the same sort of reading material. As for what you may do to me, detective, I come from people who are not so easily intimidated. Good day."

The detective sighed in mock resignation and, bowing slightly, left the cell. A door clanged shut at the end of the corridor.

She had told them nothing, admitted nothing, but still she was trapped while Curry walked free. Siringo had been right. She knew Harry would never allow the little man to flee with their treasure, never let Curry live as long as he remained a threat to her.

Etta waited for the guard to take his seat down the hall. Only then did she sit upon her cot, making certain she was not observed. She reached below her petticoat and felt for the long smooth sheath camouflaged by the fine tooling of her purple boot.

The slender blade was still there. If it should come to that, she knew she would use it to dispatch the greatest of the Pinkertons—or, if need be, herself.

On the third day of her captivity, Etta was awakened by a commotion in the prison corridor. She heard the sound of men's heavy footfalls and, cutting through this, the impatient and beautiful voice of a woman.

"Unless I have somehow not been informed," the voice proclaimed, "this country, sir, remains a democracy!"

Now, despite her vow not to reveal emotion before her jailers, Etta's eyes filled with tears to see a tall, willow-like figure briskly approaching her cell, flanked by two well-dressed men in bowler hats. Her hands clasped the bars as Eleanor Roosevelt's green suede boots click-clacked down the long hallway. Etta's heart leaped at the sight.

Gaining the cell, Eleanor nodded to her friend as if she were an errant child and then turned to Charles A. Siringo. Despite what seemed a new-found bravado, Etta saw that her Little Nell was trembling.

"These two gentlemen," Eleanor said to Siringo, "are Mr. Graham P. Yardley and Mr. Israel Solis-Cohen. By now you will have surmised that they are my personal solicitors. Mr. Yardley holds in his hand a writ to re-lease Miss Place into my personal custody signed by Mr. Justice Alois Kriter. As there are no legal charges against her in New York State, and Miss Place is an orphan under my lawyers' protection, you will release her to me immediately until such time as the district attorney and the police may make a legal case against her."

Mr. Solis-Cohen, the shorter of the two attorneys, produced a sheaf of legal briefs from his large attaché case and spoke to Siringo as if the de-tective were already in the prisoner's dock. "I can assure you that any re-sistance to myself or to Mr. Yardley will end with your own person *legally* ensconced within a public jail and investigated for prisoner cruelty and possible unnatural improprieties. And be assured, sir, that Mr. Reid of the *Herald* awaits only a message from his friend Miss Roosevelt to reveal your methods of kidnap and torture in public print."

Siringo was stunned. "With all due respect, Miss Roosevelt," he said, "Mrs. Place is not an orphan but in the care of her husband, who, you may not know, is in reality a notorious highwayman and thief named Harry Longbaugh."

Yardley spoke again. "Miss Place and your Mr. Longbaugh are not and have never been legally wed in any jurisdiction within this country, and any relations they may have had are not of such duration to be included in the definition of common law. As you will see from document number six, our firm is now sole legal guardian of Miss Place. You will see also that all signatures—that of counsel, of Miss Roosevelt, and of Miss Place—are present and in order."

Etta was astonished to see, in Solis-Cohen's grasp, a sheet of paper that contained these signatures. Hers had been so expertly forged that Etta could not tell it from the genuine article. She had never seen the document before in her life.

"You may hold your cutpurses and pickpockets at your mercy, Mr. Siringo," said Solis-Cohen, "but Miss Place is a gentlewoman from a fine family, as is obvious from her association with Miss Roosevelt. Further, we have legal documents, also signed by Mr. Justice Kriter, that any and all fingerprint records, photographs, and negatives of Miss Place are now the copyrighted property of Miss Place and are to be released to us, her representatives, forthwith."

Most of the next hour was taken up with a flurry of telephone calls, hushed conversations, arguments, and insults. As time went by, Etta hoped Eleanor would speak to her in the gentle manner of the past or even hold her hand through the bars, but she spoke only with the two lawyers and to Etta's disappointment kept her face deliberately turned away.

And then suddenly, amid the angry smash of telephone receivers and the curses of the Pinkerton agents, they were leaving.

Mr. Solis-Cohen instructed Etta to don her coat and shawl against the February chill. Then the four walked quickly down a corridor and through a basement door. Etta's eyes teared in the sunlight as they emerged into the cold air of a world she thought never to see again. Filled with joy and relief, she could hardly wait to embrace her friend, but as they reached the curb Etta was again disappointed. She was to ride in one carriage with Yardley while her friend rode in another with Solis-Cohen.

As they left the old brick building behind, she turned to the attorney. "Frankly, Mr. Yardley," she said, "I am baffled. Is it truly possible that I am free?"

"Well, Miss Etta, you are not technically *free,* as you term it," he said. "You have merely been released into our custody while the Pinkerton Agency decides whether to press charges against you in court. Happily, they usually don't. Most of the common villains they apprehend are simply held for as long as they choose while the agency provides our lazy and corrupt police with any evidence they might need for trial. This was their plan for you. But as they are a private entity, it was in fact quite illegal for them to hold you at all. And so Miss Roosevelt engaged us to secure your legal release."

"But can you actually do this?" she asked him. "Never have I heard of anyone escaping the Pinks, legally or illegally."

Mr. Yardley thought for a moment and then smiled. "How to put this except plainly? Your friend is the niece of the president of the United States and a member of a very old and important family."

"But surely that alone is not enough to obtain my release?"

"Not in and of itself," the lawyer said. "But, practically speaking, your liberty is primarily a matter of politics and business. At this moment, Mr. William Pinkerton is in discussions with certain government agencies about providing security for them. He is also locked into something of a battle with the president himself in matters concerning upcoming antitrust legislation. That is what all those telephone calls were about. You will be pleased to know that the president says that any aquaintance of Miss Eleanor could not possibly be a train robber, let alone a murderess.

The fact that Colonel William Cody has informed him that it was you who saved his life also counts in your favor.

"Then, of course," he continued, "there is the matter of the sworn affidavit, submitted and signed by you, detailing your treatment at the hands of a Mr. Fred Harvey of Topeka. As you make abundantly clear in this statement, Mr. Harvey attempted to engage in certain physical matters with you in his Chicago office, matters which you, as a moral young woman, would never engage in outside the sacred institution of marriage. Fortunately, you had a witness in the person of one Mrs. Loretta Kelley, a woman of spotless reputation formerly in Mr. Harvey's employ and, coincidentally, the very person who signed you to your contract. You will be happy to know that Mrs. Kelley is now quite contentedly—and very comfortably—retired in Larchmont, New York."

"You bribed her?" Etta exclaimed.

Yardley looked at her as if he had been deeply insulted and pointedly ignored the question. "As far as Pinkerton is concerned," he continued, "your case is closed until such time as the city and state authorities bring a case against you, thus forcing your extradition to Colorado. It is my considered opinion that this bringing of charges against you by their clients, the Dixons, is likely, but for today at least, you are a free woman."

The carriage lurched to a stop. Etta pulled back the dark curtain and was greeted by the sight of two ragged, freezing urchins fighting in the filthy slush. Directly above them was a sign:

ALHAMBRA RUSSIAN AND TURKISH BATHS.
Swimming Pool, Masseur/es, Restaurant.
OPEN DAY AND NIGHT.

Eleanor appeared at her window. "Come along, then," she commanded, her face still a mask of dispproval. "You're as filthy as a honey-wagon horse."

Etta's captivity had caused her to lose track of time. But she surmised from the marked absence of other customers that it must be the workday hours between eight in the morning and seven at night, times when the Alhambra was usually empty, times they had always adored. Stepping into the dressing room, she found herself alone. Not even an attendant shared the giant space. Peering into one of the large mirrors, she saw how right her friend had been about her appearance: Her clothes were soiled with the dirt of filthy rooms and cells; they also bore signs of the perspiration produced by struggling to avoid showing fear of Kid Curry, fear that would surely have doomed her.

She cinched her "toga" and quickly made for the hot-water pool and the scented soaps, hoping to wash away the stink of captivity and the bruises of evil and insanity. As she brushed and soaped her way back into the human race, her soul saw fit to cleanse itself as well. In a torrent of tears, Etta released everything: the fear of being destroyed by Curry, the shame at being trapped by him, the guilt at being caught by the Pink bastards and exposing her lover and his companions to the possibility of capture. Etta tried to stem the flow, to be the good and cheerful outlaw that Harry and Butch would want her to be. But they were men. Perhaps a man may laugh away fear and shame, even pain or joy. But, criminal or no, Etta was not made of such hardened stuff. She relished the tears, hot even in the steaming water—and somehow pitied the men who could never enjoy such release.

Etta sensed a disturbance in the surface of the pool. She looked up to see a golden leg break the water. The long body that followed seemed to pass before her eyes in the manner of one of those nickelodeon novelties in which the film is magically slowed to achieve a comic effect.

Finally, Eleanor's face appeared through her tears. The broken smile was filled with sympathy and the huge blue eyes were nearly as full as her own. Her Little Nell put a large warm hand to either side of her head and brought Etta's face to her shoulder. Etta held tight. Racked by new sobs, her body shivered even in the heat that surrounded them.

Etta could not have told anyone how long she lay in her friend's embrace. Eleanor stroked her head as though Etta were a child and massaged her back as though she were her mother. Finally, Etta mustered the courage to look directly into those beautiful eyes and found the voice to speak.

"Oh, my dear Nell, I feel I have done you such a great wrong. I have injured you a great deal."

"Yes, my darling," Eleanor whispered, "a great deal."

"But you must believe me that even though I *am* what they say, a criminal and a robber, all I ever felt for you was honest. God's truth upon my life."

Eleanor smiled again. "Yes, my darling, yes. I could no more cease to believe that than I could leave you to weep alone in this water."

"If you now know the truth about me," Etta said, "you must also know that, however I may long for your company, I cannot stay. A terrible man is abroad in the world. Mr. Siringo has informed me that only two days from now this villain will be aboard a train bound for Trenton, and my Harry—"

Eleanor nodded her golden head. "Yes," she said, "I know. Your champion awaits. Fear not. My agents have found him, and at this moment he is tucked away in a safe place. By tomorrow morning, you and he will begin your life's journey together, away from all this ugliness."

Etta opened her eyes wide in joy and then buried her face in her hands. Eleanor put a hand on her friend's shoulder and heaved a small and strangely humorous sigh.

"He must be wonderful, my darling, to be worth so many lies."

Etta wiped her eyes and laid her head once more upon that broad reassuring shoulder.

"I will ask only that you stay with me long enough to be comforted and made clean and correctly attired," Eleanor said. "It would not do for your Harry Longbaugh to see you as you are. And fear not for your Little Nell. When you are gone, I may avoid loneliness myself, as a gentleman of my acquaintance has shown a degree of interest in me that I have hitherto never experienced. But I shall always be your friend and, as I have shown tonight, should it become necessary again, your champion."

"Dearest, please don't think me ungrateful," Etta said, "but how did you know . . . how did you find . . . how did you . . . just . . . *how?*"

"Among the very rich, my friend, there are avenues toward everything. Of course, I became frantic after reading of your abduction in

Brooklyn and immediately set out to find you. Luckily, within our family there are retainers for all purposes, from dressing one properly to investing one's assets and so on. I simply employed the retainer we have always used to find those who need to be found. He did this quickly, naturally, and with the utmost discretion."

"May I also take from this that you used the resources of our government via Uncle Ted just to find poor me?"

"Let us just say that the Roosevelts may reach up into the highest offices or down into the lowest depths. And don't look so surprised that we might know where to look to wash our dirty laundry. What may become a fortune must begin somewhere.

"And, what does Monsieur Balzac say? Behind every great fortune is a great crime."

From the

PHILADELPHIA *CHRONICLE AND ADVERTISER*

February 15, 1902

"DEATH HORSE" STOLEN IN RADNOR TOWNSHIP!

ANIMAL THAT KILLED MISS MORROW DISAPPEARS FROM POLICE STABLE!

COMMITTEE IS FORMED, OFFERS REWARD!

DANGEROUS STALLION WAS SLATED TO BE DESTROYED BY OWNER, SAY AUTHORITIES

The notorious horse that trampled a young Main Line socialite to death during a demonstration of horsewomanship has apparently been stolen from the stable of the Radnor Township Police barracks.

Radnor policeman J. L. Randall discovered the black stallion missing from its stall yesterday evening as he returned his own horse to the barn for the night.

On February 1, Miss Emily Katharine Morrow, age 17, only daughter of Mr. and Mrs. Hobart R. Morrow II of Bryn Mawr, was riding the horse during a dressage exhibition at the Radnor

Hunt Club when the animal bucked her from its back and trampled the girl to death.

The stallion, named Bellerophon, had long been known in local horse circles as one of the largest, strongest, and most ill-tempered of equines when he was purchased by the dead girl's father last year. Mr. Morrow believed that time had gentled the horse, who, it has since been learned, kicked two stable mates to death in 1897.

Thus far, Radnor police have no clues as to the possible identity of the thief, but a thorough investigation of the scene suggests that the animal was taken and did not, in and of its own will, escape.

Police also revealed that two other horses were purloined from the stable and they presume that the thieveries were simultaneous.

Mr. Morrow, a widower, has been in seclusion since the sad incident and has so far had no comments for the press.

Meanwhile, a formal committee headed by retired Commonwealth Justice E. Wilston Keith is offering a substantial reward for any information leading to the capture of the stallion and its thieves. "There will be no questions asked of the informant," Judge Keith told the *Chronicle and Advertiser.* "There are those who believe that an animal, not possessing a soul, cannot be thought to be evil. But from what I have heard, this horse is the cursed exception: a devil horse here on earth. It must be destroyed."

Information may be submitted by letter to the *Chronicle and Advertiser* at our address.

Of all the unpleasant tasks that could fall to a highwayman, Butch Cassidy hated bossy detail most. Certainly, he had a way with animals. It was never a difficult job to find a cow and lead her toward the railroad. It wasn't even much work to bind the cow so that she stood immobile upon the tracks. Any one of the Bunch could have done it. The reason Cassidy was always tasked with bossy detail, as Ben Kilpatrick had named it, was his facility with knots.

Butch's uncle had been a sailor, and the two of them spent many a night practicing the myriad rope combinations all able seamen must know. By the time he was eight, little Bobby Parker (as Butch was then called) could entwine a perfect half hitch or bowline, lace an impeccable clove hitch or anchor bend.

It was knowledge he would come to reget. Because of it, he was always elected to fasten the cow to the rails. Only he knew how to design the trap so that the animal could be released with a single pull of a single knot that would then undo all the other knots. Using this system, the poor beast could remain on the tracks long enough for the conductor to notice her and apply his brakes, but not so long as to become an explosion of flesh spread the length of the locomotive.

Still, the job was disagreeable and time consuming. It involved much bending and stooping and, depending upon the animal's degree of terror, a strong nose, as there was often more than one steaming pile to work around. Butch had attempted many times to instruct the other members of the gang in the sailor's art, but when it came to bossy detail, all of them professed themselves miraculously halt and lame.

As Butch dealt with his beast, Etta was struggling with hers. Never during his violent life had she ever seen Bellerophon so agitated. Even when he was three years old and vicious as a rattler, she had never known him to lash out so indiscriminately. She wondered if perhaps it was the unfamiliar terrain or the stench of the nearby slaughterhouses and factories. Too, Hobart Morrow never could handle a horse. Perhaps he had been crueler to the stallion than even a demon deserved. What she did know was that ever since they had arrived in Trenton, Harry had not allowed his mare to be within six feet of the stallion. Any nearer, and the black would attempt to bite her or kick in her knees.

"When this job is done," Harry said, "someone should put a bullet in the head of that devil. Speed's a good thing, Etta, but not when hell is the destination. I'll do the deed if needs be."

Etta glanced at him sidelong as she shook and rolled on the horse's big back. "No, thank you, Mr. Longbaugh," she said. "Any dealings with this animal will be mine and mine alone." But Etta could not help but worry over the horse's worsening temperament. When she had taken him from the Radnor police stable two nights ago, Bellerophon had been as easy as the task itself. A skeleton key, a carrot, and a small English saddle had begun the adventure. A black horse ridden by a black-clad woman in the black night had seen to the rest. As they made their way down back roads toward Philadelphia, Etta had thanked God for the mild night and wondered if this was what it was like to be invisible.

But the next morning, Bellerophon began kicking the walls of his stall. When the livery's owner, Sam Gibson, came to investigate, the horse wheeled in the paddock and made straight for the old man, trying to trample him through the wooden door. It had taken all of Etta's charm and twice the usual fee to convince Gibson to let the horse keep his berth. Even then, he had agreed only if she personally took on the duties of feeding and watering him and mucking his spot. "You said he'd be here two days," Sam said. "Well, all right. Two days and he's out. This is a stable, not a looney bin for horses."

Now, as she heard the train whistle in the distance, Etta pulled up on Bellerophon's bridle and looked down at the silver watch on her breast.

The Number 26 was on time. They would have fewer than five minutes to take their positions. As the sound of the whistle grew nearer, her breath began to come short. As it always did before a robbery, a special warmth spread inside her body, making its way from her center outward, transforming into a tingle at the edges of her limbs.

"Mr. Longbaugh," she called out to Harry, "the fever is upon me. I assume that after this assignment is over, I may call upon you to bring me some relief?"

"Always at your service, ma'am."

She nodded to him and laughed. "Robbing a train in New Jersey. This should give the coppers a few tales to tell their grandchildren."

Etta dug her boots hard into Bellerophon's sides and cursed the stallion as he reared. His forehooves hit the grassland like roundhouse punches, and he sped in the direction of the Number 26 as if shot from a cannon. Etta cried out in joy and whipped him forward. After years upon the backs of other horses she was home. In his hoofbeats she could hear the voice of her father; and for that moment of memory she was the horse thief of Chestnut Hill jumping the hedgerows of The Cedars, shooting at paper targets.

From their mounts, the bandits could see the girdled cow begin to struggle in fright, emptying its bowels and bladder upon the wooden ties. The ash from the smokestack stung their eyes as they too whipped their horses forward. Now, it seemed, all of Bellerophon's rage was channeled into his muscle and Etta bent low to his mane, feeling more than ever like the rider of a whirlwind.

Etta and Harry had nearly reached the train's caboose when they heard the agony of metal upon metal. The engineer laid hard upon his brakes, and long sparks flew from the rails. With only a few hundred feet before impact, Butch Cassidy tripped his three ropes and pulled.

The sailors' knots untied and fell from the terrified cow. She took off in the direction of home as the train concluded its long slide, finally stopping only yards from where the outlaws waited.

Leaping from the mare's back, Harry clambered over the coal car and into the cab of the locomotive. The engineer and fireman were astonished at his sudden company and quickly raised their hands at the sight of his revolvers.

"Friends," he said to the men, "this isn't your train. It's owned by some men who earn more in a day than you will this year and next. So there ain't no reason to go heroic and make a funny move. Sorry about the guns. We'll only be here a few minutes. And while we are, I hope you'll take a serious look at this literature."

Reaching into his inner coat pocket, Harry produced two copies of a pamphlet entitled "Socialism for the Working Man" and handed them to the pair.

Inside the train, Etta proceeded to calm the passengers in the second-class car as Butch began searching the train for Curry. At the sight of her pistol, the women began to scream and the children to cry. The men looked silent and angry, their vulnerabilities exposed.

"Ladies, please comfort your little ones," she told them. "We are here neither to rob you nor to harm a single soul, especially not the children. I regret that these pistols are necessary, but believe me when I say they are for your safety as well as ours. If you will bear with us for just a few moments, we will take what we came for, something that is rightfully ours, and be on our way. Thank you all so very much for your kind cooperation."

With a smile like a sympathetic schoolteacher, Etta turned to the conductor. "Now then," she said. "I believe you are carrying a certain Father Halligan."

From the
TRENTON TIMES
February 28, 1902

LADY TRAIN ROBBER REMAINS AT LARGE!

NO CLUES AS TO WHEREABOUTS OF DARING BEAUTY!

CATHOLIC PRIEST IS ROBBED OF ALL!
MISSING AND FEARED DEAD!

POLICE AND PINKERTONS BAFFLED AS TO WHY
MAN OF CLOTH VICTIMIZED!

By Times *correspondents*

Less than a fortnight after her daring robbery of a Union Pacific train near our city, the so-called Lady Train Robber remains a national mystery.

As this newspaper has previously reported, the woman, whom eyewitnesses described as "tall, well dressed, and attractive," stopped the Number 26 Union Pacific train outside Trenton at approximately one o'clock on the afternoon of the 16th. She rode what one passenger said was "the biggest horse I ever seen what

248 · Gerald Kolpan

wasn't pulling a beer wagon." Astride the rearing black beast, the woman managed to halt the train and climb aboard. She was aided by two male assistants.

To the astonishment of all present, the woman seemed bent on robbing only one passenger: the Reverend Seamus R. Halligan, a Catholic priest en route to Chicago and points west, who was relieved of three very large satchels, the contents of which are at present unknown to investigators. According to conductor F. X. Hochsteader, one of the thieves then dropped the large bags through the compartment's open window, presumably delivering them to a waiting confederate.

It was then that Father Halligan, in an act of both defiance and courage, broke for the train's corridor and jumped from the ledge of the rear baggage car. To the horror of the travelers, another member of the gang leaped after him from the locomotive cab. When last seen, the ruffian was in dogged pursuit of the unfortunate clergyman. Passengers said that the two men ran into the thick pines lining the tracks and disappeared from view.

The suspect is described as a tall man with slicked-down black hair, dark eyes, and a pronounced birthmark above his mustache. Witnesses said he wore a dark suit and cattleman's boots.

Hitherto calm and collected, witnesses claimed that the mystery woman became visibly anxious when her male confederate took flight after his victim. Even so, before taking her leave the young woman apologized to nearby passengers (taking especial care to reassure the ladies) and wished them a pleasant journey with "no further inconveniences or interruptions."

Upon reaching its destination in Trenton, the train was again searched by local authorities. Mr. Arthur M. Sims, head of the regional office of the Pinkerton Detective Agency, which is aiding local authorities in this case, pronounced the robbery "a disgrace" and hinted that he might replace the man in charge of the investigation.

Meanwhile, police and city fathers here and elsewhere have become increasingly concerned that the Lady Train Robber could be transformed into a heroine instead of a villainess due to the daring nature of her crime. She is widely believed to be the only person of either sex ever to have successfully held up a train in New Jersey, and flattering artist's conceptions of her astride her gigantic black steed have filled newspapers across the nation.

Within days of the incident, so-called dime novels featuring fictional accounts of her exploits have appeared on newsstands and at booksellers. Each of these, telling completely different stories and written by different authors, purports to tell the true story of the female bandit. These books have sold out within hours of their appearances. In Atlantic City, fisticuffs erupted between three men over the last copy remaining at a besieged bookstall.

As of this writing, the search continues for Father Halligan. Officials have vowed that they will not rest until they have located the unfortunate cleric and divined his condition. However, pursued as he is by a professional criminal, authorities fear he may already be dead.

The Catholic Diocese of New York has called for prayer by people of all denominations.

Excerpt from: *The Comely Lady Train Robber!* or *Virtue Forced to Crime! Being the true and eye-witnessed accounting of the great train robbery at Trenton, New Jersey by the mysterious and beautiful Annie-Laurie Smith, Associate of Outlaws.*

By W. Worthington Bake, also author of "The True Diaries of Virgil Earp" (concerning the terrible events at the O.K. Corral), etc.

As Published March 1, 1902, in *Colonel Custis' Weekly*, Volume XII, No. 9, Custis & Ellery, Publishers, Boston, Mass. Price: 10¢

CHAPTER II
ANNIE-LAURIE'S FATEFUL ENTERPRISE

As Annie-Laurie Smith stood in wait astride the great black steed, she remembered the awful words of Solomon Gast, which even now rang in her shell-like ears.

"Should you fail to bring the gold and silver required to keep me and mine from the gallows, then your poor mother shall not once again gaze upon your fiery red hair and blue eyes!"

Never before had Annie-Laurie been so afraid. Still, she spoke with defiance.

"I shall do as you ask," she said. "But mark you, Solomon Gast, that I do so with a heart heavy as an oaken door. It is not so for myself that I grieve but for the mother you hold captive and the innocents soon to be terrified by my cold steel." (SEE: *Colonel Custis' Weekly,* Volume XII, No. 8.) "But if one gray hair of that sainted woman's head is harmed, I vow to pursue you and your thieves with a band of mine own and thus be avenged, though it may take a hundred and hundred lifetimes!"

Solomon Gast snickered. "Fear not for your mother. I shall keep my promise as a man of honor. But hark! The train approaches. Ride now . . . *or she dies!*"

Annie-Laurie glared once more at the smiling villain and pulled up on the reins. "Hey, up there, Thunder!" she called to the great horse, and the two roared forth like a Roman candle, streaking toward the moving train, its locomotive belching cinders. Gast's two evil minions, Big Dirk and Johnny Prout, made haste to overtake the young woman.

Within moments, the huge black had gained the parlor carriage. Annie Laurie said a prayer and then seized a gun-metal handhold. With that, the lithe young woman swung from her fine English saddle and onto the narrow platform between cars. From inside her shoulder bag, she produced twin .45s, each loaded for death, and emerged panting into the crowded car.

"Ladies and gentlemen," she announced. "My name is unimportant. I have come here not to foment terror amongst you but merely to seek your cooperation in the handing over of such cash and valuables as may now reside upon your persons. I ask please that no gentleman resort to heroics, so that this day no Christian soul shall meet Him that shall, in time, judge us all."

Annie-Laurie passed amidst the frightened multitude. As her shoulder bag filled with cash and jewelry, her heart softened at the tears of the ladies, the protective stares of the men. But worst of all were the wails of the children, their fearful little faces buried in their mothers' bosoms. Oh, how she longed to tell these little ones that she too was a prisoner!

Moving amongst the passengers, Annie-Laurie was relieved to

feel the great train gradually slow its momentum. Gast's confederates had succeeded at their assignment and gained the mail car, where they were to empty the safe of all cash and bonds.

But as the trio made their way through the cars toward the locomotive, they found their way barred by a man of the cloth.

"You have the advantage of me, sir," Annie-Laurie said to the Catholic priest. "I have no desire to injure a holy man, even he as is not of a denomination with which I am affiliated. But we are desperate road agents, and not in the habit of allowing even the most spiritual personage to thwart our intended designs."

The blue-eyed papist smiled briefly and then spoke to the gang's pretty leader as to a congregant of a Sunday. His brogue was rich with the heather and peat of his native Ireland.

"My name, good miss, is Monsignor Seamus Halligan of the parish at Littleton, Colorado, and I fancy myself at this stage of life a man of some experience in matters of human character. Forgive me, but I read in your beautiful face only the greatest anguish at these most nefarious deeds you have been called upon to perform this day."

"And what of it?" cried Johnny Prout, his one good eye glaring into the soft blueness of those of the consecrated man. "Whether she be a good or bad girl don't matter a cat's whisker. She is today an outlaw, and an outlaw she shall remain e'er more!"

The wise priest only shook his head. "No, servant of the devil," he replied. "That which is in the heart belongs to our Lord and is seen clear as crystal by Him. And though *you* may have consigned yourself to your dark master's pits of flame, this girl may yet be salvaged, no matter your cruel coercion!

"I ask you now, young woman," he implored, "with the price of refusal your immortal soul, to pray with me. To ask forgiveness of Him that I know you have called upon many times in an hour of need. It is even at this moment not too late to seek His succor."

Annie-Laurie's eyes filled with tears. "Yes, good father," she said, "I shall pray with you. Pray unto this hour as I have never prayed before."

Yet before the sacred words could pour forth from the clergyman's lips, Annie-Laurie heard the sharp call of her evil master through the carriage window. "Dirk, Prout!" cried Solomon Gast to his grubby lieutenants. "Let us away!"

"Yes, Cap'n," Big Dirk called back, his mouth foaming with cruelty and insanity. "All is here and ready!"

"Then silence that papist," called Gast to his fellow transgressors. "We have much riding to do before gaining our hiding place. Away, I say! And again, away!"

And so, in the midst of prayer, Dirk and Prout seized the kind priest. To the horror of the assembled, they robbed him of his meager belongings, dragged him from the carriage, and, with a mighty shove, threw him from the train!

Their evil business thus completed, the two now moved toward Annie-Laurie. One on each side, they forced the struggling girl toward the mail car, where Gast and additional confederates awaited on horseback.

As she and the cutthroats swung into their saddles, Annie-Laurie spat her words at the outlaw chief.

"Curse you, Solomon Gast!" she shouted at the smiling blackguard. "Someday . . . and I pray it be soon . . . I shall have my rich revenge!"

NEXT WEEK: A MOTHER'S RESCUE?

Kid Curry needed a hideout, and Lord knows he had heard more than enough about Tap Duncan's farm. Curry had never had an abundance of respect for Tap Duncan. He had abandoned the gang just before the Tipton job to return to his native Ohio, a place he never tired of describing. Except for the fact that Hole-in-the-Wall had one less gunman, Curry was glad to see him go, the better to remain unexposed to his maudlin homesickness.

"Yes," Tap would say, "there's a little farm I've had my eye on around Kenton. Good weather and water. Three–four hundred more dollars in the kitty, and it's Hardin County for me." He said it over and over again.

Back then, it was all Curry could do not to kill him. Therefore, shooting him now had presented little conflict. Curry needed a place to hide out; Tap had one. Tap had half a dozen horses; Curry wanted one. Tap protested; Curry fired.

Had Duncan died somewhat closer to the house, Curry would have had to bury him, but Tap's body had fallen far enough away so that the odor reached his former residence only when the wind blew from the east. His killer had decided he could live with it.

Tap's corpse was the first sight that greeted Harry Longbaugh as he rode past the derelict fence that enclosed the dead man's property. He dismounted for a closer look although there was little need; he could tell at a glance whose work this was. A single shot, clean to the forehead, no fuss and less mercy. Harry needed no more information. It was as if the open mouth of Tap Duncan had whispered to him, *Harry, you have found your man.*

It had been no mean feat. From the moment they leaped from the train near Trenton, Curry had remained ahead of Harry by two steps and what seemed like a bouquet of four-leaf clovers. A sprain caused by the jump had laid Harry up nearly a full day while a terrified doctor in Ewing bound his ankle in gauze and sent him off with a quantity of laudanum sufficient for the chase. A farmer on his way to the Camden market took pity on the limping man and gave him a lift as far as the ferry. Harry crossed the Delaware and arrived in Philadelphia, where he knew the Pinks would be watching for him at every train station. He took in the show at Dunker's Museum, ate a hurried dinner at Kelly's on Mole Street, and arrived at the police stables on Callowhill around eleven. Harry introduced his iron to the old copper on duty and politely asked which horse was fastest. He chose the animal indicated and, with apologies, bound and gagged the officer. The horse proved as fleet as advertised, providing his rider with nearly a full day's start on the law.

Harry Longbaugh knew his man. With no one to trust, Kid Curry would make for Ohio and Tap Duncan, the closest living member of the Wild Bunch.

Harry was just about to begin feeling sorry for the corpse when a high-pitched voice rang out. "No closer." Curry stood in the cabin doorway, holding an Army .45 at eye level.

"You know I'm out of range or you'd have shot by now," Harry said. "I'm here to kill you, Logan. There's no other way."

"And if I lay off your little woman?"

"You won't. And it doesn't matter now anyway. You're a sickness. Need to be lanced, like a boil."

Curry raised his pistol higher and gave something between a laugh and a wheeze. "And I suppose you think you're the doctor."

Harry nodded and took the measure of the wind.

"Then it'll end here, Harry Longbaugh. Because I know I can't never rest until you're over there with Tap. I'm fed to the teeth with you and Cassidy and the whole goddamn world looking down on me."

Harry paused and, reaching down, pulled the Colt from his waistband. He held it shoulder height, its barrel pointing toward the sky. "Your pistol full?" he asked Curry.

"Always."

Harry brought his left hand to the barrel of his gun and clicked open the loading gate. He let three bullets drop to the dust, replaced the lock, and turned again toward Curry.

"Now you're bigger than me. I'm three to your six. How's the weather up there?"

Logan smiled. "What's the play?"

Harry lowered the pistol and hefted it in his hand. The three bullets made a difference in its weight. "Hide and Seek."

On his final word, Harry ran toward the cabin. In only a few yards he would be within killing range. He could see that running inside would offer Curry little protection. In life, Tap had not been diligent about maintenance, and the house was a death trap of holes and missing windows. The front door was gone, the rear one rotted soft as cheese. Every wall had cracks and crevices that provided a clear view of whatever lay behind it. Hiding in Duncan's place would be like seeking refuge in Wanamaker's window.

As Harry tucked and rolled toward the shelter of a hay bale, he heard Curry's first shot.

"That's one, Logan. You're getting shorter."

Curry dove for the well that stood to the right of the cabin. He knew as well as Longbaugh that the cabin would provide no concealment. He rose from behind the well long enough to see Harry emerge from the bale and sprint toward a broken-down wagon. He fired again and the bullet ricocheted off one of Harry's silver spurs, setting it spinning. Harry dove behind the wagon, rolling in clouds of brown dust.

"Shrinking," Harry shouted. "Smaller and smaller."

Curry cursed and spat. He looked across the brown dirt of the farmyard toward the half-ruined corral. If he could reach the horses, he could jump one over the crumbled railing and shoot Longbaugh from horseback. He dashed from the well toward the rough fence posts, firing a cover shot as he ran.

"Three," Harry called out. "We're even, Harvey Logan."

Curry rolled in the dirt and into the corral. He tried to mount a big roan bareback but the animal reared at the first report from Harry's pistol. Curry fell to the earth in time to see Longbaugh's boots at the other end of the fence. He fired two more times but the hooves and screams of the panicked animals were as threatening as the iron of the Sundance Kid. Harry hunkered down beneath the belly of a frenzied mare, but Curry was too quick. In the sea of crazed horses all was a blur of boots and legs and dust to burn the eyes.

Then Harry saw him through the mist. He trained his Colt on Curry through the dirty air but his second shot went wide. As he tried to rise from the crouch, his ankle sent agony to his brain and gave way.

He looked up in time to see Kid Curry grinning atop the fence. The little man had him in his sights. Harry tried to dodge behind a big gelding, but it bolted along with the rest of the shrieking herd. The panicked animals had parted like a hooved curtain and revealed him to his enemy.

Two shots shattered the morning air. The horses crashed through the rotted fence in a shower of brown splinters.

The carcass of Tap Duncan stank to high heaven. Even Randall Brinks and Coky Ford had trouble enduring the smell, and that was saying something. In Kenton, Ohio, it was a truism that—as long as they could turn the money into a drink—Randall and Coky would do most anything, from delivering piglets to emptying the chamber pots and slops from the hotel. Once, when Billy Tracey's mule pulled up lame, Coky had even pulled a milk wagon all day for seventy-five cents. And because their drunkenness sometimes caused personal biological accidents, often their own odor was so offensive that only the most desperate would hire them, and then only for work to be done while decent people were asleep.

Still, this was no time for delicacy and work was work. When Sheriff Herbert Brownell received the telegram from the Pinkerton office in Columbus, he had asked Brinks and Ford to go out to the farm where that hermit lived and pick up the body the Pyle boy had found that morning. When they arrived, they paid no mind to the fresh grave that lay within a few feet of the body, even when the Pyle boy drew their attention to it. They were being paid to place a dead man in a box and drive it to the cemetery, not to be real estate inspectors. For their suffering they would receive one dollar each: a king's ransom, representing, as it did, whiskey for an entire afternoon.

By the time J. P. McParland and Lowell Spence arrived, Randall and Coky had transported Tap's husk from the crumbling farm to the Kenton graveyard. The word had spread quickly that this Duncan was in reality a famous western outlaw, and citizens had come from miles around for a good look and a small party. By late afternoon, the pie and beer and lemonade hawkers had figured out where to stand so as to be upwind of the stiff. They located their businesses accordingly.

As the two Pinkertons walked through the cemetery gate, the crowd applauded politely. Spence stared straight ahead. McParland lightly doffed his hat as Sheriff Brownell acknowledged the voters by clasping his hands above his head. "I need the truth of what happened here," McParland said.

"Truth's pretty much in front of you, mister," Brownell said. "Don't see why you needed no additional identification. I mean, we read over him and everything. We figure from how much he's rotted and some of the bites the critters took out of him, he's been lying out there a good few days."

"And who owns this farm, sheriff?"

"Fellow by the name of O'Toole. But I only know that from the county records. Man only came into town a few days a year. Didn't mix with any of us. Couldn't figure how he made his living, as he didn't much bother with trade or crops, neither. When we rounded up his horses a few miles from here, come to find out they was all stolen. Guess that's how he was making his way. And now you tell me he could be this Tap Duncan out of someplace in Wyoming."

Lowell Spence came as close to the body as the stench would allow and gazed upon it for a moment. He nodded silently to his partner.

McParland walked back through the cemetery gate. Rounding the corner, he crossed the muddy main street and stepped into the telegraph office.

WESTERN UNION
TELEGRAM

TO: MR. CHARLES A. SIRINGO   MARCH 4, 1902
PINKERTON DETECTIVE AGENCY
405 W. 43RD ST.
NEW YORK, NY

HAVE POSITIVELY IDENTIFIED BODY IN KENTON, OHIO. NOT DUNCAN AS REPORTED PREVIOUS. DUNCAN USED ALIAS OTOOLE. WHEREABOUTS UNKNOWN. BOTH SPENCE AND ME AGREE DECEASED IS HARVEY LOGAN AKA KID CURRY. SINGLE SHOT, CHEST. WILL ARRANGE FOR PICTURES BY LOCAL PHOTOG AND SEND SEPARATE. NO REPORT OF CASSIDY, LONGBAUGH OR WOMAN OF ANY DESCRIPTION. WILL PERSEVERE.

MCPARLAND

Almost before the wire could be sent and paid for, the news began to spread that the bandit in question was even more notorious than first declared. A killer, they said. With thirty bodies on his gun. When the lawmen departed, Elihu Craft—his card read *the only camera for fifty miles*—set up his equipment to document the scene. With a flourish, Craft produced a flask of firewater from his kit bag and a dollar from his purse and prevailed upon Randall and Coky to forestall the body's interment for the overall good of the town's commerce. As the pair passed the bottle between them, Craft propped the box up against the wagon so that Curry was in a near-standing position. Then, for fifty cents, local citizens high and low queued up to record themselves with the famous outlaw. Most held their breath or their noses or pretended their fingers were six-guns drawn on the infamous thief and murderer. After an hour, Sheriff Brownell had had enough. He banished Craft and his camera from the street and ordered Brinks and Ford to permanently entomb the madman of the Wild Bunch.

It took nearly forty years for the last of those photographs to disappear from the shop windows of Kenton. Once World War II came, it seemed somehow frivolous to display an image of a jug-eared boy making "devil's ears" behind the head of a corpse whose name no one could remember. Sometime in 1942 the last of the yellowed portraits (Garrett Smith, the long-deceased town butcher, pretending to be very frightened) was tied with twine, placed in a wheelbarrow, and hauled away in the third Victory Paper Drive.

The snow had just stopped falling as Eleanor Roosevelt stood upon the stairs of the great house. Her only outer garment was a crocheted shawl, but cold, in its many forms, was something she had long become used to.

As she looked out upon the vast property, the blanket of white reflected the full moon, each crystal throwing off a tiny particle of light until it seemed she could see for miles. It was not the first night Eleanor had stood here. On her previous visits the portico had become her refuge, her place of escape from the old mansion's gloom and the suffocating presence of Sara Delano Roosevelt.

Within the boundaries of acceptable convention, her fiancé's mother had made clear her disapproval of her son's choice. When Franklin had announced that he intended to marry her, Sara had been horrified. Like the rest of the family, she saw Eleanor as something of a poor relation: the product of a silly girl and a sad drunk, an ugly waif shifted from home to home in grudging efforts at a relative's keep, the carrier of an alcoholic germ and a weak chin.

Eleanor did not have to be told outright what Sara thought. Nor did she need to hear the cruel words to feel them like blows to the stomach. It was all very fine to marry a distant cousin; it had been done many times within the clan. In this manner, the bloodline was kept clean, and so far the unions had produced no apparent imbeciles. But Elliott's daughter? This gawky, homely girl, shy and fearful, afraid even to inform the help of the week's menus? A bleeding heart who spent countless hours among immigrant trash? Sara had been told she labored not only amid the Irish (who were at least of the white race and could speak a form of English), but among violent Italians and scheming Jews. How could her handsome son even consider such a match, when all the young women of their society clamored for his charm and gaiety—to say nothing of his allowance.

Ever since the betrothal, Sara had made these objections clear to their subject in ways both blunt and subtle. And so, on each of the year's visits, Eleanor had silently withdrawn to the great portico to breathe in whatever comfort the current season could offer. In spring it had been the perfume of the flower blossoms; in fall, the musty smoke of burning leaves.

Now, in winter, it was the freezing embrace of the cold, but something more: the satisfaction of knowing that over the next three nights she would steal her future mother-in-law's home in the name of a noble purpose. In Sara's absence, two criminals would be sheltered. The food Sara so zealously guarded would become their food. A man and woman not man and wife would share a bed beneath her roof and—if Eleanor was an accurate judge of her expected guests—fornicate in a bed paid for by the Roosevelt fortune.

On any other night, Eleanor would have heard the sleigh before she saw it, the cheerful jingle of its bells cutting clearly through the cold night. But its owner, Clyde Dowling, was a man to be trusted, and she knew he would follow Eleanor's instructions: no noise.

"Your passengers are political refugees under my protection," she had told him. "They will be traveling incognito. Their train is due at five in the evening, and I have described you and your sleigh to them. Therefore, you shall have no need to ask their names. You will also please remove your bells and anything else that may call attention to your mission. Neither Mrs. Roosevelt nor my fiancé are to be informed of their arrival. And of course, Clyde, you will be compensated for your additional trouble."

Clyde Dowling's sleigh now turned at the carriage circle that led to the front door. From the steps, Eleanor could see the figure of a woman bundled against the cold, her hands hidden inside a fur muff, her face covered to the eyes by a scarf of purple wool. Beside her sat a man who seemed tall even sitting down. His beaver fur hat was of the kind usually worn by plainsmen, and his black mustache hung with icicles. Dowling called to his big dray to whoa up, and the two dark figures clambered from the sleigh, the woman not waiting for the man to offer her assistance.

"Welcome, Etta," Eleanor said. "And you, Mr. Longbaugh. Welcome to Hyde Park."

Etta and Eleanor embraced. Harry Longbaugh bowed toward his hostess and then excused himself to retrieve the couple's two large carpet traveling bags.

"I must apologize that there is no one here to take your luggage. But I have determined that your visit's need for secrecy justifies trusting as few people as possible with knowledge of your presence. Luckily, my sainted future mother-in-law is on a shopping trip in France and my future husband is pursuing his business in Albany. There are no neighbors close enough to see our lights, so there will only be two actual witnesses to your presence here."

"Two?" said Etta. "We've only met that lovely Mr. Dowling."

"Well, my darling, we must eat," Eleanor said, leading the pair inside. "Therefore I have engaged a very capable young cook who speaks only the language of her native Spain. Even if she should some fine day be questioned by the police or your Mr. Siringo, she will not have understood a word of what has been said here. And by that time you should be safely at sea, en route to South America and what one hopes is a happy future."

"But the risk, Nell," Etta said. "This is not even your house. If Franklin and his mother should ever discover that you have been here without their permission—how would you even begin to explain it?"

Eleanor laughed lightly as she led them before the fire in the gloomy living room. "All my life, dear one, I have—what is it the French say?—played the game by the rules. Well, now, for your sake, I must break them. After all, why should you be the only rich girl to turn outlaw? Don't I get a turn to whisk the wallet and rob the train? Now that I've transgressed a little, I can see why you have loved it so much. To finally take what you want. To risk all—life, love, reputation—to achieve what is vital to you and *only* you. To finally say, Damn all convention—"

Eleanor stopped speaking for a moment and turned to Harry.

"—and to do all this to aid a beloved friend and the one who is beloved of her—is that not worth some small risk?"

For the first time since they arrived, a slight smile crossed Harry Longbaugh's face. "Much obliged, ma'am," he said, as he gently took her hand and bowed again. "We are most beholden to you."

As dramatic as the circumstances were, dinner passed in remarkably polite conversation: the quality of the rice, the year of the wine, the relative culinary abilities of Señorita Maria Elena Guerro. In a few instances, the Spanish Harry had learned from his times among the *putas y banditos* of the Southwest proved useful, even if only as a source of kind praise for the shy young cook. In either language, Eleanor found Harry difficult to engage in conversation, but he brightened when she asked about his plans for South America.

"What we envision, ma'am," Harry said, "is what my good comrades call a commune. It's where we gather together the locals that's been oppressed and tell them the truth about capital and labor and how they can control the means of production. Grow their own vegetables, slaughter their own beef. I reckon there's plenty of poor folks down in Argentina that need informing as to how they can be free without falling beneath the heel of the rich man. I'd rather do it in this country, but in the current situation it don't look as if that's possible, what with the misunderstandings about our past career and all."

Eleanor took a bite of her meal, swallowed, and then held him in her blue gaze. "It does sound ideal, Mr. Longbaugh," she said. "But I wonder if it is truly possible for one man to liberate another solely through knowledge . . . without violence or revolution or an educated ruling class leading that liberation. And I also must ask if such fine sentiments can ever bring redemption to a common highwayman bloodied by past misdeeds?"

Etta froze. She knew that, had Eleanor been a man, such an assault upon Harry's honor would not have been tolerated. In their world, the issue would be settled by fists or iron. But Harry's glance became only slightly more piercing as he laid his napkin in his lap.

"I reckon I don't know the answers to either of those questions, Miss Eleanor," he said, "but it don't seem much different from what you do with those poor foreign girls Etta's told me of. You're only one woman. A fortunate one, sure, but how much power do you really have against the sweatshop owners and factory bosses? You've got to have a hill of faith to think that a few dance lessons and some translation will bring them a better life. Truth be told, we might both be fools for trying. As for redemption—well, I was once told the book of life was a long one and if you wanted a better ending you could write some new pages. I pray the Lord is watching me, looking right over the shoulder of Karl Marx. But then I guess I'm luckier than many."

"And how is that, Mr. Longbaugh?" Eleanor asked.

Etta saw Harry fix her in his sights more deeply than he had done all evening. Fix her as if she were the rear window in a mail car. Fix her as if to fire a fatal shot.

"I've got Etta."

The silence that followed was short, and for an instant tears came to Eleanor's eyes. Etta felt great pity for Nell but was also proud that Harry had calmly and justly defended himself against the rudeness of her friend.

The Sundance Kid rose from the table. "If you two ladies will excuse me, it has been a very long day. With your kind permission, I'll take my rest. Miss Eleanor, I thank you for your kind hospitality and the chance you've taken in hiding us out. I look forward to spending more time with someone who Etta loves so much. Besides, I'm sure there is much you ladies would like to jaw about without the interruption of a rough fellow such as myself. Please do not bother to show me the way, ma'am. I am an old tracker and can certainly locate so large a thing as a bed."

Harry bowed once again and headed for the stairs. Eleanor wiped the grief from her eyes with her napkin as she watched him ascend the stairs. "Well," she said, "he certainly is cheeky."

"Yes," said Etta. "Cheeky. But what he said to you, you well deserved.

And make no mistake, my love. Had your name been Evan or Evander Roosevelt, you might very well be picking a bullet out of your forehead around now."

Eleanor nodded. "Besides his rather astounding beauty, I can see why you like him so much."

"I love him, Nell. To say I merely like him would be like saying I merely like you—or that you merely like Mr. Roosevelt."

For the first time that evening, Etta saw Eleanor's horse-toothed grin. "Then, my dear, I must love him too. May I apologize to you for my silly jealousy?"

Etta laughed, relieved, and nodded yes.

Eleanor slowly rose from her chair and walked to a large cherrywood sideboard. She opened the top drawer and reached inside, retrieving a wide oak-tag folder tied in pale blue ribbon. She unknotted the bow, laid the folder upon the table, and sat down beside it.

"Mr. Yardley has made all the arrangements for your passage. You sail from New York three days hence on the S.S. *Soldier Prince*. It is by no means luxurious but should be sufficiently comfortable for the journey. Your tickets and transfer documents are in this green envelope. You will be traveling under the names of Mr. and Mrs. Hardy. First names are Donald and Georgina. A telegram in your name has been sent to Mrs. Taylor, informing her of your intent to stay the night with her before the sailing. The wire has been acknowledged and she writes that she looks forward to seeing you both. In short, all is ready."

"And the legal progress of Laura Bullion?"

"Mr. Solis-Cohen believes that her release can be arranged in as little as a year, two at the most. It may sound like a long time, Etta, but it is nothing compared with what would be required to release Mr. O'Day, Mr. Lant, and the rest of your companions. Mr. Solis-Cohen says only God could secure their release, and his connections only go up as high as the governor."

"Then I shall be patient. Laura must be as well, though I admit I am getting worried about her. The other day I received a letter from her that ran to over one hundred words. I can only take such verbosity as a sign of anxiety."

The two women rose from the table.

"I did wonder something, Nell, if you don't mind a quite personal question?"

Now it was Eleanor's turn to laugh. "What, at this point in our history, could possibly be too personal?"

"I certainly do regret that I shall not have the opportunity to meet your Mr. Roosevelt. From all I have read in the columns, he is the most charming of men and kind besides. Could you tell me if such gossip is true? And does he make you as happy as you have now seen my Harry makes me?"

Eleanor sighed and walked over to a tall window. It had begun to snow again. "Yes, it is all true. He *is* handsome and he *is* charming and for my life I cannot understand why he chose *me*. His mother is nearly purple with rage over our engagement. She believes he can do far better, and how right she is. When he walks into a room, all the men want to shake his hand and all the women want to be his wife. And I know for a fact that a few of the young ladies of our set have already played that role for him in the bedroom. Of course, when we walk into a room together, the reaction is even stronger. The men still want to shake his hand, the women still want to be his lover, and then their eyes settle on me. I am not blind. I see the puzzled looks on their faces, all asking the same question: *What on earth is he doing with her?*"

Etta embraced her friend. "Did it ever occur to you," she said, "that perhaps he sees you as I do?"

Eleanor shook her head and put her hands over her eyes.

"From the moment I met you, I was captivated. When I first saw you at Rivington Street with those young immigrant girls, your words to them were like hope itself, your movements like joy made dance. When I looked into your eyes I saw more than I had ever seen in anyone's, male or female, old or young. I saw all the joy and suffering of all the people in the world. And in you I saw one who could defeat that suffering."

Etta took Eleanor's head in her hands. They stood there for a long moment until Etta broke their embrace. She kissed Eleanor lightly on her forehead.

"You are the most beautiful woman I have ever known."

Her friend's smile was enough to tell Etta she understood.

Eleanor took Etta's hand and led her through the long corridor and out onto the portico. There they gazed up at the moon, brighter now, shining through the gently falling snow.

6

LETTER TO JOSIAH LONGBAUGH
12 State Street, Phoenixville, Pa.
5 March 1904
Near Cholio, Argentina

Dear Father,

It has been two years since my last writing to you and I don't have no excuse. I can only say that that me and my comrades have been busy what with the setting up of life in this foreign country. Us gringos (that's Americans here) have been making headway with the language and find that the Argentine people are warmhearted and friendly and willing to share their last tortilla with you.

But like poor people all over the world, they are oppressed by cruel masters who force them at the threat of the bread in their children's mouths to work all day in the fields and mines here. Everywhere in the world it is the same. The rich get richer. I am now more than ever convinced of the things I learned in New York City.

We came to this beautiful land with quite a stake. Bought a small ranch outside Cholio and invited many of the local people hereabouts to work with us. On our farm nobody, not even us that owns it, earns any more from the fruits of labor than anyone else. All is share and share alike. Here they have what they call campesinos, which is like our tenant farmers back home, only they have it even worse. When we got down here it was usual to come across children dying in the street and old men begging for a few centavos outside the bars. We take these people in, feed them and clothe them, and put them to work. And every day we have school. Not only the children go but everyone. We teach the people to read and write and figure, but we also give them political lessons. We tell them about socialism and the wonderful paradise for the worker that the earth will soon become.

And if the Union Pacific bosses knew their money financed all this, would they be happy and proud? No. Capital would rather see Labor dead than happy and contented and with its fair share of the goods.

I guess it all sounds dead serious, Father, but we have fun too. At night after work, we dance and sing and some of the men play on guitars. The children dance in a ring-round-rosy. They make fine moonshine down here. It is the champagne of the poor, just like it is in Nevada or West Virginia or even Pennsylvania. And if it's strong, it has to be to conquer the bitterness of the lives they have been forced to lead. In Argentina, I begrudge no man the whiteness of his lightning.

We now number in the hundreds and the caballeros—that's the landowners here—hate us because we have taken away so many they made slaves. A rich man named Don Alejandro Espinoza haunts us day and night. He sends his henchman, an animal called El Tigre—"the Tiger" in Spanish—to take our people back to his farms and mines. We have been forced to put barbed-wire fences around our property. They claim our campesinos owe them money for food and for the rent of the squalid huts they once lived in. Sometimes they bribe the judges and win in court, sometimes we bribe the judges and win. Either way, anyone who tries to retrieve a soul from our commune will have to have better guns and braver souls than we do.

Father, I once was ashamed of being a thief. Now I am proud.
A few months ago we ran out of the money we brung with us
and, as you know only too well, a farmer can barely live on the
selling and eating of what he raises. We might have done fine to
just scratch, but to build decent buildings, teach, and provide
doctoring takes money. Now, whenever we rob a bank or hold up
a train, I am filled with happiness because I know the money will
help fill a child's hungry belly.

This work comes natural to Etta. Yes, she is from the ruling
class but she knows how to care for people. Maybe she is made
that way or maybe it is the good influence of her friend, Miss
Roosevelt, who I have wrote you of many times. She nurses our
sick and old and plays with our children. She carries water for
the animals and teaches the Spanish alphabet without being expert in the language. Still, she can drive me loco when it comes
to her own education. I can't get her to look at the texts of our
great revolution. She says she is too busy doing socialism to read
about it. Or she joshes me and says that she knew a Mr. Engels
back home and he was a very fine butcher. But I guess the proof
of the pudding comes when you eat it, and my love could not be
a better example of a worker in our movement. Her soft hands
have gone hard.

Of course for some, old ways die hard. Butch has just this
week lit out from here. I suppose he wasn't never quite as dedicated to the cause as Etta and me. Plus he built up a dam's worth
of vengeance with the amount of señoritas . . . and, worse, seño-
ras . . . what he was romancing. When he filled up Mrs. Gutierrez with what turned out a red-blond boy, Mr. Gutierrez took it
less than kindly. I tried to tell him that jealousy was a booshwa
affectation, but he was having none of it. Cassidy got out with
his hide, and it was all I could do to keep Mr. Gutierrez from
carving up his wife with a machete. But I know where to find
Butch when I need him.

I hope this letter finds you all as well and prosperous as can be under the present system. I have enclosed several pamphlets for you, Father. I hope you will read them. Please notice I have circled certain passages in the one entitled "Farmers! The Land Is Yours!" I do this because they remind me of things you said when your burden became almost too heavy for bearing.

I long for you and all at home more than a hardened highwayman should. Please see after your health and remember me in your prayers as I remember you in mine.

Viva la Revolucion!

Affectionately, your son
Harry Longbaugh

'From the
NEW YORK TIMES
March 18, 1905

PRESIDENT ROOSEVELT GIVES THE BRIDE AWAY: NIECE WEDS HER COUSIN, FRANKLIN DELANO ROOSEVELT

CEREMONY AT PARISH HOME

THE BRIDE, MISS ELEANOR ROOSEVELT, DAUGHTER OF PRESIDENT'S ONLY BROTHER

One of the most notable weddings of the year was celebrated yesterday, when Miss Eleanor Roosevelt, daughter of the only brother of President Roosevelt, and Franklin Delano Roosevelt, a cousin of the President, were married by the Rev. Endicott Peabody of Groton, Conn., at the residence of the bride's cousins, Mr. And Mrs. Henry Parish, Jr., 8 East Seventy-sixth Street.

The bride is an orphan, her parents, Mr. and Mrs. Elliott Roosevelt, having died a dozen years or more ago. She has been living with Mrs. Parish since her grandmother Mrs. Valentine G. Hall gave up her city home and went to the country to live.

President Roosevelt gave the bride away. The ceremony, which was at 3:30 o'clock, and witnessed only by relatives and a few intimate friends, in reality took place in the house of Mrs. E. Livingston Ludlow, Mrs. Parish's mother, whose house opens directly into her daughter's by wide sliding doors. The two large drawing rooms on the second floor, done alike in pale amber-yellow satin brocade, were thrown into one large salon running the width of the two houses.

The bride, walking with the President, and preceded by her six bridesmaids, came down the wide flight of stairs leading from the third floor to the second and across the large foyer hall at the rear of the Parish drawing room, through wide doorways and on to a large mantel at the west side of the Ludlow drawing room, where the ceremony took place. First in the bridal procession came the Misses Alice Roosevelt and Corinne Douglas Robinson, followed by the Misses Ellen Delano and Muriel Delano Robbins, and last the Misses Cutting and Isabella Selmes. The attendants were in white faille silk frocks trimmed with lace and silver, and wore tulle veils attached to white Prince of Wales ostrich feathers, tipped with silver, and carried large bouquets of pink roses.

Following came the bride and the President. The bridal gown was a white satin princess robe, flounced and draped with old point lace, and with a white satin court train. The bride's point lace veil was caught with orange blossoms and a diamond crescent. She wore a pearl collar, the gift of the bridegroom's mother, and a diamond bowknot, the gift of Mrs. Warren Delano, Jr. Her bouquet was of lilies of the valley.

The bridal procession passed through an aisle formed by the ushers, who held white satin ribbons. The bridegroom, who came from the large foyer hall of the Ludlow house to the salon to meet the bride, was attended by Lathrop Brown as best man, J. Roosevelt Roosevelt, a half brother, not having arrived from the South in time to fill the place. The ushers were Edmund Rogers, Nicholas Biddle, Lyman Delano, Owen Winston, Charles B.

Bradley, W. D. Robbins, and Thomas P. Beales of Boston. A small reception followed the ceremony.

The house was decorated throughout with ferns, palms, and pink roses. The bride's grandmother, Mrs. V. G. Hall, was in black velvet and point lace. The bridegroom's mother, Mrs. James Roosevelt, was in white silk, covered with black lace. Mrs. E. Livingston Ludlow was in mauve satin and point lace, and Mrs. Henry Parish wore a changeable pale blue and pink silk crepe, with lace sleeves and yoke.

After the reception the newly wed couple left for a bridal trip of a week only. They are to sail in the late Spring for Europe, where they will spend the Summer. Meanwhile, on their return from their bridal trip, they will occupy an apartment at 40 West Forty-fifth Street.

The thin young man with the wild hair and pince-nez was now well into the second hour of his lecture, but his audience had forsaken him not long into the first.

The speech would have been tedious at any length, but it was made doubly so by periodic translations from the Russian offered by Miss Yelena Ouspenskaya, a starved intense woman with bright blond hair and snow-pale skin. As the third hour approached, many of the campesinos had drifted off to sleep. Others had escaped into the gathering night to smoke their tobacco or make love.

With darkness falling, the Russian at last bowed and took a seat upon a large rock that had been set with an Indian blanket. There was no applause except from Harry Longbaugh, who beamed at his guest and then spoke sincerely in a Spanish polished by three years of communicating with the wretched of the earth.

"Comrades," Harry said, to the few that remained, "I know that you will join me in thanking Mr. Trotsky, or should I say Leon Davidovitch, for coming all the way here from Vienna, where he has been in some bad exile. I'm sure that the story of his unjust incarceration in his native land and the details of his escape thrilled and inspired you as it did me. There ain't no greater authority on our movement in this world than Señor Trotsky. And he is right! The revolution must be not just a revolution of 1908 but a permanent revolution! Never again must the working classes let their guard down long enough for the powers that be to seize what's by rights our'n!"

Had the expected applause actually arrived, Etta Place would not have heard it. The fever in her brain and belly had been building for days and, although she had tried to ignore it by work, it had been no use. At first she had thought the sudden cramps were merely a particularly difficult female cycle; later, a long-hoped-for pregnancy. But by the time the local midwife had declared it an inflamed appendix, Etta had reached a state of near-constant agony. All the attempts to cure her by herb and incantation had failed, and it soon became clear that she would need to return to America for proper medical treatment.

"I cannot allow you to make this journey alone," Harry had insisted. "You are far too sick to handle the trip. There's all that time on the train, and then the boat. No, you'll need me along."

Etta stroked his face. His eyes were filled with worry and his forehead felt nearly as feverish as her own. "I won't be alone. There are any number of ladies here who would willingly accompany me to New York. But for you to play nursemaid would be foolhardy. John Swartz took a photograph of *you*, my love, not me. It's *your* face that adorns every post office and Pinkerton cubicle between Boston and San Francisco, not mine. Eleanor's lawyers have the only pictures of me the Pinks ever took. I can get well and be back here in a few months. But if you come with me and are killed or taken because of it, I might as well die of what ails me."

Harry ultimately sought the wise council of Trotsky. The great man agreed with Etta that a return to America by the Sundance Kid would be far too dangerous and then presented his own solution: He would personally accompany his charming hostess back to the United States. What better way to return the kindness of Comrade Longbaugh? In fact, he was so pleased to be of service that the subject formed the basis of a monologue and translation that occupied the better part of the next hour. Etta pleaded a headache and went to bed.

Feigning pain proved an excellent rehearsal for the thunderbolt that split her head in earnest the following morning. Etta reckoned it was caused by a combination of her current sickness and a general overexposure to high-flown philosophy. With her temples pounding and her eyes blurring, she struggled to gather the belongings she would need for her long trek by train and boat. By the time the day of departure had arrived, it was like a labor of Hercules merely to pin Harry's gold and silver watch to her bodice.

The rainy season had begun in Argentina, and with a deluge pounding down around them the lovers found it nearly impossible to say their customary romantic goodbye; and as the cramping pain within Etta prevented her from standing, all of Harry's affections were bestowed as she lay doubled over on a gurney borne through the train yard by four campesinos.

And then there was Trotsky. Whenever Etta and Harry attempted their farewells, the great man would clap them on the back or offer his hearty congratulations for their devotion to both love and social change. When they finally did manage a goodbye kiss, Trotsky wept and embraced them as Miss Ouspenskaya explained in broken English that such effusive emotion was simply "the Russian way." When the trio at last boarded the train and Etta managed to push her head out the carriage window, there was Trotsky behind her, waving wildly. The final image Harry Longbaugh would have of his departing love was that of a two-headed, three-handed monster crying out not a plaintive farewell but a cracked and merry *dossvidanya*.

Over the next ten days Etta would have many reasons to wish she had made the journey alone. Ill and pining, there were few times when she found the company of the Russians even mildly soothing or helpful. As the days ground on she often wished for the return of her old physical strength, the better to grab the grand Marxist and fling him over one of the country's cliffs, throwing in Miss Ouspenskaya for company.

For a man of the people, Trotsky was surprisingly fussy about his accommodations. At first, Etta put this down to reasonable anxieties regarding security. Given his reputation, it was no more than prudent that he remain largely out of sight for the majority of the trip. Counterrevolutionaries had made more than one attempt upon his life this year, and there was no reason to expect that they wouldn't try again, even here on an isolated railroad.

Still, Etta couldn't reconcile the legitimacy of such concerns with Trotsky's continuous tantrums over trivialities involving dining and

housekeeping. Once, in his private compartment, she saw him go through five pillows, becoming progressively more irritated over their respective degrees of comfort. On the first morning of the journey, Etta felt well enough to join Trotsky and Miss Ouspenskaya for breakfast, a decision she soon regretted. Throughout the meal, the revolutionary continually berated the dining car waiters as if they were peasants of the steppe, sending back seven soft-boiled eggs before finally consuming one and then, satisfied, ordering another, whereupon the entire process repeated itself. In between courses, Trotsky expounded on the coming hegemony of the laboring classes. But the kind of inflated talk that had sounded charming and well intentioned from a disciple like Harry now seemed pompous and grating from a man who had just overturned his fruit compote for being insufficiently warmed. After that one meal, Etta usually pled the pain of her appendix rather than risk the company of such a spoiled windbag.

Thankfully alone within her compartment, Etta was alternately chilled and fevered, the pain continually traveling throughout her abdomen, but she reserved her weeping for the thought of separation from Harry and only worried that the tiny and useless organ within her would burst before she could reach the surgeons of New York. Should that happen, all would be lost: her life, her love, and the task she had been sent to complete.

Even if her mission should go off without incident, it would still take months. First, there was the appendectomy, then her recovery, and finally the retrieval of the money—*her* money—that lay buried in Colorado. Over the outlaw years, her share of the plunder had amounted to a more than tidy sum, and the interest she had earned as a moneylender to owlhoots far and wide nearly equaled the principal. That money was now badly needed. The commune had run out of the fortune they had brought with them. What little solace she took now rested in the notion that her treasure would be the instrument by which Harry might bring comfort to bitter lives.

The ten days of travel passed nearly as slowly as waiting for a rope in that Grand Junction cell. Even exhausted and in pain, Etta was never so

glad to see the bustle of Manhattan's battery. The trip had been hell, not least because Trotsky had seen fit to visit her every night. He would sit sanctimoniously by her bed and attempt to soothe her with old Georgian folk tales that invariably concluded with the triumph of the peasants and an uplifting moral for the underdog. In return, she had left strict instructions with the purser that under no circumstances were Trotsky or his translator to know the time of her departure or the gangway from which she would exit the ship.

It had been his fear of Sundance that had induced Peg Leg Elliott to meet the vessel. With all the bad luck she brought him, Peg had resolved never to have any more truck with Etta Place. But with Curry dead and Charlie Siringo chained to a desk, the only one who could still make it hot for him was Harry. The telegram that came to McCreedy's had threatened nothing and promised him a fine reward if he would only rent a carriage and retrieve a "friend" of Etta's from the boardinghouse of a Mrs. Taylor. Following this, he was to engage an ambulance and attendants, take them to the ship, and accompany Etta to the hospital. He couldn't figure out why Sundance kept referring to him as *comrade,* but he knew better than to disobey. Besides, after his cowardice before the Pinkertons, Peg figured this kindness to Miss Etta might square him with the outlaw gods.

As promised, the "friend" was waiting for him on the steps of Mrs. Taylor's. She wore a dark veil and was dressed in a simple suit. During their ride it proved nearly impossible to engage her in conversation. Her hello to him had been a mere nod, and his comments about Etta's health and the current state of the weather had been met with either a terse grunt or dead silence.

When the attendants carried Etta down the gangway to the ambulance, Peg was shocked by her appearance. Her peach and rose complexion had turned pale and sallow and she seemed smaller, as if her tall robust figure had been placed in an oven to shrink. As their eyes met he found he couldn't speak but he still managed a tiny smile of reassurance. Etta returned his gesture with an exhausted wave.

The two attendants made a turn toward their waiting ambulance.

Etta gazed up from her gurney to see a veiled face appear beside its door. Her mysterious friend took her hand.

"Hello, Pretty," said Laura Bullion. "You look like hell."

Despite her pain, Etta laughed, and while the laughter hurt the words were reassuring. Truly, there *were* some things in life that did not change.

The worst had to be over now, didn't it? How cruel could a surgeon's knife be compared with an appendix inflamed by a thousand miles of waves, railroad ties, and the fiery communist breath of the Father of the Revolution?

Harry Longbaugh imagined that in all the years they had ridden together, he had never seen Butch Cassidy ride the same horse twice.

Many times, of course, Butch had spoken of the need for different
mounts for different missions: this horse for courage, that one for speed,
stamina, bravery, and so on. In fact, Butch had expounded on the subject so
often and at such length that once, in Wichita, Harry had crept into the local
livery and replaced his friend's steed of the moment with a seventy-five-
pound block of lard. Carefully immersing his friend's new hat exactly
halfway into the viscous fat, he attached a note to the crisp still-exposed brim.

It read, simply, *What's this horse good for?*

Now, as Butch approached from the east, Harry could tell that the animal he rode had been selected for its calm. Small and unremarkable, its
loping gait and down-turned head spoke of a disposition placid and reli-
able, a friend who wouldn't bolt at the first sign of conflict.

As their horses neared each other, Butch saluted Harry and smiled.

"Well," Harry said. "If it isn't Santiago Maxwell."

Butch chuckled. Even he was amused by his current alias. "You're
going to like this one, H.L.," he said. "It has everything you like. No violence, easy pickings, lots of money, and a couple capitalist villains to
take off, ones you are particularly unfond of. And you don't have to shit
where you sleep."

Harry frowned and held up his hand. "I have two hundred people
back at the commune," Harry said, "and our crop's not in yet. We've had
shit weather and poachers snatching our animals. My folk are facing
empty bellies. So I'll thank you to skip the guessing game."

"All right," Butch said. "You're as much fun as ever. Anyhow, the job's a few days' ride north. Bolivia. And the suckers are Don Alejandro and his big bitch, Tigre."

Now it was Harry who smiled.

Since the day the commune was founded, no one had resisted its mission more than Don Alejandro Espinoza, a proud and stubborn caballero who had made it his business not only to prevent his campesinos from deserting to Harry's socialist paradise but also to try to kidnap back every poor wretch he believed rightfully his. Three times, the white-haired don had led midnight raids upon the compound, scattering people and livestock that would often take days to recover. Espinoza had even instructed his minions to burn the makeshift schoolhouse, traumatizing the children and causing over twenty terrified families to flee the commune's protection and return to servitude.

But if the master was bad, the servant was worse. Don Alejandro's right hand was a former bandito known throughout Cholio as El Tigre. He was as tall as Ben Kilpatrick, but heavy and blockish, a bank vault in a gold sombrero. It was the Tiger who was usually sent to carry out the strategies of his *patrón*. He did so with relish, wasting no opportunity to destroy or kill, duties he preferred to carry out with his bare hands. One day in the plaza, Etta had actually witnessed him snap a man's leg with a single pull.

More than once, Harry had attempted to assassinate El Tigre, but the henchman never ventured abroad without a cordon of personal lieutenants supplemented by assorted *federales*. Reaching the villain on his own ground was nearly impossible. The hacienda of Don Alejandro was a virtual fortress, defended by gun turrets and surrounded by sentries.

"What's the play?"

"It's crackerjack," Butch said. "A mule train. Tomorrow. Right on the outskirts of Alpoca. In that train is somewheres around eighty thousand pesos, paper and gold. Now, I knew you wouldn't want it if it was payroll for the poor folks of Alejandro's mine. Once we take it, that's what they'll claim it is, because the don hasn't paid a centavo of tax on it. But my informants in the capitol tell me it's all rents: payment from your campesino friends for the hovels and garden plots and shitholes that ol' Al lets them live in."

"We figure to run into Tigre and the boys?"

"That's what's so beautiful," Butch said. "Since no one would take it for anything more than a caravan carrying pickaxes and spades and such, it's hardly guarded at all: a couple scared rabbits in sombreros. I even know which mule holds the swag. All we need do is tie up a few citizens, scare holy hell out of the rest, and fetch the mule along. You get enough *dinero* for your people to make it through growing season; I get enough for a ticket to Texas. And the best part is, we both get to aggravate Alejandro and the Tiger and they'll never even know it was us."

"Texas? Butch Cassidy go *los Estados Unidos?*"

"I'm fed up with it here, Harry. At this point, I'm ready to take my chances with Charlie Siringo."

"Who am I this time?"

"Enrique Brown, anybody asks. Same as you was in Cochabamba."

Harry nodded and reached down to adjust his bandolero. "Once we're clear, how long before you make it home?"

"No grass under these boots," Butch said. "One-third for me, two-thirds for them women and babies of yours, and I'll be singing 'The Star-Spangled Banner' about as well as I ever did."

Harry gazed off toward a mountain and sighed. "When you get there, send word to Etta. Tell her I'm well, that we stole this mule, and there's no hurry for her treasure. Find out how she fared with the surgeons and then get hold of me. You know how."

Butch grinned. "No big kiss? No *I love you, dear darling?* No *my heart withers here like a parch-ed cactus?*"

Harry turned his dark stare toward his partner. "Which mule?"

"Second row, left side. Black nose and ears."

The Sundance Kid spurred his horse west toward Alpoca. His partner pulled alongside. Butch laughed at the darkness in Harry's face but soon, and for reasons he could not name, turned quiet himself. At a heart-shaped rock, they turned to the north and broke into a trot. Before long, they were engulfed in dust, galloping toward the easiest pickings of their lives.

From

EL DIARIO

La Paz, Bolivia, March 25, 1909

(translated from the Spanish)

YANKEE BANDITS KILLED AFTER MINE ROBBERY

AMERICANS TAKE LIVES OF FEDERAL SOLDIER, CIVILIAN IN DEADLY SIEGE

STOLEN MULE LEADS TO FIREFIGHT AND DEATH OF ROBBERS!

A stolen mule led to the pursuit and subsequent deaths of two American bandits who had attempted to escape from federal troops after the holdup of a mine caravan near Alpoca on Wednesday.

The activities of the two gunmen have plagued the southwestern part of the country for over two years. According to the mine's owner, the pair successfully robbed the mine's payroll from a mule train en route to Tupiza and made off with over 80,000 pesos in cash and gold.

The two men also stole a silver-gray mule from the train. At around three in the afternoon, the robbers arrived in the barrio of San Vicente, 15 miles west of the holdup scene. Señor Cruz Alvarez de Alonso, the owner of the local hotel, recognized the mule as belonging to the mining company and, seeing it without its rightful owner, suspected it had been stolen. While the gringos ate in his restaurant, Señor Alvarez rode to find a federal cavalry company who were encamped 10 miles east of La Paz.

When the federales arrived in Tupiza, they confronted the desperadoes, who were found smoking cigars on the patio of the hotel. It was then that one of them, a tall dark-haired fellow with a black mustache, shot and killed a large hulking man who was later said to work for the mine's owner. At the same time, his smaller fair-haired companion fixed at a soldier. Witnesses said the soldier spun around and fell dead in the dust.

Thus began a siege that lasted from late afternoon until far into the night. Soldiers surrounded the patio, keeping up a nearly continuous volume of fire. Others of their comrades threw brushwood torches into the hotel's yard, attempting to smoke the bandits out.

At about eight in the evening, his ammunition running low, the tall dark man made for two Winchester rifles that lay just across the patio area. As he picked them up and dashed back toward his partner, he was shot several times and killed instantly. His friend apparently used the last of his bullets to end his own life. At dawn, the soldiers found his lifeless body slumped behind a barricade of chairs and tables.

Mr. James K. Hutcheon of the Aramayo Transport Company identified the two as Enrique Brown and Santiago Maxwell. Hutcheon said they had worked for him as foremen of his wagon train. He added that they were fine responsible employees who always performed their tasks well. He noted that Maxwell especially was always available to aid fellow workers with moral support and even loans of money.

The bodies of the bandits will be on display at the Plaza de Tupiza until four o'clock tomorrow. General José Carlos de Ochoa said that he hopes the public sight of the decomposing Americans will serve as a lesson to any and all criminals operating in the region, especially foreigners.

Diary,

It astonishes me how little Colorado changes. It is as rocky and mountainous and dusty as I recall, and I love it as well as ever. I thank God for this consistency. It brings comfort to me when all else in my life has changed.

My dear brave outlaw, my protector and champion, is dead, fallen to federal guns in Bolivia. He risked his life on one last robbery so he might maintain his dream of a land of equals in a place where one soul may still own another and where a child's very bread can be taken from his mouth by the whim of another's avarice.

Ever since that day, my life has been a contest with despair. I have been unable to sit or stand, read or eat. Once I received the news of his death and that of our dear Butch Cassidy, I have wanted only to ride: to mount a horse and ride and never stop, to ride that animal to death and mount the next one and the next and gallop into infinity until every horse in the world was gone and I had become a ghost.

Had I still been in the outlaw lands perhaps I could approach such a fantasy. But in New York City all I could manage was to hire whatever poor mount was available in the stables of Central Park and walk him along its winding trails, incautious of policemen and heedless of capture. Thus isolated, I did not have to explain my tears to anyone. Horses don't evince concern, and women cry enough as it is.

But this is hardly the worst of it. Sometimes I believe the only thing that can equal my yearning for Harry Longbaugh is my anger at him: that he should be shot down under a stupid alias like Enrique Brown in the course of a routine robbery. I am livid that he had so little patience and faith in me that he could not wait until I recovered and returned with the money to keep his precious commune alive.

Then, in the midst of my wrath, I will spy his photograph, the double portrait taken of us by Mr. Stieglitz, a lifetime ago. I will beg forgiveness from his rough spirit and vow to continue his work, using my purloined treasure to bring justice to the meek as he would have wished.

My plan now is to find among the rich those few who see how the greed of their class is destroying the country that allowed them to prosper. Etta Place, as much as I have loved her, is fast becoming an obstacle to those plans. My next role will need to be far more conventional and genteel if I am to rob these fat marks in such a way as to benefit others. And who better to play this new part than one who was raised for the role? I can pour tea in the proper way and speak to these worthies in sentences perfumed with the subtleties of our class. My weapon now will be the tongue, not the gun, and the beneficiaries will be not some ragtag bandits, but the starving of the slums.

Still, here in Colorado, my mission was plain and crass: I had come to locate my treasure and retrieve it. If only I were in better condition to do so. Barely two weeks out of hospital, I truly looked as terrible as I felt. My waist had dwindled to a kindling stick, my eyes were sunken in pits of gray, my clothing swam on me as I rode these lonely trails, and I nearly swooned with the weakness besetting my limbs.

Oh, how I wished for the strength and stamina of Bellerophon on this ride! My rented horse was as pokey as molasses, and there were moments when I thought I would never reach my hiding place.

And had it not been for the assistance of my beloved Hantaywee I might have been proven right.

She was a sight I shall never forget. Seated atop a magnificent red and white paint, her hair flew in the wind like a flock of blackbirds. Her garments were no longer rags but the raiment of a woman of status and privilege. Her dress was of white buckskin, fringed at the arms and shoulders, each tendril terminating at a single red jewel. Girding her neck and waist was a network of small beads in half a dozen shapes, forming a myriad of sacred patterns: crimson, turquoise, and the yellow of new corn. Beneath the dress she wore fringed trousers, and on her tiny feet were moccasins of the same white hide, each toe decorated with beaded flowers in what seemed a hundred colors.

At her first sight of me, she galloped forward. Her hair and fringes and feathers took the wind and she became a vision from a savage dream: a warrior woman, stunning and unstoppable. Could this really be the pathetic Little Snake my brave Harry had rescued from that devil Curry, the mute victim who could be comforted only by lullabies intended for the most helpless of infants?

Still, this was not the end of my amazements. As Hantaywee halted her pony, she smiled and called out to me. "Hello, Wiwastelca! Is Hantaywee, your daughter! Hello! Hello!"

I replied in kind and, dismounting, we embraced. It was only then I noticed the small bulge beneath the dress and realized that my little friend and the good Dave Atkins had been busy at their marriage.

Her smile broadening, Hantaywee took my hand and placed

it on her belly. We laughed and wept. "Wiwastelca," she cried. "I am soon mother, Mother so you are grandmother!"

I begged her to slow down so I could follow. And then I tried to pronounce her new name for me and failed. I soon learned that in the Lakota language "Wiwastelca" means "beautiful woman." People had been kind enough to call me this before, but never had I felt so highly complimented. Then, in a stream of broken words, Hantaywee informed me that she and Dave were married a moon after they left Hole-in-the-Wall (by whom I couldn't imagine). They had taken her fry-bread recipes to El Paso and now employed people numbering the fingers on both her hands in the preparation and delivery of her trademark delicacies. Soon they were to open what I could only surmise was a restaurant. The baby would be born with the snow.

This was the happiest I had been in many months. Happy in a way I thought I could never be again. A new life would soon begin that would never have seen the light of this world had it not been for my beloved and his rescue of a wretched slave. For a moment, I dared to think of the child growing inside her as not only hers and Dave's but in some way mine and Harry's, and that single thought became the first beacon to pierce the darkness that had enveloped me.

I told Hantaywee that the little man who had caused her so much pain was dead, his spirit gone to the white man's hell. He could never find her or hurt her again. Then I could feel my new happiness fade as I informed her of the death of Sundance, the one who had rescued her and loved me. Now it was her turn to give comfort, and she held me close for a long time.

At length, business intruded. I wiped my eyes and said we must now search for the money I had secreted in this place; without it many would go hungry, but if it could be found, children would eat and learn and honor the memory of Harry Longbaugh.

Hantaywee began to giggle and soon broke into a dance. She danced until she became a blur of hair and fringe. Then she dashed for a nearby rock wall and reached into a crevice between

two enormous boulders. One by one she began to drag out the
four duck bags I had placed there so long ago. As she produced
each bag, she laughed a little louder, and when the last one was
extracted she turned to me, beaming with pride.

I stood before her, mouth agape. All she had had to guide her was
a letter I had sent to her husband, written in a language she could
not read, and a hastily drawn map. When I had stopped dancing
with her long enough to finally ask how she had found my hiding
place, her answer was so simple it made me feel a great fool.

"I looked," she said, "and I found."

Before long we had loaded the duffels onto my little horse:
eighty thousand dollars in bank and railroad currency. There
would be no long goodbyes as there was not enough language between us for small talk, and Hantaywee soon made it clear that
she must return to El Paso and her cooking. As we embraced
again, I ran my hand once more time over her belly. She mounted
her pony in one smooth motion.

I tightened the cinches on my saddle and gazed after my Sioux
daughter. She rode toward the summit of a small hill, first at a canter and then a full gallop. Across the wind I could hear an excited
series of yips and cries, the proud sounds of the warrior, sounds
that assured me she was now equal to any challenge in the world.

Gaining the hilltop, Hantaywee whirled to face me. She lifted
her rifle high above her head, and with a final cry she was gone.

I mounted my little horse and made for town. With luck,
I would reach the train before it stopped to take on water. Riding
through the sandy rocks, I began to realize that, although my
mourning was far from over, I must regain myself as Hantaywee
had; and that the only way to achieve this was to make my Robin
Hood live in the fat faces and full bellies of the children of want.
And if I am never to know love again, then I must be content
with its memory.

I spurred my pony to a canter, then a gallop, and yipped and
cried and whooped to the top of the hill.

As she sat across from him at Luchow's, Lorinda Reese Jameson realized that Ralph Worthington Carr met her most basic criterion for friendship: Butch Cassidy would have liked him.

Even those who had worked their hardest to see Butch hanged often remarked upon his good nature and his willingness to see the best qualities in even the most callous and degraded of reprobates. Therefore, Etta thought, it stood to reason that if Butch Cassidy didn't like you, there must be reasons aplenty. But in the end, one failing stood above all, and for those thus disdained he reserved his most withering comment. "That fellow," Butch would say, "has no sense of humor. And people without a sense of humor are the most dangerous folks in the world."

It was this singular trait that had made Butch Cassidy fear Charles A. Siringo. In no encounter had he ever heard anyone, law or outlaw, remark that the detective had smiled or joked with a prisoner. If a murderer was declared innocent or guilty in a court of law, no observer ever detected either triumph or disgust on Siringo's face. Lorinda could only imagine the detective's sourness at his recently forced retirement.

Ralph Worthington Carr was everything men like Siringo were not. Lorinda had met him through her association with Alfred Stieglitz. In her first social foray, two years after Harry's death, Etta had chanced upon Stieglitz at his Gallery 291, the avant-garde bastion that was at that time featuring the work of his partner, a Mr. Edward Steichen. Although she was still pale and thin from illness and a long period of mourning, the photographer had recognized her immediately as half of the handsome couple who had sat for him at DeYoung's studio. Pointedly ignor-

ing Etta's grief, he had immediately initiated an enthusiastic and ultimately unsuccessful romantic pursuit.

But even if much of her association with Stieglitz consisted of fending
off his advances, in his company Lorinda managed to learn much about
the new movements in art, photography, and film. In the salons of the
day she listened to intense discussions and arguments about the direction
of the world's culture and politics. The creativity the artists poured into
their work seemed to nourish her. Their conversations revealed new
worlds to Lorinda, and their camaraderie was like a tonic to her soul.

On the night Lorinda met Ralph Carr, she had been invited to a
soirée at the studio of a Hungarian named Kertész. After it had been determined that no one else in the room spoke French, Lorinda was asked
to serve as translator for the famous Monsieur Valpain, a visiting painter.
The discussion began amiably enough, but within a matter of minutes it
devolved into a thunderous argument between the artist and a non-
French-speaking critic for the *New York World,* all over someone named
Picasso. As the painter screamed at his opponent *en français,* Lorinda du-
tifully screamed back at the critic in English. When the critic became sar-
castic, Lorinda raised her eyebrows and shrugged in scorn. *Merde* became
shit, idiot became *imbécile,* every word pronounced in what the artist
later told Lorinda was a perfect *accent gallique.*

As the audience respectfully watched the absurd bilingual tableau, a
tall man stood at the rear of the room, grinning broadly. Several times he
clapped his hand over his mouth so that his laughter would not give offense to either the visitor, the critic, or the charming translator.

Apart from his height and the flaming red of his hair and mustache,
it seemed the man was doing his best not to be noticed. His suit was as
black as a funeral and, although of a good gabardine, nothing like the bespoke garments worn by many of the rich aesthetes in attendance. His
shirtfront and collar were plain and his tie a subtle stripe. He might have
been a successful salesman or a respected young professor. The blue eyes
smiling over the top of his hand gave him an impishness odd in one so
large. When the three-way confrontation was at last over, the tall man
made his way across the crowded parlor and straight for Lorinda.

"You will please excuse me, miss," he said, "but I felt that I had to congratulate you, not only on your excellent French but on the manner in which you played your role. Honestly, I was not certain who was the angrier, Monsieur Valpain or yourself."

Lorinda looked at the stranger for a moment. The only pair of eyes she had ever seen that were bluer or more beautiful belonged to Eleanor, and there was something so humorous about him that for the first time in months she wanted to laugh. She settled for a wide smile.

"Thank you, sir—I think," she said. "We've not been introduced, but as you may have noticed we are a rather informal bunch. My name is Lorinda Jameson."

"Hello. I am Ralph Carr, Chappie to my friends, and I've heard about you."

"Really, Mr. Carr. Important information or just idle gossip?"

"Hopefully, a little of both. You're the girl who doesn't like men with money."

Lorinda crimsoned to be so addressed by someone she had barely met. At Hole-in-the-Wall, any man who displayed such insolence this early would soon have been called upon to back it up with fist or iron. Still, Lorinda found that her smile remained.

"Well, then," she said, "judging by the looks of your suit, I think we should get along spendidly."

Ralph Worthington Carr stared at her for a moment and then burst into deep, full-bellied laughter. It seemed to fill the room and wash over Lorinda like a healing balm. It was, she thought, the sound of something she hadn't heard since she first left Philadelphia for Colorado: the joyful noise of a clear conscience.

"Well, Miss Jameson, I do hate to disappoint you, but I am, unfortunately, very rich indeed. I can only hope you will permit me to show you what can be achieved when a spoiled brat decides to share the wealth. As for the suit . . ."—he paused and raised his eyebrows like a born comedian—"I won it playing poker with a priest."

Now Lorinda began to laugh too. And as she did, a corner of her shroud of mourning seemed to fall away.

Over the next few months, Ralph Worthington Carr helped Lorinda regain the mirth nearly lost to sadness. For Chappie, no effort to amuse her was too foolish or embarrassing. He told awful jokes, danced the buck-and-wing in public, tried to sell a nonexistent insurance policy to a mounted policeman. Sometimes his antics would produce no reaction from her, other times only a wan grin or pitiable groan. There would even be days when Lorinda would banish him from her presence, unable to tolerate such silliness when the man she loved was dead. But as their association continued, Chappie began to awaken places of joy within her until, in spite of herself, he was laughing her in and out of hansom cabs, laughing with her over dinners, even doing his best to make her laugh in the dignified silence of museums and galleries.

But as much as he loved to laugh, Chappie Carr loved to sing even more. This was probably the reason why Lorinda now found herself in Luchow's for the third time in as many weeks. The restaurant had long been a bastion of good German food and beer, the kind of place where no one looked over your shoulder to see if more socially prominent personages were coming through the door. A place so fond of gluttony that no one batted an eyelash if a lady was undainty enough to order two portions of their famous Swedish meatballs and indelicate enough to finish them all. In Luchow's, Lorinda could eat like an outlaw, like someone who had learned to delight in the food before her, ever aware there might be times when there was none. No small trencherman himself, Chappie marveled at just how much of the heavy fare this slender woman could dispatch in a sitting, but he simply added it to the increasing list of traits and mysteries that formed his fascination.

At Luchow's, the patrons would rise every half hour or so, raise their foaming steins, and launch into *Trinkenlieder.* Chappie neither spoke nor understood a single syllable of *Deutsch,* but he sang as loudly and happily as the waiters and their immigrant clientele. Those songs he hadn't learned by heart he would simply improvise, making fine guttural noises in his throat, trailing along two notes behind the melody. This would never fail to leave Lorinda weak with laughter as Chappie waved his arms and sang louder and louder.

When she had finally caught her breath, Chappie buttered a slice of *Bauernbrot,* tore it down the middle, and handed half to her. "You see?" he said. "We rich fellows aren't so bad."

She accepted the dark bread from him and set it to the side of her plate. "Yes, you are," she said. "Most rich men aren't worth the powder to blow their brains out. I associate with you, Mr. Carr, not because you are rich but because you are crazy. I estimate that at the rate you are giving your money away, you should be stony broke straightaway and therefore much more in keeping with my usual taste in friends. Your gifts to Rivington Street alone are enough to make Mrs. Roosevelt suspect you have had your way with me."

"Would that she were correct. Actually, my dear, at my current pace of philanthropy, I will be officially flat on January the first of nineteen seventy-five, when I shall be happily pushing ninety-nine. And I daresay if I can continue to eat this good food and sing these happy songs in the company of a certain redhead, I shall reach that age easily and with pleasure."

"Your father must be fit to have your head. The scion of the Carr Burton Brokerage a class traitor!"

"Please"—Chappie laughed—"you'll turn my head. As to Father, I do believe he's given up. On the day I received my own income, I resolved that any capitalism I engaged in would never again be transacted from a desk on Wall Street. Meanwhile, my investments have beat the old man's at every turn. Is it my fault that he chooses to pile his money up while I use mine to help people? I think it's fun. Anyway, I've made so much money for his friends, he's afraid to take my name off the door. And every one of those commissions goes toward having more and more fun."

Lorinda had begun to laugh again when she saw Ralph Worthington Carr leap from his chair and tackle a swarthy and muscular man in a dark coat and slouch hat. The two crashed to the restaurant's tiled floor, bringing with them a tablecloth and several platters of sauerbraten. As the man attempted to rise, Chappie grabbed him by the belt of his trousers and smashed his fist into the stranger's chin, causing him to fall once more to the floor. Lorinda sprang from her seat to aid Chappie and saw

the tiny bottle in the man's hand. It was as clear as water and bore no label, only a plain cork. Cursing, the man tried to bring his arm back to throw the vial, but Lorinda brought her boot up toward his wrist and kicked.

The women in the crowd began to shriek as the dark man spit an oath in a strangled Italian. *"Puttana!"*

Lorinda kicked him a second time, and the bottle went flying toward a damask wall hung with heavy velvet curtains. As it shattered against the fabric, she heard a sickening hiss. The splatter of vitriol began eating through the material almost immediately. By the time the police arrived, the damask would be eaten to the plaster and the curtain riddled with dozens of jagged holes. The smoking pattern of destruction was as plain as a signature. The mark of the Hand.

With one final shove, the man in the slouch hat scrambled to his feet and managed to push Chappie over the table. Free of restraint, the man leaped over a giant planter and knocked down the two waiters who attempted to stop him. The last Lorinda saw, he was racing past the restaurant's window onto 14th Street and into the Manhattan night.

When the overturned tables had been righted and the proper authorities called, Carr took Lorinda into his arms.

"Please, Chappie," she said, "we must leave. Now. Before the police arrive and start asking questions."

He nodded and bundled Lorinda into her coat. Under the entrance canopy, he commanded the doorman to hail a hansom. Inside the cab, Lorinda was quiet. Chappie held her close.

"That was quite a performance, my dear. I hope you never kick me like that. If I didn't know better, I could have sworn that bottle of acid was meant for you. I suppose I acted as if it was."

Lorinda was thoughtful for a long moment and then smiled into those beautiful blue eyes. "My darling," she said, "it is time for a talk. There are a few things you should know about me."

THE W. B. CONKEY COMPANY
MANUFACTURING PUBLISHERS
Hammond, Indiana

January 23, 1910

Mr. Charles A. Siringo
Siringo Ranch
General Delivery
Santa Fe, New Mexico

Dear Mr. Siringo,

I very much hope retirement finds you well and that you do
not find yourself at loose ends after living such an adventurous
and active life. I certainly envy you your well-deserved leisure
and hope you will find the writing of your book for us a relaxing
diversion from the hard work required on a ranch.

In your letter, you asked me how to go about organizing the
material and what—and what not—to include. I suggest that
you simply begin at the beginning, from your first year with
Pinkerton in 1886 through this, the year of your retirement. In
the main, it is not necessary to be overly concerned with gram-
mar, spelling, syntax, or the general structure of the book. All we

at Conkey are concerned about is that you tell your story as best you can, in your own way and in your own words. You may confidently leave the technical work to us.

As to what should be included, I can frankly state that what our readers enjoy most is action and more action. Therefore, I hope that you will include your many exploits amongst the well-known heroes and lawmen of the day: Buffalo Bill, Heck Thomas, Wyatt Earp, Chris Madsen, Bill Tilghman, et al., as well as your successful pursuits of such desperadoes as Ben Kilpatrick and Laura Bullion, O. C. Hanks, Will Carver, Harvey Logan, etc. I was especially taken by what you related to us about your putting the so-called Wild Bunch out of business. You have landed scores of outlaws either in jail or in the ground, and I beg you not to be bashful concerning these incidents.

Finally, we are firm in our conviction that you be neither reticent nor apprehensive about reporting the shabby treatment by the Pinkerton Agency that forced your resignation. We are among the largest printers and publishers in this country and maintain our own staff of skilled attorneys for the purpose of our authors' protection. Rest assured that your right of free speech shall be upheld at all times and that Conkey will not allow you or any of our other authors to be muzzled.

Please note the enclosed side letter that outlines your schedule for delivery of chapters. We believe that yours is a reasonable deadline, but if you should come upon any difficulties, please feel free to write or wire me at any convenient time. I look forward to reading of all your stimulating activities.

Very truly yours, I remain,

R. D. Olson
R. Dudley Olson
Editor-in-Chief
The W. B. Conkey Company

In the large office of Don Vittorio Cascio Ferro, Lorinda began to wonder if the color of evil was not black, as the legends had always said—but gold.

True, some of it was artificial. The base of the Tiffany lamp upon the mahogany desk was mere paint, while the statue of a leaping greyhound on the sideboard was probably bronze. But much of the room's gold was real. The ornate gilt frame surrounding the baroque portrait of the don was clearly authentic, as were all the metal parts of the telephone. Every drawer handle and particle of inlay was genuine.

Ferro himself fairly radiated with golden accoutrements. Tie clasp, stickpin, watch fob, buttons on vest and jacket—all shone through the gloom with a glaring authenticity.

As she sat before him, Lorinda sorted her thoughts. How difficult will it be, she asked herself, to try and save one's life while asking this modern Croesus to part with treasure he believes has been duly earned and to forgive a debt owed for more than a decade?

His courtly manner belied all that the dailies had reported about him. At forty-seven, he was the most powerful foreign-born criminal in the country. The papers said he had been personally responsible for the particularly brutal dispatch of one Signore Benedetto Madonia, an alleged counterfeiter who dared attempt to practice his trade in New York City without permission. This was a clear violation of what the Sicilians called *pizzu*, the paying of tribute to the ruler of a territory, in this case Ferro himself. It had been reported that Don Vittorio had stabbed Madonia numerous times, cut his body into pieces, and deposited them in a barrel to be found by his confederates. The newspapers did not explain the significance of such a grisly death, and the authorities could make no case against the Black Hand chieftain, as there were no eyewitnesses. On the day the police conducted their canvass, there was not a single person in the neighborhood who was not at work, out of town, or visiting relatives in the old land.

"*Buon giorno,* Signorina Jameson!" Don Vittorio said. "You will have, perhaps, a cup of coffee . . . an anisette?"

Lorinda had spent much time among the Italians of the Lower East Side and knew that to refuse such hospitality would be considered an insult. She accepted both offerings with a whispered *grazie* that made Don Vittorio smile through his black and gray beard.

"To what do I owe the priviledge of such a visit?" he asked. "It is not every afternoon that a humble immigrant like me gets to meet such a celebrity. I truly wish we could have met under different circumstances and without all this unpleasant history. Then you would have been a member of my organization! Someone who can shoot, ride, and rob a train like a man while possessing a face to tempt Satan? Oh, my dear young lady! Considering the kind of helpless *gavones* I am surrounded with, I am truly sorry this did not happen. Tell me, did you really kill that newspaper shit heel? I heard it was self-defense. Not that this is of course, any of my business."

"You seem to know all about me, Don Vittorio," Lorinda said. "I am surprised that you never gave this information to the Pinkertons. It would have provided some money while you were attempting to collect on my father's debt."

Don Vittorio's face darkened. "Despite what you may have read, money is not everything to us. Yes, I know the press says we are greedy savages, not fit to breathe the same air as you native-born. But I would sooner take a stiletto to my eye than give the Pinkertons so much as the manure from my horses. When they aren't breaking some starving workingman's strike, they try to take the bread from my mouth. This year alone they have jailed ten of my people, including a boy no older than fourteen who only fetched tobacco and the daily papers. He was . . . how do they say? . . . simple. The Pinkertons returned him to me like a shell, so frightened he has not spoken a word since. Such *schifósi* will never receive information from me or any member of my *famiglia.* Not for a million dollars, not for ten million dollars! *Adante tutti a fanculo!*"

Don Vittorio paused for a moment, catching himself in the unpardonable sin of revealing his anger to a stranger.

"But enough. You have not come to hear me deliver grand speeches, especially in a language you do not speak. I understand you have a proposition for me."

Lorinda straightened in the enormous leather chair and looked at Ferro directly. "I am not even sure that you are aware of this situation, Don Vittorio. It is largely a Philadelphia matter, and I am certain you only intervene in business ninety miles south when it becomes a crisis. Still, I know all things related to my hometown fall under your purview and that you have the power to give orders or have them rescinded. I am here today to ask you to rescind an order—the one that calls for my imminent death or disfigurement."

As the don listened calmly, Lorinda related the story of her father's outstanding debt, his inability to pay, his suicide, and the subsequent instructions to destroy her. She told how, only three weeks before, an attempt had been made to throw sulfuric acid upon her in a restaurant and that only the quick action of a friend had averted disaster.

"In the long period of time since I was deemed worthy of death, I have become a woman of some means. I would not insult Don Vittorio by expecting him to commute my sentence without remuneration. At the time of his death, my father owed your associates approximately twenty thousand dollars. The large valise at my feet contains this exact sum. I will gladly leave this money with you if you will lift the weight of your organization from my shoulders. And I hope that you will accept my sincerest apologies for any trouble or embarrassment I may have caused you during my pursuit."

Don Vittorio was a hard man to amaze. Over three decades in business he had heard every manner of entreaty: the half-jovial appeals of gamblers pleading for more time, the protests of storekeepers beseeching him for extensions on their protection payments, the sobbing and begging of those well aware that, by his hand, they were doomed. But never had a beautiful young woman come into his office and blithely suggested that they horse-trade for her life.

The don lighted a black twisted cigar with a gold-headed match. "There is the small matter of interest, Miss Jameson," he said. "I have been told that my men have been after you for more than a decade. You can imagine how humiliating it is for a man in my position to have his people outwitted and outrun by a mere girl. And then there are the two young men who lost their lives on that Christmas years ago. True, they probably would have been killed anyway. The younger one had informed on us to the Pinkertons, and the older one was so stupid he could look in a mirror and shoot himself. But even forgiving the deaths of such *cretini,* the amount you owe us has grown much larger than the original principal. If I were a bank, you would not use me so."

Lorinda smiled sweetly. "I concede all these points, Signore. But I am limited in the amount I may offer you. I have come before you in good faith and without lieutenants to protect me. Still, there is more than profit in this for you. With the payment of this debt, it will become known that you and you alone have done what both an army of lawmen and the Pinks were unable to do: bring Etta Place to heel. And should anyone inquire, I will tell them how ten years' interest has brought me to financial ruin while speaking not only of your firmness but your mercy."

"And if I should not prove merciful?"

Lorinda's reply was businesslike. Kid Curry had taught her the price as well as the value of terror.

"Then I shall soon be dead by your hand. Your death, of course, will soon follow mine, as no amount of pleading on my part will stay the highwaymen and outlaws with whom I once associated. I believe it is what the Sicilians call a *vendetta.* And please, make no mistake, Don Vittorio. Their determination is as granite as your own. You may surround yourself with the Army of the Potomac, but they will trap you as they do the mountain lions in the wild. Like your own code, theirs does not change. So the final result will be waste on both sides. The death of a young woman yet to bear children; the killing of a still-vital man whose five grandchildren will mourn him."

Don Vittorio's face betrayed nothing, but he could feel the truth of her words in his stomach. He had learned over the years to trust that organ more than the brain or, God forbid, the heart. He weighed his response for a moment. A colossal show of anger might perhaps break the resolve of this young woman, but his gut told him no. Perhaps a reasoned negotiation would bring about better terms, but this would be far more mortifying to him than merely granting or denying her request. And he believed her when she vowed that her friends would see him dead. She seemed like an honest girl, and to him the definition of honesty was the keeping of promises.

"The money you have brought me will be sufficient," Don Vittorio said. "I won't live or die by the rest, and there are enough deeds keeping me out of heaven. After all, you were not the one who incurred the debt. I ask only that you tell no one of my generosity. Mercy is like a lollipop. If I give it to one child, soon all the children will want one."

Don Vittorio rose to indicate that the interview was over. He strode from behind his desk and bowed, his lips an inch from Lorinda's hand. She thanked him and made for the door. Then she turned back toward the gilded desk.

"Don Vittorio," she said, "I wonder if you know of the wonderful work that the young Mrs. Roosevelt and her committee are doing at the Rivington Street Settlement House."

"Settlement house?"

"Yes. The work there is so very important. Many of the young women and children they help are, like yourself, of Sicilian origin. Others are Slavs or Poles or Hebrews. They teach these needy immigrants to dance and to speak English, take them on trips to the country, and tell them about our Constitution. They steep them in all that it means to be an American. Oh, if you could only see the wonderful things that go on there, Signore!"

The don stared at Etta, perplexed. "And what has this to do with me?"

She smiled again. "I only wonder if you might deem it possible to make some contribution to this special place. Even a small amount of money would be of great aid to these unfortunates. If only you could extend your mercy past me toward those so in need of it, I imagine that the heaven you now feel closed to you might open its door a few inches."

Five minutes later, Lorinda stood in the narrow lane below the rooms of Don Vittorio Cascio Ferro. From his office window she could still hear his peals of laughter descending to the street. So helpless with mirth had he been, she feared he would be unable to write a check. As it turned out, there had been no need.

Trembling slightly, Etta held tight to the valise that still contained the very money that had bought her life, the bag he had handed back to her as his laughter began. As she set the case's lock, her glove brushed against the side pocket containing the large-bore derringer she had brought in the event Don Vittorio's answer had been no.

Lorinda tucked the bag up under her arm and started for Rivington Street. Less than twenty feet along, she ducked into an alley and vomited, releasing all the congested fear of that day's meeting and somehow, she thought, all fear to come.

As befits a demon, it had been hell to coax Bellerophon into the live-stock car.

Lorinda had made it clear that she would pay for as many men as were necessary to complete the task; in the event, the job required eight brave and hardy souls. Even at sixteen years old, the stallion remained intent on defending a territory that seemed to encompass all the land for a mile around. And he would still kill to be king.

She had often wondered how she could miss such a devil, but the years in South America had only increased her longing to admire him, to feel the danger radiating up through his strong back, to hear his defiant whistle. But then, Lorinda had always been a magnet for the world's demons: demons truly evil, like Kid Curry, and gallant devils like Father and Ben and Butch.

And Etta.

But Etta had died along with Harry Longbaugh, disappeared in a hail of Bolivian bullets as surely as if she had been there. With Etta had gone her wildness, replaced now by the civilized calculation needed to separate the rich from their gold for purposes higher than greed or adventure.

Bellerophon was now the single reminder of that outlaw world, an aged but still untamed spirit, rearing and kicking in the morning sun.

In Argentina, she had hoped the stallion would be well cared for and not neglected or destroyed for his fury. After she had stolen the animal from the Radnor police, she and the horse had made their way to upstate New York and the little farm of Kicking Bird, a Mohawk she had met while traveling with Buffalo Bill. Unlike most of his fellow performers,

Bird was never inclined toward drink or dice and was known about the fairgrounds as one who kept both his money and his thoughts close to his vest. The exception to this reserve had been Etta Place; he would spend hours describing to her the small and beautiful farm he was about to buy near Oneonta, New York, the village of his birth.

When Lorinda had returned for him she found Bellerophon still safe in Kicking Bird's keeping. The old brave was only too happy to release the black devil to his mistress. He told her that during his eight years on the farm the stallion had tried to kill one of his two geldings and had kicked a hired man senseless. His wife, an Irishwoman, had many times asked Bird to shoot the animal. In light of his refusal, she had taken to praying the rosary twice a day.

Now, inside the train, the horse's paddock was a sea of signs that warned the daring or the stupid that any attempt to feed or admire the occupant could end with a bite to the eye or a kick to the head. BEWARE, the placards declared, DANGEROUS HORSE! APPROACH AT RISK OF LIFE AND LIMB, and STOP! DANGEROUS HORSE! TO BE FED AND WA-TERED BY OWNER ONLY. The protection of the illiterate was considered as well, via a series of dramatic skulls underscored with crossed bones, drawn white on a field of black.

As she watched the cities and fledgling suburbs of the East melt into the empty tableaux of the West, Lorinda realized that this was the first long trip she ever taken under her given name. She had been Etta Place for twelve years, ever since an old lawyer with a sense of humor had bestowed the name upon her. Lorinda had become so accustomed to her alias that for weeks after her birth name was restored she hesitated to respond to it. For all the trouble Etta had caused her, it was not easy to give up the name under which she had lived the most significant days of her life.

After all, as Lorinda Reese Jameson she had felt only ambivalence and loyalty to her father and in return received only his reticence and self-pity. Etta Place had been the name under which she had been well and truly loved. It had been Etta, not Lorinda, who had felt the sweet kiss of Harry Longbaugh, Etta who had taken on the banks and filthy jails and steam locomotives and triumphed.

In the end, it was Eleanor who restored her to the name with which she had been christened. Just as she had in the Pinkerton jail, Nell had exercised the Roosevelt power that allowed Lorinda to bury Etta forever. Lorinda watched the process with amazement, getting a rare look at how well the rich cover their tracks, even from the most astute of blood-hounds.

Using the advice of longtime family advisors, Eleanor quickly turned Etta into a work of fiction, a non-person with no papers, no loved ones, and no date of birth; a living alias whispered of in outlaw camps and ru-mored to have robbed trains; a creature of dime novels and penny dread-fuls. Even her Pinkerton file had been mislaid, along with all its copies.

The questions had been carefully planted at the polo matches and charity balls, a whispering campaign in reverse. Truly, what could such a low caricature have in common with Miss Lorinda Reese Jameson of Philadelphia, she of the Agnes Irwin School and cotillions at the Union League? Only a woman of the finest sort could be considered worthy of pursuit by the wealthy and eligible Mr. Ralph Worthington Carr. And only such a one could afford to repeatedly refuse his offers of marriage.

Of course there had been that unpleasantness with her father, but did he really kill himself or was it merely an accident? That business in the scandal sheets? The usual sensationalism. Now, respectable newspapers up and down the eastern seaboard began to print "the truth." All the right people knew the facts: that after her father's passing, kindly cousins in Colorado had taken her in. There were letters to her from both of them, and photographs of the three of them together. Upon their sad and sudden deaths she had returned east, a unique representative of two worlds, able to display the genteel charm that was the hallmark of Chest-nut Hill and the rough-and-ready independence of the western horse-woman.

In her small and elegant Village apartment, the best of society min-gled with the finest artists, writers, and thinkers. For the rich, the words *Let us to Lorinda's* came to be synonymous with an evening of the excit-ing and unexpected. For the creative, that same phrase could mean, at the most, lucrative patronage; at the least, a fine and much-needed buffet. And wasn't it common knowledge that Miss Jameson had used these occasions not to further herself socially but to benefit the poorest of a city awash with both robber-baron money and privation's sweat and blood?

When the train reached Fort Morgan, Lorinda carefully instructed the railway workers to keep clear of the sliding door of the livestock car. She saddled Bellerophon inside the paddock and rode him out and down the ramp. The eight men scattered as he pawed the earth and reared, snorting and whistling. Lorinda shouted to the nearest man and asked him the name and address of the most convenient livery. He nervously replied, and she shouted for her bags to be sent there. Bellerophon made a full circle of the railyard and then bolted headlong for the town, two thousand miles of unused energy boiling in his veins.

When she arrived at the stable, Lorinda arranged to rent a horse and bridle from the astonished proprietor, first making sure that the animal was a mare and therefore less likely to become a sparring partner for her old friend. As they passed by the few buildings that comprised the town, Lorinda fought to restrain Bellerophon from breaking into another dash at the sight of the wide plain and the scent of earth and brush. When the mountains came into focus, he seemed to calm, but still she held tight to his traces and a clump of his mane. It would not do at this juncture for him to frighten the mare or, worse, run her off, leaving Lorinda without transportation that knew its way home.

Once the trio had cleared all signs of man's creation, Lorinda dismounted. With a leather strap, she tied Bellerophon to a sickly birch and left the mare to graze on the few blades of grass sturdy enough to grow among the rocks. Speaking to the black gently, she removed the silver bridle from his head and uncinched the English saddle from his back. Then she paused, knowing that this would be the final time she would ride an animal this magnificent beneath a sky this cloudless; this blue and big.

Lorinda released the leather strap and gave the stallion a light tap on the flank. Again he reared. For the shortest time their eyes met; and though his gaze seemed filled with murder, she saw no death in them today. With a final full cry his forelegs hit the ground, the contact of his hooves sharp as pistol shots. He pawed the earth once, twice, and then made for the horizon, fading through the dust like a change of scene at a nickelodeon.

Lorinda looked after Bellerophon until he vanished and then turned to saddle the mare. Beneath her, the horse felt narrow and light. In his flight, Bellerophon had not looked back. She resolved to do no less.

What sense would it make now to live a false life with a real name?

Diary,

Perhaps I have been working too hard or gone too long without my Chappie (he wrote today from Argentina to inform me that the milk powder had arrived and the roof tiles for the school were the wrong size). Or perhaps I am merely getting to an age where one's eyes play tricks, the stage in life where one can no longer trust the senses not to lie. Still, I must tell you of the singular and grand illusion that visited me today as I stood among my friends in Union Square.

There must have been four or five thousand volunteers in the parade. From the reviewing stand they looked glorious: citizen soldiers of every color and creed. I readily admit I would have given much not to feel the ache inside me as I watched them march along the street in their makeshift uniforms.

Perhaps the vision came to me because in that moment I needed a distraction, a diversion from the stark reality that the fine manhood I saw in those streets were an army of the dead . . . far too small and weak to comprise the bulwark against fascism they so hope to be. But even through my tears I realized, as did every one of them, that for the right-thinking there is no help for us but to fight. Hitler is on the rise; the Germans have destroyed Guernica; and if Franco and his minions are not stopped in Spain, I fear they will spread their systemic hatred to the whole world.

Weeping, I held tight to the First Lady's hand. By her presence here today, Nell had withstood no end of criticism from the papers, the politicians, even our own party. They had shouted that this so-called Abraham Lincoln Brigade was nothing but a motley crew of communists, fuzzy-thinking socialists, and all manner of societal misfits. The Herald Tribune had called Eleanor's attendance "misguided." That knuckleheaded flyboy Lindbergh had referred to her as "a pinkster in petticoats." Franklin, of course, handled the situation with his usual aplomb. "You know my missus," he had told the reporters, "she has her own ideas about things." God, he is the most charming and practiced of liars! Could this be why Nell has stayed with him so long, or is it because being the wife of a president affords her power to accompany deeds?

Last night, as we have for three decades, we rendezvoused at the Alhambra. Luxuriating in the hot water, it struck me how much our bodies have changed while our spirits have not. Still, I was slightly embarrassed when Nell bluntly stated how lucky I had been.

"Twice," she said, "you have found love with a man. I never have."

How I wished for her sake that she was wrong. But as always she spoke the truth. Franklin's infidelities had finished them as man and wife years ago. Their marriage now was merely another political deal, something brokered on neutral territory. Lamely, I told her how much our country's poor loved her. She only sighed and asked me how warm I thought "one-third of a nation" could make a bed.

But I was going to tell you of my vision, was I not? Even now, it is fading like the dreams that seem so vivid in sleep but, upon waking, escape memory.

As the brigade rounded the square and approached the platform where we stood, I caught an errant sunbeam in my eye. This caused one of those dark spots to appear before me and partially block the center of my vision. Suddenly, on one side of the obstruction, I noticed a tall man, different from the others, primarily because he was quite old amid the young—older certainly than myself.

Still, his bearing was erect and his uniform pressed and immaculate. His hair and mustache were, I noted, gray as the coat of a Confederate general, and his flat wide-brimmed hat sat upon his chiseled head like the very crown of experience.

As my watering eyes blinked in the sunshine, he disappeared momentarily, only to emerge on the other side of the sunspot. As the assembled masses began to sing, I saw his mouth open with the joy of our cause. Then, just before he turned and left my sight forever, I noticed something familiar about his handsome face.

Just above the trim mustache, I perceived a tiny mark: black and round, riding midway between nose and lip. The sun caused my eyes once again to blink and water. For a second I considered making my way into the throng to confirm my suspicions, but I could manage only a small wave in the direction in which I believed he had gone. By the time my vision had regained full strength, he had marched, straight and strong, into the cheers and vanished.

As I stood staring after him, the good people of New York launched into the final verse of a familiar and hopeful tune. To be sure, I was trembling, trembling as I had not in thirty years. But as my tears at last fell free, on my breast and on the watch I have worn for so long, I took Nell's arm in mine and joined my voice to hers:

While we seek mirth and beauty, and music light and gay,
There are frail forms fainting at the door.
Though their voices are silent, their pleading looks will say,
Oh, hard times come again no more.

It's a song, a sigh of the weary,
Hard times, hard times, come again no more.
Many days you have lingered around my cabin door,
Oh, hard times come again no more.

Author's Note

I got the idea for *Etta* over a decade ago. I was watching a television special on the Hole-in-the-Wall Gang when the narrator said something that caught my attention. He claimed that virtually nothing was known about Etta Place, the alleged girlfriend of the Sundance Kid.

At the time, all I knew about Etta Place I had learned from the 1969 film *Butch Cassidy and the Sundance Kid.* I saw Katharine Ross play Etta (and do a fine job of it), but I couldn't imagine there could be so little known about the legendary figure herself, especially considering there was quite a bit of information on her two male cohorts.

I thought, "What a story. But that can't be right." Shortly after that, I went to the Free Library of Philadelphia and began researching the subject.

It was true. Etta Place was the very definition of a mystery woman.

Not that there weren't plenty of stories. I read tales of her being a schoolmarm or a prostitute or both. Some theorized that there were women who later lived under other names but could have been Etta in their youth. There was even a man who claimed that she was a niece of English royalty and that he was her nephew.

But the fact remained that there was no record of where Etta Place came from, there was little data on what happened to her, and no one knew where she was buried. There wasn't even proof that her name was real or a nom de guerre. I made notes and drew a few pictures and began to think about writing a novel.

Then for years I did nothing, but that didn't stop Etta from haunting me. Finally, I could take it no longer and began the research for what would eventually become this book.

To give Etta a past, I went with what little was known. There is no question that Etta was an extraordinary beauty. She was said to dress fashionably and have fine manners. I also read that she was a crack shot and a fine horsewoman who rode using an English saddle. It was that saddle and those manners that led me to think she might have once been a wealthy girl. And where would a turn-of-the-century girl learn to use both horse and gun if not from a father who had no son and had raised her like a boy?

The choice to have her come from Philadelphia was easy. I live here and we are known for two things besides cheesesteaks and soft pretzels: old-school aristocracy and minding our own business—two qualities Etta would need in abundance.

Writing Etta as a prostitute or teacher had already been done by others, so I decided to make my heroine a Harvey Girl because I thought it was an interesting way to launch her into the western landscape. It would also allow her to fall in with all kinds of people: some good (Loretta Kelley, Laura Bullion) and some bad (Earl Charmichael Dixon).

With some of these basics laid down, I constructed a time line about Butch, Harry, and Eleanor using all the facts that I could find. This done, I liberally inserted various factoids about Etta along with completely fictional material. Yes, Etta and Harry did go to New York and did leave for Bolivia on the *Soldier Prince,* but the relationship with Eleanor, the *Wild West* show, and the socialist politics are all my invention. Etta never robbed a train in New Jersey or saved Teddy Roosevelt; and if she became a celebrated philanthropist, we'll never know because she disappeared from history after 1909.

The rest of the dramatis personae in this novel have been similarly trifled with. In the case of Kid Curry, I knew very well that he had actually died a suicide, and the manuscript read that way originally. Even so, in the end I decided to have him perish in a duel with Harry Longbaugh: a showdown that never happened.

Etta, Butch, Sundance, Laura Bullion, Curry, Eleanor, Peg Leg, Buffalo Bill, Charles A. Siringo, Annie Oakley, Don Vittorio Ferro, and the various Wild Bunch members actually lived, just not exactly the way I say they do in these pages.

Rodman Larabee, Loretta Kelley, Earl Charmichael Dixon, Dante Cichetti, Hantaywee, Eli Gershonson, and Ralph Worthington Carr are all products of my imagination. I hope they are worthy of accompanying the historic figures that appeared in this story, especially the woman who inspired it.

GK
Philadelphia
May 2008

Acknowledgments

Many people were helpful and supportive during the years I worked on *Etta*.

My wife, Joan Weiner, was lovingly patient with me from the time of *Etta*'s conception through its publication. It's wonderful to have good things to share with her.

Our children, Kate and Ned Kolpan, deserve a medal.

Ruth Kolpan, my mother, died as I was finishing this book. She was encouraging till the end.

My agent, Katharine Cluverius, had faith in me and in *Etta* from her very first reading, kept me sane through rewrites and "overthinking," and did it all while awaiting her first baby. Thanks also to Liz Farrell, Larissa Silva, and everyone at ICM.

Editor Robin Rolewicz helped me form this work into something much better than it was when she acquired it and did it while awaiting *her* first baby. Anika Streitfeld polished *Etta* to a diamond shine and was my gentle guide through the new world of book publishing. I am a very lucky writer to have had their help.

At Ballantine, heartfelt thanks to Libby McGuire, Kim Hovey, Brian McLendon, Lisa Barnes, Dana Blanchette, Catherine Casalino, Christine Cabello, Jillian Quint, and Katie O'Callaghan.

Special thanks go to Linda Carner, Harris Devor, Denise Goren,

Charlie Hardy, Lori and David Rech, Beryl Rosenstock, Jonathan Rubin, Bruce Schimmel, Gini Graham Scott, and Joseph and Meg Smith. A tip of my Stetson also goes to Ron Cohen and Lisa Moroz. They know why.

Thanks also to Twyla Tharp, whose book *The Creative Habit* helped me conquer the fear of tackling my first novel.

I'm not sure if "Hard Times Come Again No More" was ever an anthem for the Socialist movement in this country but if it wasn't it should have been. It is a beautiful, inspiring song and I salute the spirit of its author, the great Stephen Foster.

And finally, much obliged to Etta Place for being such a great mystery.

ABOUT THE AUTHOR

GERALD KOLPAN is an Emmy Award–winning television reporter in Philadelphia. Prior to his television career he wrote for newspapers and magazines nationwide and was a frequent contributor to NPR's *All Things Considered. Etta* is his first book.

ABOUT THE TYPE

This book was set in Garamond, a typeface originally designed by the Parisian typecutter Claude Garamond (1480–1561). This version of Garamond was modeled on a 1592 specimen sheet from the Egenolff-Berner foundry, which was produced from types assumed to have been brought to Frankfurt by the punchcutter Jacques Sabon.

Claude Garamond's distinguished romans and italics first appeared in *Opera Ciceronis* in 1543–44. The Garamond types are clear, open, and elegant.